# Daniel

**The One Who Got Away**

# *Daniel*

**The One Who Got Away**

Claire Van Etten

JONES MEDIA
PUBLISHING

DANIEL THE ONE WHO GOT AWAY Copyright © 2016 by Claire Van Etten.

All rights reserved to Claire Van Etten. Printed in the United States of America. No part of this book may be used or reproduced in any manner whatsoever without written permission.

This book is a work of fiction. Names, characters, and incidents either are the product of the author's imagination or are used fictitiously. Any resemblance to actual persons, living or dead, events, or locales is entirely coincidental. The publisher does not have any control over and does not assume responsibility for author or content.

Cover art and illustrations by Claire Van Etten.

Jones Media Publishing
YourBookBluePrint.com

ISBN: 978-1-945849-99-2 paperback

# Contents

**Part I  Life at the Prow** ...... 1

    Chapter 1:  Friday Morning ...... 3

    Chapter 2:  The Prow ...... 11

    Chapter 3:  Sheila at Dinner ...... 25

    Chapter 4:  Daniel Visits Paul ...... 31

    Chapter 5:  Disaster at Sheila's Place ...... 41

    Chapter 6:  Thomas and Memories ...... 47

    Chapter 7:  A Second Visit ...... 57

    Chapter 8:  The Call ...... 61

    Chapter 9:  Paul's Death ...... 67

    Chapter 10:  The Memorial Service ...... 71

    Chapter 11:  A Dream ...... 81

    Chapter 12:  Grief ...... 87

    Chapter 13:  The Wine Buffet ...... 91

    Chapter 14:  Encouraging Words ...... 101

    Chapter 15:  Staff Meeting ...... 109

Chapter 16: Out of Town ........................................................... 117

Chapter 17: On The Ferry ........................................................ 123

**Part II Time Out** ................................................................ **131**

Chapter 18: Glass House ........................................................ 133

Chapter 19: The Cold Day in Hell ......................................... 141

Chapter 20: The Clean-up ..................................................... 147

Chapter 21: The Fix-up .......................................................... 157

Chapter 22: Alone on the Beach ........................................... 169

Chapter 23: The American Camp ......................................... 179

Chapter 24: Dinner with Luke .............................................. 185

Chapter 25: The Morning After ............................................ 197

Chapter 26: Trini and Oscar ................................................. 205

Chapter 27: The Respite ........................................................ 213

Chapter 28: Time Out ............................................................ 225

Chapter 29: Ruth .................................................................... 233

Chapter 30: Cherry Pies ........................................................ 241

Chapter 31: The Return ......................................................... 255

Chapter 32: The Mini Magellan ............................................ 263

Chapter 33: The Fourth ......................................................... 277

Chapter 34: Juan de Fuca ...................................................... 283

Chapter 35: Cape Flattery ..................................................... 293

Chapter 36: The Wicked Way .................................................. 303

Chapter 37: In the Orchard.................................................. 311

Chapter 38: Sheila's Confession ........................................ 317

Chapter 39: Deeper Confessions......................................325

Chapter 40: At San Sebastian ......................................... 337

**Part III Sailing Home ................................................. 341**

Chapter 41: Blackberries................................................343

Chapter 42: At The Garden Club .................................. 351

Chapter 43: Nan ............................................................... 361

Chapter 44: Calling Otis..................................................373

Chapter 45: At Nan's Church ........................................379

Chapter 46: Last Days ................................................... 389

Chapter 47: Picnic at the Lighthouse........................... 405

Chapter 48: The Lighthouse Dream ............................ 415

Chapter 49: The Sunflower Sail ................................... 419

Chapter 50: The Final .....................................................427

Chapter 51: Back In Town ............................................. 441

Chapter 52: Flower Power..............................................453

Chapter 53: The Trade ...................................................461

Chapter 54: On Friday Night .........................................465

Chapter 55: A Christmas Wedding ..............................475

# PART I

# *Life at the Prow*

## CHAPTER ONE

## Friday Morning

DANIEL stepped out onto the walkway and firmly latched the door. He waited to hear the sound of the foyer door alarm engaging and then walked out to the street's edge looking back up at the façade of the building. It was a typically dark Seattle morning, clouds low overhead, rain imminent; the building sitting solid and comfortable in the pale early light. This was a two-storied brick apartment court, now smartly converted to condominiums. The structure was one of those built in the late 1920's, a U-shaped design, with a rectangular formal garden filling the court, and a little narrow sidewalk leading from the street to the main foyer door, dividing the garden in half... symmetrical, orderly.

Filling the court were two tall, old, spreading magnolia trees, one on each side of the walkway. A traditional low trimmed boxwood hedge outlined the court neatly. The building had been recently painted a soft dove gray. Each of the four front units had a huge plate glass picture window facing onto the street. Glossy black shutters and black painted trim framed these windows. A touch of brass hardware and curvy black iron grillwork finished the look... traditional, pleasing to the eye. A shining brass plaque on the front of the building declared, "The Graystone Arms..."

Looking up, Daniel's face could not conceal pleasure and pride. The only other person watching was Henry, his dog, standing patiently beside him, a charcoal gray standard poodle. Henry of course approved of everything that Daniel liked. He was a constant companion. And, Daniel had reason to be so pleased. The Graystone Arms belonged to him. It was his property, an inheritance from his Grandmother's estate. She had owned several properties there in the Seattle area. This one had always been his favorite and she had wanted him to have it. She had entrusted him with the total restoration of the place four years ago, just before her death. The project had come together well. Everyone had thought he was too young to undertake the renovation all by himself, but he had done the job in just less than a year, enjoying every minute of it. The front second floor unit on the left was Daniel's own dwelling. He was looking up at that big picture window now.

Just then, Thomas stepped into sight in the window above him. He was still in a striped nightshirt with a coffee cup in hand, his shock of blond curly hair, tousled. He smiled down at Daniel and waved. Daniel smiled and waved back. Thomas adjusted his glasses, a familiar gesture. Then still smiling, he moved away out of sight. Now only the reflection of sky and heavy morning clouds remained mirrored in the glass. Daniel's smile faded. "I need to do something," he breathed.

Suddenly, there was a lashing gust of rain hitting the window and blowing everything around in the courtyard. A low roll of thunder sounded not too far away.

He looked back up again at the picture window above, watching the rain hitting the glass.

Looking down at Henry he said, "How do I get into these things? He's in our place…he's wearing my nightshirt, and drinking out of my favorite cup."

With a clenched jaw he added, "I hope he remembers to turn off the coffee maker."

Raising one foot and then the other, Henry waited there on the sidewalk. His eyes were shining like two black buttons. He was groomed in an all-over tight trim, with just a little pom-pom at the end of his tail. He began straining a little on the leash and growling slightly, signaling that it was time to go.

Daniel had already thrown on his raincoat; now he opened his umbrella with a snap. In that moment he turned away toward the day ahead and with an effort, firmly cleared his mind. Off they went, the wind propelling them from behind.

This morning was like most mornings. Daniel walked to work almost every day, no matter the weather; it was his only form of daily exercise. Henry was naturally waterproof, and so he always accompanied Daniel. They started out down the street towards Daniel's place of work, a restaurant, just a few blocks west of his home there in the First Hill District near the waterfront.

This man, Daniel… was a beautiful man. It could be said, a beautiful "young" man. He looked very young, maybe twenty-two, when in fact, he was thirty. Five-foot ten, fine ash brown hair swept back off his face; his eyes were clear, soft, gray and seemed completely open to the world, framed by delicate brows.

A strong, well-shaped chin and fine regular nose, these were the signature features of an English schoolboy minus the ruddy cheeks. Daniel was gravely pale; it was that milky-white fair skin so often seen in the Pacific Northwest, where the daylight could be hazy at its strongest, leaving skin pristinely undamaged by the sun. His figure would have been called "lithe" in another age, not an athlete, but strong, elegant, physically ready for the challenge of life. There was something though, a coolness, maybe even a stillness, which was not quite what could be called "ready..." Not the full-throttled energy of youth. Restrained, but beautiful, a classically beautiful man.

In this town, it wasn't necessary to dress with the formality of a sports coat and tie for work, but Daniel enjoyed dressing and today under his raincoat he wore a tweed coat, a narrow black knit tie and gray slacks. The air was damp and swirling gusts of rain still called for some bundling up, even if it was supposed to be spring.

Their route to work was a jagged one at first, and led under the freeway at one point, which Henry hated due to the loud din of traffic rushing by over them. After the freeway, it was downhill all the way as they passed other solid old buildings, some columned and arched, a few newer office parks with intensely green, trimmed landscaping and blooming spring bulbs, crocuses, daffodils, tulips. On this dark morning their colors shone like neon against the green shrubs. The way led onward to downtown and the waterfront. The closer they came the more sea sounds and smells came into their attention; seagulls were making their racket. Henry was sniffing the air with every step and Daniel too breathed deeply of the rain-soaked air, the wheeling and diving sea birds could be seen in the distance. And the sea, a dull lead color, could be seen between the buildings along the shore.

Their routine included several detours along the way. There was a tiny corner coffee kiosk three blocks from work. Natalie, the server at the Bean Box saw him coming and started his order. This was not "Starbucks," just a little brown hut, with orange hot cups labeled, "Can't beat the Bean Box..." The coffee was good though, very good. Natalie handed him his regular, Kona with a splash of Pinion and plenty of cream. Natalie could barely turn around in the crowded kiosk; her ample form filling the space. The black and red tattoos running up her arms were the main graphic ornament of the tiny shop.

Daniel smiled, "Hey Nat..."

"Hey, Daniel. Hey Henry. Thank God it's Friday...TGIF."

She handed Henry a dog treat. Henry was not put off by her Goth hair and nearly black lipstick. He gladly took the treat from her. If dogs smile, he was smiling.

"Yeah, Friday. You need to come to dinner tonight. A very special load of halibut is coming in today."

"You know I can't afford your place; just bring me a doggie bag," grinned Natalie.

"You'll be long gone," he smiled. "I'll be late."

He took his coffee and moved on. Ahead he could now clearly see the waters of the bay, dark and low between the high buildings as they neared the business district. Down the street he picked up a weekend flyer. Daniel liked to look over the events offered around town, even though he could seldom get away from the restaurant to attend anything, and never on a weekend. He still liked to know what was going on.

There was something exhilarating about walking along rain-washed streets, out in the open air, breathing in the fresh rain scented air. His eyes were following the reflections in windows glistening in the morning gray light as he and Henry made their way down the streets into the very heart of town. The trees along the street side of the walkway were fresh washed too, sending drips onto his umbrella. Flowers were bent down, falling out of planter boxes and hanging pots; the earliest daffodils and tulips signaled the soon return of sunny days and the sun's warmth. Tourists would be piling in too, in a few weeks. The town would be full; the days at the restaurant buzzing with activity.

In the middle of the next block, he turned quickly into a floral shop. Actually, it wasn't a regular flower shop, but one of those hole-in-the-wall shops with a roll up metal door. Flowers were displayed on the sidewalk in white plastic buckets. He and Henry ducked into the dark, heady-smelling shop every day to pick up flowers for the restaurant foyer. This was something Daniel loved. The colors and spicy fragrances were as stimulating as the caffeine in his coffee each day. Today the bunches of brilliant red, tall gladiolas could not be ignored standing in their white plastic bucket. The stalks were already opening their blossoms. He selected two bundles and waited for the flower seller to wrap them in bright yellow waxed paper cones. The man took his time and silently reached over to pluck a white carnation and put it into Daniel's lapel. This was also part of the day's routine, rain or shine.

Finally reaching the restaurant, Daniel paused on the sidewalk giving Henry the chance to do a head to toe shake which sent a shower of water flying everywhere. As they approached the front doors, Daniel slowed his pace, savoring the moment of arrival. The ornate sign overhead read, "THE PROW."

## CHAPTER TWO

## The Prow

THE truck traffic was beginning to clear out at 9 A.M. in front of the restaurant. Most of the morning deliveries had been made, so things were settling down at this hour on Second Avenue. As he had done leaving home that morning, Daniel paused to look up at the façade of this place. Letters above spelling out "THE PROW" met his gaze and like the Graystone Arms, amazingly, he was the owner here.

This was the doing of Grandmother again. They had opened this business together five years ago. He had at first owned it jointly with her. This commercial property had been one of several which she owned in Seattle from early years. Her father had been an old-timer in the days of Seattle's development. He had owned many downtown buildings, and she had inherited several from his estate. Now it had come to him and he had nurtured it along, built it up, and created it, really, from old retail space. A hundred years ago it had been an old high-ceiling stationery shop.

In the beginning, Grandmother had been Daniel's money partner, and he the managing operator. Since her death, he was now sole proprietor. He missed her presence, his octogenarian partner. His relationship with his grandmother went far beyond gratitude; actually, he never called her "Grandmother..." Her name was Willamette Stanton Drews. For some reason, people usually called her "Bet" but early in life he had named her "Willie" and possessively called her "My Willie..." His family had laughed at this name, but he persisted. Sometimes he thought she was his one true friend. Without her support he would be nowhere. Now, since her death, he just had all the memories of her, of closeness, conspiracy, childhood fun and the life that they had shared. Of course, he also had the properties and money she had given him and he had all the strength she had poured into him. Willie was gone, but Daniel loved her intensely still.

Daniel had been shuttled off from Seattle into Willie's realm as a young teen by his parents. He had been sent to Santa Barbara to a private boy's boarding school for high school years and spent the weekends and holidays with his little grandmother nearby. Willie had gone down from Seattle to Santa Barbara with her husband, Charlie, for retirement. They wanted to live in the sun and Charlie wanted to play golf. But Charlie had died only two years later, cutting short his time in the sun. Willie remained in Santa Barbara and Daniel became her on and off companion.

Daniel knew he did not want to go to college. He wanted to become a chef, and eventually to have his own restaurant. Willie had understood that even though his mother and father had been dumbfounded. After high school graduation, before he went away for training, Willie had thought he ought to make sure he liked restaurant life and suggested he get some practical experience. So, after high school, he lived with Willie and got a job working at the famous "Buzby's" of Santa Barbara for a year and a half. His instincts were right on. He had loved everything about working in the restaurant.

By then, The Culinary Institute, New York, was his school choice, at least for the first year, and Willie was willing to send him. Later he had moved out of dorm life, got a place in Manhattan and pieced together an education attending boutique cooking schools on and off for the next two years. That is also where he had met and eventually gathered all his top staff. He had never regretted the path he had chosen.

After culinary school he set out for France. There he worked first at the back of a Parisian fishmonger's shop and then in a steamy bakery for a few months. Finally, he took another short course at the Cordon Bleu there in Paris. Freed at last from classes, he had set out on a rambling six months' tour of Europe, traveling in the cheapest class, seeing things from street level, and checking out fresh, local food along the way. At times some of his new continental friends joined him, but mostly, he went alone, wheedling local recipes where he could. The heaviest items in his backpack were his notebooks. "Grand Tour" it was not, but he had arrived back in the U.S. only a little older, with gritty practical experience. And, he had finished immersing himself for years in various forms of schooling. Now, it was time to put all this to work. He had a vision of what he wanted. Eventually, it had resulted in this gem of a bistro back in Seattle, his home town. And so Daniel had been launched into the food business through the grace of Willie. Now, he rambled no more.

The façade of The Prow was gleaming in the diffuse morning light. It stood out among the storefronts darkly, elegant fittings adding a rich shine. The storefront was flat to the street, but there were pilasters of mahogany between the beveled glass windows. Each pilaster was topped with a hand carved Corinthian capital of the same wood. The multi-paned windows winked and sparkled at him. To the south, double wood doors, slightly recessed from the street, opened into the foyer entrance. The over-sized brass door handles were cast in the shape of ship's anchors. Centered above the doorway in black and gold Spenserian script "The Prow" had been painted.

Daniel never got tired of this place or the work inside. He never thought of traveling anymore. This was his world, complete. The rain showers had stopped and the sun was bearing down on the veil of moisture over the city that morning as Daniel turned the key. Henry did his head to foot shake, flapping his ears vigorously. Looking up at Daniel he gave out his sharp bark as they stepped through the doors.

Inside was an amber world. The foyer walls were a deep gold and the glass wall sconces shone an even deeper amber light all around. Caramel-colored velvet benches and settees lined the walls for the comfort of waiting guests. The floor was polished black and tan marble squares, set diagonally in a checkerboard pattern. A long twisting flounce of apricot silk hung festooned from the high ceiling, adding to the rich reflected light.

There, in the high-ceilinged entry, loomed the obvious symbol of the restaurant's name. Huge and somewhat intimidating, it was the wooden prow of an old sailing vessel, embedded into the wall and jutting out high into the room. It was the carved figure of a woman, one arm raised, stretching forward and bearing a lantern in a gesture of guidance for the ship. Her glaze was fixed ahead. In her other arm she cradled an infant closely against her side. The woman's body was swathed in classical carved draperies, flowing back into the massive form of the ship's curved prow. Carved leaping fish figures were worked into the wooden folds of the woman's gown. This wood and that of the whole structure was teak, polished and oiled. It had been a bit of an engineering job to install this large piece, and it was intentionally fixed with a slight tip to the side, as if a ship on a roll in the sea. Across the room the Maître D's station stood. It was a balance to the jutting prow, made of the same wood as the old ship, looking like a raised captain's turret, carved with the same fish and mythical sea creatures in panels.

Daniel went to the back side of this station and brought out an old towel he kept there for the purpose of drying Henry on wet days like today. First the paws and then an all over scrub was enough to clean him up for the restaurant's fine floor. He barked again and ran on through to the back.

Daniel was not the first to arrive at the restaurant this morning. He could hear voices and the noise of kitchen work coming through the opened kitchen doors at back through the restaurant. He lay the brilliant gladiolas down on a chair and went through to the kitchen and offices. Pans were banging; there was a sound of chopping and water flowing as soups were being prepared. Henry sniffed but trotted to his round bed basket in the office, while Daniel went first to the kitchen.

This kitchen was unusual for a commercial restaurant. It looked more like the kitchen of an old country house somewhere. Remembering kitchens in Europe, Daniel was determined not to have a dank, hard-light, hard-steel, windowless workplace in his place of business. He had worked hard and struggled with the inspectors to create something different and better for all the staff and employees. Yes, the floor had to be standard commercial quarry tile, terra cotta-colored, but there were many unique features here. There was the high glass square-paned window looking out the alleyway which was now a small container kitchen herb garden. Garbage containers had been banished to a short walk down the alley. Daniel did not want his staff catching whiffs of garbage in the kitchen while they prepared some of the city's best foods. Large clear skylights lit the workrooms. And beneath them, green, herb-filled hanging planters hung from weighted chains which could be raised and lowered as needed. The building was two storied and so as a result the kitchen ceiling was very high. Light and bright, that was what he had wanted, lots of good natural light. There were more wooden surfaces than steel and plenty of room for flower pots. There were nasturtiums for garnishes, pots of chives, basil and thyme, and some red geraniums for cheer. The huge ceiling vent fans turned slowly this time of day, casting moving shadows as slow-moving steam rose up to them. They would be whizzing faster later in the evening.

The human personalities working below in the beehive of a kitchen were of a diverse mixture as well. Trini and Oscar were head staff members. Trini was both sometime sous chef and business office manager. Her husband, Oscar, was head chef. Daniel had given over that job to him early on in order to concentrate on management. He still worked with Oscar to develop dishes for the menu, but Oscar ruled the kitchen. He and Daniel had been friends and colleagues in New York. Oscar and Trini were natives of Cuernavaca, Mexico. Sarah from Iceland was the pastry chef. Dora and Janus were food prep. Daniel had first met them on his trip through Transylvanian Romania on a food tourism jaunt. They had kept in touch and finally he had persuaded them to make the move to Seattle. They knew everything to be known about the preparation of vegetables. An assortment of young waiters and kitchen assistants rounded out the company.

Daniel greeted everyone quickly. Then the staff all gathered with Daniel to look over the freshly arrived fish and spent some time discussing the day's menu. A big beautiful batch of halibut had come in. They were all "ohhing" and "ahhing" over that. The mussels looked great too. Then Daniel left the kitchen, asking Trini to make a cup of tea for him as he made his way to the office, grabbing a couple of fresh pastries along the way. There he looked briefly at a stack of mail, checked the accounts on the computer, reviewing figures from yesterday's business. Finally, he reached for a tall blown glass vase, filled it with water and started out to the foyer with it. He heard the office phone ringing, and walked back, but then chose to ignore it. He could see from the number that it was Sheila. "She wants reservations," he thought. "She never calls except to reserve her favorite booth. I'll call her later." He said to himself grimly. "The restaurant is not even open yet. I need to finish." He went out onto the restaurant floor with a clenched jaw, trying not to think about Sheila.

It was, as Natalie in the Bean Box had said, Friday. Time to get everything lined out for the end of week crowd that was sure to come for both lunch and dinner. His head was buzzing with details especially for tonight. In the quiet of the empty restaurant, he walked gingerly to the foyer with the filled vase. He un-wrapped the damp flowers and began the task of arranging. Pretty simple, as the bouquet would consist of just one variety of flower. The crisp stalks did need some trimming to put them at the right height for the vase. They fanned out beautifully and in very little time were glowing and symmetrical on the wooden Maître D's station, a frenzy of bright red. Each day, with the setting of the welcoming bouquet, a gift to all who walked through the doors, Daniel felt that The Prow was ready for business.

There were two dining areas flanking the large foyer with tables throughout the center and booths along the walls. A long, dark wood seafood bar divided the two areas. A drinks bar covered the back wall, also in dark wood with lots of brass in the fittings. Behind that, through a pillared entry was a small banquet and overflow room for private dinners in the same theme, but papered with a parchment, sea-faring mural above a dark wood wainscoting. At one end of the room, in a niche, stood a marble statue of Neptune with his trident.

The dining rooms were aglow, the result of acute attention to detail. This was reflected everywhere in the checkerboard floor, amber light, caramel plush seating, dark woods and black and white table linens. The walls were lined with black and white photos and old engravings of the historic harbor and Puget Sound framed in plain black frames. Many of these came from his grandfather's collection of early photos when life in Seattle was rough and tumble and muddy.

The Prow china was white with a black rim, and a tiny black ship emblazoned in the center of each dish. The only frivolity was more fantastic apricot-colored silk gathered and draped down from the high ceiling over the seafood bar.

He left the vase by the Maître D's station, and then turned his attention to the dining room. Checking each table, he flicked a damp cloth over a few chair seats as he wandered the room, inspecting with an eagle eye. Two waiters in long white aprons were also checking table arrangements and taking one more turn through with dust mops between rows.

This was Daniel's daily inspection round, a pleasant routine, which he enjoyed. His face showed an intensity that the staff had come to know during this hour of preparation. He liked to pause at the back of the dining room, looking out towards the light coming through front windows, appreciating the order and readiness of the place. He always experienced a curious surge of delight at the sight of glittering reflective glassware and crisp linens, the rich wood and marble floor. It appeared to him like a stage, prepared for the drama of people, talk, food and drink which would be played upon it once again today. He was always grateful to be part of this. Actually, to be orchestrating it all.

Today's lunch specials would be simple: butter and garlic steamed mussels with French baguettes. And the restaurant's well-known signature dish, Prow Chow, an excellent fish and shellfish white chowder. Oscar was working on something special with the halibut for dinner. You could smell the cooking now. Solid Seattle fare. It was Friday, the doors would open at eleven-thirty and they would be ready.

Daniel wandered back to the foyer checking the vase of flowers once more. He turned it this way and that, re-arranging a few stalks for best advantage, then sat down on one of the foyer benches. Relaxing, he smoothed his tie, crossed his arms, and leaned back looking up at the Prow Figurehead.

This beautiful thing was the key to the theme of the restaurant. Without it, he felt this would be just another trendy bistro. When he had been working with the designers on the décor, he knew exactly what he wanted in here. They just had to go out and find it. And they did. It had to be the prow of a ship, an old ship. So they put out the word to boatyards from coast to coast, but in the end, they had found this piece close to home. When they had taken Daniel out to see it, tears filled his eyes the moment it came into view. Why? He didn't know. Searching the records, they learned that this was the prow of the two-masted ketch, Augustus, out of Maine. She had sailed through the newly opened Panama Canal in the early twentieth century and ended her days in the Pacific coastal cargo trade. The piece had been refinished and then brought to the restaurant where it was carefully re-constructed. When finished and installed everyone had been stunned at the effect of it coming out of the wall like that, lifting up and on a roll, just as if still in the sea. All else in the restaurant was fitted around this theme: the billowing silks, the polished brasses and the wood.

Daniel knew he needed to return Sheila's phone call. He dreaded it. He would have had a struggle to describe their relationship. She was Willie's daughter and also a native of Seattle. Yes, Sheila was his mother, but hardly "Mom..." Daniel was the only child of Sheila and Paul Cross, two Seattle business people. That would best describe them. Paul Cross had founded the Northern Shore Maritime Insurance Brokerage there, years before Daniel was born. Sheila had originally gone to work for Paul at the agency straight out of college and then the two had married. Paul was twelve years older than Sheila, a bachelor; he had never been married before. He had spent his youth as a naval officer. Later, when Daniel was a young teen they had divorced. Sheila, ambitious and restless, had broken away from the insurance brokerage and started her own commercial real estate firm. She was a successful, hard-driven woman. Daniel had mostly been raised by nannies and finally by his grandmother. "Willie," his rock and his friend, was now gone, and there was no hiding the truth that "family" was now just a fragmented mess.

He would call Sheila soon. Right now he was enjoying the day, and continued sitting quietly in the entry, looking out through the double glass windows in the doors. It was early and he could collect his thoughts here in the low light of his favorite place for a while. He would act as Maître D' at lunch today. He liked doing this at the lunch hour, greeting and chatting with the lunch crowd, building good feelings and a sense of caring hospitality which he knew was the heart of service. The touch of hospitality, Daniel felt to be essential in his place, and he worked at it. Actually, it was not like work, he loved it. In the evening, the colorful and stout Bea would take over as, Maître D' with her pouf of red hair, cat's eye glasses, rhinestone rimmed, and her fitted dark suits. Everyone loved her. Andrea, in black crepe, tall, blond and willowy, would assist her, acting as seating hostess, gracefully slipping through the aisles to bring guests to their tables.

Today though, there was more to think about than restaurant preparations and Sheila. There was Paul.

Paul was his Dad, but he called him "Paul," just as he called his mother, "Sheila." Daniel had been born in Seattle and spent his childhood there, the only child, with his parents in a very contemporary condominium at the south end of Queen Anne Hill. When he had turned thirteen his parents sat him down and told him that he would now be going off to a boy's boarding school in Santa Barbara, California. This would be a great opportunity, they said. Willie lived in Santa Barbara by then. After Charlie's death, Willie had stayed there and so would be close by. Daniel could go to stay with her on weekends. It would be a chance to meet new friends, maybe do some sports, and Willie would be there for him all the time. He would be happier, they said.

Actually, Sheila had done all the talking and Paul sat by, taciturn as usual. "It's a good school," Sheila had said. She had carefully researched it, and she was sure Daniel was tired of hanging out with them, two busy workaholics. Oh, and by the way, since he was growing up now, let's just go with first names, Sheila, Paul, Daniel. It would be more grown up. Daniel had looked quickly up at Paul with a startled, white face. Paul had said nothing, so Daniel was unsure if this was his idea, hers, or agreed on by both of them. Sitting there now in the amber glow of the foyer, he remembered that moment, the shock, the disorientation. He had felt like he was falling through a big crack which had opened up in the earth and that it was going to close up with him down in it. And that is exactly what happened. Sheila had disposed of him neatly and Paul had let it happen.

It was after this, during Daniel's first year away at school that Sheila had asked Paul for a divorce. Looking back, this was certainly going to happen. Any glue that had made them a family had now dissolved and eventually, inevitably, amicably, they were divorced. Daniel suspected that Paul was crushed by this, but no such thing had actually been expressed. It was a sad business. The two had been divorced for many years now, and neither parent had remarried, both seemed content to be married to work. Theirs was now a threesome of distant and cool relationship at best, and a pattern of formality had been set.

Paul… Daniel could not ever remember having spent a day in his presence which was comfortable, normal. It is possible that

Paul cared for him, but how would he ever have known it? His standing with his father was vaguely uncertain. Paul was always distracted, narrowly focused on his business, with Spartan living habits. He was never directly harsh or directly unkind to him, just apparently completely uninterested in a kid, a boy, hanging around the house. Daniel may have just imagined it, but there seemed always to be an attitude of faint dissatisfaction coming from Paul. Not quite strong enough to be out and out rejection. He just did not know for sure. Daniel did know that Paul had scrupulously, if not lavishly, provided for him. And this counted for something. He just didn't seem to like Daniel very much, or, more importantly, need him.

Now, Paul rarely popped up on Daniel's radar screen. When Daniel threw aside college, Paul had just shrugged, and it looked as if he considered his obligations to Daniel to be finished. They rarely saw each other. He didn't come to the restaurant. Theirs wasn't a family that celebrated holidays together anymore. But now, something had happened. Something major. In December Paul had apparently not been feeling right. He went to the doctor. In January, tests were done. Paul had pancreatic cancer.

## CHAPTER THREE

## *Sheila at Dinner*

LATER that morning, Daniel returned Sheila's call. Yes, she wanted a reservation, but no, not for lunch. She was coming for dinner, she was bringing special clients. There was a big deal brewing. Could Daniel make sure that everything would be just right tonight? He bristled at this. "I make sure that everything is just right for everyone, every day, all the time," he shot back.

"Well of course you do, Daniel. Of course you do. Thanks so much." She hung up without any further chit chat, as usual.

He tried to calm down, but she could always get to him. It was her attitude of dominance over something that was not hers, so imperious. It was his restaurant. She had no clue about how he ran it or how much of himself he put into it. And, she did not care. Finally, he brushed it off and spent the rest of the day there, serving as host at lunch, which was very busy and pleasant. People loved the specials and were commenting on them, especially the new Brussels sprout cole slaw. Lots of talking, lots of people coming and going.

After lunch, he visited with the staff in the kitchen. They rested their tired feet perched on the kitchen stools, talking and eating bowls of the chowder. Then he went on into the office. His office was small and neat, windowless, with red glossy-painted walls and English antiques. His glass-topped desk was small and immaculately clear of papers and mail. On the credenza behind the desk, wicker dividers held all the essentials and current paperwork, neatly filed. A small Oushak rug in gold, tan and red accented the floor. Henry was dozing there in his basket. Daniel listened to some music for a while, with only one table lamp lighting the room. Then he stretched out on an old brown velvet sofa he had there for just such a purpose between service hours. He seldom went back to the condo during the day, especially on Fridays and Saturdays. Today, he had a sound nap but woke feeling groggy. A mood of anxiety had dropped onto him. He tried to analyze it. There was his father to think of, and his illness. There was the problem of Thomas, which he had been successfully shoving to the back of his thoughts, ignoring his growing discomfort in the relationship. Then there was the on-going irritation with Sheila. He knew he needed to address these worries, but not now. It was time to get going for the Friday dinner crowd. He went to the private bathroom just off the office and freshened up. Then he went out onto the dining floor and began preparing. Most people wandered in after 5:00 P.M. to start with cocktails.

At exactly 5:30, Sheila and company came through the doors. Daniel saw her come in. He was near the kitchen doors, putting away a cart and did not immediately come out to greet her. She had brought along Mary Ann, her secretary and Jeff, her assistant. Apparently, the important clients were meeting them there later. Daniel took the opportunity to silently assess Sheila as she moved along to her booth. She never sat at the bar. She was a short, one might say petite, woman, 50ish. Maybe petite was not the right word for her as she was fine-boned but curvy, with a round pretty face, a small waist and rounded hips, rather busty, with shapely legs. Fine-boned, but strong, full of energy. She always wore the most impractical high heels and he could not remember ever seeing her in pants during the business week. Her preference was a fitted, tailored suit, the skirt falling right at the knee. Today her suit was collarless in baby blue light wool. Her hair was exactly the same ash brown tone as Daniel's, but unlike his fine straight hair, hers was a short cap falling in loose curls. She had the same large, wide, gray intense eyes. In a whimsical frame of mind, he sometimes compared her with the classic cartoon character, "Betty Boop…" Yes, a fair haired version of "Betty," right down to the face-framing curls. Quite a feminine appearing woman. This, however, belied her nature and personality, which included a stern outlook on life, dogged strength and a razor sharp wit. Adorning the whole image was an array of stunning and very expensive jewelry, most of it Italian.

Her movements were dainty and somewhat darting, like a swallow. She would swoop in, find her place, all the while engaging in a fast friendly banter. Once seated, she "reigned" with a calm authoritative manner among the staff and with her people. Watching her, Daniel could not deny the strong physical resemblance he bore to Sheila, the creamy skin, the hair, the gray eyes, and something about the nose, but that is about as far as any feeling of affinity with her went. She had always been an enigma to him.

Still, Daniel knew that Sheila was proud of him, proud of the restaurant, though she never said as much. He knew she talked him up among her clients and sent him a lot of business. She was a regular client, coming in about twice a week, usually for lunch on Friday.

Finally, he went over to greet her at the table. He put on his welcoming smile. She smiled back. Mary Ann and Jeff looked up from their menus and greeted him too.

"Good to see you, Daniel. You are looking well."

She had put on her cordial face to match his smile, but he could see her mind was preoccupied.

"The halibut is special tonight," he offered. "And the Sole in Papelotte is always good too."

"Oh! The sole sounds wonderful," Sheila replied looking over the menu." We will have a hard time deciding. We're waiting for our guests first, of course." She smiled up at him again, a dazzling smile. He was dismissed.

"I hope you have everything you need," he said. "Just let us know when you're ready." No sense of familial relationship had been expressed.

He moved away, mentally shrugging his shoulders, leaving her party to the waiter. "That's enough said," he thought. A few minutes later, he saw the clients arrive. A man and a woman, mid-fifties, sophisticated, dressed with a somewhat East Coast dark formality. They huddled over their drinks and business. He left them to it. Soon they had ordered and were laughing it up over dinner. Daniel watched Sheila do her magic, as she held their attention with stories and expressive gestures. Her face and jewelry were sparkling. They were mesmerized. He shook his head and went on to the foyer to say goodbyes to departing diners.

Sheila's party stayed late, relaxed now and slowing down their talk over coffee and night-caps. Soon, they made their way all together out to the doors. They had enjoyed their time and the food, Mary Ann and Jeff said. Sheila turned to him with a flourish. She introduced her clients briefly, now having linked arms with them both.

"And, this is my son, Daniel," she said. "We owe our lovely dinner to him and his staff. He is the proprietor here." Still smiling, she swept her arm around the room. "Don't you love the drama of this theme?" she said, "Daniel designed the décor himself."

He smiled and nodded. "Please come again, won't you. You are always welcome at The Prow."

The clients glanced around again appreciatively and murmured their thanks for a lovely evening... And then they all departed together, conversing intently.

Daniel picked up a glass and napkin left there on a bench in the foyer. The same old emptiness came over him. As usual, he felt like a little child, looking in from the outside on the life of his mother and the things and people which were important in her life, as she swept by, not ever having really seen him. Or so it seemed to him.

Sometimes, he wished she just wouldn't come at all. This was his place.

## CHAPTER FOUR

# Daniel Visits Paul

THE next week, Paul phoned Daniel, which was something of an event in itself. Daniel could not remember the last time he had called. He asked if Daniel could come over to his place for a drink and a visit. Another first. Sheila was often in the restaurant, but Paul had been there only for the grand opening, a few years ago. He was still running his agency and did not dine out very often so they rarely crossed paths. Daniel agreed to come by, but was instantly on guard, wondering what this could be about. "This has to have something to do with his illness," he thought.

He was right. There had been the diagnosis of pancreatic cancer in early January. Not the best way to start the New Year. Since then, Daniel had dropped by to visit him a few times at his office, offering to treat him to lunch. This had not gone well. Paul certainly did not want to discuss his illness then, or have any kind of emotion-producing talk. He had been polite, but had begged off, using the excuse of wrapping up important work. He expressed thanks for Daniel's visits, but did not encourage him.

Daniel had tried to do the dutiful thing, to reach out, but Paul's nature made it hard to get close to him even now. This was frustrating and Daniel knew this sickness was not going away. The whole circumstance was worrisome, but somehow the reality of what the future would hold had not settled in with Daniel; he just had not seriously faced the looming outcome. So, he had been ignoring the situation, imagining that perhaps Paul would try some stop-gap or exotic treatment and "overcome..." The last time he had seen Paul he looked a bit thinner, but not really changed that much. Now, he wanted to talk. He was never one to shrink from the truth, and with Paul, there was always a purpose, a goal to be worked on. Daniel guessed that he wanted to talk about the business of impending death. Of course, Paul would want all his affairs to be in order for any eventuality. He would probably want Daniel to know some things about his estate.

Daniel went over on Saturday afternoon, between the lunch and dinner hours. Paul answered the doorbell himself. Daniel could not help registering the shock of Paul's physical decline. He had not thought about how he would find him, but the reality was stunning. He was very white and had probably lost more than twenty pounds. There had always been an angular look to Paul, but now his raw-boned frame was utterly pared down. His hair had thinned some and his eyes were not the same. There was an opalescent dullness to them now... This was the biggest change, as Paul's sharp, bright eyes had always been a focus of his strength. Now, that focus was gone. However, he was neatly dressed in a crisp white shirt and a pair of those grandpa jeans with a partly elastic waist. This was ironic, since his waist was quite slender at this point. Daniel was relieved that he was not in bed with pajamas and bathrobe. Paul ushered him into the living area of the condo and asked what he would like to drink.

"Just coffee, if you have it," Daniel said.

"Good, I'll have some too," Paul answered with some of the old vigor.

Paul's housekeeper, Jim, brought two cups and a tray. They sat near the large window in the diffuse afternoon light coming off the Bay. Paul had been in this condo since he and Sheila had split up. It was obvious that he was comfortably at home there. It was a starkly contemporary environment which Paul loved, and it suited him. Located just above the wharfs, the building was geometric, modernist, with its large windows facing the waterfront. Gray-blue walls, chrome and glass, pristine off-white carpeting. The condo's bird's eye view of the harbor and all the activity of ships and boats was complete. Nautical design drawings of every age lined the walls, as well as a few large paintings of ships and boats of every sort. Daniel sat down on the sculpted navy blue sofa. Paul cradled himself in a contemporary version of a brown leather La-Z-Boy. This was his only concession to the discomforts of his illness. They sipped coffee and listened to the harbor sounds. Paul asked about the profit status of the restaurant. Daniel replied with news of the newest menu items. There was a lull and more sipping. Then Paul said an interesting thing.

"I miss your mother. I still care for her."

Daniel, completely flustered by this, said, "Well, does she ever visit you? Have you seen her?"

"No," smiled Paul. "I just think of her." His dull eyes crinkled up at the corners. He continued smiling.

Then he opened the topic of the business at hand. The goal here it seemed, was to identify some parts of Paul's estate and make things clear to Daniel. There seemed to be no reason to argue with him or make pretense about his bleak future. His changed appearance said it all. Daniel was prepared to listen to him seriously.

Mainly, Paul wanted Daniel to know that he was bequeathing the vacation property on San Juan Island completely to Daniel. This was "Glass House," another modernist home with its surrounding property on the southeastern coast of that tiny island. It stood on five acres of land, narrowly laid out along the coast. The properties included the house, an orchard and beach fronts. The house was still completely furnished.

"We had some good times there on the island, didn't we?" Paul said.

Daniel was not prepared to argue about this either, though that was not the way he remembered it.

"I want you to have the place, to go and enjoy it whenever you can. Get away from work, when you need to. It is a healthy place and a great retreat. I always liked going there." Paul smiled hopefully at this.

"Oh, yes. It is a beautiful spot, Paul. A treasure... I really appreciate your thinking of turning it over to me." Daniel tried to smile too. "I will do my best to take good care of it always."

Paul nodded at this, and lay back on his chair, looking up at the ceiling. His white hands lay quietly on the armrests. He seemed satisfied with Daniel's response.

"A beautiful place by the sea." Paul whispered.

They had started visiting there early on, and Paul bought the house when Daniel was eight. Daniel's mind was casting back to memories there on the island. He was thinking of the chilliness of early summer on the terrace, playing with toys in a brisk wind by himself, wearing his noisy, rustling, nylon windbreaker. Paul and Sheila would be inside, making cocktails at the long, prominent bar, their frenzied conversation over a stack of papers, their hard laughter. He was thinking of his feeling of aloneness out on the gray slate terrace, cold, and a million miles away from his parents, though in reality they were only a few feet away on the other side of the huge plate glass windows. He was thinking of his little boy room inside, the twin bed with bright, quilted, red coverlet. More like a monk's narrow cell than a place for a child. The high horizontal window was way too high for him to look out of. He remembered the odd, framed Picasso print on the wall, somehow menacing. The scratchy, dense, wool carpeting underfoot where he would play on the floor at night, while Paul read silently, legs crossed, in a corner of the living room and Sheila sat silently also at the dining room table for hours playing solitaire. Very little talking, no laughing. They didn't have a television out there on the island. They wanted it to be a retreat in nature, but it did not feel natural at all. Jazz recordings were playing on the stereo in the evenings. Dave Brubeck. The entire atmosphere could be summed up by the word "sullen..." At least, that's the way he remembered it.

"Yes, it was a beautiful place by the sea," Daniel replied. Then he remembered the little Penguin class sailboat that they had down at the beach. He had painted it red, yellow and blue himself. He wondered if it was still there. Only he had used it, and it had been fun once he learned to sail a bit, and could maneuver it along the coast. Paul never went with him and Sheila was afraid of it. And here was the small beach house too, backed up against the rocky cliff. It was little more than a one room changing cabana, but it was natural and rustic and you could pretend to be shipwrecked there. There was a beach down below at the little shallow cove, partly sandy, partly gravelly in places. It was not the best place for swimming, the sand soon gave way to submerged rocks on either side of the little inlet, but it was a good digging spot for tunnels and sand building. On one side of the cove there was a little jetty for the sailboat.

After the divorce he had gone back to the island for summer vacations several times, but things were very different after that, he was fourteen by then and not interested in building sand forts on the beach anymore. He would go with Sheila for a week, then she would be restless and ready to return to the city. Paul would show up, the parents would switch parental duty with each other, and they would awkwardly spend a couple of days all together before Sheila left. Then he and Paul would stay two more weeks. This was tough. He could tell Paul wanted him to be there, to have the experience of being on the island and by the sea. That was definite.

By then Daniel was a teenager, hard to entertain and no longer playful. Paul brought a lady who stayed with them, cooking and taking care of the house while they were there. Paul and Daniel had very little to say to one another so Daniel had spent most of his time down on the beach, hanging out at the beach house, fiddling with the boat or sailing, sometimes fishing.

Paul spent his days reading and sunning on the terrace or doing mainland business on the phone. Sometimes Paul would go hiking alone. Daniel would ride his bike all over the island by himself. He liked to visit down at the marina with Otis, the caretaker, and his family, hanging out with them, passing the days at their houseboat.

Dinner was awkward too. In a formal tone, Paul would question him about things. Daniel's replies were always somewhat guarded. A few times, they made an attempt to play board games together. Two summers of that were enough for both of them. From then on, the property had not been used much at all. Paul would go alone at times. He liked to go and get apples in the early fall from the orchard on the property. Otis and his son Luke, who was just a few years older than Daniel, kept the place up nicely and watched out for it.

"I remember the Penguin," Daniel said. "I wonder if it's still there."

Paul chuckled. "Oh yes, I can see no reason why it wouldn't be. A great little kit boat that was. Probably back behind the beach house. So, you will have a House on a Hill and a Ship to Sail...!" He laughed again.

Daniel smiled too, watching him. He was glad that his mood was light.

"Otis is retired now, I see him here often on the mainland. A great friend. He lives near Anacortes. His son Luke is taking care of Glass House now. You can trust Luke."

"What about treatment plans for your problem, Paul?"

Paul's face turned serious at this. "I am not doing the extreme treatments recommended. This tumor was already so advanced there is no use in torturing myself with that kind of thing. Let nature take its course and I will stay here as long as I can at home. Jim is taking good care of me."

In fact, Jim, the housekeeper was hovering in the kitchen doorway now. He brought in the coffee carafe and poured another cup for them. Daniel realized that he was worried about Paul over-exerting himself in this meeting.

"I have been wrapping up loose ends and I think I have done everything I need to do with my estate. I wanted to talk with you personally while we have the time. I wanted you to know about Glass House." He paused, thinking.

"It's too bad your mother doesn't want to take over the brokerage. She is so capable. But, she has gone in another direction and I don't think she would want to turn back to this. My two best agents, Andy and Bill are interested in buying the company. I would love to sell it to them. In any case, they will take care of it, until it can be sold." His face brightened. "I don't suppose you have any desire to jump in and take it? Sheila could coach you."

"Wow, Paul, what an offer. I appreciate it but you know it would be a big stretch for me. I'm up to my neck at The Prow."

"Sure, of course, just thinking."

With that, Daniel could see that the Paul was finished. He became quiet, his hands softly patting the arm rests of the chair.

Daniel finally stood and walked to the window.

"You have a great view here, Paul. I love this harbor." Turning towards him he said, "I hope if you need anything, you will call me. I can come over most any time during the day. Drive you to the doctor or whatever. The Prow is at your service to provide meals, should you want to try them. You know the chowder is really delicious."

He was standing, looking down at Paul in his chair. He wanted to reach out and touch Paul's frail shoulder, or put his hand on his head for a moment but he knew this would make him terribly uncomfortable, so he did not do anything of the sort.

"Oh, no, no. I am going to be fine here. Jim and I are doing splendidly." He said this rapidly and Daniel knew he would never call him.

"I had better go, time to get back to the kitchen. Down at the restaurant, Saturday night is a big one for us."

Daniel smiled and walked over to Paul's chair. He did take his hand. It was very cold.

"Thanks, Paul, for this wonderful gift. I really appreciate the planning that you have done in giving me this. And thanks for the personal time." Daniel shook his hand. Paul's grip was still strong.

"Oh good, so glad you are pleased. It's a great property." Paul was back to the all-business, impersonal mode, not looking at him anymore.

"Help Daniel out will you Jim?" He lay back in his chair and closed his eyes.

Daniel walked to the door, giving Jim a look.

Jim quietly said, "Steady decline, but he is not in pain."

Daniel whispered, "Call me if I can do anything, O.K.?" Jim nodded solemnly and shut the door.

Standing outside on the porch, Daniel paused looking back at the door.

"I guess my Dad is dying," he said out loud. "It looks like he is not going to make it." He said this to the empty air, trying to take in the reality of it, but it was still not sinking in. Not real. He wished he had called him "Dad" during the visit, even though that title had not been used for many years, but it probably would have caused him distress. Best to leave well enough alone.

CHAPTER FIVE

# Disaster at Sheila's Place

SHEILA was not domestic. After her divorce from Paul, she had sold their old Queen Anne Hill condo and moved into a hotel, temporarily. This proved to be such an attractive lifestyle for her that she eventually bought a suite of rooms on the top floor of one of the boutique hotels downtown, the historic Murdoch. She had decided on this space immediately the first time she came to look at it. The rooms were just the right size, with high ceilings. Not too big so that she would be knocking around in a big space, just nice and snug. There was a "token" kitchen: all she needed was a toaster and coffee maker. It was a northwest corner unit on the top floor with French doors to the balcony. The final selling point was the view. Open, floor to ceiling views of a huge sky, the Bay and the Sound beyond, with green strips of island off in the far distance. You could walk out onto the small balcony into fresh air and have one or two pots of flowers. And besides, the hotel conference rooms and the restaurant would serve well for her business meetings. This way she had daily maid service; even her laundry was taken care of without ever needing to go out of the building.

She bought furniture and linens for her new place. She got the toaster and the coffee maker...perfect. She asked the hotel to bring in a decorator, and soon the place was charming and comfortable. Sheila loved lemon yellow and the walls throughout her place were a clear lemon chiffon hue. There were crown moldings at the ceiling and wide trim around the baseboards and doors, all painted brilliant white. The furnishings were dark wood. She insisted on sparse ornamentation. There were two simple tapestry wall hangings, some pictures with narrow black frames and accents of blue and white china. A ficus trimmed up to tree form filled the space in one corner. She had felt that she was home at last. Since her college days she had not been this happy.

Within months Sheila had put together an investment group to buy and renovate the hotel. She worked that deal and ended up as a twenty percent owner in the hotel. They refurbished the building and its public areas, keeping the traditional look in place. Strangely enough, her grandfather, William Stanton, Willie's father, had been one of the original owners of the place. She had vague memories of Thanksgiving dinners in the banquet rooms there as a child. She was happy.

The problem was that Sheila had her home, and Paul had his home too. But, since boarding school days, apparently Daniel was not really included at either of these places. Daniel had been transferred to the care of schools and, of course, Willie. Daniel came to understand this. Most of his school mates were in even worse condition. They lived a circular pattern from school to summer camp and then back to school with perhaps a two week

Christmas period with parents once a year. At least Daniel had Willie. He lived with her all summer and stayed with her for the term holidays of Easter and Christmas. At Christmas there would be a dinner at a private club in Seattle, or everyone would meet at Willie's house in Santa Barbara. Paul was always invited to these occasions and he usually showed up. The visits were brief and formal; it was fine. The pat on the back and the nice gift and that was it. Early on, Daniel used to turn this all over and over in his head, trying to understand what it was about him or what he had done that had caused this to happen.

Daniel never dropped in on Sheila at home. Nevertheless, when Daniel left Paul's condo he felt compelled to go directly to see Sheila. He had taken his car, even though Paul's house was just blocks from the restaurant. So, without calling ahead, he drove to Sheila's hotel. Maybe he would catch her there on a Saturday afternoon. The desk clerk rang her room and she was in.

When she opened her door, he could see the discomfort if not anxiety on her face. He could see that she had been reading on the couch; the paperback lay splayed open there, a glass of soda nearby. She was dressed in leggings and a tunic sweater, with wedgie house slippers on her feet.

"What's up?" she said, scanning him up and down.

"May I come in?"

Her eyes widened. "Of course! I am just surprised you are not at the restaurant."

"They can manage without me for a bit," he smiled. "I just wanted to come by for a visit. I have just had a visit with Paul at his place."

"Oh! Well, come on in. Would you like something to drink?"

Daniel was coffee-ed out so he asked for a glass of water. In a moment, she brought it and they sat down. Sheila's "wary button" had been fully punched. Her tension was palpable.

"Paul is dying, Sheila."

She was squirming in her seat now. "Oh? How do you know that?" she demanded, involuntarily crossing her arms in front of her.

"You ought to go see him, and then you would understand."

Sheila pursed her lips and looked down. "Daniel, you know when two people divorce that means that they are no longer responsible for each other's welfare. Paul is not my responsibility!"

"He's dying now, Sheila," said Daniel evenly. "He's dying."

"Well, that's no surprise given his diagnosis is it?" She leaned back into the sofa, arms still tightly crossed. She had regained her poise and was fully defended. "Just what is it that you expect from me?"

"I don't really know. I just thought I should come and let you know how it is going for him. Jim, his housekeeper, is there taking care of him. But he told me that he misses you. That he still cares about you. I guess that doesn't go both ways. I'm sorry I bothered you."

Sheila had sunk back into the sofa cushions in front of one of the floor to ceiling windows of the living room. Daniel could see the bay behind her. It was getting dark and he could see the lights coming up along the shoreline, and the abrupt ending of light where the water began. The lights of a few ships glittered in the dark areas. Her view faced north with the curve of the shore leading up the peninsula. In the daytime hours you could see not only the bay, but the Sound beyond. Suddenly, he was exhausted and wished he had not come. He stood up wearily. Sheila got up too and stood in front of the door.

"Daniel, all children want their estranged parents to reconcile. I understand your concern. Try not to worry. Paul and I understand each other, we always have. Everything is as it should be."

A little softer she said, "Thank you for coming by to tell me about this." She was standing very straight now, chin up.

He shook his head. "Why do I even try with you?" he said bitterly and pushed past her and out the door.

Outside in the hall, his anger brought him to a state of trembling. He wanted to reach back and pound on her door childishly but stopped himself and turned and walked away quickly to the elevator. He couldn't wait to get out of the building. As he got into the car, a flashback from his childhood began to unfold itself.

He was sitting in his car, but in his mind he was sitting with Sheila and Paul on a Sunday morning. Just sitting on the sofa between Paul and Sheila was a sharply remembered experience. He was in the middle of a force field of parental personality issuing back and forth. It was Sunday; he was still in pajamas, a weak, cloudy light coming in through the living room window. Paul was reading the Sunday Paper, some kind of bony, dry, hard vibration emanating from him. Sheila was going over a manual on her lap, from her something like a sharp, sparkling lit fuse flared out. Daniel was in the middle fiddling with a Rubik's cube, playing and feeling but not looking up. He must have been nine or ten years old. In a few short years Paul and Sheila would divorce. Not even this benign Sunday family time could be tolerated or at any rate desired, each parent appearing to prefer the single life and separate pursuits. It seemed that there simply was no need, no connection strong enough to keep them going forward together. At first, there had been an unpleasant separation, then a comfortable and amicable divorce. They remained friendly, just as they had been in their marriage. Daniel had eventually solved the Rubik's cube and finally tossed it away. But, he had never been able to solve the puzzle of Paul and Sheila.

His mind returned to the present. Sitting in the car he sighed deeply. He had done what he could. It was fully dark now. He started the car and headed back to The Prow, thinking at last how thankful he was to be heading toward that place of sanctuary.

After he left, Sheila took his glass and her glass of soda to the kitchen. With a quick motion she dumped both drinks in the sink. Then she poured herself a real drink, some bourbon on the rocks, and walked out through the sliding doors onto the little balcony. She stood a long time looking at the twinkling lights and the dark sea. Early the next morning, she dressed and went to attend early mass at San Sebastian's church nearby. She went to mass on Monday morning too, then she went on with her business as usual.

## CHAPTER SIX

# Thomas and Memories

DANIEL arrived back at The Prow at just about seven. There was already a great crowd of diners seated and more waiting and chatting in the foyer. This warmed his tired heart. Saturday was typically a family night and some kids were dashing around the foyer and playing on the floor. Everyone was jolly and it was getting loud. He had brought in huge white oriental lilies this morning for the foyer and arranged them in a black ceramic vase. They were a stunning sight in the evening amber light of the restaurant. He waved to people as he came in. Many were regular customers. Bea greeted him from the Maître D's station but did not cease her work. Going through, he saw Thomas sitting alone, obviously waiting for him at a back booth. Curiously, it looked like he was wearing a nylon zip front workout shirt. This was out of character for him. Daniel waved to him, but quickly went on through to the kitchen. Everything was moving well there. The staff was calm and he had not been missed or needed. He relaxed and looked over the plates going out for service. Everything looked fine. He smiled and gave a nod towards Oscar behind the stoves as he twirled from task to task. He smiled a big smile back and banged the spatula in his hand on the stove in an enthusiastic greeting. Daniel realized he had been holding his breath, something he was known to do when stressed. He took a deep breath and at the same time noted the wonderful aromas coming from the kitchen.

Trini approached him and putting an arm around him said, "Everything is fine. Why don't you go on and have dinner with Thomas? You can help me finish up later." She knew where he had been and was "mothering" him.

Daniel slipped into the booth across from Thomas. Trini was right behind him with a drink. She set it down and left.

"How did it go?" Thomas asked.

"Oh, peachy. It was a two-part series. First Paul. Then I went to Sheila's place."

Thomas winced. "Ouch, do you want to talk about it?"

Thomas was a blond with a halo of pale blond waves, chin length. He wasn't the sculpted Nordic kind of blond. His was a rounded form, wide through the shoulders, but there were no sharp angles to be found on his strong body. He also had a rounded, sweet face. It was a comfortable, attractive face, framed by the curls and heavy black-rimmed glasses which could not hide his intelligent, kind eyes. There was a downy blond moustache, clipped close. He reached out and patted Daniel's hand, smiling. His fingers were a little sausage-like too, with square perfectly manicured nails. Clean, white, wide hands.

Thomas was working on an art preservationist's degree at the university. He loved the world of British painting. His undergraduate degree had been done in English literature, but he had come to love the visual arts more. He was supporting himself with work as a computer graphic artist and copy writer; he was good at this. The two had noticed each other at a soirée during the past Christmas season at one of the upscale galleries in Capital Hill. They hit it off immediately that evening. Daniel had been attracted by Thomas' comfortable presence and sweetness. They had shared some great times throughout the holidays and then quiet intimate times in the cold winter together. Thomas had a very small place of his own in Capital Hill. Daniel had only been there once. It was jam-packed full of tools, art materials, and old musical instruments which he collected. There was a faint but attractive smell of resin and linseed oil. Now though, they were spending more and more time at Daniel's condo in the Graystone Arms. Thomas occasionally spent the night. Neither had much free time, but these days Thomas had been making time to be with Daniel. Of course Daniel did not have the academic background which Thomas possessed, but he did enjoy reading and he admired Thomas' acute sensibility in the art world and with beautiful objects and paintings. And there was something else about Thomas, some quality which Daniel could not fully describe. It was a mixture of responsiveness, comfort, emotional depth and a subtly androgynous prettiness.

Now though, he moved his hand away from Thomas' patting gesture. As usual, something was happening with Daniel. He was beginning to feel both stifled and bored with Thomas. Thomas' eyes registered a hurt, surprised look. Daniel looked away ignoring this and continued scanning the dining room, checking on how things were going in the moment.

"We don't need to talk about my parental visits," he said. "Same old, same old. Paul is very sick though."

"I am so sorry, Daniel."

"It is to be expected. Pancreatic cancer. He is clearly declining. He has good care though." Daniel was looking away, still scanning the dining room. "I don't think I want to go out or anything tonight. Let's have dinner and call it a night."

Thomas was quiet. The waiter came over quickly, seeing Daniel's motion to order. They both ordered the flounder sautéed with butter, mushrooms and thinly sliced leeks. There was some small talk. Thomas had gotten a new graphic design account with an online eyeglass framing business there in Seattle. It was going to be a nice creative venture and would include both website graphics and print media. He chatted happily about it.

Finally, Daniel asked Thomas about his new black, zippered nylon shirt. It was an innovation for him.

"I've decided to join a gym and try to tone up a bit," he said, a little sheepishly. "I went for the first time this afternoon. I've got a trainer. We didn't do much today, just got acquainted with the guy and the equipment."

"Oh, wow. That's new. That's great. Good for you. You'll probably enjoy that."

The coffee was brought to the table, two decaf cappuccinos. They sipped. No further conversation.

"Well, I guess I'll get along home then. Sounds like you have had a stressful day and need to be alone." Thomas said this questioningly, hopefully.

Daniel nodded, looking away.

"O.K., dinner was superb. Thanks. I wanted to be here for you tonight. I know this is a really difficult time for you. Give me a call, O.K.?" He was hurt.

"Yeah, I'll call you tomorrow." Daniel didn't want to look at his eyes. "Maybe we could take a walk along the bay. I feel like getting outdoors. How about you?"

"Great! I need that," Thomas smiled. "That will add to my exercise régime." He slid out of the booth and was gone.

As he was leaving, Daniel thought he noticed a bit of moistness to his eyes. "Such a nice guy," he thought. "This is giving me guilt and I sure don't need it at this point." He went out to the kitchen, the rush had settled down by then. He spent the rest of the evening hanging out with the kitchen staff and helping to close things down. As usual, Oscar and Trini gave Daniel and Henry a ride home the few blocks to his condo after closing up.

They went in and Daniel made a cup of jasmine tea. Henry had been given his last trip outside back at the park near the restaurant so he got into his pillow bed with a grunt and settled down to sleep. Not so Daniel. He began to think back over the events of this incredibly tense day. He was no longer angry about Sheila. What could be expected? She is who she is and it was foolish going over there thinking things might be different. It was not worth the effort to be so angry. He shook his head and snorted. Henry opened one eye to look at him, and then returned to his slumber.

Daniel looked around his living room. Like everything else, he had designed it meticulously. It was meant to be his home, his dwelling place, a place to relax. Unlike his father's taste for hard contemporary line, Daniel's place was a haven of multi-layered, contemporary warmth and natural things. To offset the cool atmosphere of Seattle, he had painted all walls in tones of pumpkin, gold and the amber which he had used also in the restaurant. There was a feeling of warm stone. The sofa and chairs were tweedy and substantial. Woods were pine with a light finish and so were the floors. The lamps were those three-dimensional paper columns for soft light and a sculptural presence. The walls were mostly bare. There were some framed shells over the sofa and he had some carved pine baskets and woven pine needle trays on the tables. He had wanted it to be warm, but simple, not visually complex, a place to rest. There was only one huge, split-leaf philodendron for a decorative focus. Its dark green shape twisted upward, nearly reaching the ceiling.

Now his mind wandered back to Thomas. He sighed. He was so tired of this cycle, the attraction, and then the rush to pleasure in the exotic newness of a relationship. Then finally, the inevitable loss of interest and the unpleasant and often sad ending. He hated it, but he wanted to do the right thing.

It had been a long day but he could not give up yet and go to bed. Memories kept flooding back from previous relationships. He sat there motionless, cradling his tea cup and remembering. In the beginning, there were the early days away at school. First, when he arrived in this new environment there was an ever-deepening loneliness, a feeling of alienation from the other boys. But then, he had found his group.

In the beginning there was confusion, shame, but also pleasure. There were crazy escapades usually led by the older boys, the laughing, the dares, the drinking, the strangeness of another person's flesh, but the thrill of doing something taboo. Daniel never liked drugs. He hated smoking. Nevertheless, this life was a severe form of rebellion. Of course, always ending up the same way. There were several boys who had meant a lot to

Daniel, the first people on earth who had ever showed they cared about him, other than Willie back in Santa Barbara.

Paul and Sheila had given him very little moral direction or training. Lying was clearly condemned and stealing. He remembered the devastation when Paul had caught him taking some chocolate candy bars when they had visited with some friends for dinner. He must have been about eight years old. He had seen them in a drawer when the hostess was working on the dinner in the kitchen. Later, while the adults were talking in the living room, Daniel had gone back into the kitchen and taken three candy bars out of the drawer. He ate one, and put the rest in his pocket. Later when they were driving home he took the others out of his pocket and showed them to his parents, offering them one to eat there in the car. Paul had become enraged and stopped the car. He told him this was stealing and the feeling was that it was the very worst thing you could do. Paul turned the car around and drove back to the friend's house. He made Daniel go up to the door alone and ring the doorbell. He had to give the candy back and tell the host he was sorry. Then he ran crying back to the car. They drove home. Paul in a cold tone told him that stealing was against the Ten Commandments. He had never heard of the Ten Commandments before. But, that was the end of Daniel's life of thievery.

Sheila was a Roman Catholic. She regularly attended church, but for some reason, she did not see to it that Daniel follow her in that. She took him to mass when he was small, but no explanation was given about what was going on there in the church. He was just taken along with her. It was pleasant enough, but he had never made a connection between being there and anything to do with his conduct. He had seen the wooden Jesus there, hanging on the cross. It didn't make sense to him. He did wonder though, if Jesus had also stolen something. Not candy bars, he was sure of that, but maybe something much more valuable. These trips to mass had ended for him when he went away to school.

He remembered when he had first brought home someone that he was involved with. It was when he was in high school in Santa Barbara. He had come up to Seattle with his schoolmate, David, for spring break. Daniel wanted to give David the tour of Seattle. They had stayed with Paul. He remembered the moment when Paul had realized what was going on with them. Daniel had seen the dawning in Paul's face and then came the formal stiff-arm distancing. Nothing had ever been said. However, after this, Paul's disinterest seemed even clearer to him. The decision later to forego college and become a chef had apparently put the icing on the cake for Paul, and Daniel figured he was almost completely abandoned after that.

There was certainly no "birds and bees" talk from anyone. So it was catch-as-catch-can regarding sex, responsibility and morality. He had learned from others, from society as a whole and had formed a personal code of his own, which sometimes worked and sometime left him grasping for an anchor that was not there. But, eventually, he thought he knew what was right and what was wrong, how to treat people. He thought he knew, but was not always sure. Now, with Thomas, his moral sensibilities were immediately under siege. Thomas did not deserve to be treated badly, and Daniel did not want to treat him badly, but he was beginning to see that their relationship was soon to be over. This cycle was beginning to get him down. How to do it? How to be decent. That was the question.

Since Daniel lived most of his teen years and beyond in Santa Barbara with Willie, she was really the first to understand Daniel's lifestyle. He brought home friends to the Santa Barbara house. She said nothing. Sometimes she tried to fix up dates with him with granddaughters of her friends. They were cute girls and he liked most of them. He smiled thinking about how they always wanted to kiss him and wanted him to kiss them. They were needy. They were star-struck by his good looks. He did not know why he felt so strange about their rounded hips and their otherness, but it did feel strange to him and he could not help it. Sometimes Willie had tried to begin a conversation with him about all this, but he successfully derailed that with humor, and Willie did laugh and just let it go. She loved him and never turned away from him. Her love was solid, this he knew for sure.

Then there was Douglas. What a trip he was! Daniel had met him at a party just after he returned from Europe. Douglas was 18 years older. A professor of literature, handsome, graying hair, tall. An altogether romantic figure, he had seen Daniel literally across a crowded room and was immediately zeroed in on Daniel's striking delicate looks. Douglas was the only one who had wooed him in an old-fashioned way. Always reciting poetry to him and telling him how he put him in mind of Shelley. Within a couple of weeks, Daniel moved in with Douglas and the wining and dining began. Douglas bought Daniel many gifts and even brought him a "poet's shirt" one day. He wanted Daniel to read poetry to him in the shirt, but Daniel was not the poetic soul that Douglas imagined. Daniel declined the poetry sessions but tolerated Douglas' reading and playing tapes of poetry readings he had held before. Douglas was dominating, but softly, and Daniel felt much appreciated, much loved.

One day they went clothes shopping together. Douglas was a clothes horse. He was looking for a suit for a special conference coming up. When he emerged from the dressing room wearing a dark brown suit, Daniel froze. Douglas was very taken with the suit and was rattling on about how professional he looked and was twirling around before the mirror. The salesmen were agreeing and pumping out compliments. Daniel became deadly quiet and as they arrived home after shopping, he knew he was leaving.

His time with Douglas was over. In a few days he had left, moving back in briefly with Willie. There was no talk about it at home between him and Willie. Douglas was devastated and called, leaving messages for two weeks, before he finally gave up. That was when Daniel had made the final move back to Seattle. And, that was when Daniel had started seeing Charlotte, his counselor. After a few weeks of sessions, they hit upon a devastating memory. At Charlotte's recommendation, Daniel avoided older men after that.

With that remembrance, Daniel shuddered, quickly returning to the present and mentally turning off indulgences into the past. He picked up his cup and took it to the kitchen, turned out the lights and made his way to bed.

## CHAPTER SEVEN

# A Second Visit

TWO weeks had passed since Daniel had visited Paul at home. He had phoned several times, Jim always answered. He said Paul was about the same. He was weaker, but still moving around the house. Jim was driving him everywhere he needed to go. He was mainly resting and reading. Jim took him to the doctor as needed, stayed late and arrived early every day. He had not needed to spend the night yet. Paul didn't want to take calls on the phone, but Jim would tell him that Daniel had called. Thanks so much. Oh, and his mother, Sheila, had dropped by last week. And Otis.

Daniel decided to make soup for Paul and take it over to him. He and Trini worked up some slow cooked chicken bone broth. Then they added just a few vegetables, blended it, finishing it with some mild spices and heavy cream. He called and told Jim he was coming over.

The day was clear and bright, so Daniel just walked over this time carrying his thermos jug of soup with him. Jim came to the door and brought him in. Paul was in his recliner leaned back and dozing. This time he was wearing a forest green jogging suit. Daniel thought he looked about the same. He couldn't tell right off. Paul did seem more drugged, not so alert. He was obviously weaker.

"Got some soup here for you Paul. Cream of chicken. Are you hungry? It's very bland. I know you don't need spicy stuff right now."

Paul smiled at him.

"I am not ever hungry any more. But I'll bet it is great. Let Jim put it in the refrigerator till dinner time. Thank you for your trouble." He reached out his hand to touch Daniel's hand. Paul's hand was cold.

"Are you cold, Paul?" Daniel asked.

"Cold all the time," he smiled. "Just not moving around much to get the blood going." Another smile.

"So Sheila was here for a visit, right?"

"Yes, she came by the other day. Was it Wednesday, Jim? I think it was Wednesday. It was good to see her. She brought me some peanut brittle, my favorite. She remembered that. It was a nice visit. I loved seeing her." His eyes were glistening; the smile remained.

"I'm glad you're here too. I have wanted to let you in on what I have arranged with the medical people. I'm doing O.K. but this situation here with Jim won't last forever. I can't expect him to be my nurse. I am probably going to need somebody with me all the time later, you know. If possible I will go to the hospice center. It's all arranged. If that's not enough, I'll have to go to the hospital. I hope I don't have to. We'll see. I don't want you or your mother having to do anything to make this all happen.

It's all arranged and Sheila knows that too. Like I said, it's all arranged."

"Are you in pain, Paul?" Daniel was watching him closely. "Are you taking pain meds?"

"Yeah, some... I just feel very very weak."

He looked weak. Daniel was trying not to be alarmed. There was nothing to be alarmed about. Paul's life was waning. Nothing could stop that, but he couldn't help a rising feeling of alarm. He reached over again to touch Paul's arm. It was so thin. Daniel almost wished he had not come this time. How was he going to live with this anxiety, not being here, not knowing?

Paul was talking again, kind of mumbling. His eyes were nearly closed now. Suddenly he opened his eyes wide, focusing on Daniel's face.

"I want you to know that I am not afraid. I am going to be alright. Actually, everything is going to be alright. You remember Otis, our caretaker on the island. Otis will speak for me, when I am gone. Stick close to Otis, Daniel, O.K.?" His eyes were steady and soft.

"I'm sorry, Daniel. I'm sorry for all my failures with you. I hope you can forgive me." He closed his eyes again.

Daniel reached out and touched the top of his head this time. That was as close as he dared get to an embrace. Paul did not react to this. Daniel then stood up and walked out, tears coming rapidly. Jim was waiting by the door to show him out. He was maintaining a stoic face, but he patted Daniel on the back.

"I will call you immediately when things change. You can trust me."

"I know. Thanks so much. This is hard. This is really hard. See if you can get him to try the soup, all right?" Daniel sounded a bit panicked.

Jim nodded. "I know. Take care of yourself. I'll call you."

## CHAPTER EIGHT

## The Call

A week later, in the early afternoon, Daniel was working in The Prow kitchen, filleting fish and chatting with Oscar. The office phone rang; Trini went in to answer. She came back quickly.

"It's Jim. He needs to talk to you, Daniel."

Jim quickly told Daniel that Paul was having trouble breathing and that they were leaving for the hospital. An ambulance was there to take him and Paul's doctor had been notified and would be there as soon as he could.

Daniel left the fish in the care of Oscar. Trini drove and dropped him off at the hospital, which was actually just blocks away from Graystone Arms. It was a huge medical center, but Daniel made his way quickly through the maze of echoing hallways to the emergency center desk. There was Jim standing in the waiting area. He had followed the ambulance over in his own car.

"He just started having trouble breathing about an hour ago," Jim said. "They asked me to stay out here." He looked bewildered.

Daniel talked with the receptionist and was told to wait briefly until they could get Paul registered in. Not to worry, he had been provided with oxygen from the time he entered the ambulance. Paul's doctor had arrived. Daniel and Jim sat together. The whole thing was unbelievable to Daniel. Jim was surprised too. He said things had been going smoothly until today. Paul had not been able to eat since the night before due to nausea. They had thought it was just the medication. He had been increasing pain meds.

In just a few minutes, a nurse came and motioned for them to come in. There was Paul in a bay of the emergency room, with a nasal oxygen hookup. He was curled up, obviously in pain and so thin. An IV drip had been put in and the nurse said he would feel relief momentarily.

Daniel saw the doctor sitting outside at a desk working on something. Then he got up and came to meet Daniel and Jim. They moved away from Paul's bed and the doctor looked from one to the other of them gravely.

"It looks like the cancerous growth has invaded his lungs," he said simply. "This is causing the pain and cutting off his ability to breathe. In any case, it will not be long with this development, a matter of days most likely. There may also be some pneumonia. We will keep him here. Hospice can't handle this. We will keep him comfortable now through the IV and with the oxygen. We have told him what is happening and that he is going to feel better with these drugs and that we will keep it that way. I am very sorry. I wish we could do more." His face showed a sincere empathy. He shook Daniel's hand and then Jim's. Then he went back in with Paul.

They stood there in the hall looking down at the floor. Neither one knowing what on earth to say. Within minutes, the doctor pulled aside the draped curtain and motioned for them to come in. Paul was relaxed now, breathing heavily with the oxygen and nearly asleep. He looked very white.

"We're putting him in a room on the third floor with other critical care patients. I suggest you speak to him now and then let us get him settled. He is going to be knocked out for a while. No need to stay right now. Check with the nurse to get his room number."

They went in and put a hand on each side of Paul, on his shoulders. He did not respond to their presence. They looked across at each other and quietly left. In the hall, Jim told Daniel that Paul had planned for this. He had pre-arranged for a private nurse to come in if he needed it. It was all set up. Jim would call the nurse. Paul did not want any of them to be staying up with him at night at the hospital. He thought that would be inconvenient and tiring and everyone needed their rest in order to work, he had said. It was all arranged.

Daniel nodded, teary. "O.K. then, I will be back later this evening. And, I will call Sheila and tell her what has happened. Will you call Paul's office and let the guys know up there?"

"I will be glad to. And I'll see you later tonight also." Jim gave Daniel a ride back to the restaurant. Neither one spoke as they drove the short distance. As Daniel climbed out of the car he thanked Jim and they exchanged a look. It was a look of resignation and fear mixed.

Daniel called Sheila. Her response was just to thank him for the call. She didn't offer anything else. Daniel couldn't really think about her right now. He went into The Prow office and sat down on the sofa. Trini came in and sat with him for a while. She told him to stay put, that the staff would handle everything for the dinner crowd. On top of everything else, he was agitated that he could not attend to his business in The Prow as always. He continued sitting. He didn't know how long he had been there, but he finally got up and put Henry on the leash and told everyone he was leaving for the day and walked out. He and Henry trudged up the hill to his condo. Henry was quiet too and seemed to know that he should stay that way. They went in and Daniel called Thomas at home. He was working there on the new graphics job.

"My Dad's in the hospital," he said on the phone. "Paul is in the hospital. Everything is going downhill fast. I think I am scared."

Thomas said he would come right over. He did come right over and embraced Daniel in a warm bear hug and held him there for a time. They sat down on the sofa in the late afternoon light.

"I can't begin to say how lost I feel and how scared." He was clasping and unclasping his hands.

"Why are you scared?" Thomas asked.

"Seeing Paul like that, all curled up in a ball, hurting so bad. It was shocking. Paul is not like that. Paul is strong and tall...and hard...stoic!" He began to cry.

"Well, not anymore," said Thomas gently. "He is vulnerable to pain, just like any of us." And Thomas began to cry too.

Thomas went into the kitchen and rummaged until he found a carton of tomato basil soup. He heated it and fixed some toast and tea; and they ate. "Let's go back to the hospital. We can walk, it's just a few blocks."

Daniel nodded. "O.K., Let me change my clothes. I smell like fish."

They made their way to the hospital. They found Paul's room on the third floor. Jim was already there, looking very nervous. Paul was now drugged to the hilt. He could barely see them all looking down at him.

"What are you boys looking at?" he slightly smiled. "Don't you have anything better to do than watch a guy die?" He laughed a bit. He was looped. His color had returned a bit, not so white now.

They all three just patted him in turn, on the sheet-wrapped leg, on the hand, on the bony shoulder. He sighed and snuggled down in the bedding.

"You can go on home now, there's nothing here to do." And he drifted off to sleep.

They sat awhile talking in low voices; then the private nurse arrived. Her name was June. She was tall and slender and obviously efficient. She seemed kind. She took Daniel's phone number and the restaurant number. She promised to call him with any and all news. There was nothing else he could do. They shook hands all around and left.

For the next three days, Daniel would wander in and out of the hospital when he could, looking in on Paul. He was obviously well cared for there and was always knocked out, asleep. Daniel asked a few times if Sheila had been there. No one remembered having seen her. Jim was in and out too, and they said a big man had been there. That would have been Otis.

CHAPTER NINE

# Paul's Death

ON the fourth morning, the hospital called Daniel at the restaurant office. Trini came to get him with a pale face. He knew what was coming. Nurse June's message was simple. "You'd better come now."

Daniel decided to take a cab to the hospital. Oscar and Trini needed to stay at the restaurant. It was the best way under the circumstances, but the cab's ticking meter drove him wild with its constant measured beat of time and distance. He jumped out immediately when it arrived and dashed through the hospital's glass doors. With a grinding feeling in his stomach, he approached Paul's room. Jim was sitting in the nearby waiting area. Daniel was surprised when Sheila came out the door of Paul's room, just as he was going in. They nearly collided. She was hard-faced but teary.

"I'm not going back in," she said. "I'm finished. You go." She didn't leave though, but took her place in a chair in the waiting lounge. She offered Daniel no embrace, no touch of sympathy, as he knew she should do. She merely took up her vigil in closed-off silence.

Daniel did not know what he had expected at Paul's end, but certainly not this. It was as if Paul was literally melting away. He was smaller in the bed than when he had arrived there. There was just less of him. It was hard to believe that Paul had ever been a six foot tall, strong, raw-boned man. The cancer in these last days was literally swallowing him up. Things were less complex in the room now. Equipment and lines were being quietly removed. The IV was out. He could tell Paul was conscious, though.

"Who is it?" Paul said in the strangest voice Daniel had ever heard come from his father. It was a guttural, chirping sound.

June, the nurses and two technicians were there. "Move in closer," a nurse said, quietly. "He is not seeing anymore."

Daniel moved closer, barely touching the bed. Paul's thin hand was there and Daniel took it in his own.

"It's me, Daniel," he said. Paul was able to turn a sightless face toward his son.

In that same strange voice, he said, "My Danny." And with what strength he had left he pulled Daniel down closer to him. "I love my little Danny," he whispered.

There was a sort of smile on Paul's thin translucent lips. His eyes, though sightless, seemed to be focused above and beyond the ceiling. Then he was quiet. He patted Daniel's hand several times, then lay still, closing his eyes.

"My beautiful boy."

Daniel was so stunned that he could not begin to take in what was happening; he had never been called Danny before. He had never heard this voice before. He stepped back and watched.

The medical staff were doing things, then most of them left, leaving only June, one hospital nurse and Daniel. Daniel was focused on what was happening to his father. He just sat by the window watching for what must have been an hour. He could see that Paul was leaving, just coming away from his flesh, and then in a moment he was gone. Daniel saw the final exhalation, then the face composed itself and all was still. The hospital nurse moved in to check his pulse and Nurse June quickly came around the bed and put her arms around Daniel warmly.

"I'm sorry," June said, giving the strong and needed embrace that his mother had failed to give.

Right then he hated Sheila with a fury. But as he looked at Paul's body, still at last, so diminished and apparently weightless, he knew that he could not resent him ever again. What he felt was surprise and pity and sadness. He also felt that a small, but very heavy stone had been dropped into the center of his being. Its weight was unbearable. And whirling all around this stone were questions, and loss.

Someone had gone out to tell Sheila in the waiting area. The male hospital staff were silently readying the bed to be moved out of the room. They did not speak or meet Daniel's eyes. He sighed and then went out into the hall himself. Sheila was standing there. When Daniel approached her she just nodded her head over and over, as if to say, "Yes, he's dead. Yes..."

Finally, she said firmly, "Don't worry about anything. I will carry out all of his arrangements. His wishes have been given to me by Sam Ellis, his attorney, and we will follow them. He wanted to be cremated and then a memorial service. You can take part in the details if you want to. I'll call you." With this she gathered her coat and bag and turned to go.

Daniel said, "Wait. I want to have a reception and some food after the service down at The Prow. We'll close for the day."

"That would be nice, Daniel. I'll call you soon." She turned and left.

Daniel went back into Paul's room. He found his hand, shrouded now by the sheet, taking the hand in his own. The feel of that hand was all that Daniel needed to know that now Paul was really and truly gone.

Just then Otis arrived and he and Jim came in. Jim was wiping his eyes, and he patted Daniel's back, saying nothing. Otis hugged Daniel hard and a sort of rumbling sound, heavy and rich, starting coming out of him. He was humming! He was humming some old hymn of his. He smoothed his big hands over the sheet covering Paul's body on the bed. Back and forth he smoothed the sheet and tucked it in as he smoothed, just like a woman would tuck in a sleeping child.

Then his deep voice said loudly, "God Almighty, God Almighty." Neither Daniel nor Jim could bear this and they walked out of the room. They could still hear Otis humming and chanting, "God Almighty, God Almighty…"

## CHAPTER TEN

# The Memorial Service

DANIEL did not feel like driving, so he and Thomas took a cab to Paul's memorial service. He hadn't asked for a ride from anyone else. He just didn't think of it. It was a strange way to arrive at your father's memorial service, he thought, but typical of the disjointed nature of his family. The cabbie let them off at the gate. They wanted to walk in through the memorial garden, taking their time.

The cemetery was located on a high spot in Queen Anne Hill, in the midst of a beautiful garden. And though Daniel had dreaded this event, the beauty of the surroundings was a comfort as they made their way towards the site of the mausoleum, in the center of the cemetery. It was a perfect spring morning. Blossoming trees stood out brightly against the intense green all around and beds of tulips and crocuses colored the way along the paths. The sound of traffic in the distance was only faintly heard. They could see a group already gathered there, at least fifty people.

Paul had chosen to be cremated. So, his remains would be interred in the columbarium there in front of them, a double bank of highly polished stone, and two tall rectangles with a trellised grid connecting them overhead. It couldn't be called a building as it could not be entered, at least not by the living. Just two big, high blocks with square niches on every side of the polished stone for the remains of the dead.

The urn Paul had selected for his ashes was black marble in the simplest possible shape, a sturdy rectangular box, with a flat lid on which a small engraved metal plaque gave his name with dates of birth and death. The urn sat on a larger rectangular marble stand in front of the opened niche space, also rectangular. These niches were openings in the tall, polished mausoleum wall, an even larger rectangle. Each niche was sealed with a smooth bronze plate after interment... plain, neat, strong, geometric... just right for Paul.

The assembled crowd was waiting quietly as the Navy chaplain walked among them. He wore dress blues with a white brocade clerical stole. He was shaking the hands of some, embracing some, quietly speaking a word to Sheila and few others. Sheila stood significantly to the side, eyes down, hands folded together, while Daniel, bringing Thomas with him, walked through the crowd, placing himself closest to the urn. He wanted to fully experience this. He knew what was in the urn. He had gone to the crematorium the night before for a short official ceremony as a witness to the veracity of the transfer of the remains. Sheila had called him and asked him to take care of this detail. He had signed the papers declaring that these were indeed the ashes of Paul Cross. He had looked into the urn before it was sealed...pale sandy grit, with one or two tiny slivers of white solid bone. This had surprised him. He had thought it would be powdery ash like after a wood fire. He had needed to see this. It was some kind of closure.

Daniel did not know everyone present, but picked out a number of Paul's old Navy friends, people from his office, business associates, several neighbors from the condo, Jim, the housekeeper, Sarah, Paul's old secretary, now in a wheelchair, Paul's attorney, Sam Ellis, and Sheila. It was the first time he had ever met Paul's nephew and niece from Idaho. The family resemblance was there. They looked more like Paul than Daniel himself; both were tall and blond with angular bodily attitude and stance. Sheila introduced them quietly to Daniel and Thomas. Of course Otis was there too, with his wife, Marion. Daniel had never before seen him dressed in a suit and his huge form in formal dress created a presence not to be ignored. He was to speak, as arranged, for Paul. Daniel noticed that Sheila was wearing a beautifully cut midnight blue silk suit. There was a corsage of two white camellias at the lapel. He thought the idea of wearing a fresh corsage here somewhat odd, but shrugged it off. "Who knows what she means by it," he thought.

Thomas was hovering near Daniel, clearly moved already to tears. He reached out to put an arm around Daniel, but Daniel moved away from him. He was not in the mood to join in Thomas's emotional display. Thomas glanced at him quickly.

Soon the chaplain took his place by the urn and the service began. He began with a psalm.

"There is a river whose streams make glad the city of God,
The holy dwelling places of the Most High
God is in the midst of her, she will not be moved…"

More prayers and readings were given. Paul had not wanted "falderal", so no furling and unfurling of flags was done. The chaplain simply offered Daniel the tri-folded flag; it felt strange in his hands, rougher than he had thought, and dry.

Otis stepped up to give his talk. He was wearing a wide smile, standing there in his dark suit. You would think he was about to perform a wedding, from the joyful look on his face. Then in his rich voice he spoke movingly of Paul's naval service, his business achievements and then turned to the subject of his character. Daniel was listening intently.

"Paul was a quiet man. A person hard to get to know," he said.

The crowd gave out a soft chuckle, but Daniel's shoulders slumped and he looked down.

"There was always more of Paul than he expressed to the world. He was a stern but loyal man, and he was my friend. I am so sorry for his suffering. His death was too early. He had plenty left to do here on this earth. I knew him first in the Navy. When our family moved out to San Juan, I started working for Paul. He had a young family too. Paul was always protecting and providing for his family and beyond. He made life easy for our family too with his generosity. I loved the man. Some thought him hard. I didn't. I knew he was just a disciplined man. He gave his best and expected the best from those around him."

Daniel's eyes filled with tears.

"What you may not know is that about three years ago Paul and I started to spend more time together. After Marion and I moved back to the mainland, Paul and I, we'd meet and go to coffee. Even before his sickness came on he was aware that his life was like a brief candle, burning down. We talked a lot. He had many questions about the universe...whether there was anyone out there running things. He talked about these things with me."

With this Otis smiled his enormous smile. "I tried to point him to God, to Christ.

He's my Lord, you know."(Another huge smile and he patted his chest over his heart) "Somehow, I was not able to help Paul. He was looking out far past me and my puny words. Something did happen though to Paul, and I want to tell you about it. He wanted me to tell you about it too.

"One day he called me and asked me to meet him. He told me that something had happened to him. He said one day he had been driving in heavy rain. He lost control of his car. The brakes were wet and failed. Then he skidded into a car in front of him. There was not too much damage, fenders and bumpers smashed up; but a young guy with some children was driving the car he hit. They both got out to survey the damage. No one was injured, but it was scary. The guy's family was in the car. Little kids were peeking out through the back window. To get out of the rain, Paul suggested that they climb back into his car to talk and exchange names and insurance information. As the young man sat there in Paul's car writing, something began to happen. Paul said he felt something that he could only describe as a 'connection.' A connection to everything good, to life, in a way that he had not felt before. He said he felt a warmth coming to him, and a power over him. And, just then, the young guy had paused from his writing and looked straight at Paul. Then he said, "Someone was looking out for us all today." Paul said he was stunned and immediately knew it was true. Someone, some Good Person was in control, when he had lost control. When he went home, this experience stayed with him. After that Paul had peace, even later when the cancer arrived on his doorstep. A few months later, I guess you all don't know this, but Paul called me and we talked some; he asked me to baptize him. I am a lay preacher at our church; he knew that."

At this there was a rustling in the assembled crowd.

"So I invited Paul to our church service one Sunday and I baptized him in the presence of our congregation. That day he made a public statement of faith."

Now there was complete stillness among the mourners. Daniel was stunned.

Otis took a paper out of his pocket and looked back up at everyone.

"So therefore, my friends, I can with complete confidence read to you the poem which Paul asked me to read here for him. I believe our friend, our family member and a fine sailor has entered the eternal life safe and sound."

Shaking his head and with one last smile, he read:

*"Sunset and evening star,*
*And one clear call for me!*
*And may there be no moaning of the bar,*
*When I put out to sea,*
*But such a tide as moving seems asleep,*
*Too full for sound and foam,*
*When that which drew from out the boundless deep*
*Turns again home.*
*Twilight and evening bell,*
*And after that the dark!*
*And may there be no sadness of farewell,*
*When I embark;*

*For tho' from out our bourne of Time and Place*
*The flood may bear me far,*
*I hope to see my Pilot face to face*
*When I have cross the bar."*\**

Then Otis gently touched the urn before him and said, "I love you, brother. Rest in peace..." He folded his paper and stepped back into the group beside Marion. She patted his arm.

Daniel looked over at Sheila and saw that she was looking away. Even so, he could see the pained, twisted expression on her face.

The chaplain continued, finishing with a short prayer of committal. He briefly removed his stole and wrapped it over the urn, making the sign of the cross over it. Then he lifted and placed the urn into the niche. Daniel thought it looked small and somber in there. The crowd was then invited to greet the family and there was a time of greeting and condolence. An announcement was given that a reception was to follow the service at The Prow Restaurant. All were invited. There was a final benediction, then everyone began to disperse, talking quietly as they left.

From the corner of his eye, Daniel saw Sheila step up to the niche, detach her white corsage and place it inside, next to the urn. Then she walked quickly away, speaking to no one.

Daniel asked Otis and Marion for a ride back to the restaurant for himself and Thomas. Two other naval officers, who had been watching at the side stepped up to the niche, standing by until all was secured. The chaplain remained also, watching. Daniel was reluctant to leave, but cemetery workers

---

*\*Crossing the Bar, by Alfred, Lord Tennyson*

were approaching with tools to close and fasten the niche. He could not bear to watch that. He kept looking back, feeling an incompleteness, a restlessness coming over him.

"So this is what it means to be bereft," he thought. With a sigh, he and Thomas left with Otis and Marion for the restaurant.

They entered The Prow and Daniel saw that Trini and Oscar were on the job, acting as hosts. They had done a fine job of preparing a buffet for the crowd in the private banquet room at the back of the restaurant. Daniel had told them to work up something of their own choice. They had done well. There was a huge bone-in Virginia ham, thinly sliced, with a creamy mustard sauce. Prow Chowder was served in two-handled soup dishes. There was a Grown-Up Mac and Cheese dish with Havarti and Ementaler cheeses and mushrooms, steamed fresh spring asparagus in a lemon sauce and a finely shredded cabbage salad. All solid and plain foods, comforting foods, meant to honor Paul and to appeal to the needs of everyone on this day. For a dessert Trini had returned to her roots, preparing coconut flan from her mother's special recipe from Mexico. And there were two four-layer chocolate cakes. Trini was hovering over everyone, with a pale face of concern, wearing a black skirt and frilly white blouse with a standup collar. Oscar manned the buffet. Trini had arranged some fresh spring flowers for the tables. Everyone relaxed into the room at last, choosing drinks and plates of food, clustering in groups and talking about the service, about Paul, and Otis' stunning story.

Sheila had taken a table with Paul's niece and nephew and was trying to introduce everyone. She looked better now and Daniel nodded to her and left her to her tasks of hospitality.

Daniel stood with Otis and Marion, sipping a drink, making small talk. They talked about the past few months and Paul's decline. Thomas worked the room, chatting amiably with everyone, trying to be helpful.

There, next to Otis, Daniel quietly said, "Thanks for your kind words for my Dad. I really did not know him that way. Maybe I really did not know him at all. Actually, the problem is, I did not know how to be his son," he said with a tight voice. "Paul was a mystery to me and I don't think he liked me very much."

Otis smiled at Daniel. Actually, he smiled over him, he was so big. He patted Daniel's back gently.

"It is like I said; Paul was a complex guy, unexpressive at times. I am so sorry you two did not do well together, but I would have to believe that he loved you." Otis just kept patting Daniel's back softly as they stood there side by side.

Finally, Daniel turned and looked Otis straight in the eyes.

"You know Otis, that I am not the kind of man Paul had hoped for. He did say he loved me though, right before he died. There in the hospital. It was weird."

## CHAPTER ELEVEN

## A Dream

THE night after the memorial service, Daniel had a terrifying dream. A nightmare. It began innocently enough. He was entering a favorite men's store downtown. As he walked through the door, it was apparent that things had changed. All the merchandise was gone, nothing but empty racks lined the walls. Then he saw that the owners were gathered together at one end of the store sorting through some bolts of cloth. It seemed like he was looking over their shoulders, innocently trying to see what they were doing. The fabric was beautiful stuff and he began to talk to the two owners asking about what was going on. They were reluctant to talk to him, and replied brusquely that they were no longer a retail shop and that he needed to go. Still amiable, he told them he would like to order a sports coat to be made from one of the bolts of cloth. The owners furtively ushered him to the back door. He was not to be allowed to go out the front door where he had entered. He had been their good customer, but they did not seem to know him now and showed him out the door abruptly.

Going out, as often happens in dreams, the scene had changed completely and he had no idea where he was. He tried to walk around to the front of the building to find his way, but now he found himself in a totally different location, lost. The streets were not just unfamiliar but also strange and he realized that he had somehow slipped into a foreign country! It was as if he was in some kind of primitive indoor mall crowded with people. There were high windows all around, unlike most closed-in malls. All the windows to the outside were filthy, so the view out was obscured. He desperately needed to contact someone he knew, someone who cared about him, for help. Every face milling past him was unfamiliar, no one spoke English. He began to feel the horror and panic of being lost. He hurriedly walked through crowds, up and down a number of staircases. There was not a single familiar face. He was a nobody, nothing, invisible.

Finally, he came out into a harbor-like scene, boats and ships everywhere. No one could direct him or lend him a phone to call for help. Finally he saw an older woman who was obviously handicapped and sunken low in what he thought was a wheelchair. She beckoned to him, smiling. She had a phone he could use. Bizarrely, she said he must get down into a chair like hers, next to her, to use the phone. He looked at her face. It was covered with something white and he realized she was a leper! Even so, he was so desperate that he got into the device she showed him. Then he realized that he was locked into a big metal square cage. The phone had disappeared. He was down, immersed in the waters of the harbor, like a lobster in a pot. He began drifting until he was being carried away in the metal cage faster and faster through the water, bobbing along in a swift current, being pulled out to sea. The harbor and sea were loud, menacing, overwhelming. With that he awoke suddenly with a shout. Sitting up, he was drenched in sweat, his heart beating out of his chest. He lay back in the dark, thankful to be awake and alive. Lying there in the dark, he immediately thought of the Tennyson poem Otis had read at the memorial. There was no peace in this "crossing the bar" but only separation, the sensation of being trapped, and terror.

Thomas was there, sleeping soundly; he had not stirred at all when Daniel yelled. Daniel got out of bed, throwing on a bathrobe. It was chilly in the condo, so he went to the kitchen, turned up the furnace, and started water for a cup of tea. There in the bright artificial light of the kitchen, he finally began to cry. He was sitting tightly wrapped in his robe, shoulders hunched, just a picture of misery at two A.M. He made his cup of tea and continued to sit and weep, drinking it. Henry appeared at the kitchen door, looking at him curiously. He came into the kitchen and licked Daniel's knee and then lay down under the table watchfully.

Daniel tried to sort through the dream and the events of the day before. He could make no sense of the whole thing; clearly his mind was exhausted. He wanted to be alone and have the space and time to fall apart. The thought of Thomas in the other room was causing him more panic. Thomas had to go. He would take care of it in the morning, but that familiar guilt pressed in on him. Thomas was the nicest and kindest man he had known. It did not matter; he had to go.

He went into the living room and lay down on the sofa with a throw tossed over him. He dozed on and off until dawn began to brighten the room with gray light. Then he sat up shivering, the wrap over his shoulders. Thomas appeared at the doorway. He was in a T-shirt and boxer shorts and was blinking and obviously trying to get his wits about him from a deep sleep.

He was about to speak when Daniel said in a low voice, "Go get some coffee going. We need to talk."

Thomas' eyes were wide open now and silently he went into the kitchen. Daniel could hear him getting the coffee maker going. Soon he reappeared with a tray of coffee for both of them.

Daniel was ready when Thomas came in stiffly and sat down. "I'm sorry, Thomas. I am so fond of you, but I need..."

"Yeah, I get it," Thomas interrupted. "You want me to leave." He took a drink of coffee and sighed. "I have just wanted to help you, to be there for you. I am sorry if I have been in the way." He was blinking back tears.

"You are a great guy," Daniel began.

"Please...don't go into all that kind of stuff. I'm going to go get a shower and get on out of here. We've turned a corner. No problem. I need to get back to my place anyway. I've got a ton of work that needs my attention." He said it quickly with a grimaced smile.

He stood and left Daniel huddled alone on the sofa. Soon water was running in the back of the condo and then some sounds of dressing and hangers coming out of the closet. Thomas had never moved completely into this space. He had just brought over a few things. There was the sound of a bag being abruptly zipped. When he reappeared fully dressed, he was wearing his new black workout shirt. Daniel had turned away towards the window.

"Thank you for everything. I just need to be here by myself," he said in a flat voice.

Thomas put out a warm hand and stroked Daniel's hair and gave his shoulder a squeeze. He started to walk out, but stopped at the door. With his hand on the doorknob, without looking around at Daniel, Thomas said, "Please don't worry about me. You have enough on your plate." There was a pause. "I'm making friends at the gym. My trainer, Roy. We are getting very close. I think we have something together." Then without another word, he left, shutting the door quietly.

Daniel leaned his head back on the sofa and groaned loudly.

"This is not working anymore. This is not working," he said out loud.

With that finality, Daniel took a deep breath and sighed even more deeply. He let the tears come again. He felt the return of the possession of the full space of his home and that brought some peace.

He had not really planned to go in to the restaurant today, but now he knew for certain that he couldn't go. They did not expect him. They would be fine. He went back to the bedroom and got in bed. Henry came in, jumped onto the bed and made a nest for himself at Daniel's feet. Daniel covered up his head and slept most of the day.

## CHAPTER TWELVE

## *Grief*

FOR the next week, Daniel took a cab to work every day. He knew his daily walking routine would be good for him, but he just couldn't do it. His legs felt like lead and the sounds of town, traffic and street business, which had always exhilarated him, were now jarring. Actually, Daniel was shocked at himself, shocked at what Paul's death was doing to him.

After all, he reasoned, before Paul's sickness it was not as if he was thinking of Paul a lot, or wanted to see him all the time. Daniel had not lived with Paul since he was thirteen years old, so the relationship had become formal, not really familial, for years. They seldom saw each other until Paul had gotten sick. He could not say that he had had a depth of relationship with him to justify such a feeling of loss. He just could not sort these feelings out. He tried to put the terrifying nightmare out of his mind permanently.

All was quiet and running smoothly at The Prow. The staff was trying their best to make things easier for him. They were sad too. Of course, Henry came along for the cab rides, and his presence in the office really helped normalize things. Daniel was holed up in his office mostly. Trini was always popping in, looking in on the two of them, and it seemed that she brought Daniel a cup of tea every time she looked in. He spent a lot of time sitting in the office, looking through restaurant catalogs and scribbling notes, checking inventories. He couldn't think creatively about anything and sent Trini out for the daily flowers and let her arrange them every day, for now.

He quickly got over any guilt about Thomas. He had resolved not to try to pick up that relationship again. Too intense, too emotional. He would move on one day with someone else, but was so glad to be alone at the condo for now. At night he listened to music on his stereo system, sometimes classical, sometimes jazzy piano. It was good to rest in his own living space. He avoided drinking, as that brought him to a maudlin, teary state which he found disgusting.

As for Sheila, he had not contacted her since the memorial the Tuesday before. She had not bothered to call him, either. A few days after the memorial, Daniel received a certified copy of the disposition of Paul's will from Paul's attorney, Sam, and saw Sheila's name listed as a recipient of a copy too, of course. She had not called to talk about it, or anything else.

There were a few other beneficiaries. Jim his housekeeper received ten thousand dollars and all of his clothes, furniture and household goods, including his primitive Chinese jar collection. Sarah, the secretary, also received a gift of money and two oil paintings which had hung in Paul's office. They were ones that she had particularly loved. The Cross nephew and niece from Idaho received twenty thousand dollars each. Several charities which Paul favored received nice gifts including a fund for military personnel, The Navy League. The rest was divided between Sheila and him. Paul gave Sheila his Seattle condo. Daniel received the San Juan Island property as promised and Paul's old Mercedes sedan. There were some personal things for Daniel too: Paul's Navy scrapbook, the etchings of ships from his condo, and all of his cameras with his boxes of photographs and slides. In addition, the cash settlement was very large for each of them. As Paul's insurance business was sold, the proceeds were to be split between Daniel and Sheila. It brought tears to Daniel's eyes to think of Paul making all his arrangements.

## CHAPTER THIRTEEN

# The Wine Buffet

A private party was on the calendar at The Prow two weeks after Paul's memorial service. It was a fundraiser Sheila had put together for the Downtown Preservation Society. It was to be a wine tasting buffet, scheduled for Thursday in the late afternoon.

Daniel wanted to cancel. He was barely functioning. And, it wasn't up to him to decide, but he felt it did not seem right for family members to be holding public celebrations right now. Sheila had set up the event for the organization months ago. It was a group that her real estate firm liked to promote annually. The planning was all already complete for the affair. It was to be an appetizer buffet with a complementary wine bar, brought in by several vineyards to show off their newer wines.

It was for this kind of event that Daniel had originally designed silk draperies with a heavy lining to run across the back half of the dining room. They could be pulled across to create a semi-private room. They were made of the same apricot-colored silk hanging from the ceiling. An opening was usually arranged off-center near the kitchen side of the room and several of the larger potted trees were usually moved to stand on either side of the opening for an accent. When not in use the draperies were pulled and stacked gracefully at the wall on either side, held back with heavy gold roping. It worked out well for up to fifty guests. The bar was inside this space, making drink service very convenient. So, everything was set up. He just did not want to do this right now.

Finally, Daniel had called Sheila and suggested that she cancel, or that she could postpone for a while, since it was so soon after Paul had died. She hurriedly argued that invitations were long mailed out and most arrangements confirmed. They needed to follow through on this, as planned. She was adamant. There was nothing to be concerned about, she said. No one will even think twice about it. Important clients were coming into town for this. They were new to Seattle; they did not know Paul. It was unfortunate timing, but let's follow through on this.

Daniel felt defeated by her pushing through for the event, but he let her have her way. He did not have the energy to grapple with her over this right now. Everything was scheduled for four to six P.M. Thursday. The night before the wine tasting party, Daniel felt terrible; his head was pounding. All was in readiness at the restaurant, so he left early, deciding to trudge back up the hill to his condo on foot with Henry for the first time since Paul's death. He thought maybe the walk in the cool twilight air would do him good. He did breathe in the fresh air and the walking helped him to begin to stretch out muscles which had been tense for days. Trini had bagged up a portion of rice pudding which she had prepared for him. He brought it in and feasted on that, watching the city darken out his window. He was dreading tomorrow and dreading the night too. He was afraid for some reason that he might have another nightmare. He considered calling Thomas in a knee-jerk reaction to his feelings, but he resisted doing that. It was over. Finally he went to bed and slept peacefully all night.

On Thursday morning Daniel walked with Henry to work... back to the normal routine. His mind was set now on putting everything together for the wine buffet event that night. When he arrived at the restaurant Trini had already done the foyer flower arrangement. It was beautiful, a huge display of tall, elegant, blue delphiniums in a cobalt blue glass column. This cheered him considerably.

The dining room setup was in place with draperies drawn across to create the private room and the staff was putting finishing touches on the tables. Poster displays of Downtown Preservation projects stood on easels near the entrance. The wine reps were already there arranging the displays at their makeshift bar. Daniel greeted them all. Glasses were sparkling and ready at hand. Trini was using the cream-colored cloths, a more elegant look than their normal pure white. She was busy and trying to make everything smooth for this event which she knew was charged with emotion for Daniel. He could see her serious expression, unvarying as she worked around the tables.

Arrangements had been made for Andre, the guitarist Sheila had hired for the event. He had arrived and was tuning up at his seat nearby with the gold draperies as his backdrop. Some plants were placed there too, just to make it a little more like a stage. Everyone was working hard to make this thing look right. There was tension in the air... Daniel was still so uncomfortable about doing this. He knew Andre though, a real professional, who would play soft smooth guitar while everyone wandered through the dining room. It would be appropriate. It would be fine.

Just then Sheila arrived. Her two assistants, Jeff and Mary Ann, came through first, fanning out into the dining room like two bird dogs, checking every table with eagle eyes. Sheila followed, dressed in a yellow linen suit. She was tottering on the highest possible spike-heeled shoes, also yellow. She greeted the wine people and was in the process of dealing out more fast paced instructions to Jeff and Mary Ann. She had not seen him yet, but as he watched her, an idea came to Daniel. Avoiding her, he quickly headed out to the kitchen.

When he entered the kitchen, he knew exactly what he needed to do to make this whole thing right. He took his coffee and sat down the already busy crew who were working together on the pastry items.

Looking around at everyone, he said, "Let's dedicate this work today to Paul. I know you all did not know him and he was only here once or twice in the restaurant, but I would like this to be about him today. OK?" They all nodded and looked at each other knowingly.

"And I am going to donate the food we serve and the drinks to the Preservation Society in honor of him."

"Oh! That is really nice, Daniel, really nice." Oscar was nodding and smiling. "A great gesture, my friend." It was clear that everyone realized that this was the right thing to do. Trini confirmed this with an ear to ear grin, her first smile today.

"That makes this right," thought Daniel to himself. "It's good now."

Guests began arriving, Andre began playing something in a soft style and all was well. Sheila was turning up the charm by the minute. Daniel could see her out of the corner of his eye, flitting around the room now like a yellow bird. The "Important Clients," the ones from out of town, arrived. Sheila escorted them around the room introducing them to everyone. Once again, her distant cooing sounds reminded him of a bird. The day had been unusually warm and the guests were wolfing down the drinks and hors d'oeuvres.

Daniel, as he had promised himself, stayed in the background, on the fringes of the crowd, watching and directing the staff where needed. Tiny desserts were being served now, and the wine people were bringing out their dessert wines and champagnes. Daniel was helping them circulate trays of drinks.

Sheila, sensing the winding down of time, went to the easels and had Andre strum a loud introduction for her to get everyone's attention. Then she began her spiel. With the biggest smile and wide gestures she described the current activities of the Council, praising this and that person's work, and bringing up the applause. She began talking about the Evans Building.

"We are so pleased to begin raising support and planning the work on this lovely old building here in our midst in Seattle, which has become so sadly neglected of late. Our architectural firm, Daily and Sterns will be guiding us in this. Say hello to Dave and Ben who are here with us today."

Waves, smiles and applause.

"The Evans is a gem which we must not lose! My father Charles Drews was in fact long ago involved with the Evans building as well as many, many other landmarks of our beautiful city. And this is what motivated me to begin this work of preservation and restoration. I come from a line of Seattle business people who have always tried to give back to the community."...Dazzling smile.

Daniel could see that she was beginning to look a bit hazy at this point. Too much champagne, too much ego.

"As a matter of fact," Daniel saw her eyes flicker slightly. "As a matter of fact, this very building where we are now enjoying a lovely time together was a family possession and project of ours. I am pleased that we were able to turn an abandoned dusty stationery shop into this magnificent restaurant, in keeping with the traditions of our downtown district. I think you will agree that the result was well worth the work and effort to bring a property back to its full potential and commercial use."

Daniel froze in place. Expressions of surprise and applause came from the crowd. Sheila was beaming.

Daniel carefully set down the tray of filled champagne glasses which he was carrying. His face was livid. He then picked up a butter knife and used it to chime one of the glasses sharply for attention from where he stood. Everyone hushed and turned toward him. With a supreme effort, he smiled.

"I want to follow up my mother's remarks with a welcome for all to The Prow." He spread his arms in a welcoming gesture. More smiles all around. Applause.

"I am afraid in my mother's usual enthusiasm and zeal she has made a few historical mistakes."

Smiles and light laughter from the crowd. Sheila was standing to his right and did not turn toward him. There was an instant electrical charge to be felt in the atmosphere. He had broken the rules. Calling her "mother" was probably the least of it.

He continued, "This property never belonged to Charles Drews. It belonged to Sheila's mother, Willamette Stanton Drews, an inheritance from her father, William Stanton, whose name I am sure you know as a pioneer in this community's early days. It was my grandmother who preserved this property and handed it over to me to establish this restaurant here. It was she, Willamette, whom I affectionately called 'Willie,' who did this work, who sent me to learn this business, and who was my wonderful partner in restoring and developing this property and The Prow Restaurant until her death just a few years back. She was a native of Seattle and she also loved this downtown district where her father made his fortune so many years ago."

Looking around calmly he went on, "Another thing which my mother failed to mention is that we here at The Prow are pleased to provide the food and drink for this occasion, as a gift to the Council. This year it is our pleasure to support your work of preservation, through this event, in honor of my father, Paul Cross, a Seattle businessman. My father passed away just a few weeks ago. But, he would have wanted you all to be his guests and to enjoy this gathering in his name."

He smiled a tight smile again and raised a nearby glass of champagne.

"To Paul Cross."

"To Paul Cross," everyone repeated solemnly, raising the toast. There were some murmurs and questioning looks exchanged among the guests. Then they went on with their conversations as the buzz in the room picked up again and the guitar music continued on.

Daniel instantly turned to Sheila and approached the spot where she was standing. Mary Ann and some others standing with her fell back and turned away, embarrassed.

"Why are you here? What are you really doing here?" he demanded. "Why do you keep coming here, acting like you own this place? When this event is over I want you to get out of my restaurant. I am sick of you. You have the audacity to come in here and claim the credit for the creation of this place and my business in front of all these people! I don't understand you! I don't want to try with you anymore. And, don't think about sending me a check for all this. It was done for Paul." He was in her face. He spoke quietly but his face was red now and he was shaking. He turned away in disgust for a moment, then looked back at her.

"You know Sheila, I used to fear you. You are so destructive!" He said it with disdain. "I don't fear you any more...I hate you." There was a deadly calm now in his face.

Sheila looked at him calmly. Then she blinked slowly once, pressed her lips together, picked up her purse and walked out without a word. Mary Ann and Jeff followed her immediately, heads down, not meeting his eyes.

Trini had approached Daniel by now and was at his elbow.

"*Mijo!*" she said softly," *Mijo...*"

People were watching him. They had not heard his words to Sheila, but the body language was perfectly clear. He looked straight ahead and walked out to the kitchen.

Trini and some of the other staff went quickly among the guests seeing to their needs, displaying big smiles. The party was over though and everyone soon began to drift out.

When Daniel reached the kitchen, he just kept going and walked out into the alley. He did not want the kitchen staff to see him. He was trembling and hot and he began to cry. He put his face on the cool brick wall and cried some more.

In a few minutes both Trini and Oscar came out to where he was. They had begun the process of finishing up the party, but the regular dinner hour was still going strong. He could see they wanted to be helpful to him, but the kitchen was calling.

"I'm sorry guys," he said, shaking his head. "I messed everything up. You did such a great job and it was all for Paul. I messed it up!"

They were on either side of him, patting.

"It's just that she gets to me. I am finished with her bullying. I meant what I said. I don't want her here anymore!"

"*Pues*, I know, Daniel, but she's your mom." This was from Oscar.

At this, Daniel snorted, "One of these alley cats that wander through here is more of a mother than Sheila Cross!" Trini and Oscar both groaned at that.

"Go on back to work. I'll be in a minute. We've got to finish this shift. I'll be O.K."

They went in without another word.

"I meant what I said!" Daniel called out after them.

He breathed deeply a few times. Wiping his eyes, he then went back inside too. He washed his face and hands and straightened himself up in his bathroom off the office. Then he sighed, took a deep breath and went back out on the dining room floor looking pale and wrung out, but with a weak smile. At the end of the evening Daniel came into the kitchen and spoke to everyone as they were finishing up.

"Let's have a staff meeting in the morning. We need to talk."

That night, Daniel had another dream. This time it was not a nightmare. He dreamed he was walking on the pebbly beach of San Juan Island. He and Henry were walking north on the landward side of the island near Glass House. They were coming to the "Bone Graveyard," a name he had given to the bleached out tree trunks which were washed up in great numbers on that part of the beach when he was just a boy there. They were walking slowly. He was feeling the rough gravel under foot and hearing the crunch. In the distance, Daniel saw a figure. It was a man walking towards them. As he came nearer he saw that it was Paul. He was wearing a white shirt, shirttail un-tucked and khaki pants which were rolled up a bit past the ankle. The pants had gotten wet around the bottom in the spray from the sea as he walked along the shoreline. He did not look like the Paul who had died in the hospital. He looked much younger, he was lightly tanned and seemed to be perfectly healthy. He was wearing glasses and on his feet were old white Converse basketball shoes, saturated with sea water. Daniel was afraid as Paul approached. He felt his heart pounding out of his chest. He had that old worry of not measuring up, not being O.K. with Paul. Paul came on, closer and closer. The sunlight was reflecting off his glasses as he walked but as he came near Daniel could see his eyes and a warm smile on his face. He raised his hand in the classic two finger "Peace" sign. He walked right up to Daniel, still smiling. With that Daniel jerked awake, lying in the dark with that same pounding heart.

## CHAPTER FOURTEEN

# Encouraging Words

Early the next morning, Daniel got Paul's car out of the garage behind the condo. It was a cream-colored BMW sedan 2006 vintage, roomy and elegant. Paul would probably never have bought another car in his lifetime. He liked to keep things that worked for him and pleased him. He didn't need a new car every other year. Jim had brought it over soon after the memorial service. It was a bit dusty since weeks had gone by without it being driven. He filled it with gas, had the oil checked and drove to the Queen Anne Hill cemetery. As he approached the columbarium where Paul had been interred, he saw that Otis had already arrived and was sitting on a nearby garden bench.

Daniel had called him the night before and asked that he meet him this morning. They shook hands without a word and just sat for a bit looking at the dark granite wall before them.

Finally Daniel said, "Thanks for coming down here so early in the morning, Otis."

"Not a problem. I get up early every day. It's routine for me, part of aging."

It was a clear day, as yesterday had been, and was probably going to be quite warm. Paul's name had not yet been etched into his square. Daniel didn't know how they did that. So far it was just a blank polished brass square, among all the other squares.

"It feels good to come back here," Daniel said.

"It does indeed. I always enjoy being in a cemetery. It makes you think about eternal things, and in fact, you feel close to eternity. It is a place of peace, rest, solitude, all that good stuff. Lots of people come out and have a picnic in these places, at least where I am from," Otis chuckled. "The memorial for Paul was no picnic though. It was tough, especially for you I think?"

"Yeah, I'm having a hard time. How do you lose someone that you never really had? That's the question. That's the tough thing for me. I'm going to take some time off, get out of town for a while. I'm leaving in the morning. I just wanted to ask you about some things before I leave, stuff about Paul. I need to get some things straight and I thought maybe you could help me get some clarity," Daniel sighed.

"He was so different on those last visits we had at his condo, towards me I mean. I am so confused about all that. I don't get it. We hadn't seen each other in ages, and never like that. He never even came to eat or just to visit me at The Prow. Actually, that's not true. He came for the grand opening, just that one time. I guess he thought he had to come. We had separate worlds even though we were just a few blocks away all the time. And the stuff he said to me the day he died...it was shocking! On top of seeing him die, it was shocking." He paused, thinking a minute.

"And, then there was seeing him decline like that. I wasn't prepared for it nor did I ever expect to see something like that! I've never been around anyone who got sick. Not even Willie. I knew she was getting older and all, but she just died in her sleep. I'm glad. I could not have stood seeing her suffer or anything like that." He looked at Otis beside him.

"There is a huge amount of suffering in this life, can't deny it." Otis was gazing at the polished wall.

"Why? Why does it have to be this way?" There was desperation in this question.

"Some bad stuff happened way back when, back at the beginning of people. It messed us up. Messed us up with the creator of all things too. Twisted life around big time." Otis was still steadily focused on the granite wall. "We got disconnected. We got to get re-connected."

Daniel snorted. "Yeah we are disconnected. I was born into a house where everybody was disconnected from each other. I had no place. I don't know why they even had me. It had to have been an accident!" He laughed ironically.

"I just got in a big fight last night at The Prow with Sheila!" He looked away, sheepish.

Otis turned now and looked at him. "Oh yeah? What was that about?"

"I don't know. Well, yes of course I do know. She just enrages me and as they say, last night she got on my LAST nerve." He laughed. "I'm sick of her. It is a mystery to me why she has continued to patronize my place. Yesterday I told her never to come back to my restaurant again."

"O.K. I think you're right. You need to get away." Otis laughed a deep chuckle. Daniel laughed too. It was a relief to laugh about it.

Then Daniel was serious again. "Why did Paul get baptized like that? Why did he want us to all know, when he never talked about those things himself?"

Otis uttered a deep low sound. Then he spoke.

"First off, Daniel, I know you think Paul did not care about you, that he was disappointed in you all along, but that's not true. We talked about it together. He didn't much know how to be a father in the way that most of us think of fathers. So I'm sure he didn't talk much at an intimate level. Like I said at the memorial, he was a stern, closed kind of a guy. He had love in his heart, but he failed to show it directly most of his life. He was always aware of that. But like I told you all, something happened to Paul." He smiled his big smile. "He got re-connected...big time." He laughed. "Then he re-connected some more over at our church. He was baptized! Connection with a capital 'C'." More deep chuckles. He was shaking his head. "Hallelujah! He wanted you to know it before he died, but he was a guy who just had a hard time expressing himself. Poor boy!"

Otis continued slowly, and Daniel could tell right away by a change in his tone that he was going to try to be careful, going to try to be cautious with his next words. He framed it impersonally, "Some people..."

"Listen, some people need to try to show strength all the time, twenty-four/seven, or maybe it is just what they imagine is strength. They think it is the right way to be. You've heard of the 'stiff upper lip'? This is part of that thinking. Not just the 'upper lip', but the whole self... 'stiff'. Who knows why Paul adopted that stance in his life? Maybe it was just his personality. It is not a very fulfilling way to do life, but I certainly cannot explain your father. Nobody can."

Daniel was silent, leaning over with elbows on knees, head down, thinking. He nodded.

"Yeah, I know. I just thought maybe you might have some insight."

He cupped his hands to his mouth like a megaphone turned in the direction of the granite wall and shouted, "We're talkin' about you over here, Paul!" They both broke up in laughter.

"Here's the deal, Daniel. It is possible that at the end of his life, Paul realized he didn't have to hold back his feelings any more. There was no more need for the stiff upper lip. He took a chance and revealed his hidden feelings about you. I think maybe for once he trusted God all the way in this. He just let go and let God, as they say. He did love you, just like he said that last day. If I was you, I think I would cherish those last few meetings, those last few hours, as if it was a lifetime. That's what I would do."

He smiled his big smile. Then turned to the granite wall again and shouted out, "How'd I do Paul? That just about right?" His big rolling laugh started coming out of him.

Daniel laughed too. But then his laughter faded. "I have had a couple of disturbing dreams since Paul died."

He described to Otis the nightmare he had that night after the memorial, the weird circumstances in a foreign place, the woman with the leprosy and the final lost-ness of floating out of control through the harbor and out to sea. Then he told about last night's strange dream of meeting Paul on the beach. When he finished with the telling he shook his head as if to shake off these terrifying, strange thoughts and images.

Otis was quiet for a while, and then he reached into his pocket and drew out a small book. It was a very small Bible. He paged through it silently, and then began to read out loud.

> *"Some went down to the sea in ships and plied their trade in deep waters;*
>
> *They beheld the works of the Lord in their trouble, and His wonders in the deep.*
>
> *Then He spoke, and a stormy wind arose, which tossed high the waves of the sea.*
>
> *They mounted up to the heavens and fell back to the depths;*
>
> *Their hearts melted because of their peril.*
>
> *They reeled and staggered like drunkards and were at their wit's end.*
>
> *Then they cried to the Lord in their trouble, and he delivered them from their distress.*
>
> *He stilled the storm to a whisper and quieted the waves of the sea.*
>
> *Then were they glad because of the calm,*
>
> *And He brought them to the harbor they were bound for."*

"This is Psalm 107, Daniel. Your first dream reminded me of it." He then prayed, head down, bent over. "Our Lord, I ask you to help Daniel in these days. Heal his hurting heart. Bring him at last into the safe harbor you have prepared for him. Amen."

Otis put his big hand on the top of Daniel's head and left it there. It was very warm. "You go on out there to the island. You are going to be O.K. God's going to meet you there. Go out there and rest yourself."

CHAPTER FIFTEEN

# Staff Meeting

DANIEL had set up the staff meeting at the kitchen for nine A.M. He was feeling much better, having met with Otis. Actually, he felt that somehow heavy pressures he had been feeling from all sides were lessening. However, he knew what needed to be done next and he would go ahead with his plan. He did start tearing up when he first walked in and saw everyone gathered there waiting for him, sitting gravely around the main work table. But he straightened himself up right away. He had asked everyone on staff to come in at nine, regardless of their shift, even the busboys. He wanted everyone together so that there would be no confusion, no misunderstanding, about what he was now going to do. He quickly realized that it was important to show leadership and a steadiness at this time, so he assumed a businesslike manner. First, he needed to apologize.

"I am very sorry for my behavior during the buffet last night," he said. "This is not the way that we treat our customers and visitors to The Prow, no matter who they may be. That is not what we are about here. Our mission is hospitality. I really messed up last night and I want you all to know how regretful I am. All of you worked very hard to bring excellence to the event and make it special for me and an evening of honor for my father. I want to thank you so much for that. I hope the evening was not completely ruined by my actions." He spoke softly.

"No, it wasn't ruined, Daniel! Everyone had a good time and the food was excellent. Nobody knew what was going on until at the end there. And not everyone was aware of it even then. You just lost your cool, man! You're only human!" Oscar was talking, the rest of them all murmured in support of him.

"Thank you all. You're the best, as usual."

He finally smiled and sat down with them at the table.

"Nevertheless, I need you all to know that I am in a crisis, personally, since my father's death. I think I need to take some time off. I should have realized the need to do that earlier. But... here we are now and I have asked you all to meet so that we can organize things for me to take a leave for a little while. I want you to know that I am depending on you."

"You CAN depend on us, Daniel!" Sarah put the emphasis on the "can."

She had made his favorite pastries, poppy seed rolls that morning and now she handed him a plate of them with a smile.

"We are so sorry for your troubles, Daniel. So sorry. We love this restaurant too! We will not let you down. I can't imagine what it is going to be without you, but we will do our best."

Daniel picked up a roll from the plate, and then passed the rest on around the table.

"I am going out to the San Juans to a house my Dad has given to me. It was his vacation house for years and now I am inheriting it. I want to see it again and spend a little time there. I plan to be gone for a couple of weeks, possibly longer."

"We are going to miss you, Daniel. We are going to miss you." Trini was speaking with a trembly voice. She had her hands together in front of her as if in prayer.

Daniel's eyes, always beautiful, were lit up now as he looked around the room at them all.

"There is no way I can express my thanks to you," he said. "You are really my family. I hate to leave you. I hate to leave The Prow, but I will be back."

Then he spent some time going over details and procedures to be used during his absence. He assigned duties to make everything clear. Finally, he thanked them all again, went around and shook hands with everyone and exchanged tender hugs. Then he motioned for Trini and Oscar to follow him to the office. Henry was already there napping and the three of them took a cue from him and flopped down on the sofa and chairs. From Daniel there was a deep sigh.

"Whew, that was harder than I expected." He lay back on the sofa and stretched out his feet in front of him.

"First of all guys, I do not expect you to pick up these responsibilities without compensation. Your salaries are going up a couple of notches. You will be stepping into expanded roles. You are going to be paid for it."

"Daniel! We don't expect that!" Trini looked from him to Oscar. Oscar shrugged.

"That's the way it will be," Daniel said flatly. He began to go over banking and money matters with them.

Oscar questioned him about the menu and his expectations and about some of the food vendors. "Do you think they are going to respect me, like they do you, Bro? Can I trust them on the pricing with you gone?"

"It's just a short time. I don't think there will be any changes in just a few weeks. You can both always call me out there if anything comes up. And, I trust you to make decisions on your own. You can do it. You guys will be O.K... Now go on, get out of here! Do your jobs." He had a big grin on his face.

"We wish you all the best, Daniel. We know how upset you have been for a long time about your family." Trini put her hand on his shoulder. "*Que Dios te cuide, bendices, y sana su corazon.*" Daniel knew enough of her Spanish to know this was a blessing and a prayer for the healing of his heart. They embraced and left him to go and attend to Friday lunch.

As Daniel sat at his desk in The Prow office, he knew there were several other things he needed to attend to before he left. One was a phone call to Thomas. The whole thing had been bothering him, especially the way things ended that morning after the memorial service.

Thomas answered the phone a little breathless. He had obviously run to get the call.

"Hey there my friend, how's it going?" Daniel wanted to be casual, not start with something heavy.

"Oh, Hi Daniel!" Thomas sounded pleased. "I'm fine, how about you?"

"I just wanted to call and thank you for your help during this past time with my Dad. I really appreciate all you did, for being there, really."

There was a short silence. "Well, I hope you are doing better now. Losing a parent is a very big deal in life." His voice was neutral, but not unfriendly.

"Actually, I am not doing very well yet. I have had some crazy bad days. In fact, that is sort of why I am calling. I think I need to get away for a bit. I am leaving town today for a little break." Daniel laughed nervously at this, surprising himself. "I just wanted to touch base with you and thank you properly."

"Wow, well I'm glad you are getting away then. Who's going to take care of the business?" He was still a little breathless.

"You know, Trini and Oscar are pros. They can handle it all for a while. It's hard to admit that, but I am not indispensable. How is your work coming along?" He was just being polite with this question. He really did not care.

Guardedly Thomas replied, "My work is fine and my life is fine too, in case you wanted to know about that." He lowered his voice. "I'm here at the gym. I'm spending a lot of time here. I know it seems like an odd combo, but Roy really, really likes me. And I like him too."

The voice went lower still. "I think he loves me…is in love with me." There was an embarrassed low giggle. "I like him too, a lot."

"I am so glad to hear it, Thomas," Daniel said wearily. "I want you to be happy. You are one of the nicest men I have ever known. Best of luck to you always." He meant it.

"Thanks," Thomas said shyly into the phone. "I'm no athlete and everyone knows it, but I'm trying to get into shape, for Roy… Daniel, can I tell you something?"

"Sure. Let's hear it." He was wincing now.

"You are a gorgeous guy. Really. And so smart and capable… and rich!" He laughed.

"But I want to tell you… you know, we are not getting any younger. There is more to relationships than looks and sex.

You know? Being with you was hard at times, because you..." he paused. "I don't want to hurt you especially now when you are in turmoil, but you are a little...cold. It was really hard to stay connected with you because of that, a little cold, a little distant all the time." Then quickly, "I'm sorry, you don't need that at a time like this, but I want you to be happy! What is it that makes you so inaccessible?" he blurted. "Oh, I'm sorry. I'm making this worse by the minute." Thomas was getting flustered now.

"Well, Thomas, I hear you but I don't have an answer for you. I think that is why I am taking this step and going away to look after myself," he said dryly.

"Good, Daniel. Good. Listen, thanks for the call. I am so glad you made this effort. I will always think of you with good thoughts, happy thoughts. I've got to go. Love you...I'll see you around, O.K.?"

Daniel hung up the phone. He was shaking his head and smiling. He was very glad he had called Thomas. So glad. Now he could be free of any sense of discomfort about the way things had ended. Really free.

Next he paid a personal call to his bankers. He needed to set up full access to accounts for Trini and Oscar. Then he phoned the suppliers to tell them what was going on. He also called Sam Elliot, Paul's attorney and had a long visit, telling him what he was doing, in case he needed to contact him for anything. He called Jim and let him know too. He thanked him again for everything he had done and wished him well. Jim was still busy packing up Paul's things. He said that he too was planning to take some time off, when he finished clearing the condo.

Daniel had already alerted the caretaker of Glass House, his old childhood friend and Otis' son, Luke, out on the island. He had told him that he was coming and asked him to straighten up a bit and get some food in for him. He had also taken a few special things from the restaurant's pantry in an ice chest back to his condo. There would be some good meals on the island.

The next morning Daniel finished up all the business needed in order to get out of town. He slipped into The Prow very early and looked over the accounts one last time. He had remembered a new recipe which he had been working on for a special. It was a marinated Red Snapper steak with black olives and capers, a very tiny bit of crushed cumin and lots of garlic, very Spanish. He wrote it out and left it on his desk for Oscar. Henry was writhing around the office, panting and looking up at him. He knew something was up. Daniel patted his head reassuringly. He snapped on Henry's leash and went out of the office, closing the door behind him.

They made their way through the empty and darkened dining room and out to the front door of The Prow. He could hear voices from the kitchen, people were arriving for work. Daniel looked back one last time at The Prow figurehead in the foyer, a sublime form in the low light of morning, the infant tucked up in the mother's strong arm. The one person he was not going to call before leaving was Sheila.

Now at last he was looking forward to the journey. He had already packed in the early hours of the morning, so with nothing else left to do, he began to wonder, "What will it be like out there?" He would be there before dark.

## CHAPTER SIXTEEN

# Out of Town

DANIEL decided to drive up and take the Anacortes Ferry, the one they always took when he was a kid. It was Friday, and he knew he might meet with congestion at the ferry, with tourists and students heading out to the islands. It wasn't summer yet though, so he thought it would be fine. Henry was allowed to sit in the front passenger's seat for now. He was merrily looking around as they moved along the freeway, enjoying his "top-dog-nearly-human status." Peering out the windows, he occasionally barked at random cars as they passed them. He was unaware that soon he would have to be stowed away in his dog crate on the ferry.

Once they were away from Seattle, the green of open spaces was instant refreshment for Daniel. The horizontal landscape was so much more calming than the vertical cityscape. Actually, he loved driving, just not city traffic. Once beyond Marysville the forests and green took over completely. It was short drive, just about an hour and a half, if you didn't hurry. He moved into the slow lane, breathed deeply and realized that there was no need to hurry now at all. The sun was shining, at least for now. Clouds moved in and then moved on. A typical fine spring day. As he drove his mind wandered and he began thinking of times past, of long ago, and thoughts of Willie, thoughts of Sheila too.

He knew all about Willie. At least as much as she had told him, which was a lot. He was remembering how much they talked and talked when he was with her in Santa Barbara especially. They talked while playing cards in winter in her cavernous, high-ceilinged den, with a fire going in the little plastered and tiled fireplace, and out on the patio on long summer evenings. She would stop to look through her telescopes periodically on those summer nights.

She had gotten her bachelor's degree in astronomy, an improbable field for a little wealthy girl of her generation. For college she had gone back east to Maryland to a small school which was known for its astronomy department. They had one of the nation's earliest planetariums on campus, she told him. She had majored in astronomy with a minor in French, but she never took a job in science or anything like it. And yet, she owned a library of volumes on the subject of the universe and she continued to use her telescopes well into her old age. It was simply an intense, passionate interest. She said she wanted to know what was out there. He remembered her tiny form hunched over with a blanket over her shoulders to guard against the chill air, peering through the lenses in the night.

Instead of a career, she worked on and off her whole life as a volunteer in various charitable works. She liked hospital work, especially spending time with children. She did not join committees or "boards," preferring hands-on work. She played bridge, she played golf.

Willie was little. Who knows what happened to all the little delicate white women like Willie from generations back? Little, short-waisted, bird-like girls. Maybe the genes in them had morphed, creating the slender, long-waisted, narrow-hipped girls running around town today. In any case, Willie was five foot one and small-boned. He could see her in his mind's eye, with delicate sharp features. Her skin was thin, and soon wrinkled. As a child, she must have been one of those little, be-ribboned girls with fragile features from the century past when such girls were dolled up from birth. Actually, "doll-like" was a good description of Willie. Her hair had once been just like Daniel's, a fine ash brown. As a girl it had been so fine and lank and hard to fix that it had been curled with hot curling irons that frizzled it. She often talked about how she hated dealing with her hair. Later, she succumbed to permanent waves. At the end, her hair was steel-gray, short, thin and curly. Her eyes were hazel and Daniel remembered how she hated to wear glasses, even when she needed them, complaining bitterly of the inconvenience of taking them on and off for reading, always losing track of where she had left them last.

He was remembering the scent of her perfume as he drove along. Guerlain's L' Heure Bleue was a surprisingly strong and heavy choice for a little woman like Willie. And he remembered the smell of cigarettes. She had smoked, right up until the time of her death, not a heavy smoker, but always an after dinner smoker. Her preferred dress was a two-piece, light wool suit by Paul Parnes. She had a ton of them. Conventional to say the least. But she did have a bright red cashmere twin set that was his favorite thing on her. She wore it with denim pants; they were not really jeans.

Willamette Stanton Drews was her name. Others, including her husband, called her "Bet," but for some inexplicable reason Daniel had always called her "Willie," or "My Willie..." He had given this name to her as soon as he was able to speak at all as a toddler. She was his Grandmother.

She was a wealthy girl who married an aspiring and ambitious young man, Charles Drews. Sheila was their only child. Charlie followed in the footsteps of her entrepreneur father, buying and selling Seattle real estate. He made his own fortune and was happy to move down the coast to Santa Barbara, California in retirement.

They enjoyed the town and the sun down there. He had died at sixty, just when they were beginning to enjoy the leisure life. A pulmonary embolism took him in the blink of an eye. Willie stayed on in their Santa Barbara house and Daniel loved living with her in her big old mission-style place. It was good for Willie too, to have a companion. This was where Daniel had begun to cook. He would shyly bring some concoction in for Willie to try as a snack in the afternoon. She was appreciative and encouraged him. Later, he would cook entire meals for them. She loved it. She had died three and a half years ago. She simply died in her sleep and the maid found her. Thinking about her now caused the tears to sting his eyes as he drove.

Try as he might, Daniel could not really directly remember Charlie. He was a blur, in the background, always working. He only remembered the exotic tale that Charlie had been child of immigrant parents from the Middle East. Their original name was "Druise," which had been anglicized to "Drews," and they had come from the Druise people, a non-Muslim sect in Turkey. Funny he should remember that. Apparently Sheila was much like her father with a drive and appetite for business, she had followed in his footsteps. She looked like Charlie too, more robust physically than Willie and with high coloring and curly hair. Everyone said she had been a beautiful baby.

Daniel was trying to come back to the present to enjoy the beauty of all the green, and the open sky, but his mind kept wandering. He really didn't want to think back any more about, about Willie or Sheila or Paul or anyone. He wanted to let go of the past and look forward. He wanted to rest and have a time of peace out on the island. He switched on the radio found a "beautiful music" station and began to hum along with the tune. He would soon be arriving at the ferry dock.

## CHAPTER SEVENTEEN

# On The Ferry

ONLY a faint difference of tone separated the pearly gray sky from a sea of brushed steel. There had been a change of weather, typical for spring time. Clouds had drifted over, blocking the sun. Daniel was leaning on the rail of the ferry at the bow, looking west far out to the horizon. The San Juan Islands lay like dark mushroom caps on the surface of the sea. He could feel the rumbling weight of the ferry with its cargo of cars and trucks as it plowed through the waters of the sound toward the islands.

Daniel had never been out to the island without his parents. How many times had they all traveled this route together? Mostly in summer, never in the spring. Realizing there was no further sense in leaning out over the rail, impatient to arrive, Daniel walked inside to the lounge for a cup of coffee. There were a few tourists and just a handful of students going home from the mainland for the weekend. Daniel began thinking about what lay ahead, what he might find at the island house. How he would get along there by himself? He was convinced that he had to go, to try to pull his feelings together, to shore up his mind. It was still shocking to think how he had behaved in the days after the funeral. Not expected by him or anyone. Not normal. He would return to normal after some time alone on the island. He was sure of it. It was probably time to let go of some things, to dump the negativity of some old memories and get back to functioning normally and efficiently, which was the mode that brought him the most happiness, the most peace. The decision to leave the restaurant in the hands of Oscar and Trini was a wrenching one. They were loyal, serious and capable, but he knew that he was the soul of the restaurant and his presence made it live and breathe, because of his love for the place. He guessed for the moment it would have to be an "oh well" season. He had to get back his composure and get to what Thomas would call his "personal center..."

Thomas...he was not too unhappy about that situation. He was glad that relationship had come to a close. With time to think, he knew that he had been the one to change, to begin to withdraw, feeling agitated and trapped, like he always did. Suffocated actually, and this made him feel pretty bad because Thomas was such a great guy, a beautiful friend, a thoughtful man, so kind. He deserved better. Daniel hoped he would be happy now.

Henry had to be kept in a dog crate and remain in the car on board for the ride, but Daniel knew that his companionship was going to be essential to his feeling better on the island. They would swim in the sea and stick together in the house in the evenings. The man and his dog...the perfect combo. Dog and man, free together for a season. He hoped that he could relax and enjoy the time.

A ball rolled across the floor of the lounge, bouncing against his foot. He looked up to see a little blond boy running towards him to get it. The boy did not say a word, but chased his ball, kicking it back to where his parents were sitting on the other side of the lounge. They smiled and Daniel smiled too. Daniel glanced out the window and noted that fog had dropped down on them. Billows of moisture were pressing against the ferry's thick glass window.

All at once, he was back in the condo where he had lived with his parents as a child in Queen Anne Hill. He was leaning his face against the big cold glass picture window of their living room. It was a foggy day there, too. His toys were scattered on the floor by the window, blocks and cars. The Gentleman had just arrived. Daniel must have been about five years old. The Gentleman was there to visit Sheila and Paul. Daniel's memory was vague in part. The Gentleman's face was unclear, but he did wear a rich brown suit and a brown and gold tie, he remembered that. That was the main thing he remembered, a brown suit. The man was older than Daniel's parents...gray hair. And he recalled that he wore a formal suit and tie, this was unusual enough dress in the 1980's to catch the attention of a young child.

The adults had drinks. There was talking and laughter. Daniel had been brought over and introduced. "Say how do you do to the gentleman," his mother had said. Sheila was more sparkly than usual with the Gentleman there. Looking back now, he was probably a new client of hers, come to town to be wined and dined. An important client, as Sheila rarely entertained clients at their home. The gentleman spoke nicely to him, calling him a "beautiful child." He bent down and shook Daniel's hand softly. He reached out and stroked Daniel's hair.

He asked him if he liked ice cream. Of course he did. Daniel just could not remember the man's face. The adults went about their conversation. Daniel had gone back to playing near the window. Nanny was there with him.

Time passed as the adults visited, laughing and talking. Daniel was looking out the window when he saw that the fog was lifting. Then he spotted the ice cream cart below, coming into the park across that street. He said "Ice Cream Man" to no one in particular. Sheila and Paul were used to his prattling and seemed not to hear him, but the Gentleman looked over smiling and repeated, "Ice Cream Man," looking at him. Later, as the Gentleman was making ready to leave, he asked Paul and Sheila if he "could take the young man downstairs to the park for an ice cream cone from the vendor..." Daniel remembered Paul's expression of surprise and a sharp look, but Sheila was delighted and said, "Why of course..." You could see, though, that she wondered why the man would bother. She was obviously pleased with what she considered a courteous gesture.

They glanced out and saw that the fog had lifted. Of course he could go. Did he want to go? Yes, he was not afraid to go out with the man just across the street for the ice cream. He had gone many times with Nanny. Nanny was hovering and offered to go along too.

The gentleman laughed and said, "Oh, this is just a boy's outing..." He would be right back.

Sheila waved him on out the door with an amused, indulgent look.

They went down in the elevator. The Gentleman held his hand softly and spoke so nicely to him, as if he were a friend and not a bothersome little kid. It was nice. They crossed over into the park. He bought a large cone for Daniel. The Gentleman did not order anything. Then they wandered through the park to a quiet leafy spot where there was a bench. The gentleman put Daniel up on his lap. He was talking nicely all the time, saying what a nice and pretty boy he was, stroking his hair and bouncing him on his lap. It felt nice. Daniel was engrossed with managing the cone and the drips.

He was sitting on the brown suit. The Gentleman was patting his bottom softly. Soon his jeans were slipping down and the Gentleman was wrapping his jacket around him. Something was pressing hard at his bottom. He wiggled but the Gentleman held him tight. He tried to hold on to the ice cream cone. Something felt bad and was hurting his insides. The gentleman was humming and then rocking him hard. He squirmed, but was held tight. No one was around anywhere. He stopped eating his cone and quickly looked back at the Gentleman's face. It was all funny and smiley and then it shuddered. He was hurting as the Gentleman pushed his pants back up and leaned over him a bit, relaxing. Then he sniffed Daniel's hair deeply. Daniel could smell the Gentleman's cologne and the alcohol from the drinks and his cone was dripping and he jumped down and started walking away fast. He dropped his ice cream but kept going. The Gentleman followed, quickly taking his hand again saying how nice a boy Daniel was and did he like his ice cream? What a pretty boy he was. They came silently up the elevator and back to Sheila and Paul.

Daniel did not remember the Gentleman leaving. He never looked back at him. He went to his room and asked his Nanny for a bath now. Then he felt better. The next day Nanny saw a dark pink spot in his underwear from the day before.

She said, "Have you hurt yourself, Daniel? What happened?"

The worried Nanny told Sheila. Sheila came into his room. Daniel remembered that her face looked funny. She sat down on the bed watching him. He said nothing and kept playing with his cars on the floor, not looking up. He did not want to talk for a while. He never saw that Gentleman again and he never liked the color brown again. Daniel never wore brown. Possibly, whether consciously or not, that was the point in time where Daniel began to hate Sheila.

Daniel realized that he had gotten up and had been standing by the ferry window all this time, leaning his head against the cold glass. He was blinking back tears. How long he had been standing that way he did not know. The fog was still dense outside. He was remembering and trying to keep from feeling both the rage and sadness that always came up in him. He was trying not to feel it.

He had been admired as a beautiful boy his whole life. His fine and aristocratic features had attracted so many. He was cold to it all that. He didn't need their attention. But this memory had not been about admiration, it was a memory of violation, of betrayal, of shame. The rape of a child. He had worked hard to control the rage which festered in him.

He looked at the little blond boy, playing now on the floor of the ferry at his parent's feet. The parents were talking quietly together...a peaceful scene. Daniel shook his head and looked away in bitterness.

"Why in the world am I thinking back about it at a time like this," he thought. "Isn't there enough turmoil within me right now?"

This memory was something he tried hard to forget, to erase. He had trotted out his story many times with Charlotte, his counselor, in Seattle. It was still deadly horrifying to think of it. He remembered asking Charlotte at one session about the memory and asking her when and how he could get rid of it.

Charlotte had gotten up from her chair. She came and sat down quietly by Daniel that day, an unusual move for her.

Then she had looked him and said, "Daniel, memories are like a strong rope tied from your heart going all the way back into the past. You just have to struggle with a memory, until you finally work yourself free from it. The power of the memory is the emotion attached to it. To be free of that power is work."

Well, he certainly was not yet free. What kind of work could possibly loosen such a rope? He turned from the window bitterly.

Soon the ferry made its way out of the fog bank and there suddenly was San Juan Island, green, beautiful and sunny. They had already entered Griffin Bay. Most of the passengers, including Daniel, walked out onto the deck. There they saw the island with its harbor tucked into the lacy foliage. The ferry maneuvered deftly around tiny Brown Island and soon they were docked at the landing at Friday Harbor. Daniel went below and started the car. Henry was barking and glad to see him. They drove out of the hold and onto the dock into the sunlight with all the other travelers, in their turn. It was a beautiful sunny day in Friday Harbor.

Everything looked the same. There was a small cluster of shops, restaurants and homes gathered around the harbor and some lovely old places farther apart up the road he would take to Glass House. He did not stop for supplies. He and Henry could depend on Luke to have gotten everything in that was needed for their stay.

A mile out of town, on the old Rose Harbor Road, he made a stop to release Henry from his dog crate. Henry ran around with new zest in the meadow by the road and rubbed himself on the grass, relieving himself at a tree and barking at birds and squirrels. It was sunny now and really felt like spring here on the island. There were some daffodils strewn throughout the meadows as they drove and Daniel began to feel lighter. He felt a stirring of hope.

"Maybe I have made the right decision coming here," he thought.

# PART II

# *Time Out*

## CHAPTER EIGHTEEN

# Glass House

DANIEL, with Henry in the front seat, began driving along the level, winding road leading to the Glass House, taking in each familiar turn and homestead on the way to the island's eastern inland coast. It had been sunny and brilliant as they passed through the town of Friday Harbor, but now clouds were drifting back over the island, darkening the day. This mercurial weather was just part of the pattern of living on a small island. They drove on by meadows, woods and small white houses with porches banked with flowers, in the midst of a smooth green sea of grass. Roses were beginning to show their blooms. There was a green house around one turn surrounded by fields of straight, orderly rows of blooming flowers, a shock of color against the deep green.

Soon Daniel saw the familiar white rocky outcrops signaling the entrance to the Glass House drive. Then he was making his way up the gravel trail. Grasses were encroaching into the driveway, giving a ragged and unused look to the approach. The place had not been occupied regularly in years and it was showing. Then Glass House appeared amongst the rocks, low against the horizon.

Daniel knew everything would be in order when he arrived. Luke had done a faithful job as caretaker for Paul in recent years. He had come to work for the family as a young man, a helper to his father, Otis. Luke was a San Juan Islander, native-born, making a life for himself on home turf.

His father had originally served in the Navy in the Pacific. He and Paul had become friends on board ship during several duties. Later, Otis had discovered the San Juans and grown to love life on the island. He got a job at the marina and came to work for Paul part time too. It seemed like the perfect arrangement. He and Marion began to raise a family on the island. They all lived on a big houseboat in the marina at the southern tip of the island, a great place for kids to grow up.

When Otis and Marion finally wanted to return to the mainland for retirement, Luke took over. He loved the place and planned to always make San Juan his home so Paul had felt secure about the care of the property, even when he did not get out to the island often anymore.

Daniel had phoned asking Luke to give the place a once-over cleaning for him, bring in some groceries and to leave the key under a rock by the garage. The key was there as expected. Daniel walked across the slate terrace and let himself in through the large glass doors into the living room gloom. Henry had run off nose down sniffing through the weeds beyond the terrace.

Flipping on the ceiling lights, Daniel was instantly hit with the presence of Paul and a flood of memories. A mirrored wall of glassware and bottles were displayed behind the dominant, sleek bar. Tight charcoal gray wool carpet lay under foot; the room was furnished with an angular sofa, shaped like a boomerang, in primary red. There were several stainless steel Eames chairs in black leather. This was Paul. No comfort, but a display of restrained style, strength and weight. Oiled walnut paneling finished the back wall. Suspended from the canted wood ceiling hung a very large, Calder-style, contemporary mobile in silver and red metal. It was something Daniel had secretly aimed at with a slingshot as a boy, trying to bring it down. He never succeeded. His missiles just made the thing spin. It was still hanging in its space high above the walnut game table. The eastern wall was of plate glass windows with glass doors leading out onto the terrace. Just hard-surfaced geometry everywhere. He noticed that the glass was clean and bright. Evidently Luke had cleaned all the windows in preparation for this visit.

Daniel remembered it all, and little had changed through the years. He could not help marveling as he looked around, how amazing it was that Paul was now defined by the remains of gritty gray ash in a marble urn inside a vault back on the mainland. His life was gone, yet he lived on in the atmosphere of Glass House. Yes, Daniel felt his father's character virtually in the air of the place. "Home," Daniel said grimly to himself, "home for the present..." Daniel was relieved to get away to the island, but now looking around he began to feel it might be difficult, staying in this house. He wandered around the rooms, and even though the day had turned cool, he threw open the terrace doors. The feeling of the rushing air helped. He went down the hall and dropped his bags in his old room, then came back to the chilly living room.

He wandered back outside onto the terrace, whistling for Henry who came bounding up, panting and happy. The house was positioned low and broad on an overhang above the sea. Beyond the walled terrace, the sea was a moving mass of leaden gray. He could hear it pounding down below on the rock strewn beach, but could not see the surf from this vantage point. Clouds were rolling in and the same fog which the ferry had plowed through earlier was just beginning to envelope these shores now.

Glass House hadn't always been there on that promontory. It was built in the early 1960's by a Pacific Modernist architect, an example of the glass and steel beam style of the period. Paul and Sheila bought it from him in 1986. They had kept joint ownership for a while after their divorce, sharing the house in an amicable arrangement. Later though, Sheila had sold her share to Paul. She had no time for the island. No landscaping had ever been done around the house and property, Paul preferring the natural look of the native vegetation. However, there was an orchard.

Many years before the house had been built, there had been an old, plain, wood-frame cottage out on this spot. Actually, it had been an old military bungalow that someone bought after the war and moved out to this point, fixing it up as a vacation cottage. They had planted an orchard. The cottage was not attractive enough, nor big enough to salvage, so it was torn down to put up Glass House.

The orchard, belonging to the era of the old wood cottage was left there though, behind the house and there it still remained, growing wild and somewhat ignored. Daniel wandered around the perimeter of the grounds and found the orchard, with its newly sprouted green leaves, behind the house. The wind was up now; the weather was definitely making a shift, and the trees were creaking as branches bent. Blossoms had already fallen to the ground and were scattering everywhere in the wind. Daniel walked through the long lush grass beneath the fruit trees and watched Henry scamper, zig-zagging his way round and round the orchard. Daniel walked through the rows of trees, giving his legs a stretch and noting the gnarled and blackened trunks, sodden now from spring rains. Then he walked back inside through the kitchen back door and began exploring in the kitchen.

It was as he remembered it, a stark, stainless steel food laboratory, with a commercial utility table in the middle of the room, white tile on the floor and a black tile backsplash. The kitchen was big, more spacious than necessary for a small family. He smiled, thinking that not a lot of cooking had been done there when they visited the island. Neither Paul nor Sheila liked to cook, so they usually brought in prepared foods. He found that Luke had indeed stocked up the pantry with some necessities, and the refrigerator was clean and filled with supplies. He poked around in all the cabinets and thought about the possibilities of cooking in this sterile but well-equipped space. Luke had left a note on the table:

"Hope everything is in order and the food is O.K. You are the chef! Call me. Luke."

There was one window in the kitchen, a big double-paned glass one over the sink, facing south. Daniel glanced out. The view was of a rough, wide, wild meadow with few trees, getting a bit foggy now in the late afternoon as clouds swept over the island. He could barely make out the cliff path which led down all the way to the marina.

He wandered on through the house, searching through closets until he found the thing he was looking for... his old boyhood patchwork quilt, a bit musty and faded but usable. He draped it over the severe red sofa. He sighed... slightly better. Then, shedding his coat, he wrapped up in his quilt and lay down to rest. After a bit Henry found him and jumped up beside him, sitting there staring at him, a tall and awkward presence on the formal sofa. He made Daniel smile and he began thinking that no matter what, Henry would be there bringing his quirky animal cheer every day. This was probably the first dog that had ever entered Glass House. "It's about time," Daniel said to him, patting him heartily. Then, both man and dog succumbed to sleep on the bright red sofa.

Later, Daniel awoke, walked out again onto the seaward veranda and looked far out to sea. Hands on his hips, his eyes filled with tears. He stood long, motionless, looking east over the bay and the low dark green neighboring islands through swimming eyes. The sun finally came out from under the clouds at the horizon behind him to the west and was setting with an orange burst of light, but he did not turn to see it. He only saw the progressive darkening of the moving sea and the eastern sky becoming a deep and hazy blue.

Finally, returning to the house, he turned on more lights, which had a softening effect on everything. In the kitchen he heated some of The Prow's chowder which he had brought from the restaurant. He made some toast in the oven from the loaf of French bread. On impulse, he searched for a candle and found some utility, white, fat tapers in the pantry. He stuck one into a short crystal glass and lit it, adding a little bit of comfort to his quiet dinner at the kitchen table. The modern metal kitchen chairs were hard. Henry was standing by, his brown eyes shining in the candlelight. He did have a puzzled look on his face which gave Daniel a momentary smile. He was obviously wondering why they were here in this new place.

## CHAPTER NINETEEN

# The Cold Day in Hell

THAT first morning Daniel awoke and knew at once there had been a big change in the weather. The fair weather of spring was gone and winter had returned overnight. A freezing rain was peppering the high bedroom window, and what he could see of the sky looked dark. He had bedded down in his old childhood bedroom in his old twin bed. He could not imagine sleeping in his parent's bed or the guest room. Grabbing his quilt for a cover he walked out to the living room. It was a cold day in hell. At least it seemed like it to him...he was immediately miserable. He was sorry he had come out here. It was a mistake.

He saw that a brutal wind was whipping onshore from the northeast; clouds were ominous and low...one of those days when it does no good to crank up the heating system. Drafts were swirling in through every crevice of the house and banging the windows which were already rattling. Just looking out through the huge plate glass windows in this stark house made him feel cold. He looked around at the dark, empty living room and began to feel despair, an inner Hell...pressing in on him. His emotions were too raw to bear this lonely, memory-filled place. It was too quiet here even with the wind and the unseasonable sleet hitting the glass. It was too lonely and too sad here without one single human voice, too reminiscent of Paul. He could only think of the restaurant, its comfort and warmth, all the people working there, the busy camaraderie, the laughter, the energy, the normal pace of life.

Sleet kept hitting the glass intermittently. Yes, he had made a mistake coming out here. He trudged back to his room and took a hot shower. Then he dressed in the warmest clothes he had brought, a ragg sweater and cord pants, warm socks and walking shoes. His thought was to just spend the day here, look around a bit, and then get back on the ferry tomorrow and go back to the mainland.

He made tea in the kitchen and carried a cup with him out onto the terrace. He had put on his black, hooded windbreaker and now stood shivering, looking like a black bird in the freezing rain. Henry was smart enough to remain inside by the windows, looking out. There was very little to see from the terrace this morning as clouds had enveloped everything, and the wind-driven sleet made it impossible to even see as far as the shoreline below. His face was beaten red by the rain pellets. Trying to drink a cup of tea in this was an absurdity.

"I keep coming out onto this terrace," he thought. "I keep looking out over this water, looking for something...escape, I guess. How ridiculous." He turned and faced the house. At least the wind was now to his back.

Suddenly, anger boiled up in him. "This is MY place now," he said out loud. "This is MY property given to me by MY father who is now DEAD. I can do anything I want with it. I can change it. It's my place now." With this he laughed and tossed the remains of the tea out into the wind.

"I need to explore my property completely," he thought. "I am not going to run away until I get that done."

Back in the kitchen he made a warming breakfast of eggs and toast. He had found an old two cup coffee maker in the cabinets. The coffee aroma and taste felt especially wonderful on this bleak morning. Henry had his breakfast too. They remained in the kitchen which was warming up some now, watching out the window to the south for a break in the rain. Finally, it did let up to a light drizzle. Daniel looked at Henry and said, "Let's go."

The north end of the terrace led to a steep, dirt, beach path; they started down. It was slippery and muddy all the way, and both of them nearly tumbled several times. At the bottom the sea was still roaring and the waves were high. The beach was just as he remembered it, gravelly sand piled against the cliffs with a crescent of fine sand at the cove's center leading into the water. At the north end of the cove, among the rocks, a small jetty pushed out into the cove, a place to dock a boat if needed. To the south, rock outcroppings were taking a beating. Passage and view were cut off for the present by the rain-filled atmosphere and waves.

A few feet to the north of the path stood the beach house, little more than a shack, really. It was high up enough on a little rocky ledge to avoid being swamped by waves, even at high tide and in a storm. Daniel and Henry peered inside. The padlock on the door was unfastened. The furniture had been tumbled around, and the place was a wreck, sand and dust covered everything. The big, high, south-facing windows were caked with a salty, opaque film on the outside. Drizzle was hitting them now and making a soft drumming sound in the little house. There was little furniture here. The house was meant to be a place to change clothes, shower and fix beach picnics. Daniel saw a two-burner gas Coleman stove and the stone fireplace. An old wooden table was turned on its side, and there were a few wooden kitchen chairs. Rough cabinets lined the cliff side wall, and there was a separate changing room draped with a curtain for privacy. There were no beds, no bath or toilet. Several oil-burning lanterns were in the cabinets. The architecture was contemporary, in keeping with Glass House. The high, slanted and beamed ceiling had a large skylight above the cliff side wall, obviously put in to give more light at the rough counter that served as a kitchen. There was no electricity in the place. Unpainted inside and out, everything had weathered to a slivery gray. Outside on the beach a stone fire ring had been built in the sand, sodden now with no sign of the remains of any fires. Daniel remembered having built fires there as a teenager, making hot dogs by himself on the beach.

Now just a light mist of cold rain continued to fall as Daniel walked around to the back of the building. He was delighted to find the Penguin, his little old sailboat, beached upside down under a big tarp. He pulled it off and jumped quickly back as a large male sea otter leapt out chattering and angry. It loped off down the beach to the south. Henry followed barking until Daniel whistled him back. Both Daniel and Henry were ruffled, but Daniel laughed and carried on with his examination of the Pelican. The paint was still intact though faded a bit, same old red, blue and yellow stripe. He flipped it over and saw that its hull visually seemed to be undamaged. But it was undoubtedly in need of caulking. He was thrilled.

He saw that the plumbing coming down the cliff from above was still connected. This was a cold water line that supplied an outdoor tap and an open shower there at the back of the house. He turned on the tap and after a little shaking and groaning, water flowed out from above, rusty at first, but then clear. By now he was grinning. Off to the north a few paces was a sturdy outhouse. He peeked inside; it had been abandoned so long that the odors associated with that function had dissipated, and no otters!

This whole setup was intriguing. He walked round and round, looking the building and situation over. Henry followed, panting.

Looking at Henry he said out loud, "I think we will fix our house up. And, we will fix our boat up. I think we will spend some time down here."

Henry barked, wagging his tail and ran round and round, as usual. Dogs don't know many words, but something in Daniel's tone and expression had given him instant joy.

By nightfall, the wind had died down and the temperature was on the rise. The rain was still a soft mist but lessening and he could see that the clouds were breaking up. It looked as if it was just a one day winter, just a one day hell. They would see what tomorrow would bring.

## CHAPTER TWENTY

# The Clean-up

THAT very evening Daniel phoned Luke down at the marina. The phone rang and rang and finally Daniel began to leave a voice mail message. "Hi, just wanted to tell you I'm here, Henry too. Thanks so much for the groceries and the clean-up in the house. I uh..."

Just then, Luke jumped on the line...

"Hey Daniel! I was tying down some lines, couldn't get to the phone in time. I hope everything is in order up at the house?" He was a little out of breath. "I'm glad you got here. Too bad about the weather today...Pretty wild and wooly! This is not our usual day here in spring. It'll clear up soon, don't worry. What are you and Henry doing? Too cold to go for a walk."

"Actually we did go exploring. We went down the old beach path and spent some time looking around the beach and at the beach house. I found my old sailboat. It still looks like it could be seaworthy."

"Yeah, I bet it is, maybe needs just a little caulking. I haven't been in the beach house all winter. Nobody uses it anymore."

Daniel was listening.

Then he said, "It was very nice down there on the beach, and since warm weather is coming, I think I'll do some camping out down there and try to get the Penguin fixed up. Do you think you could help me get things livable down there?"

"Sure! I'll be there tomorrow! I'll come over in my utility boat. That's where I keep all the supplies and tools we might need, and we can put the Penguin in the water and work on the beach house too. Sounds like fun! The weather should be clearing up."

"Perfect, Luke. Thanks so much. What time can you make it over?"

"I'll get my chores here done early and will be there about ten. O.K.?"

"That's great. I'll meet you on the beach. I'll make us a lunch."

"Wow, now you're talking."

The misty rain continued to fall quietly most of the night, but by morning the clouds had cleared off, leaving a mild pearly sky. The blustery wind had quieted down completely. Daniel boiled eggs and poached some of the salmon Luke had left in the freezer. He deviled the eggs and then mixed capers and onion into the chopped salmon for a sandwich filling. There was some herbed goat's cheese. He sliced some apples and put in a bunch of grapes. He found some chocolate cookies so he stuffed them into the backpack too and put the fresh brewed coffee into an old thermos found in the pantry, hoping it would stay at least warm if not hot. He started thinking about the supplies needed down at the beach house: an old fashioned stovetop coffee percolator, a couple of cast iron skillets, heavy duty metal skewers for cooking over a fire, maybe a dutch oven with legs too. He started a list as he finished his breakfast in the stark kitchen. He could hardly wait to get back down to the beach and see how decent weather changed the feel of things. He dressed in some old clothes he had brought for any work he might need to do. No need for a heavy coat today. Just a sweatshirt would do it, and some old tennis shoes.

It was decent weather. Very decent. On the way down the beach path he could feel his spirits rise as he looked out over the calming sea and a thoroughly blue sky. Cloud banks were only visible far off to the south.

At the beach house he looked for an ice chest, but found none, so he wrapped the food and the bag of ice he had carried down in a couple of towels and left them in the house out of the sun. He took the tarp off of the Penguin gingerly, expecting that otter again, but this time he was not there. He prodded and pulled the boat out from behind the house and down onto the sandy beach area as best he could. He could have waited for Luke to help him, but he was so anxious to see it in the water.

At high tide he was able to float it out into the water and he jumped aboard. He wouldn't let Henry come along until he saw how it fared in the water. Henry was left barking and running up and down on the beach. There was no mast or sail, so Daniel rowed out a little way into the water and sat drifting and watching the hull. He dropped the keel into place. That worked fine. Something about this was thrilling, bringing back feelings of his adventurous boyhood times in the boat. He floated like that for half an hour...only a little water was coming in right along the keel line. The sun was shining warmly now. He rowed back in and docked the boat at the jetty for the present.

He and Henry went back into the beach house and he started looking around, deciding where to start. He found an ancient broom hanging behind the house but decided to wait for Luke before starting what was going to be a major job of cleaning. He had brought a tape measure and began to check out dimensions. The ceiling was very high on the south side, about twelve feet. That's where the stone fireplace had been built into the wall, with high, swing-out windows on either side of it. Ceiling height sloped to about eight feet at the north wall. The main room was roughly 14 by 16 feet. He had plans forming in his head and was so preoccupied that he didn't notice the sound of Luke's motor until he was almost landing.

Daniel and Henry walked out onto the beach to meet him. Luke jumped out of his skiff with a big dazzling smile. He embraced Daniel warmly. They had not seen each other in years. Together they pulled Luke's boat onshore. It was an aluminum-hulled flat bottomed skiff, full of all kinds of equipment and supplies...a "floating toolbox." Henry eyed Luke with curiosity and his dog "smile," wagging his tail. Luke roughed up the curly fur on Henry's head and smiled at him too. Instant friendship.

"Hey man. Long time no see!" His smile then faded and his eyes were solemn as he said, "I'm sorry about your Dad, a terrible thing to happen to him. He always seemed so healthy when he was here, but I hadn't seen him for years."

He patted Daniel's shoulder gently. "How are you doing? I wish I could have come to the memorial, but I couldn't get off the island." Then he gave Daniel another warm hug.

Otis was a black man, but his son, Luke, was a caramel-colored man. He had a smaller build than Otis too, with tight, curly hair and warm brown eyes. Luke was handsome in a different way from Otis's over-whelming strength. He looked more like his mother, Marion, with handsome, sharply sculpted features. Daniel was delighted to see him after years away from the island. Both of them had become men, but Daniel was some few years younger with a slender build. Just seeing Luke brought back even more strongly the memories of the days when he had been down on the beach and in the water.

"I guess you could say I am having 'uneven' days," Daniel said, still with a slight smile. "That's why I am out here. I need some days off. Your dad has been a huge help to me. And I am so grateful to you for continuing to taking care of the property. Thanks so much." His smile was one of true gratitude.

They looked over the Penguin at the little dock. They got in and rowed it ashore up onto the beach, prying and prodding it, and finally turning it upside down. They left it to dry out there on the beach. Daniel told Luke it had not leaked very much on his trial run that morning, a great relief. So, even though they both wanted to launch the Penguin right then and go for a sail, it was agreed that they would leave the boat for later and spend the day on the beach house first.

"I would really like to have a place to hang out down here on the beach." Daniel rubbed his hands together. They stood looking at the structure up on the low rocky ledge.

"It's in pretty good shape," Luke said looking up with squinted eyes. "Nobody has used it for years, but the structure still appears sound. How's it look inside?" They walked out of the brilliant sunshine and into the weathered gray interior. "Wow, what a dirty mess! Lots of clean-up here."

"Yeah," said Daniel, hands on hips. "I don't know exactly where to begin. I guess first we should sweep the walls and floor. Did you bring any brooms? I only have one old one."

Luke grinned, patting Daniel on the back. "Oh, I've got something way better than a broom!" They walked back outside to the skiff and Luke pulled a rolling, gas-powered, power washer out of the tangle of tools in his boat. "This will do the trick," he grinned again.

They went in and carried out every piece of old furniture, the canvas curtain and the sparse collection of cooking pots and lanterns, piling everything on the beach. Luke hooked up the washer to the outdoor tap. Meanwhile, Daniel tried to knock down the biggest cobwebs inside with his old broom. Luke primed up the washer and started attacking the siding on the outside. Years of dirt and salt poured off and ran down the beach into the sea. He rinsed the mossy rooftop too and Daniel, watching on the inside, was pleased to see that no leaks opened up in the ceiling or through the walls. Luke dragged the machine inside and handed it to Daniel. "Your turn, give it a try."

Daniel sprayed the place down starting with the ceiling and working all the dirt down the wood plank walls and out the door. It didn't take long in that little space, but by the time they were finished both Daniel and Luke were soaked with spray and dirt. Finally, they gave the windows one last blast and were glad to see that the majority of the dull film was washed away. Just a little toweling off and the glass would be shining again.

Luke looked things over. "It's super damp in here now. We should make a fire in the fireplace later to help dry this out."

"Let's eat first," Daniel offered. "We can do more after a rest."

Daniel brought out his iced-down lunch pack and they sat on the beach and enjoyed their feast. Luke loved the deviled eggs especially, something his mother had always made. The coffee was still plenty hot and they savored that too at the end of the meal. Daniel was telling Luke about his "cold day" discoveries the day before.

"It was so great to find the Penguin back there. Funny thing, a big otter jumped out at me and Henry from under the tarp. It scared us half to death!" he said laughing.

"That was Potter," Luke said, matter-of-factly, munching a chocolate cookie. "He hangs out along this part of the coast. He's got a family nested around here someplace."

"Potter, that's what you call it?"

"Yeah, Potter the Otter. That's what we all call him around here. He's a big one."

"Potter? O.K. I will be on the lookout for Potter."

He laughed again and finished off his coffee.

They went back to their cleaning. Daniel wiped down the hearth and scooped out the damp ashes into a dust pan. Luke sprayed off all the furniture on the beach. He saw that some of its wood was rotten in places. It would have to be replaced.

They draped the dressing room curtain over some rocks and sprayed it thoroughly too. It was canvas in a broad blue and white stripe. The power spray freshened it up somewhat. Daniel had decided that he would use it to rig a shower curtain of sorts for the outdoor shower when he had time. Then he went back in and walked through the house, fanning the damp boards with a piece of old cardboard. There was no possibility of a motorized fan, since the house had no electricity.

Luke got some wood scraps out of his boat and chopped them up with his hatchet. He built a fire in the newly cleaned fireplace. There was so much dampness that it took a while to catch and it smoldered a bit before it blazed up, finally burning steady and beginning to heat the room. In no time the dampness was subsiding.

They decided to leave the furniture outside where it would dry well in the open air. The day had been warm and the forecast was for more sunny days ahead. As the afternoon waned they stood around watching the fire burn down in the fresh clean house. Daniel didn't want to leave until it was completely burned out and cold. While Daniel watched the fire, Luke washed down the Penguin, inside and out, with the power sprayer on the beach. Another day, they would get to work on the little boat. For now it could dry and air out pulled up high on the beach.

They sat down on the sand, finished for the day, but enjoying the atmosphere of sky and sea in the lingering afternoon. Luke filled Daniel in about his life and work at the marina and the news that he was engaged to be married. He had never been married, even though he was thirty-plus. The wedding would be on the island at Christmas time. Daniel could tell he was thrilled about this. His fiancé was named Anna Babineaux. She was a teacher on the mainland in Anacortes. He laughed in a pleased, shy way, "Anna from Anacortes." There was a wonderful grin on his face. It was obvious that this was something longed for and long anticipated in his life. Strangely enough, he said, he had met Anna through his parents, who now lived on a tiny farm there on the mainland. She would leave her job in the classroom at Christmas and come to live with him on his houseboat in the marina. Luke's eyes sparkled as he told about it.

"I am really happy for you, Luke. And, I was wondering why your folks left the island after all these years?" said Daniel.

"Oh, my Mom was dying to have her own garden and an orchard after years on a boat with just one potted tomato plant." They laughed. "She was tired of stealing your apples all these years out of Paul's orchard! She wanted her own apples! They're pretty happy over there now. A big change. But they have friends there and my dad has his buddies. And, they love their church. How about you, Daniel? Have you been happy? Before your Dad got sick I mean." He added this quickly.

"You remember how my family was, not that close...you know? I have my restaurant and I love it. It's my life." He was looking far out over the water. "I have been able to do exactly what I had dreamed of doing, thanks to my grandmother. She was the one who always believed in me and my dreams. Sent me to culinary school."

He smiled and stood up, brushing sand off himself. "Now though, I need to be here for a little while and get back my balance." He looked at Luke.

Luke nodded with understanding. "I get that," he said softly.

"Thanks for helping me fix all this, Luke. I really needed your help. What a mess it was! I feel better already!"

"No problem, man. It's my job and my pleasure." They shook hands. "I'll be back tomorrow if you want. I think I will bring a guy who works with me. His name is Pete. He is really good with repairing all kinds of stuff, especially boats. He can take a look at the Penguin." Luke got into the skiff and Daniel pushed him off. They waved and smiled. It had been a great day. Luke was off and soon out of sight down the coast.

Daniel and Henry took one more walk through and around the beach house. Daniel took a long deep breath. It was very satisfying, the way things were coming together. After making sure the fire was out, he shut the door, left the Penguin beached there on the sand and started up the path.

## CHAPTER TWENTY-ONE

# The Fix-up

PETE Davis was a bald guy. Daniel could see that from a distance as Luke was coming up the coast the next day. Pete's tan bald head was shining in the sun as he and Luke made their way in the skiff. Actually, he was only partially bald, but he shaved his head to make things neat. Daniel was soon to learn that Pete was a neatnik, a fixer-upper, a craftsman. The two men hopped out of the boat and brought it up onto the beach. Daniel and Henry were waiting there at the beach house. It was mid-afternoon, but they had already had a full day.

Very early that morning Daniel rounded up his list of things needed for the beach house, and then he and Henry drove back into Friday Harbor. They were first customers in the stores that morning. It seemed that dogs were welcome in town, and Henry came right along with him into most of the shops. Many of the things needed were easy to find: towels, twin sheets, a nice new blanket in red plaid, soap, new broom and mop. At the hardware store Daniel found some cast iron cookware, hooks and hangers, nails, rubber boots, a big flashlight lantern, a king-sized plastic garbage can with a lid, and another smaller can too. He bought five gallons of kerosene, a dozen fat candles and some matches, and also new batteries for the portable radio he had found in a kitchen cabinet up at Glass House. It would give him some music and news down at the Beach House when he wanted.

At the thrift shop he found and bought an old army single bed frame. The kind made of iron piping. It was painted the typical "army green..." The people there at the shop offered to bring it out tomorrow with their truck.

He needed a few orange crates, but had to go to one of the fruit packing places just out of town to get those. He bought six. In one of the fancy boutiques he bought a small framed wall mirror; he intended to continue shaving, even if he was leaning towards a "Robinson Crusoe" style life.

This was a start. Probably many other things would show up at Glass House if he would just rummage around. Back at home, Daniel brought a couple of loads of his purchases down to the beach house. More remained above. He could see that he was going to get plenty of exercise just going up and down the path.

Actually, his spirits were unaccountably buoyed up. He was not thinking about Paul or Sheila. He was not thinking about death or problems. He wasn't even thinking about The Prow or worrying about how things were going along without his presence. For today, he was just enjoying all this preparation and the beauty of the island and the sea. It was a familiar thing for him to focus on creating, fixing and grooming things. It was his preferred operating mode. He had not expected this new twist to life, but he was so glad for it.

Now on the beach, Daniel went out to greet Luke and Pete as they landed the skiff. Up close, Pete was much older than he had thought at first glance, probably fifty-five at least. He had clear green eyes, a deeply-wrinkled brow and strong arms and hands. His hand felt like a steel hawser when they shook. He was tanned and well built. Luke made a nice introduction and Daniel thanked them both for coming. Pete stood there silent, but smiling.

They looked over the furniture. Some of the chair joints were loose and needed re-gluing and reinforcing. One leg of the table was split. They looked at the shower area which was completely out in the open. Fine in your swim suit, but no privacy there. The outhouse was fine also…maybe a new smooth-sanded seat was needed! Daniel explained that he was going to haul one of the twin beds in the guest room down. He told them about his frame purchase of that morning. And, that he did not need shelves or chest of drawers. That's what he had bought the orange crates for. He just wanted the bare minimum. This was his place now, and he wanted to have it usable. He figured he would be coming over to the island on days off, holidays, but he didn't want to make a maintenance burden for himself. Nothing too fancy.

In the beach house there was a long wooden counter with shelves underneath on the cliff-side wall. The Coleman stove sat on one end of that. Of course, there was no refrigerator. But Daniel had a plan for that. Then they turned to look over the Penguin. Pete's eyes lit up looking at it and he finally spoke.

"I used to have one," he said, "built it myself." Moving his hands over the hull he said, "Where'd you get'er?"

Daniel couldn't remember where Paul had bought it but it was local.

"My Dad got it from an islander, an older guy who had made it years before. That's all I know about it. I painted it when I was thirteen." He grinned.

They smiled too, looking back at the boat…red, yellow and blue.

"Very chipper," said Luke.

Daniel told them that he had found the slender aluminum mast in the garage up at Glass House. He had found the nylon sail, and some rope and rigging there in a box as well. The fiberglass keel was still in the boat and was in good condition, though it needed cleaning. The tiller was still attached.

"It needs re-caulking," said Pete, still examining the hull. "Even if it doesn't leak at first, it will leak when you start moving it around and the water presses against it. The old caulk is brittle. I'll start today. We can give it a coat of paint later…any color you like." He said it with a grin.

Luke suggested that they take the furniture which needed fixing back with them in the boat to the marina where they had electrical tools and a shop. He looked up with a beautiful smile, running his brown hand over the rough table.

"I can't take the table of course, too big, but I think I can just re-glue that leg right here and clamp it, O.K.?"

It was O.K. with Daniel. He was glad for any and all help.

The two men got their stuff out of the skiff and started to work. Daniel went back up the path to start bringing down the rest of his purchases. Henry stayed put, watching the men with great curiosity there on the beach. The sun was now moving to the west, throwing both shadows and glare on the work below. It was a calm spring day.

When Daniel finished bringing down everything he could handle, he asked the guys to take a break and help him get the twin mattress down. They came up to Glass House and Daniel could see as Pete walked through the house that he was taking in the contemporary architecture with interest.

"This is a well-built house," he commented. "Don't do it like this anymore." He nodded his head appreciatively, scanning the beams and woodwork. "Craftsman-like" was his final judgment.

They managed to haul the mattress down without it getting caught and torn in the bushes. It was a bit of a task and they laughed and grunted as they struggled down the narrow twisting trail. At the beach, Daniel ran ahead and laid down a plastic tarp, one he had bought just for this, on the floor. He noticed that all the wood in the house was nearly dry. The floor was a little cool, but the tarp would keep the moisture out until they could get the frame. He intended to sleep in his new house tonight.

He planned to make an ice chest out of the big trash can he had bought. He would bury it in the sand outside near the door and fill with ice packs and food. He had read of campers doing this. The ground would make a good insulator. He would do that tomorrow. For now, he wanted to help out on the Penguin. He watched how Pete scraped and pulled out the old caulk without damaging the wood. After a bit, he joined in the work too. With three it would be a fast job. Just before sundown all the caulk was out. They cleaned up and called it quits for the day. Luke and Pete piled the broken chairs in the skiff, pulled the tarp back over the Penguin and headed out for the marina and their supper. Daniel waved them off from the beach. They waved back and headed out in the fading light.

Daniel hiked up to Glass House and made a quick dinner of salami, cheese, bread and soup. He ate it there in the kitchen but hurried back down to the beach house at twilight bringing his pillow and a lovely bottle of cabernet, along with some old sweats to sleep in. The nights were still cool. He brought the new percolator and some ground coffee too. He felt like a kid on a campout, something he had never actually done as a boy. Now he was doing it as a man, and alone, but it felt great. There was a little kindling wood left, so he made a small fire and sat on the floor on a pile of towels with his wine and just let the evening flow away. Henry lay beside him, lightly snoring. Daniel had made up his bed earlier and after opening some of the high windows for air, he sat there in the light of the fire's embers.

He was feeling strangely excited in a childlike way. He kept trying to control this delight and stuff it down, but he couldn't do it. It alarmed him to feel like this. He had been so down, so confused, back in Seattle...so sullen, so angry. Now he felt as if experiencing this rising joy made him suddenly too vulnerable. His father had only been dead a couple of weeks. Joy seemed wrong. He tried to reason with himself, "It's O.K. for me to feel this way. I am here alone on this beach. No one sees me. I'm fine for now. I can feel any way I want."

He sat there in a reverie with his knees tucked up under his chin until the fire burned down. Then he got up and shut the door. He lay on his back there on the floor on his bunk and looked out at the blazing array of stars through the banks of open high windows. Another childish thought came to him as he lay there quietly. Actually, it was a memory. He remembered lying in bed as a boy, maybe six or seven years old, looking out his bedroom window. Back then he would pretend he was going out into the night sky, sort of like Peter Pan, flying off. He would fly straight up as far as he could. He had no concept of God, but would strain to see if he could go out as far as God was, whoever He might be. Finally, he would go so far in the dark sky that it scared him out there all alone, and in his imaginings he would rush quickly back to his bed and cover up his head from fear. Tonight, though, he just rolled onto his side and was soon asleep.

The sun came in strong and early there on the beach. Daniel woke up with sunlight coming in on his face. He didn't know why but he just felt deliriously happy. Hopping up, he opened the door to the fresh air and he and Henry went outside, Daniel to the outhouse, Henry to the nearest bushes behind the beach house. Then, they were both irresistibly drawn down to the water. At the center of the curving beach in the little cove was a smooth-sloping sandy entrance to the sea, with few rocks. Daniel stripped off his sweatpants and followed Henry's example, running straight into the water. It was undeniably cold, but felt wonderful. Looking up as he floated, Daniel saw that the sky was clear again...another blessedly calm clear day, at least for the morning. Often the afternoon could bring in weather.

Later inside, Daniel revved up the percolator. He had readied the Coleman stove the day before. The coffee was not too bad. Strong and thick, only a little bit gritty. He would have to work on his perking technique. He ate some plain bread with a slice of ham. Henry ate his dry stuff and wandered back out to sniff things out for the morning. Daniel dressed and immediately started in digging a deep hole next to the door. It was easy digging in the sandy beach. He used the coal shovel from the fireplace set. Soon he was able to flatten the bottom of the hole and insert the plastic trash can. He used the old broom stick to pack the sand in all around it, and it was done. He had buried the can with about a foot of it sticking out above the level of the sand and he topped it off with the plastic lid. He searched out some flat rocks up on the slope behind the house and laid them all around the can as a nice clean platform. He decided to keep going with the rocks, extending them on to make a small rock porch in front of the door. Pleased with his work, he dashed up the path, packed the bags of ice he had stored in the garage freezer into a large duffel bag and dragged it down to the beach. He filled and packed down ice in the can. Then he added a couple of heavy duty trash liners for a water barrier and viola! An outdoor refrigerator.

Mid-morning the skiff arrived with Luke and Pete. They hiked up the beach in the brilliant sun and admired his refrigerator and new porch with hoots and laughing.

"How'd you think of that?!" Luke asked.

"Oh, I saw it in a magazine a while back," Daniel was shyly pleased.

"Say, we brought some beer, and some food, can we put it in there?" Pete was gazing down into the iced contraption.

"Sure! I haven't brought my stuff down yet. Fill it up!"

"Well, we brought some things to cook out here later if that's ok. We want to work until we get the Penguin done and try her in the water today. O.K.?" This was Luke.

"Wonderful," Daniel beamed. "Would you like a cup of coffee for now? I made some on the Coleman."

They accepted the offer and coffee was served for them in hot cups. It was nice and hot and they didn't seem to mind the smattering of grounds.

Pete went directly over to the boat and was setting his materials out to start the caulking. He was focused on work. So, the fascinating job of inserting the new caulk began. They had brought oakum, long strands of tar-soaked twisted hemp, which Pete knifed carefully into the narrow seams with caulking tools. It was a process which looked strangely similar to sewing. First he laid the oakum in like a seam, rhythmically tapping it so it was uniform. Then he went over it again and tapped it in so completely that it was no longer visible. It was an art that Pete had down pat. Luke joined in the work on the other side and wasn't too bad at the job either. They both said this new caulk would last for years.

Daniel went up and gathered the rope and rigging for the Penguin and brought it down. He went back for the mast. It was aluminum, a fourteen-footer, but very light. He slung it over his shoulder and made his way down to the beach with it slowly and carefully. Then he connected up as much rigging as he could remember how to do sitting on the beach, as Luke and Pete continued stuffing and tapping. Soon it was done. They flipped the boat back and forth on the beach, checking each seam carefully.

Then it was time to place the mast into its fitting and begin rigging ropes and sail. Daniel remembered a lot of how things were to connect up and did his part helping get it rigged with Luke as his guide.

Finally, they looked up from their work and Daniel said, "Is it ready?"

"I think it is as ready as it's going to get!" Luke replied with a grin.

The three of them hauled the Penguin out into the sea and got aboard. The water came up high on the gunwales with all three of them in the small boat, but it was fine. Daniel was at the tiller. They dropped the keel into its sleeve and took off south. Luke was managing the sail and started checking all the rigging. As they had hoped, a slight breeze had come up that afternoon and the boat skimmed along the coast. At first they stayed close to shore, sailing close to the wind, then they ventured out into the bay and tacked back north. Pete was keeping an eye on the seams, but everything was tight and his face showed the satisfaction of a job well done. Luke was chatting on and on about childhood days when they had sailed and fished out of this little boat. Daniel was silent, a lump in his throat as he marveled at getting this done, something he had never imagined at all.

As the sun dropped behind the land mass of the island, they turned and headed back. A first voyage, no problems, no leaks. Pure joy for Daniel and an obvious pleasure for Luke and Pete too. Back at the cove, they pulled up the keel and slid the Penguin up next to the jetty where it would stay, tied down overnight. No rough water was expected.

Pete and Luke had brought more wood in the skiff for a fire and soon they had a blaze going strong in the stone fire pit. It was time to relax and have a beer. Daniel sipped the last of his cabernet. They had brought a batch of cleaned and prepared fish from yesterday's catch. When Daniel saw what they were doing he quickly climbed up the path with his flashlight and brought down some things from the kitchen of Glass House. Back down on the beach he held up a canister.

"This is the secret breading mix we use for frying fish at The Prow," he said smiling. "I'm not giving out the recipe!" They chuckled.

They had also brought potatoes, which they sliced thin and fried in the pan along with the fish. Daniel cooked some frozen tiny peas and onions, adding bay leaf and butter, on the Coleman in the beach house. There was no dessert, but Daniel made another pot of strong coffee for them. He had brought down a carton of heavy cream to swirl into it.

They sat talking of the day's work and the attributes of the Penguin there on the beach around the fire pit. There was praise for the fish breading mixture and Daniel was chided for hoarding the recipe. Lots of laughter. Packing things away, Luke and Pete said their goodbyes and pushed off in the skiff. A sliver of moon had risen and they made their way out into the cove by its light. Then they motored even farther out into the bay to avoid any rocks along the shore in the darkness. He could see them turn south by the bow and stern lights reflecting off the water. Soon they disappeared in the darkness.

Daniel stayed by the fire, thinking over the day with one more cup of coffee. Henry had already retired to the beach house for the night. He had taken over the foot of Daniel's bed for himself. It was very quiet now as Daniel stirred the fire with a stick, sparking rising embers and watching the flames alone. The past three days had been very different days from his normal life. Very different. Obviously he was in an all new environment. But, there was something else. He continued musing and watching the dying flames. He was thinking about how much he admired Luke and Pete's skill in caulking the boat. The rhythm of their work had been mesmerizing. He had joined in too, near the end.

He was proud of how he had remembered the work of guiding the tiller after all these years away from the island. Their brief sail along the coast had been so strangely fulfilling to him, it had brought tears to his eyes. Three guys in a little old boat. He shook his head, tears coming again.

Coffee or no coffee, he was tired. Dousing the fire with sand, he went on into the beach house to bed. Lying on his flat bed with Henry at his feet, he had one more thought before sleep took over: What a relief to have no one admiring him, looking at him, or looking up to him for instructions on what to do next. Just a guy among guys. And nobody was giving him the once-over.

CHAPTER TWENTY-TWO

# Alone on the Beach

UNDER the cold outdoor shower the next morning, Daniel began to think soberly through his plans.

"O.K... Good...Fine," Daniel said to himself. "I can live down here now." He was clearing his mind of all that had happened since he arrived on the island.

He began to talk to himself out loud. "I came here to get away. Things are fixed up so I can bare to stay for a couple of weeks. Maybe I can get some peace down here. This place is better than I remember it being...more habitable. I've got to settle down and get my life under control again! That is what I need to do here."

He thought about the shocking way he had been feeling and acting back in town with a shudder, and he thought of the agony of his arrival on the island a few days before.

"It's time to rest and straighten up! But...I have a few things to finish up first. The bed frame...it'll come today. I need to dismantle it to bring it down here. I need to take a check to Luke and Pete. I need some firewood."

Henry was looking at him curiously and growling, causing a big smile to break out on his face. He dried off and snapped Henry with his towel. Dressed and ready, he went up quickly to Glass House, Henry at his heels. Leaving Henry in the house, he took the car down to the marina. He wasn't sure how a big dog would do on a small houseboat. He found Luke at home on the boat. He needn't have worried about Henry as Luke's dog came wagging up when he arrived. He was a big chocolate lab and seemed to navigate just fine on their floating home.

At first Luke protested about the check, but Daniel was adamant so he took it and got a couple of cups of coffee, and they sat down out on the deck.

"I can't begin to thank you and Pete for all your help. Getting the Penguin restored and working like this is really a boost that I was not expecting. And this little place is very livable now. It happened so fast! I'm very grateful to you guys. My plan is to stay out here about two weeks...get myself together, so to speak. I need to be alone awhile and settle down. I was getting out of hand after Paul died. Everything got messed up. I need this break." As he said this, he felt his eyes tearing up.

"When I leave to go back to the mainland, maybe if you and Pete have the time you could bring the Penguin down here and give it a new paint job, O.K.?"

Luke looked at him warmly. "Sure thing," he said. "What colors shall we use?" This created a moment of laughter, then they chatted a bit more over their coffee. Daniel mentioned that he would be searching for firewood.

"You don't have to go far, just up the beach to the north is the 'Bone Yard,' remember? It's all that driftwood that comes in off the bay. It is yours for the taking. It comes in as fast as people haul it off. Have you got an ax?"

"Yeah, there are some tools up in the garage and I did find an old ax the other day. I'm good. So, I'll call you when I am leaving for home so you can take a look at the place after I leave and close it up right. O.K.?"

Luke nodded. "You know I will."

Daniel repeated his thanks and soon took his leave back to Glass House.

A half an hour after he got home, the truck arrived, lumbering slowly up the drive from the thrift shop. They unloaded the frame in the driveway.

"I'll take it from here," Daniel smiled. "I've got to take this thing apart and haul it down to the beach house for a bedstead."

The two delivery men looked at each other. "Why didn't you say so," one said. They picked up the bedstead and began to put it back in the truck bed.

"Wait, what are you doing! I want the bed!"

"Yeah, we know," said the older and taller of the two. "This is an island. We do boat delivery. We are coming around to this side of the island this afternoon with some stuff. We will bring it to your beach front. It'll save you some work."

"Oh, O.K. Thank you. The little beach house is right down…"

"Yeah, we know. We know everything that is along these beaches."

They smiled, finished loading, got in the truck and drove off.

Daniel stood there for a few moments hands on hips thinking this through.

"We are on an island," he said, looking down at Henry. "Things are different here."

Man and dog loped down the beach path to their new little house. Daniel looked things over carefully.

"It's so cozy," he thought.

He loved the weathered wood walls, the stone fireplace, the south-facing windows. He had brought down his new orange crates the day before and a few clothes and shoes for the beach. He stacked up his crates along one wall like a bureau and folded his things to fit in to the spaces in the crates. In the dressing alcove, he put up the coat hooks that he had bought and hung up his coats and sweatshirts. Next, he walked out behind the house and studied the shower. It poured right into the sand and there was no curtain. He would bring some more of those flat rocks and make a floor for the shower when he had time. The curtain would have to wait. No one was going to see him showering back behind the house. And if they did, it wouldn't matter. This was a private beach so they could just keep going and look the other way! He hammered in a few more hooks beside the shower for his clothes and towels. Back inside he made a cup of tea on the Coleman and sat quietly enjoying the space of his new home. It was not yet noon, but he became so relaxed there that he just lay back on his mattress and went fast asleep. He woke an hour later more refreshed than he could remember for a long time.

After lunch, he and Henry started north up the beach with the ax and a tarp. The weather was still fine and clear. The Bone Yard began about a half mile north of the beach house, just beyond some jutting rocks. The whole place there was a wonder, strewn as far as he could see north to the next headland with twisted trunks and branches lying in the sand. Some of the branches from the fallen trunks reached well above Daniel's head. It was a horizontal white and silver forest. Daniel picked a washed up trunk that was not too big to handle and started breaking it up with the ax. He also just picked up loose branches lying around in the sand. The wood was white and very dry so he knew it would burn fast and hot. He stacked the pieces on his tarp, then he and Henry started back down to the beach house slowly dragging their treasure of wood. He stacked it up close by the door, and it made an impressive stack. He would have wood enough for a number of days, and there was plenty more where that came from. The amount of wood up along the coast was so much greater than he had realized when he was up in the Bone Yard with the enormous sea-washed trunks everywhere. One twisted branch that he had brought was especially beautiful in shape. He pulled it off the pile and took into the beach house. He rigged a way to hang it over the fireplace mantle. It looked natural there, so he left it.

"We have everything we need here," he said. "Everything we need for this time."

Later, Daniel went up and filled his biggest duffle bag with food from the pantry and fridge and dragged it down to the beach. He stored things away in his home-made beach refrigerator and organized the rest in his rough kitchen. He heard a boat coming down the shore. It was the Thrift Shop guys with his bedstead. They pulled up to the jetty and brought the frame intact right up onto the beach and into the house. They accepted his thanks and a piece of banana bread for each of them. He had made it the morning before up in the Glass House oven. Then they headed on down the coast with their deliveries.

That night, Daniel and Henry were finally alone in their new place. It felt good, really right. Daniel made a ham bone and bean soup. He had sliced all the meat off the bone of a good ham and packed it away for sandwiches in the outside refrigerator. The soup would be enough for several days. He gave Henry the marrow from the bone. There was some fresh pineapple that he had brought down. Dessert was more banana bread and a cup of hot ginger tea. The wash-up was easy for one guy's dishes, just a heating of some water on the Coleman and a swish of soap. The light from the kerosene lanterns was poor. It didn't matter. They sat outside on the beach in the dark watching the sea and listening to its movement. The Penguin was beached nearby, a dark, whale-like shape lying on the sand. Daniel had rowed it up as close as possible at high tide, surging onto the beach. Then he was able to pull it a little further up with a rope through the damp sand to where it would be safe.

Finally, they went in to bed. This time, Daniel decided not to lock the door. He just shut it. He had been sort of anxious before, thinking about his dream of Paul walking down the beach toward him, so tanned and healthy, wearing his casual white shirt.

"He won't come in here," he whispered. "He is gone beyond us. It's O.K."

He felt his eyes filling with tears, but that was O.K. too.

Now there came days of resting, days of drifting, not aware of the clock, of time...nothing to attend to... nothing to respond to. The only contacts with others were a couple of quick trips in the car to the little grocery store for eggs, bread...essentials. One day he bought some local vegetables at the weekly farmer's market.

He had left his phone up at Glass House and would just check it daily or whenever he was up there. He had set up a system with the restaurant. He didn't call the restaurant. They would call him once a week on Monday with a brief report on things. They knew they could call him if they needed him and he would call back within a day. He could listen to his portable radio at night if he wanted to, but he found that he enjoyed the quiet even more.

After a few days of sleeping late, lethargically burrowing down in his blankets, and seeing a strong sun coming in through the windows before he got out of bed, he began to rise early each day, watching the sun coming up over the bay. The air at that time of day was so pure, so brisk that it made him feel more alive than he could ever remember feeling. The word unencumbered came to his mind and that is exactly how he felt. He and Henry walked a lot up and down the beaches, exploring tide pools, picking up things here and there. He was surprised to see blue, green and amber lumps gleaming up at him from the gritty sand. These were sea glass, worn pieces of discarded broken glass, tumbled by the sea. He began to collect them, putting them in his pockets and later propping them up on the shelves and windows of the beach house in rows. Sometimes he found tangled and rusted wire washed up. These too he gathered, and dragged back to his house. Smiling, he thought what wacky sculptural mobiles he could make, one day. Not today though, these were resting days.

Some days they hauled the Penguin into the water and skimmed along the coast exploring. He tried a bit of fishing.

The ancient fishing gear was still up in the garage, so he brought it down to the beach house and rigged up some rods for sea fishing. He caught a few fish when he sailed out to the middle of the bay. They were nice little Greenlings, a good white fish, not too big. Daniel breaded and fried them out in the fire pit. They made a fine fresh dinner and with bones out, Henry got some too. There were mussels everywhere along the coast, but Daniel was just not up to the gathering and cleaning process right now, maybe on another trip. Clamming also seemed like too much work. He was happy with his bland, simple food these days... plain pasta with oil, sliced tomatoes and cheese, omelets, soups.

Other days when they climbed up above to Glass House they walked out back and wandered through the long grass in the orchard, checking the ripeness of the cherries from time to time. He took a book, and would read there leaning his back against a tree. Some days he would spend in the Glass House kitchen, baking bread and muffins. There were days of pedaling slowly along on his old bike down the silent roads of the island, Henry accompanying alongside on a leash. He had found that bike still leaning against a wall in the garage covered with a tarp. All it needed was some air in the tires and a squirt of oil to the chain.

There were some swimming days too. He would take the Penguin north along the coast until they found a deserted beach or cove. Then they would swim and float; every day the weather becoming warmer and more summery. He took a snorkel and mask and floated face down, looking at the huge rocks and the array of colorful creatures attached to them below. There were schools of fish moving, swaying and darting rhythmically under him and occasionally a pale octopus drifting along.

At night Daniel would make a nice fire in the fire ring and sit in his old bleached out canvas folding chair, feet to the fire. He began to notice the skies above each night and it reminded him of his times with Willie, out on her patio watching the moving heavens with her, hearing her low, running commentary on the constellations. The brilliance and multitude of the stars out here away from the city was overwhelming. Out here, he became even more aware of the movement of the lights above them, the measured, regular paths of stars and moon. All life slowed down for him.

One morning he woke up hearing an unfamiliar sound. It was a scrabbling, scraping sound. He knew immediately what it was. It was Potter the Otter trying to get the lid off his outdoor refrigerator. He opened the door a crack, but that was all it took for Henry to jump to the door barking furiously. Potter had been poised on his hind legs, with his head cocked to one side. He was gone down the beach in a flash. Some distance away he stopped, stood up on his back legs and began to scold loudly in his chattering way. Daniel went out and yelled back at him, carefully shutting Henry in the house.

"Get along, you robber!" he yelled, but he couldn't help laughing. "I'll fix you!" That afternoon he crafted a chain and lock to secure the plastic lid. Even a clever otter could not pick that lock.

From time to time, in the quiet, waves of feeling would come over him about his life, about Paul, about Sheila, about all the past. As he thought back to days not just on the island, but throughout the years, he could not begin to understand Paul and their relationship. He did not resent Paul anymore; he just could not comprehend the way they always were together, the formality, the distance and the apparent neutral disinterest. A consistently disjointed relationship. The few expectations Paul had for Daniel had been so weak, and finally...unfulfilled. How could a man be that way with his only child, his only son? And yet, he was a generous man and had been so kind in his last days! He saw these memories as unsolvable puzzle pieces and after trying to come to some understanding, he would push these pieces aside whenever he could.

Sheila was another matter. He resented her deeply. He knew in his core that she had neglected him, ignored him systematically throughout his life. Damned if it wasn't true that she had tried to get rid of him whenever and however she could! He despised her for it. He couldn't grasp why she kept coming regularly to his restaurant. Was it just to try to dominate him? Maybe. She was the "Queen Bee" after all. The best thing to do about this was to stay completely away from her, and he resolved to do this from now on. He could not imagine her returning to The Prow as a customer after what he had said to her.

These anguishing thoughts were not frequent though. He was mostly living in the moment, enjoying the days. He did think about Thomas some, and others, wondering about their lives. All in all, he was glad to be alone right now. It was what he needed, he knew that. He didn't worry about The Prow for some reason. It was his work, his creation, his pride. It had even been his identity, but he simply could not be there right now.

CHAPTER TWENTY-THREE

# The American Camp

ALMOST all the lands to the west of the Glass House property stretching across the narrow southern tip of the island were National Park lands. At the far west edge of the park was the American Camp, a collection of plain little historic buildings and their well-groomed grounds commemorating the early days of the island's history. In those early days American and British troops engaged in a strange skirmish triggered by the killing of a pig, the "Pig War..." Soon afterward, the boundaries were set between British and American territories and peace returned, but the little military camp was preserved along the west coast of the island, a sweeping open area of grass, dunes and rocky cliffs descending gently to the sea.

Daniel had not been to the American Camp for many years. He had gone out to see it with Paul and Sheila once as a little boy. He had a clear, old memory of the vast feeling of space and of a jumping-off place pointing towards the Pacific Ocean beyond. Open ocean could not be seen because of Vancouver

Island, and the Olympic Peninsula to the south, but you could feel it in the air rushing in. You could smell it.

One morning, he decided he would get away from his daily pattern of sailing, swimming and walking on the beach. It was time to visit the American Camp side of the island. Driving was something he was avoiding. He wanted to go slow and quiet wherever and whenever he could. He would take the bike. It was the same old bike he and others had used for years. It really was ancient and beat-up...the tires were suspect for a long ride out to the American Camp. He decided to check the tubes. They were shot. He found a couple of new inner tubes in a box and after changing those out everything seemed to be working just fine. He pumped some more oil into the old chain, bagged a sandwich and a water bottle and set off. Henry had to stay home in Glass House for this trip. Daniel was not sure what he would encounter, and it could possibly be a very long hike for Henry. He thought he would visit the camp and then bike down to the Cattle Point Lighthouse and explore that, circle around south to the marina and then home on the cliff path. If he could navigate it, it would be an all day circuit.

He took the main road north around the perimeter of the park. Along the way he enjoyed the little gardens he saw at small homesteads, splashes of color in orderly arrangement around tidy homes. He passed the old flower farm which stretched almost to the eastern edge of the island. Bulbs were blooming and the early roses. The greenhouse appeared full of blooming flowers. Some women were bent down working in the flowers as he passed. He told himself that he needed to visit the flower farm another day. Maybe they would sell a bouquet to him...flowers were missing from his life here on the island.

Soon after, the road swung west and he followed it all the way down to the trails of the seaside camp. The bike was creaky and old, but it held together. Daniel had thrown on a very soft, old t-shirt of a nondescript color. Before leaving he tied a windbreaker around his waist in case of weather. His shorts were the baggy ones that fit loosely. He was pedaling slowly, stretching his legs as he went. It felt good to extend these seldom used muscles, to let out the tension, the warming sun bright on his skin as he rhythmically pedaled to the west.

Finally, he arrived at the American Camp. It was stark there with few trees and that "National Park" plainness. There were little wood frame buildings painted a pristine white. The whole thing had a museum-like feeling. There were no other visitors, just the preserved stillness of a monument. Beyond the Camp, at the western shore, wild grasses and gently rolling meadows led on and on. Below that were low cliffs of black bedrock where the sea ran swiftly up and surged onto the narrow shoreline. He sat with his sandwich on the grassy plain and watched the sea and the distant shores of Vancouver Island, dotted here and there with houses near the shore. Much further south he could see the hazy blue Olympic Peninsula beyond the Strait of Juan de Fuca. Everything southward had an open, wild feeling, as if no one had ever been there. He didn't see a single boat on the waters at this hour. They would be coming around soon, though, the ferries regularly plowed by on their course from the mainland to Victoria. At this moment, only the tiny lighthouse rising out of the dunes to the south told of human doings.

He biked on down the trails and soon was circling the Cattle Point Lighthouse. Nearby was a picnic area with tables among the grassy dunes. The plaque at the little lighthouse told that it was a relatively modern structure, built in the 1930's, but that a lantern signal had been there much longer, lit through the years to warn boats and ships of the narrowing channel and the rocky tip of the island. The current structure, surprisingly, was not very tall; he had expected a tall cone shape. It was blocky, angular and traditionally painted...a brilliant white. He sat a while here too, just looking, just resting. He noticed a pair of golden eagles swooping around the shores and little shore birds running in and out of the tide. It was a peaceful, remote environment, but there was a difference in the sea here compared to the inland channel down below Glass House. This sea to the south was open, moving and wild.

He tried to think back, to imagine how things would have been during the island's pioneer settlement days. Obviously most of the building and bustle had been at the north and around Friday Harbor. This, on the other hand, was a place of perpetual solitude and stark views. He was glad he had come. It felt good once again to be unhurried, un-noticed, and free...like those eagles up above.

He laid his bike down in the tall grass and began hiking his way to a place where he could climb down to the narrow beach. The black boulders were daunting, but he wound his way through them and came out on the gray sands below. Walking along, he saw a different view of the lighthouse from this low position. It looked big and sturdy, an essential help to those out on the waters. The tide was coming in so he didn't stay long on the beach. He reached down and picked up a baseball-sized smooth stone from the wet sand. It was just a small piece of the kind of dark basalt stone that ringed the beach in boulders and flat bedrock. Turning it in his hands he was struck by its smooth density. He would take it home and put it on the mantel of the Beach House fireplace, a memento of his day on the far, wild side of the island.

Finishing his sightseeing, he headed back to the main southern road and biked eastward toward the marina along the island's southern tip. He didn't want to breakup his time alone, so he did not check in for a visit with Luke and Pete. Instead, he skirted around up above the marina and finally headed into the cliff path. It was a narrow track but he was able to stay on his bike most of the way, just walking a little over the rocky spots.

Moving north, he could see Glass House lying low on the horizon. It looked dark and imposing, even though low and horizontal. A great property, and he was glad to own it, but he was still really not yet comfortable in the place. It was late afternoon when he turned into the garage, stowed the bike, and rescued Henry from his incarceration in Glass House.

"I went out west," he told Henry, with a pat to his head. "Been there, done that, got the souvenir rock." Then they trotted on down to the Beach House for a camp fire dinner.

## CHAPTER TWENTY-FOUR

# Dinner with Luke

FINALLY, one morning after two weeks of solitude, Daniel realized that he was not only alone, but also lonely. It seemed that it would soon be time to return to the mainland and the normal world at the restaurant. Physically, he was much improved. He felt relaxed and rested. His nerves had calmed down and he had mellowed out some. Air, water and sun had done their healing work.

He could not say that there was any change in the unresolved problems in his mind, but that would be a lot to expect in just a couple of weeks. Right now though, today, a human voice would be so nice, just a handshake or the smiling face of a friend. He had to admit that he was still feeling very restless inside.

He needed to say goodbye to Luke. Maybe he should invite him over and make him a nice "thank you" dinner? He would call Luke. He had not seen him since he had gone down to take him his check. He knew Luke was always busy at the marina and going back and forth to see his girlfriend in Anacortes. But, he called anyway. He invited Luke over for dinner that evening.

He had said, "Hey! You don't have to do all that work! Come on over here and we can eat on my houseboat. I've got some fish and we can enjoy the sunset. Bring something if you want. It's pretty down here after dark with all the lights shining on the water. Bring Henry!" Daniel was surprised, but accepted his invitation.

He decided to surprise Luke by sailing down to the marina in the Penguin for the dinner. If he had to leave it there in the dark later, he could always walk home up the cliff path. He was not familiar enough with the coast to sail after dark. There was a tear in the Penguin's old sail. He decided to sit down and do some work on the fraying sail, and spiff things up in the little craft. He got to work, fixing some of the rigging and sewing a few ragged spots.

He wanted to try out these adjustments, so he sailed north up to a quiet little cove which he often visited, where he could swim too. Of course Henry had the dog version of ESP and was jumping around thrilled at the prospect of an adventure. In the cove, Daniel dropped anchor. Henry had already leapt over the side before the boat was even fully stopped. Daniel eased over the side into the chill water and just floated on his back. He looked up into the blindingly blue sky, cloudless at this time of day.

"I am alone. Why is that? Why do I always need to get away from everyone?"

He said it out loud to the sky. He had to admit to himself in that moment, lying in the sea, that he was always alone, even when he was with people. He realized he had come out here seeking to be even more alone. This was suddenly so disturbing that he threw his head back and began to holler out loud there in the water. It was sort of an angry wail. Henry stared at him, then swam up and started whining and swimming around him in circles. Daniel ended up hooting some more at the cloudless sky, letting off steam. He swam around splashing and chasing Henry, which scared the dog, causing him to bark, and frantically try to get away from him.

"I guess as long as I have you trailing along, I am not alone after all!" he shouted at him.

Finally, they both floundered back into the boat and since they were becalmed, Daniel rowed home feeling drained.

On the south side of an outcrop of rocks in the cove, Potter was feeding in a tide pool. He could hear the hollering in the cove and he knew there were creatures in the water over there. He was lying on his back in the shallows crunching on a mussel shell he had pulled fresh from the pool. He liked to lie on his back with his belly as a table. He laid his prizes from the rock pools up there and worked them open with his fingers, teeth, or a small rock as needed; then he gobbled them up. This pool was rich with food and he had been there a while slowly making a lunch for himself. The urchins were the best, but you had to get around their spines to get to the soft meat.

Something was wrong with the human out in the cove. He knew it. He could hear it. He could smell it. There was fear...and something else. He knew about this one who had his nest further south on the beach. He had that barking creature with him all the time.

Potter wanted to know what was in the pit in the sand outside the door of the human's nest. It was food, but not the kind Potter knew. He wanted to get into it, but couldn't. The smell coming from it was exotic and tantalizing. Maybe the human would like to trade? He would bring him something. Maybe a fish or something from down deep on the sea floor, maybe a few crabs. He would bring something and leave it and see what happened. For now, he didn't bother to show himself or creep around and look into the cove. He could hear that they were leaving and he lay quietly continuing his mid-day feast. Later, after a rest, he would swim back south to where his mate was nesting with the new babies. There were two right now. He and his mate would dive and catch fish for them and then they would watch them play on the sand.

Arriving home, Daniel hiked slowly up to Glass House where he took a warm shower, shaved and put on clean shorts and a fresh canary yellow T shirt. He did some cooking. He felt better. Later Henry got a shower too at the outdoor beach shower to get all the salt off. They both looked fresh and presentable for visiting.

Later, Daniel took two big bottles of a good red table wine along in the Penguin, and a small chocolate mousse which he had concocted, wrapped up and lying in an ice bucket. It was going to be a two bottle evening, he could feel it. Since he woke up this morning, and then later in the distress he felt swimming in the cove, he knew that he needed to talk to someone.

He had known Luke for years. He had been there from the first days when his parents brought Daniel to the island. He had been about eight and Luke a few years older then. Luke always came along to help his father, Otis, when he was working on the property. Luke had been a quiet, smiling presence in their childhood, a sweet friendly boy. Maybe he could talk with Luke?

Maybe he could trust him. They were certainly friends now that they were both adults. He kept thinking about this friendship with Luke, evaluating it, really. Luke had always expressed a quiet support. And Daniel had tagged along with him around the property happily all those summer days.

Luke had observed what the Cross family was like, their strange cold ways, yet he remained loyal and kind, always interested in Daniel and his life. He knew that Luke's family was a "real" family. You could feel it in the atmosphere. There was talking and cooking in their house, listening to music, and sitting around laughing in the evenings. He knew, as he had hung around there some as a boy. Daniel was always welcomed. Both Luke and his dad, Otis, were always there for the Cross threesome when they arrived from the mainland.

Later, Daniel had taken off around the world and back. Luke had remained. He had continued to help his dad and then he had gone to a maritime academy in Seattle for specialized training. This had boosted his position at the marina. He returned to the island with a responsible job working there. He loved the boats and knew everything about them. He was not yet married, but Luke knew he liked girls and now he had marriage plans with Anna, from Anacortes. Luke had told him she was a school teacher. They were engaged and now a wedding was planned at Christmas time this year. A Christmas wedding on the island, and then the couple would make their home here.

Daniel sailed into the marina well before sundown. He saw Luke sitting in a deckchair waiting for him, smiling broadly at the little Penguin. He tied down and came aboard the house boat wearing a grin himself! He had surprised Luke and pleased him, he could see that. He relaxed. It was a relief to be with someone he knew, someone comfortable.

Luke's little houseboat was neat and tidy, though dark inside. Lots of wood paneling and sort of retro-sixties fittings. It smelled like teakwood and wax. There was a small tight salon, galley, bunks and head with shower in the back. The deck was spacious with awnings overhead. They opened the wine and sat down to talk.

Luke had been working all day, but was freshly showered and dressed in a bright blue t-shirt and gray sweatpants, waiting for Daniel. He was a handsome man, clean-shaven, with lustrous, smooth skin and medium length hair, in tight soft curls, not thick. One small gold ring hung rakishly from an ear. There was some French in Luke's people.

He had a dog too, George. He was a chocolate lab. Luke said he spent his days diving in and out of the marina waters, following him around and generally splashing things up. He thought he was helpful, but generally, he was not. A good dog, he and Henry hit it off just fine. After the perfunctory sniffing, George lay at Luke's feet most of the time. But, he would charge out on deck at the slightest noise and sway around. Henry sat by, poised and observant as usual.

It was still warm in the waning sun and Daniel and Luke had taken some of the wine out on deck and began talking about the Penguin. Daniel knew it had been inherited from an old guy Paul knew on the island years ago. He had been a woodworking hobbyist and had created it from a kit, the way most Penguins were put together. Paul had gotten it for Daniel but never ventured out in it himself. For a Navy man, he was not much of an enthusiast for recreation on the sea. Sheila had ridden with

Daniel in it a few times, just for a short jaunt. Paul would sit in a deck chair up on the cliff, on the Glass House terrace and just glance down to see their progress once in a while, looking up from whatever he was reading. Luke and Otis had actually given Daniel his first sailing lessons and they were talking about that tonight. He had been a nervous student and they were laughing about how he could not coordinate tiller and sail and fumbled around so self-consciously with the rigging when left to do it alone. Sometimes, the boom, though light in weight, would come around and nearly knock Daniel into the sea. They laughed about the slapstick nature of those early lessons. Otis had gone out with him until he was safe, then sometimes Daniel and Luke had gone out farther and fished together, though usually nothing was caught. These had been summer days of just wind and water and sun. It had been a really "O.K." time in Daniel's life. He was glad to talk about it tonight, even if the past could be unsettling. Yes, just thinking and remembering his constant discomfort as a boy around Paul was unsettling. You just could not relax with his background presence, so austere, with such an apparently blunt disinterest in anything about whatever you were doing or thought important.

Luke was also telling Daniel about what he was doing these days at the marina. They were developing a new area and creating some new docking features to give more sophisticated security for all the boats. He was chatting on and on and Daniel was glad to hear his voice and just listen.

The wine was hitting him hard after his strenuous day of swimming and rowing. He was admiring Luke's beautiful brown skin, his muscular arms and the light falling on his sculpted features. It was good to be with someone so beautiful, so strong.

Finally, they went into the galley and started preparing the dinner. Daniel helped make a Greek salad and Luke toasted bread on a grill and then some whitefish steaks. The mousse was stashed in the miniscule refrigerator. There was more wine and time to watch the sun going down over the water. They ate out on the deck and kept talking and drinking.

Daniel had not brought up the thoughts about feelings, family and the past that were troubling him so much. He was not sure either if Luke would understand his strange aloneness. They sat in the dark with only the light from the salon inside illuminating them, and just talked about life on the island and little events which had happened that week. A shark had come into the marina, causing a stir. Two famous artists were renting a guest house near the marina and came out to paint each day. People were interested in these goings-on.

Finally, settling down with another glass of wine, Daniel looked over at Luke and said, "I don't know what I am doing out here. I don't know why I came out here." He was sinking now, full of dinner and an excess of wine. He had been nervously drinking. Now, lethargy was over-taking him, and sadness was washing over him. He thought that Luke might not have heard his comment, as he didn't say anything immediately and was lying back in his chair, eyes closed.

But finally in a low voice, he said, "Maybe you're doing something very 'old-fashioned,' called 'grieving...' Your father has only been dead for a few weeks. That would be the thing I would think is going on." Luke sat up and looked directly at Daniel. Then he smiled.

Daniel drew in a sharp breath. "Grieving?" he snorted. "Well, I guess. The thing is I don't understand it, but I feel like everything has been pulled out from under my feet. You know, like life is so turned around I don't know where I am in life. I was doing well and leading a successful life until Paul died. Now I am disoriented. Strange, because, as you know, there was not a lot between me and My Dad Paul." He said this with a bitter twist in his voice."

Closing his eyes again, Luke said flatly, "You were lucky to have Paul. Not many people have someone to look after them and support them like Paul did for you, no matter how distant he might have acted. He was responsible for you. I saw that. You were lucky to be his son."

"You're right, I guess," said Daniel. "But, I can't remember him really ever taking the slightest interest in my life. I don't think he liked me."

Daniel was slurring his words now.

Looking over again at Luke, he said, "Puts a dent in my feelings about myself, ya know. I always wanted to fix that. Now it can't be fixed for sure," he grimaced. "Too late now. Nothin' can be done about it." He finished the last of the wine in his glass.

Leaning back in the chair at last he said, "Do you think it is possible that I am out here just really feeling sorry for myself?"

"That is a possibility," Luke said dryly, with closed eyes.

Suddenly, Daniel wanted to just touch Luke, to stroke his strong beautiful face, to embrace him. To get Luke's strength for himself, he needed it so desperately.

Dizzily, tippingly he stood up and said, "Hey! Let's have a nightcap to top off the evening! How about something stronger?"

They got up and walked back into the salon. Luke was preparing something at the little bar. Daniel stood swaying, right behind him. He reached out and began stroking Luke's back softly. He pressed himself against him softly, wrapping his arms around him. He buried his face in Luke's curly hair. Tears were welling in his eyes. He was so dizzy now and getting numb as he tried to speak, it was just a throaty slurring, a kind of a moan.

Luke turned around slowly and took Daniel's hands in his own. He looked at him full in the face. He put down the glasses and took Daniel's face in his hands. His face was stern, but kind.

"You are my brother, Daniel," Luke said quietly. "You are my young hurting brother."

He took him by the arm firmly and went over to the old sofa. He pulled Daniel down roughly beside him. He wrapped his arms around him and brought him up onto his lap like a child. He held him tightly. Shocking! He rocked him like a baby as Daniel first cried and then sobbed. Luke put his hand on Daniel's head and held it there, warm, firm and steady. Daniel laid his head on Luke's chest. He could feel his steady heartbeat. Luke hummed and rocked Daniel on the sofa as long as he continued to cry. There was no other sound than the creaking of the boat and George out on the deck groaning in his sleep.

"Poor boy," Luke said, quietly. "My poor boy."

This was so shocking that Daniel thought he would die. The whole thing reminded him of something similar in the past. But that had been wrong and this... this was right. He knew that it was right. Very right.

Finally, Luke let him go and they sat just side by side with Luke's strong hand continuing to rest on Daniel's head. It felt so warm and powerful, like a benediction, which in fact, it was.

"How am I goin' to get home?" Daniel said, barely able to get that out with a slur. "I am so drunk! I've made an ass of myself." He laughed, wiping his face with his T shirt.

"Well little brother, you are definitely not sailing home in the Penguin," Luke laughed a deep heavy chuckle.

Daniel, in a thick voice said, "It is great to have a brother to care for you when you are SCREWED UP!"

"You will not always be screwed up," Luke said calmly. "One day you will help me. That's what brothers do."

Luke picked up the dishes and mess while Daniel lay on the sofa. Then Luke took a very limp Daniel and the two dogs along the marina docks to the shore and up to the cliff path. The moon had risen and they trudged along, through the high, open, scrubby land under its light. The low rocks and boulders shone silvery in the moon's light as they passed along the narrow path. Above, the sky was milky with the myriad stars extending out forever into space. Luke was guiding and steadying Daniel from behind whenever he would veer off the path. Luke was humming something familiar and soft the whole time. Daniel, now out in the open air was in a near blackout. The dogs soberly trotted on, one behind the other ahead of them.

At Glass House, Luke put Daniel to bed on the living room sofa.

"You are not going down to the beach house tonight, Bro," he said. "You'd break your neck! This will do for you." Daniel stretched out and was gone under the old patchwork quilt. Henry stood guard in the dark.

Luke shut the door and walked back on the path to the marina in the moonlight. George followed. If anyone could have seen Luke's face, as he walked through the night, they would have seen both the pain and serenity.

## CHAPTER TWENTY-FIVE

# The Morning After

DANIEL woke up feeling the scratchy wool of the red Glass House sofa pressing into his face. The smell of very old cigarette smoke was coming up from it. He knew where he was and wanted to die. Both to die and throw up at the same time. It would be better to throw up first, then die, he thought. That way at least he would die cleaned out of the mess that was in him. "What an ass," he thought. "What an ass." He wasn't sure of all the details of what had happened last night, but there was enough remembrance to make him feel cold.

Henry was scratching at the terrace door, really needing to get out and whining. Daniel sat up and looked out through the plate glass wall to the sky and the sea beyond. The weather had changed. It was a dark morning, with a heavy cloud bank in the distance.

Shivering, he thought, "O.K. where to begin to try to sort this. How in the hell did I get so out of control?"

Looking down at his hands, he could see that he was bloodlessly white and in his mind this was just a symptom of the utter fear he had just fallen into.

"What the hell?" He was talking to himself now. He felt panic rising in himself.

"What has happened to my life! I have had a successful, purposeful life. A good life! Now I am out here, living in a shack on the beach, sailing around in my old childhood toy boat, stumbling around drunk, humiliating myself with a friend who has already done way too much for me!"

"What the hell," he moaned out loud. "What the hell!" His head was hurting very bad too.

It was about 9 A.M. and still chilly outside. He wandered out onto the terrace looking down and out over the sea. The fresh air made him feel sick. Nausea. Then he saw a tiny boat making its way up the coastline. It was Luke, sailing up in the Penguin.

Daniel was unaccustomed to feelings of guilt. He considered himself a fair-minded person, and yet he knew he could manipulate his conscience to his own benefit, at times. In this moment, a weight of guilt was pressing in on him like lead, and there was no denying it.

The Penguin was proceeding on gaily and soon it disappeared under the curve of the cliff. Daniel knew it was coming ashore. Luke would be climbing up the path in no time. In resignation, Daniel just sat down in one of the patio chairs, staring straight ahead. In a minute, Luke's curly head appeared coming up the path. Then Daniel saw that he was carrying the ice bucket. He was grinning, holding it up high over his head.

"We forgot to eat the mousse last night in all the hubbub," he said.

"Hubbub," repeated Daniel. "Imagine that."

Then quickly he began, "I'm so sorry for my behavior last night. That was a betrayal of our friendship. I regret it very much."

"You regret it?" said Luke, standing over him. "You regret being human and flailing around during a time of sorrow and of some really confusing emotions?"

"You know how I live, you know about my life" said Daniel, looking defensively up at Luke. His face was solemn and pained.

"I'm sorry I took advantage of your hospitality," he said stiffly.

"O.K. I forgive you then," Luke said matter-of-factly.

"Can I get some utensils out of your kitchen to eat this with?" Luke went into the house and brought out two bowls and two spoons. "Let's eat this, O.K.?"

"I can't," said Daniel. "I feel totally sick."

"O.K. I'll eat it myself."

In a bit, without looking up from his eating, he said, "You know, what I did with you last night, the rocking thing? The lap hug thing?"

Daniel winced at the mention of it.

"You know, that was an 'Otis thing.' That was what Big Otis does, or would do if he was here with us. That's the Big Otis treatment for boys out of control or boys in trouble, for hurt boys, for sad boys."

Now he looked up at Daniel.

"But I meant it too. It wasn't just the Otis treatment, I meant it too." Luke was sitting, cheerfully shoveling in the mousse now as he spoke.

Daniel could see that he was undisturbed.

"We have had lots of problems in our family, Daniel. We're used to problems. The thing is you have got to let others get close to you in those problem times. That's how we roll in our family anyway."

After Luke finished eating he just sat quietly, also looking out to sea.

"That was really a great mousse, Daniel. You're in the right business. You have a real knack for creating some very good food."

Daniel's heart was beating rapidly. He had decided to take a chance. What further harm could he do to this relationship beyond what he had already done? Sort of like vomiting he thought, maybe at least I will feel better if I just get all this out of me. How could things be worse?

"I never sat on Paul's lap as a kid." Daniel began. "We didn't do that. However, I did sit on a guy's lap once when I was little. It was very different from the comforting stuff last night. I can say that it was very different from anything Otis might have wanted to do to help me too."

Tears were welling up in Daniel's eyes. He was starting to breathe out heavy deep sighs. He dropped his head into his hands. Luke was watching him intently.

Then Daniel began to tell the story of his time with the "Gentleman," the man in the brown suit. The time when he was taken to the park way back when he was five, the leafy grotto in the park where the "Gentleman" took him. The ice cream, the betrayal, the rape, the running back across the grass towards home. The despair and the confusion. The silence and the secret. The violation that he could not stop. The hatred growing on and on for Sheila. Even at five years old, he had known that he was just offered up to that man, a stranger, without any thought for his safety or protection. Just a lamb to the slaughter. She should have known better, but as usual she was only thinking of her own advantage.

Luke was weeping as Daniel came back to this world at the end of his story. "Hell of a thing to do to a little boy. Hell, of a thing," Luke said in a choked voice. "I am very sorry, Daniel. I am very, very sorry that happened to you."

Daniel told Luke that he had worked with Charlotte, his therapist, about this and that he was trying to let it go. Actually, he was beginning to let it go. That the memory was losing its power. But now with Paul's death and his conflict with Sheila things were looming up at him again.

"I appreciate your listening, Luke. Somehow, it is really good to tell you."

Daniel sat back in his patio chair, really exhausted now.

"Thank you for your friendship. It's always been nothing but good knowing you, from our earliest days here. This is a terrible story to dump on somebody, but I just had to tell you. I guess I wanted to tell you last night. I just couldn't open it up. I want you to know what is going on in my life. I hope you can hear it without it hurting you, or our friendship."

Daniel was looking at Luke, who was still obviously moved by the things he had told him. He looked over at Daniel with a face still in pain.

"You can tell me anything, Daniel. That was what I meant earlier, when I said you need to get close to people when you are in trouble. Like I said last night also, I consider you a brother."

"Will you really forgive me for last night...for everything?" Daniel put out his hand tentatively.

They shook hands. It was an awkward moment, but a moment of sincerity . . . and then they stood up and Luke hugged Daniel hard one more time. Daniel released a deep sigh.

"I guess I need to get on back to town, back to Seattle and work. I'm just spinning my wheels here," Daniel said sadly.

"You know, I don't really think so. I think you need to stay a little longer. Why don't you just give yourself some more time? Don't go bouncing around right now. Just try to stay and relax and let life happen for a little longer?" Luke offered. "You own this property now. Why not enjoy it? You are the owner of The Prow. Can't you call your restaurant people and ask them to keep things going for you a little longer back there?"

He paused, "You know, there's been a death in the family. You need some good time off. I think things are working for you in a healthy way here. Much more than you may realize. Just why not give yourself more time? Take a time out."

With this last word he made the sports "T" sign for time out with his hands. He said it with a grin.

Daniel didn't answer. They got up and Luke started toward the cliff path. Daniel walked along with him a ways and they began to talk again of daily matters. Finally Daniel put a hand out again to Luke and thanked him for bringing up the Penguin. And he thanked him for listening, for being forgiving, for trying to understand.

Luke smiled and said again, "Think about staying."

Daniel smiled weakly too. "Thank you for everything, Luke."

They shook hands again and parted ways. The sun had peeked out now and the green low shrubs were fragrant in the breeze.

Daniel went down to the beach house and started preparing a good breakfast for himself. A cool breeze was still blowing. He ate and his nausea was gone. He spent the rest of the day resting on the beach and on his bunk.

Two days later, Daniel phoned the restaurant and asked Oscar and Trini to come out to the island the next day for a meeting. It was early in the week and they could take off a day. They were glad to hear from him and said they would come right away. They said they were worrying about him…everybody was. "The restaurant is doing fine," they said. But everyone missed him. They were praying for him. They would be there on the ferry the next day.

## CHAPTER TWENTY-SIX

# Trini and Oscar

THIS was the first trip to the island for Oscar and Trini, so the ferry ride was a big treat for them. They arrived on the 11 A.M. ferry at Friday Harbor and drove their blue Volvo off the dock and slowly through the streets of the little town and then out into countryside, taking in all the sights on the way to Glass House. It was early June and a sunny day. Trini was chattering and thrilled with the display of blooming roses at every homestead as they drove along. Daniel was waiting for them out near where the driveway meets the road, and waved them in happily. Henry was barking furiously. He recognized them.

Trini hopped out of the car first, her black glossy hair shining and bobbing in the sun. Sturdy arms reached out and gave Daniel a prolonged hug. Then Oscar came along and joined in the huddle. Trini was teary as she held Daniel at arm's length and looked him over.

"We have missed you so much," she said simply.

Their car was full of hampers, jugs, boxes and bags of food from The Prow. Everyone had sent some special dish along with well-wishes. They unloaded it all and Daniel took them through the terrace into the house. They were "oohing" and "aahing" as they walked through the living room. Trini brushed her hand along the sleek red sofa.

Her eyes were bright, taking it all in.

"What a joint!" Oscar whistled, wringing one hand.

"This is the house, but this is not where I am living," Daniel told them. Then he helped them stow the food in the kitchen.

"Wow!" Oscar was admiring the all stainless steel cabinets, the marble pastry slab and island, the commercial double freezer. "This must have cost a mint, even back in the day!" he said. "This could be a restaurant kitchen. It's got everything, *Hermano*."

They petted Henry as he jumped and shivered around. Then they toured throughout the house, and back out onto the terrace. They were in awe of the beautiful wide view.

"Let me show you something before we eat," Daniel said. He helped Trini into the dirt path down to the beach. Oscar was close behind. As they came out onto the sandy beach, Daniel gestured dramatically toward the beach house. "Welcome to my primitive home."

They were amazed and laughed at all his rigged up devices for on-the-beach living.

"Hey, you're Robinson Crusoe!"

Oscar was examining the gas burners, the buried refrigerator, and his net bag for hanging produce. They laughed at his outhouse and outdoor shower. Trini looked up at him curiously.

"This is cool, Daniel, but why are you down here not up in the swanky house?"

"I'm not sure. Some guys helped me fix this up, and I just started staying down here. The big house has the imprint of Paul. It's a little heavy for me," he smiled weakly.

"The whole place is mine, but these are my digs, for now. Just wanted to show you my setup."

They said nothing, but looked around seriously.

"O.K. I've got another place to show you too. Let's go up and feast on The Prow's best. You have obviously brought the best and most expensive stuff!"

They laughed and followed him back up the path, into the kitchen and then out the back door into the orchard. "Man, you've got it ALL here!" said Oscar spreading his arms. The orchard was beautiful in the noonday peace and sun.

Daniel proudly showed them first the cherry trees with their ripening fruit and then the apple trees, laden with little green knobby apples. "You are about ten days early for the cherries, and you can see there will be loads of apples coming early this fall, all kinds of varieties. There will be many apple pies and things baked later on." His voice was full of pride.

They spread blankets and hauled out the food. Henry was running round and round the trees in excitement, hoping for handouts, of course. First there was a bourbon-laced pate, with shards of crisp bread. Then a big insulated jug of "Prow Chow," the restaurant's fish chowder, still plenty hot. It was divine slurped up from bowls out there in the grassy orchard. There was a beautifully prepared cheese board with lots to choose from but the highlight was his favorite, a Danish Havarti. Next, they brought out a multitude of vegetable crudités, then hearty chicken pot pies and Daniel's signature chocolate mousse with a fruity wine at the end. Everyone was groaning by then.

"How am I going to get up from here?" Trini said. "My zipper is going to pop…I'll have to roll back to the ferry!"

Oscar was spooning out the last of the chocolate mousse, quietly enjoying the last morsels. Daniel shuddered, watching Oscar finishing the mousse, thinking about the mousse he had made just days ago, the mousse which Luke had greedily consumed all by himself out on the terrace that chilly morning. He was shaking his head remembering it all.

Oscar noticed Daniel's shift of mood and began by saying, "As of today, we know you are well-fed here, but how are you doing otherwise? We don't know what to do for you out here all alone. Are you O.K.? Is it helping to be here? What can we do for you?"

"I am better. Thanks. I have had a confusing time, but I am better. Don't forget also, I have my friend Luke here on the island. This is a friendly place." He sat up and tried to gather the things in his mind that he needed to say. "I thought I would just be here for two weeks," he began. "It is looking like I need to stay longer, that's why I asked you to come out. I need to know if you guys can continue as we have been, continue holding everything together for me at The Prow. How are things going there with me gone? Tell the truth!"

They looked at each other.

"It is different without you. You know that, I'm sure. You are the glue for the staff and for the customers too," said Trini. She sat up straight. "I have to say I think we are doing well though. Everyone is well trained. The systems are all in place. The quality is there in the food and in the service. Everyone wants to do their best for you and the name of the restaurant," she smiled. "I think we are doing well! And no slowdown in business."

Oscar smiled too. "I have been surprised myself at how well things are going. It's not that we don't need you, man. But it is going along smooth. As Trini said, the systems are all in place. We all know our stuff and what to do." The smile had turned into a big grin.

"Not indispensible, eh?"

They laughed. Daniel tried to look serious, but it did not work. He was grinning again. He was so happy to be with them both. "I want to ask you to continue for a while longer, maybe all summer. Can you do it? Of course, we will have to make another increase in salaries...to management levels."

They looked at each other, surprised. "Sure, Daniel. We can keep on keepin' on," said Oscar. "What are you going to be doing here?"

"Umm, I don't know what you would call it, but I think I need to get over some stuff." He looked away. "Luke says it is grieving. I think it is hitting the reset button in my life." Then he added, "It is helping me to do that here. How fortunate that I have you guys and the restaurant and that I am able to take this break. I think that being here is going to strengthen me. I am grateful."

"No problem," Oscar said. "*Andele!*"

They picked up the remainder of the meal and went inside. In the living room, they went over some accounting and talked about a couple of menu changes over coffee. They gave him the blow-by-blow of the past weeks' business and asked for permission to change a couple of items.

"We are having trouble getting good mushrooms right now," said Trini. "We would like to shop around for a better supplier."

"Do it, make the changes, just don't be going and making this into a "Taco Den," you guys. I don't trust you, Trini!" Daniel kidded.

"What! No flan?" she crowed.

"Flan is good. Coconut flan is even better." Daniel was smiling.

"*Umm, que rico!*"

The conversation wound down and they were left looking at Daniel in the quiet. Wondering what was happening with him. He never asked about Sheila and they did not offer anything about her. It had been a very pleasant day and all three were relieved to be together. It was reassuring all around.

"You are doing everything I need for you to do right now. Just keep the place going with no decline in quality. That is all I ask. Plus, get flowers for the foyer everyday." He was still smiling at them.

"We are doing that, Daniel," Trini said, smiling back at him. "We are doing all that."

They packed up and loaded the Volvo. Trini could not help clinging to Daniel a moment before climbing into the car.

"Next time, I will take you out in my little sailboat!" Daniel said.

Trini shook her head, as if to say, "no way..."

Then, leaning into the car window, Daniel said, "I'm going to send you a care package of these cherries later this month. Be on the lookout for them!" And then off they went, as quickly as they had come.

Later, on the ferry, Trini and Oscar stood by the railing watching the green island growing smaller by the minute.

"Daniel looks different," Trini said, looking up at Oscar. Meeting her eyes he replied, "Yeah, he looks a little…shaggy! I think that's a good thing."

## CHAPTER TWENTY-SEVEN

# The Respite

"So...I'm here for a little while longer," Daniel thought, hands on hips, watching Oscar and Trini's car disappear down the narrow lane. He walked back into the house. There was still some coffee in the carafe so he poured a cup and sat down on the red wool sofa with the coffee and his phone. He was thinking some things through. It was after four and Luke was home at the house boat. He answered on the second ring.

"I have just spent the day up here with my managers from the restaurant," Daniel began. His voice was excited.

"They came over this morning on the ferry. We discussed me staying here a while longer. They are willing, and I know I can trust them to keep the place going...so I'm going to stay. They've gone on back." He paused. "You should have seen the food they brought me from The Prow. It was amazing. I know they can handle the restaurant without me being there for a while longer. It looks like I will probably be here for the summer." There was a lifting of hope in his voice.

"I think that is perfect, Daniel! Are you good with it?"

"Yeah, I think I'm good. You were right. I need some time. Thank you for your encouragement, Luke."

"We'll have some good times, neighbor. No problem."

"There's another thing...I want to get the Penguin painted. Can you guys do it down at the marina?"

"Of course! We have a work shed down here and painting boats is part of what we do. Pete and I have our regular work, but we should be able to fit this in a few hours a day. We should be able to have it done in three or four days. Why don't you sail it on down tomorrow?"

"I will. I'll be there early tomorrow."

"That sounds fine with me. I'll round up Pete to help. See you tomorrow."

"Good, see you tomorrow."

He continued sitting on the red couch. He looked over at Henry who had jumped up and was sitting on the other end.

"This thing has got to go," he said, patting and stroking the red wool. "Soon. And, there are other things up here that need to go away too, like this gargantuan bar." He pointed towards the long walnut structure along the south wall. "And the Frank Sinatra mirrors, and all these dozens of glasses. It's all got to go. Sorry Paul," he laughed and slapped the couch again.

Henry looked to where Daniel was pointing. He did not understand these words but he opened his mouth and yawned loudly anyway, shifting his weight from one front leg to the other as dogs do, trying to give some support to whatever Daniel was going on about.

They got up and Daniel tidied the kitchen, putting things away. He shut the doors and they went on down to the beach house. It had been a satisfying day. There had been so much food at the picnic in the orchard that no more was needed today. Just a final cup of tea after dark.

Early the next day Daniel started unloading gear out of the Penguin, everything not necessary to sail down south to the marina. The cooler, some tools and fishing tackle, extra rope and his rain jacket were all taken into the house. Everything including the fittings would have to be removed when they starting preparing to paint the hull.

After breakfast they set sail for the marina. On the way, Daniel saw Potter sunning on a rock outcrop. He hadn't seen him around the beach house since the morning when he had tried to raid the outdoor refrigerator. Potter's girlfriend was nearby too, floating in the water with her two pups. The pups were so fuzzy that they naturally floated on the surface of the water like furry water lilies. Henry leaned over the side of the boat barking at them all. They paid no attention to him. Daniel could not remember if he had thought to lock up the "refrigerator" before he left.

"Oh well, let them try," he thought.

At the marina, Luke and Pete were waiting at the shed at the far end of the boat slips. It was well up out of the water and with the help of some kids they all worked to lift the Penguin up high onto dry land. The shed itself would be used during the actual painting phase to keep dirt and dust off. The side walls of the shed were heavy clear plastic sheeting, which could be raised or lowered as needed. After the Penguin was fully dried out they would ready it for sanding. For now, Daniel helped them unscrew all the fittings. They stowed the hardware away in some boxes, then looked the hull over and talked about paint and colors. Daniel wanted to keep his three colors, red, yellow and blue. The three of them would work together to design a new and different layout for the stripes. This was going to be a fun process. Daniel was looking forward to it, and he wanted to help where he could. Pete thought the job would take four days, working several hours a day. They didn't need to strip the paint, just sand the hull. Luke also said he would order a new Dacron sail. He knew where to get one. It was going to be one handsome boat. Daniel left them to their other scheduled work and promised to come down tomorrow to help with the sanding. He was thrilled about the prospect of this work.

Daniel and Henry awoke early the next day and hurried up to the Glass House kitchen. Daniel had decided to make some beignets for the guys to munch on this morning. He mixed and rolled out the dough, then heated the oil piping hot and dropped the dough in, one square after another. They puffed and browned. He rolled them while still warm in fine powdered sugar. It was messy, but worth it when he tasted the first one. All pleasure and calories. Bagging them up, he decided to hoof it on down the cliff path.

They arrived around 10 A.M. at the marina. Luke and Pete were already hard at work on the Penguin. They had it turned bottom up, secured with special blocks. He could hear the sanders working from a distance. The guys stopped working when they saw him coming. Daniel showed them the beignets. There were cries of delight. They ate them up, groaning; they were so light and so fresh, still warm in fact. They brought out hot coffee to go with the pastries.

The three of them were looking over the hull as they ate. A light sanding was going to be enough, they all thought. As they went back to work Daniel joined in, too. He had nothing else to do, might as well lend a hand. They used light rotary sanders, blowing the debris away with a blower frequently. They were working hard on the outer hull, first a coarse sanding, then the fine finishing.

Around noon a small blonde woman was seen walking through the docks towards them. It turned out that this was Pete's wife, Peggy. "Pete and Peg, a dynamic duo," Luke said as he introduced her. She had brought a bag of sandwiches and potato chips. The sandwiches were on plain white bread, some with bologna and the rest with fresh egg salad filling, lots of mayo, some pickle spears on the side. They told Peggy about the beignets and with mock "sad" faces said they were sorry, but that they had eaten them all up. There was not one left over for her. She walked right up to Daniel, looking him in the eye.

"You're a pretty boy," she said as she patted his face. "You better bring me some beignets next time." They all broke up laughing.

Peggy was shapely though very thin with sharp black eyes and more than a few wrinkles. She liked to be in the sun, just like Pete. The blond hair was achieved at the local beauty shop. Daniel was to soon learn that Pete and Peggy had been in "unfortunate marriages" before. Peggy came out single to the island and got a barmaid job in Friday Harbor. Pete was already working at the marina. They met and hit it off at once. Finally, they risked getting married again and as Pete would say it was a "whole 'nother ballgame..." They were happy. Surprisingly, they did not live on a houseboat like Luke, but had moved into the marina housing on the bluff above. Their rent was provided as part of Pete's job as marina handyman.

Their real home, however, and the object of much love was their sailboat, kept in a slip at the marina. It was a 28 foot Morgan, Out Island, a classic masthead sloop built in 1973. Pete had gotten her through an auction and paid a little less than the price of a good used car for her. The boat was a bit neglected, the topside a little chewed up, but he carefully refinished and restored it all little by little, as he had time. It was well fitted out. In fact, it came with a full set of china and also tableware monogrammed with a scrolled "P," which made Peg know it was meant to be their boat. It was plenty big enough for Pete and Peg whenever they had time to get away. Pete tinkered with it constantly and they took it out most Sunday afternoons. Sometimes, when he had a whole weekend they ventured much farther than the island. The craft was called "PegNPete." They planned to retire on it and sail the world.

The plain sandwiches were eaten quickly with gusto and then they went right back to their sanding tasks. At two o'clock Luke and Pete had to quit, going back to their regular tasks for the marina.

For three days they worked this way, bringing the surface of the hull down to a paintable finish, inside and out. Daniel was there every day, working alongside Luke and Pete, sanding and scraping. They didn't talk a lot, focusing closely on the work, but it was an easy companionship. Pete was the perfectionist, of course, repeatedly checking the smoothness of the surface with his work-hardened hands and eagle eye. Daniel got up early to fry the beignets every day too, including plenty for Peggy.

It was tiring, dirty, work. Daniel's fair skin was beginning to take on a golden tan since coming to the island. At night his shoulders and hands were stiff and ached a bit. There were a couple of blisters. He wasn't used to this, but it was clear that it was very healthy for him. The days were beautiful with the coming on of summer. Being outdoors on the island, working in a spectacular place of beauty in the natural world was inspiring every day. They could often see eagles wheeling over head as they worked.

The first day Luke and Pete buzzed Daniel and Henry home in the skiff in the late afternoon just for the fun of it, swinging their boat out away from shore in a wide arc, breaking up work with time on the sea, with wind and sea spray buffeting them. Along the way they saw a few seals sunning themselves. Far in the distance a pod of dolphins were leaping, and of course, there were otters. On the remaining days, Daniel and Henry hiked back home through the fields on the cliff path. There was a feeling of openness, of space, out in that wide field in the sun that thrilled Daniel. He could see Lopez Island and others in the distance, the sparkling sea channels all around and woods to the north. He could see weather changing and building up to the south out over the Strait of St. Juan de Fuca, a place of unpredictable seas, extreme tides, fogs and winds. But on the island, all was beautiful and sunny most days. Summer was putting on her full attire.

Back at Glass House Daniel began his plan for the dismantling of the living areas. He was on a roll, fixing and changing things. The first day, he found some cardboard boxes and began packing the bar glassware into them. There were a dozen really nice stemware crystal glasses that he kept for use with company, the rest he packed away to be taken to town. He also took down the movable glass shelving and supports, stacking all of it in the garage. He would visit the thrift shop again. Maybe they would take them, and just maybe he could find some other things there to trade that he could use in the house.

After the sanding work was finished, on the fourth day of work, the three men huddled to figure out the painting design for the Penguin. They decided on a more sophisticated version of the three primary colors, red, blue and yellow. This time Daniel agreed to a darker marine blue for the majority of the outer hull, a four inch wide stripe of deep scarlet red at the gunwales and a thinner line of a Naples buttery yellow just below that. They had sanded the rail down to the bare wood. That would be kept natural and varnished. The inside of the hull would remain natural too with a durable varnish coating.

When the Penguin was ready for paint, Daniel bowed out of the work. He knew that painting is a skill needing an experienced hand, and that Luke and Pete did not need his help with this part. It was time to get back to the beach and to his Glass House work for a few days while they painted and restored the rigging and sail. It would be a big treat to see his boat all shiny and new after it was painted and dried.

There was one thing left to decide.

Pete brought it up to Daniel. "Do you want to name your boat? If so, we can see that the name gets properly inscribed on the stern."

Daniel smiled shyly. "I've been thinking about that too. Penguins are not always named, but this one is special. I think I would like to name it "TIME OUT…"

Pete and Luke grinned, looking at each other. "TIME OUT it will be," said Pete. "We'll do it in white."

"I will leave it to you fellows," Daniel smiled. They took a break and ferried Daniel and Henry home in the skiff this time. They were just pulling away from shore at the beach house when Daniel started yelling by the front door. He motioned them in again, and they pulled in and jumped off of the skiff onto shore.

"Look at this!" Daniel was pointing down to the sand near his refrigerator. There, stacked on the sand, were two large freshly caught crabs. The refrigerator had obviously been attacked again full force too, but it held fast. They all laughed and Luke picked a crab up and turned it over in his hands. He could tell they were freshly caught.

"A heck of a nice present from somebody..." Then he smiled. "Potter! Potter brought this!"

Daniel was wide-eyed now. "Do you think so?"

"He wants to trade with you." Luke was laughing hard. "Yeah, he can't get into your refrigerator stash, so he is offering a trade! He brought these to you. I'd clean'um and eat them soon. They're fresh."

"Absolutely amazing! So, what should I trade him for this?"

"Oh, I don't know, maybe some ham or something like that, maybe some raw eggs."

They were still laughing as Luke and Pete brushed the sand off themselves and headed for the skiff. "Enjoy your crab dinner!" they called out from the boat. And with a wave they took off to the south.

That evening Daniel steamed the crabs in the fire pit using the big steamer pot he had brought down to the beach. He made the simple garlic butter sauce. He cooked both crabs, saving one aside to eat cold. As he sat eating on the beach, he thought he heard a distant chattering beyond the rocks to the south. Someone was watching. He took crab number two up to the regular refrigerator at Glass House, for safe-keeping. Then before bed, he arranged a plate of ham and raw eggs in their shells and laid it outside next to the refrigerator.

He didn't hear a thing all night, but in the morning the ham and eggs were gone, eggshells and all. In place of the food, a long strip of seaweed was draped over the dish. He shook his head. Henry was there watching, "I guess this is an otter thank you note...what a guy." He left for his work up at Glass House, chuckling all the way.

In these waiting days...waiting for the Penguin to be painted and finished, Daniel continued his work at Glass House, slowing down the pace of his life even more. There were many hours in the day, and he was finding himself to be in no hurry. In the mornings, down at the beach, he would fiddle with that old rusty wire piece he had rescued from the surf. He tried wrapping bits of sea glass into it at various spots to give a sparkle and weight to the thing. Finally, he hung it up high in the beach house ceiling, letting it descend down in a springy way, filling that upper space. It didn't rotate, but the sun through the windows would strike it at certain times of the day, and the glass bits would glow. It was very pleasant to look at, kind of reminding him of his apricot silk festoons at The Prow. "This is my answer to Calder!" he told Henry, who did not care. Then, he hiked back up to his demolition work at Glass House, something he was enjoying tremendously.

After a beach house shower, he spent the evenings stirring up a campfire meal and enjoying the coming of night and its display of stars. Sometimes he would fall asleep in his canvas sling chair out there on the beach, just drifting off while looking up at the sky.

He did notice that his "refrigerator" was still under attack whenever he was absent. He always locked it, but the edges of the lid had been chewed and the locks were scratched and gnawed too. Potter was trying his best to get into his cache.

"No way, Potter," Daniel chuckled. "No way."

## CHAPTER TWENTY-EIGHT

# Time Out

PUTTING the finish on the Penguin took a few days longer than Luke and Pete had projected. Pete, the technician, decided to use an epoxy finish on the bare wood, and then he applied two coats of a good oil-based paint. Of course, the striping took extra time and finesse. Finally, Luke called to say it was ready. There was excitement in his voice. It was clear that he and Pete liked this little boat. Daniel felt like a kid on Christmas morning when it was time to go down to claim his Penguin.

In the interim, Daniel had slowly dismantled the Glass House bar. Then he carefully pried off the back bar mirrors. Some broke, but most were intact. He threw salt over his left shoulder for the broken mirrors, as he had been taught by Willie. She was a scientist, but still not taking chances with luck. Bit by bit he had carried all the pieces out to the garage. The wall behind the bar was now pitted with holes; so he had puttied the holes, sanded a bit and rolled on a coat of sheet rock compound in a fine texture. He would think of a color to paint it later.

He called the thrift shop guys and they came out and took everything they thought they could sell, including the odd Picasso print in his childhood bedroom. They were kind enough to haul away the debris from the bar to put in a dumpster in town for him too. They took the red wool sofa.

"This will sell immediately," they said. "And the glasses will go too."

The room looked very strange now without the sofa and the bar. Daniel would have to get used to this before putting anything else in. Nothing was left but the Eames steel chairs, which he liked very much, and the walnut game table and chairs in the corner. He had left the Calder-style mobile hanging over the table for old time's sake. It was fine there for now. That was enough work. The most disturbing objects were gone, and now it was time to play! Time to pick up his newly restored boat and have some fun.

That night Daniel had another dream of Paul. Daniel saw himself up at Glass House, sitting cross-legged on the empty floor in the living room looking at the wall where the bar had been. Paul walked in through the terrace doors. He was dressed now in a pair of Bermuda shorts, a bright lime green golf shirt and the same old converse high tops. He was wearing those glinty glasses. It looked like his hair was growing longer; kind of at chin length. It was swept back off his face. He looked at Daniel and even in the dream Daniel felt his heart beat faster. Paul walked up to the newly plastered wall where the bar had been. He looked it over with his back to Daniel. Then as it happens only in dreams, he somehow now had a can of spray paint in his hands. He began to spray graffiti on the wall. When he was finished he turned and gestured to it, like...voila! He had flowingly painted the word "CHANGES" huge, in red. It was a brilliant red. He smiled and walked out. Daniel did not wake up with this dream, but he remembered it vividly when he awoke the next morning.

At 10 A.M. Daniel arrived at the marina, walking. The newly finished boat was on the docks ready to put in the water, suspended from the marina's hoist. They had even rigged the hardware and mast. The new sail had not arrived yet, but it didn't matter. The old sail would do for now. Even from a distance Daniel could see how good it looked. Luke and Pete were standing proudly by. Everyone was smiling, but none as broadly as Daniel. It was perfect! They examined the hull and stroked it like a new car. The finish was extraordinary... what a difference. Pete said he thought the epoxy was a good preservative touch next to the wood, and that it gave a smoother finish to the paint. Daniel agreed. The hull was beautiful and having the rail in natural wood tone made it so rich. The marine blue hull was sharp-looking. The accent stripes, just right. They walked around to the stern and showed him the name "TIME OUT" painted white in a casual, funky script. It just capped the whole thing off. They thought he should take it easy putting things into the bottom of the hull for a few more days, until all was totally cured. It was finished inside with a clear marine varnish. They had lined the floor of the hull with a few newspapers. Putting it into the water was fine though, they said. So they launched it, lowering it into the water carefully.

Daniel didn't know how to express his thanks to these two friends. He tried, but knew he would have to do something special soon to make them know how great this was, how meaningful for him. They had lovingly done this project, and he knew it. They would accept payment for their work, but that was not enough for Daniel.

Luke and Pete had even refinished the old oars of the Time Out. Daniel climbed in and somewhat awkwardly, he rowed out of the marina, then unfurled and hoisted the sail, dropped in the keel and started up the coast. What an incredible feeling! It was like a new boat. New caulking, new finish, new colors, a fresh name. Starting anew. That's what he was doing.

Henry was waiting at the beach house when he arrived and ran down the beach and into the water to greet him. Daniel dropped and tied down the sail, mooring the boat to the mooring posts on the jetty. For some reason he did not want to go cruising just yet. He wanted to sit on the beach and admire his new craft for a while, bobbing on the water there at the shore. He was a little shy of it.

Later that afternoon, he and Henry took off north to cruise the coastline. Everything about the new Time Out was so smooth, so elegant. The wind was to his back so he let the sail out, letting it fill as it would. It was such a pleasure to hold the mainsail line and watch the billowing sail work the wind. He sat at the tiller and Henry took his place in the bow. He sailed out away from the shore considerably to avoid any unfamiliar hidden rocks. The water was calm and a dark emerald green, gliding alongside the hull. It was a wonderful, short, maiden voyage. He knew he would be in this boat often now, sailing in peace and quiet in the inland channels. A rush of love for the San Juans came up in him. What a gift these islands were, what a gift! Not just for him but for everyone who came out to them.

He tacked back against the wind, trimming close and soon they were coming up to the beach house shore. Daniel wrapped the sail tightly to the boom and dropped the little anchor. He tied down fast to the jetty. He couldn't always trust it as a place for the TIME OUT to be kept, but for now, in great summer weather, it was O.K.

As he approached the beach house he saw something lying by the "refrigerator…" Henry bounded up and was messing with it. It was a small limp octopus. Daniel groaned. He didn't want to start this kind of pattern with Potter. The poor thing was a bit shredded. He called Luke for advice. "I am not really personally into calamari. We serve it at The Prow, but I don't eat it. What should I do? It's a mess."

"Don't pick it up. Don't take it. He'll get the message. Just leave it there.

And don't put any food out for him this time. He'll figure it out."

"O.K. Hope you're right…Hey, Henry and I just got back from a cruise north up the coast. It was wonderful. I can't explain how it feels now. Thanks again, Luke." He said the last part softly.

A few days later Luke called to say the new sail had arrived. Daniel sailed down for it before noon. Pete had laid it out on the grass above the marina, so that they could see it unfurled. It was a beautiful, light-weight, white Dacron. Very strong and yet very light. Just right for this little boat. It had a red vertical stripe running down its length about a foot out from the mast side. And there were three bright red telltales. Very sharp, very nice. They clipped it on with new hardware and line, so it was all set.

Luke looked like he had something behind his back. Daniel was wondering what it was when Pete spoke up.

"We didn't want you getting lost or be hitting some rocks or something out there, so we got you a set of nautical charts of the

San Juan waters. Now you're a real sailor." He handed Daniel a long canvas tube.

It contained four charts. Not just some copies that were blurry, but large, finely printed charts. They rolled them up again for him, and wrapped them back up into the tube. Daniel was thrilled by this gesture. He hugged them both hard. They looked very pleased too.

"Now Daniel," Pete added in a fatherly voice, "remember this, don't be taking this little boat out into the big strait, the Juan de Fuca, O.K.? It's too small for those waters, you'll get in trouble! And watch out for the southeast tip of Lopez, in case you are ever over there. It can be very dangerous."

Luke added, "You better not go around by the Cattle Point Lighthouse alone either. Your boat has a shallow draft, but those are tricky waters too, lots of rocks," he grinned. "We're just lookin' out for you. I know you are a big boy. A great little sail to start with might be to get over to Fisherman Bay on Lopez. The wind will be right going and there are few obstacles. You can easily tack back."

They also showed him which radio station had the best weather and boating information on their portable radios.

"Thanks again, guys." He was holding the chart roll. "You guys are the best. I really need this. I can put these up in the beach house and study them."

He thought he saw Pete's tan face flush a bit. He was clearly pleased. At this point Daniel brought out checks for all their work and they shook hands all around.

"Great work, guys. I'm so happy with the "Time Out…"

"All we need now is to 'christen' this boat," Peggy called out, coming toward them with two champagne bottles. They whacked one on the bow, Daniel officially calling out the name "Time Out..." The second bottle was shared among the four of them with toasts to the bright little sailboat.

Daniel took the Time Out sailing almost every day after this. He was not alone. The channels were full of sailboats now and motor craft too. It was high summer in the islands, the middle of June and tourist season. He often sailed up along the coast north to Friday Harbor and beyond. He sailed as far as Roche Harbor.

Daniel had not hit really rough water yet in the Time Out. There had been a few times when heavy fog dropped down on him suddenly. This was frightful and he lost his bearings for a moment. There was a compass on board, so he knew which direction to follow. Once he had looked up to see a ferry approaching fast. The huge vessel blasted its horn and he tacked quickly out of its path.

As Pete had recommended, he planned and carried out a day sail across the channel to Fisherman Bay at Lopez Island. It was charming there and he circled slowly around the Bay, stopping in to dock at the little store on the eastern shore for a snack and a look around on land.

This was a handsome little boat now, and Daniel was proud to be seen sailing in it. He noticed that the look of it brought recognition, smiles and waves from other sailors in much larger craft. They knew it was a kit boat and recognized the immaculate craftsmanship. And so, Daniel was growing more and more skilled in his ability to scoot around the island channels.

Usually Henry was his mate and he took up watch in the bow of the boat, barking at birds and the occasional dolphin skimming by. Orcas were not an uncommon sight and he was glad he had only seen them from a distance. He wondered how the Time Out would fare up close against their splashing and diving antics.

He still liked to take his little boat out for quiet days too. Days of drifting, sometimes snorkeling a little, picking up a few shellfish, swimming and resting in some of the small coves to the north of Glass House. Or, he would go out into the bay between San Juan and Lopez and cast a line, fishing most of the day, frying up his fresh catch at the fire pit at night.

Mainly though, he was practicing his tacking and gibing, and learning all with a neophyte's fervor. There were many evenings spent studying the new sailing charts by the light of his Coleman lantern. He had put his charts, the gift of Pete and Luke, up on the beach house walls where he could study them closely. Sometimes he would take one down and spread it out on his kitchen table where he could sit, drink tea and try to get a firmer understanding of the islands, the coves and bays, the water currents and the hazards. He realized as he sailed that he was beginning to get somewhat familiar with these prevailing currents, winds and tides. This was building his confidence. He would plot a course for the next outing, checking the radio report, using his yardstick, observing buoys, water depth and other markers along the course. Bit by bit he was learning his way around.

In the evening, the Time Out was docked most nights off the Glass House jetty. It was safe there and Daniel enjoyed just looking at his little boat bobbing on the water. It was amazing how this little wooden craft was bringing him so much joy. He thought of Paul, trying not to be maudlin, but simply thankful.

## CHAPTER TWENTY-NINE

## *Ruth*

SEVERAL miles down Heath Road, a young woman named Ruth Sloan lived in a white frame house. She had always lived there. The place had belonged first to her grandparents, then to her grandmother alone after her grandfather's death. Next to the house was a spacious and full green house. Ruth ran a flower farm and a florist's business there. Her flowers were wonderful. She grew some old-fashioned varieties there that people loved: "Old English" roses, Victorian annuals and bulbs. She grew things like "bachelor's buttons," which were rarely available. Her floral designs were unique and natural, not like a commercial florist would create, and so her business on the island was steady.

Wedding flower arrangements were the order of the day on Friday for Saturday weddings. Ruth had been working steadily all morning on the small arrangements for tables, little grapevine wreaths with sprigs of cedar, star jasmine and brilliant blue bachelor's buttons, charming and natural. She put these all away on trays in the refrigerator unit on the screened in back porch. Then it was time to do the bride's bouquet.

She selected and picked an armload of blue delphinium in the green house and then came back for some white oriental lilies, a little more jasmine and another handful of the bachelor's buttons. Lilies had to be handled carefully because of the smearing of orange pollen from the stamens. She brought them gingerly to the potting sink to remove the stamens first. One careless jolt and many blooms would be ruined.

As she worked, those white lilies began triggering memories of the day of Kevin's funeral. She could see them in her mind's eye. It seemed lilies were everywhere in the chapel. The lilies in her hands were casting out that same fragrance.

It was an overwhelming and heavy odor. She couldn't stop it. Her eyes filled with tears and she threw down the lilies, shaking pollen over everything. Anger rose in her until she thought she would shriek out loud. But, she didn't, instead she ran outside letting the porch screen door slam loudly behind her.

Kevin had been a true wild man. Tall, square shouldered, lanky, slender in a boyish way, with smooth brown skin. Always smiling and with a poor memory for his responsibilities. He lived in the moment...a pilot, but more than that...a flyer, in every sense of the word. He operated a flight service between islands and mainland, flying both small planes and helicopters. Whale watching, courier service, passenger hops, and anything else needed in crossing the waterways by air, which was his job.

Everyone had been taken aback when he started seeing Ruth. She was attractive enough, not a beauty, but a pretty, lively, red-haired girl. Just as Kevin was smooth and brown, Ruth was fair and downy, with peach fuzz on her cheeks and not just a few freckles. Her hair was the proverbial riot of red curls.

A native of the island, Ruth cared nothing about flying or traveling or any kind of run-around adventuring. She had no particular interest in life beyond the shores of the island. She was a florist and flower grower. She loved the gardens and the woods, being outside, or bringing something she found outside indoors. In a sort of medieval, throwback way, she wove wreaths and garlands from what seemed like twigs to anyone else into beautiful things worthy of display. Clients loved them. Her grandmother, Nan, had taught her all about the flowers and now Ruth ran the farm and florist business all by herself. There were several acres of flowers and a nice greenhouse near the main dwelling. Nan was living quietly now in the cottage across from the greenhouse.

Kevin and Ruth had gotten married. He was like a bee, she was the flower. She stayed home, he buzzed around. But it was two years of no peace and no babies. His pattern of life had been more like a dragonfly than a bee, buzzing in, hovering, then taking off. He was off to work, or for adventure, and Ruth knew that he took off for other women too. She found evidence in sweaters brought home which were not hers and paper coffee cups with lipstick that was not hers. She didn't know how to respond to this, so she did not respond.

Then he died in a flight home over the Strait. A couple of tourists had missed the last ferry and wanted to get back to Seattle quickly. He was glad to go, to get the fast cash and to take them on the long scenic route for fun. But he had then arranged a late meeting with someone he was interested in there. They had drinks and he was hurrying back home with too much liquor in him and went into the sea. Now he was gone for good, having taken off forever.

He had come into her life and thrilled her, flustered her and messed her up a good bit. He was in the process of breaking her heart, and his death broke it completely. And now, she was in the process of getting over it, and him, and returning to the life she had before him. But something had changed, and she couldn't really go back, not all the way.

Ruth was a slight, wiry girl. Today, she ran through the flower field with her red hair streaming out behind her. She began running, angry, and then she wearily slowed to a walk when she reached the open fields of high grass beyond the flower rows. It had rained the night before. She was wearing a heavy denim skirt and this quickly became wet from the dew and flapped around her legs, nearly stumbling her. After a while she just dropped into the long grass, submitting to the deadening sadness which was all around her and in her. She sat a while, knees to chin, and then lay back in the high grass. Tears came and she sobbed, just letting the tears of anger and sorrow flow out. Thoughts of Kevin and memories washed over her in a grieving flow. After a while she just couldn't cry any more. She was exhausted, and that was a relief.

No one could see her there in the tall grass. Lying on her back, she saw only sky above. It went on and on, blue, deep and so empty. Some birds flew over, very high and tiny above her. She could see all the way to the faint sliver of moon in the daytime sky and beyond. How could it be so empty? It was noontime and the sun was her only companion, warming her in the still damp grass. She drifted and slept.

She must have slept for nearly an hour when she awoke, slowly realizing that she was dirty, itching and had a terrible headache. She stood up with hair tousled and still wet from the grass. Looking at her skirt she saw that it was damp and stained. She didn't care, and she did not want to go back to work in the empty house right now. She walked on, calm now, but with a brooding headache and a dirty face. Walking aimlessly, she wandered towards the cliffs over the cove. Finding the cliff path, she headed into it without thought or direction. The path led through grass and then some scrubby trees to the cove overlook. Soon the water was visible... it was even bluer than the sky and sparkling as it stretched deeper and deeper out to sea. Approaching the edge, she heard the sound of the tide in the cove below and began to see the gradient of soft blue-green where the sea became shallow and approached the curving tiny beach.

There in the cove she also saw a small colorful sailboat bouncing on the water. Down in the hull lay the body of a man. She could see him clearly from above. He was on his back, his face and chest were white and his limbs lay motionless. Her heart dropped and then with a tremendous rush of adrenalin, she began running down the path to the beach. Was he dead? He was a young man, she thought, lying there on his back. He looked bloodlessly white. The sail had been dropped, and she did not see oars in the boat. On reaching the beach below, she saw that the boat still bobbed in the center of the cove waters. She called out, but nothing stirred. Ruth tucked up her skirt and began walking out into the water. The beach was sandy but entering the water she came upon rocks, slippery with algae. She just threw herself in clumsily and began dog-paddling out to the boat.

Fearfully, just a few feet from the boat's side she called out again loudly, "Hello...!" The man sat up suddenly, looking at her in surprise. She stopped swimming and treaded water.

"I saw you from the cliff above. Are you all right?"

Just then Henry came bounding up the beach, barking his head off. He too jumped into the water and began swimming out to them, barking all the way. Ruth's eye's filled up with tears for the second time today. Daniel just stared at her wide-eyed. Ruth turned and started swimming for the beach without another word. She was dripping, mortified and finished, just finished with this day.

Daniel called out after her, "I'm so sorry I scared you. I'm O.K." He had hoisted Henry, still barking, clumsily into the boat.

Floundering through the beach stones, Ruth never turned around but stalked up the beach and into the rutted cliff path without reply. At the top of the cliff she glanced back, but the boat was gone now. Probably the man and his dog had rounded the south end of the cove by now. There were rough rock outcroppings at the north of the cove. All was now as clear and empty as if she had dreamed the whole thing.

She knew who he was. He had spent summers at Glass House as a boy. They were wealthy people. She hadn't seen him in years. She remembered his name was "Daniel..." He used to hang out around the marina, and she remembered him biking around the roads and with his parents shopping in town. Luke had told her he had come out for a stay when she saw him at the grocery store yesterday. Luke said his father had recently died. She frowned and pulled her wet streaming hair out of her face and trudged on toward home.

The ruined bouquet was still lying on the work table, wilted and drying. She tossed it away violently into the trash, turned on the stove under her tea kettle and started over on the bouquet with new fresh flowers. She worked intently and quietly into the evening, stopping only for a cup of tea, still wearing her same dirty clothes and a weary face. Finally, stowing the fresh bouquet in its shelf carefully and shutting the refrigerator with a slam, she went to shower off all the grime and salt water stickiness. She was too tired for dinner.

Clean now, in a plain old cotton gown, she flopped into bed with a book. Beside the bed on the nightstand was Kevin's framed photograph. Ruth closed her book and picked up the photo, staring at it a long time. He was wearing his aviator sunglasses, so she could not see his eyes. He was wearing his favorite baseball cap. The smile was the one she wanted always to remember. There were no more tears left for today. She quietly laid the picture on the table, face down. She looked up to the ceiling studying the faint cracks there until she finally succumbed to sleep.

## CHAPTER THIRTY

# Cherry Pies

IN the orchard there were some cherry trees, and even more apple trees, whose fruit often fell unpicked to the ground for want of gatherers in summer and early fall when everyone had gone back to the mainland. These trees were very old now and thick trunked. Some were gnarled and bent into stunted forms by the prevailing winds and by benign neglect. Spring could be so beautiful in that high, old, hidden grove when cascades of white blossoms arrayed themselves over the wet black trunks. That season was rarely seen by human beings. Bees and other humming insects claimed the place for their own in the damp, cool, springtime. And, through the years the silence of the place had settled down into a permanent atmosphere, in every season.

Now that summer had fully arrived, Daniel and Henry were spending some time there, in the orchard. They were still living in the beach house and spending most of their time on the sea, sailing the Time Out, fishing or swimming, but they had begun to come up the path some afternoons, going in among the trees. Henry liked to go to the very middle of the orchard where there was a small clearing, full of sunshine and grass, like a miniature meadow. He would lie sprawled out there while Daniel strolled through the lanes of the trees. Daniel had taken to walking the orchard, row by row, mainly to enjoy the green light filtering through the leaves. Musing, he thought he saw a face once. He felt like someone was watching him. It was a friendly face, suggested by the wavering light.

Today, he reached up and pulled down a cluster of cherries. He tasted them and found that they were finally ripe and ready to pick. There were mostly pie cherries, tart and dense... but sweet enough. Just recently Daniel had discovered little metal stakes in the grass at the foot of each tree with painted lettering on them. Closer examination showed that someone had painstakingly printed the name of the fruit variety of each tree in black on those stakes. Daniel was pretty sure that person had been Paul. Such efficiency was like Paul and somehow seeing and reading all those metal tags did something to his heart. There at Glass House he now felt as if he was getting to know Paul better since his death than he had ever imagined he could do when he was alive.

Daniel began picking cherries though he had no basket. He just started piling them into his baggy t-shirt front and soon had a big bumpy pouch of cherries. He ate and picked the low-hanging fruit in the midday quiet. He collected several loads until he had picked enough and eaten his fill. He took them back by the kitchen door where he put them in an old galvanized gardening tub and filled it with water from the backyard hose. He brought a kitchen chair out from the house and sat and swirled the cherries until they were clean. Finally he took them out, removed their stems, dried them carefully and piled them on an old towel. The sun was so comforting and warm that he really did not want to leave this moment. Sitting in the chair, he finally surrendered to rest and then dozed in the heat. After a while, as the sun began to wane and the afternoon wind picked up, he stood up and went inside. There he found some brown paper grocery bags and filled them with his cherries and brought them in to the kitchen table. He didn't want to bruise any of them. Sniffing their rich scent, he decided, "Tomorrow, I will make pies."

Of course there was no proper oven or even a stove at the beach house, only the stone fireplace and the two-burner Coleman, so the next morning, Daniel had to do his baking at the big house. The kitchen was well-equipped and he soon found pie tins and spices. He had bought fresh flour recently but sugar supplies were scarce. To find enough he rummaged around combining the contents of several sugar bowls before he had enough for the pies. Thankfully, there was an old cherry pitter in one of the drawers. With today's haul of cherries there was enough fruit for three pies, one for Luke, one for Pete and Peggy and an extra one. He had worked most of the morning and was proud of his baker's work.

"I am a chef again after all," he muttered to himself.

He was conscious in that moment of the fact that every aspect of kitchen work was satisfying and pleasing to him. It really was his calling. After the baking, the pie crusts were beautiful, brown, high domes with perfectly fluted edges, packed full of the fine Glass House cherries. Daniel smiled as he rotated each one on the counter.

After cleaning up, he went back through the dining room to make his way out and down to the beach. On the way, he caught his reflection in the huge wall of mirrors in the dining room, in the dim light, as he and Henry passed though. He moved nearer to the glass, critically examining his image there. His crisp city look was gone. He was still shaving, but not every day, and it appeared that he might need a hair trim also. Oh well. No rush on that. Daniel was giving himself the freedom to do and be whatever he felt like. He looked at himself and Henry with a grin. Both of them had changed since they arrived on the island. Henry stopped and looked too. They say dogs don't see themselves in mirrors... but maybe they do. He certainly saw Daniel's reflection and was looking up at him wisely.

"We're getting scruffy," said Daniel.

Henry was beginning to lose his clipped coiffure too and his shape was softly rounding out. But, there was more, Henry saw it in Daniel's face, and that is why his gaze was wise. What was it that was showing now in Daniel?

Both dog and man clattered on down to the beach for a swim. Then Daniel heated water for a shave. He really preferred to shave down at the beach even though he had to go through the routine of heating water. Then he went out for a long cold shower behind the beach house. By now he was used to the cold tap water and enjoyed it.

Standing in the shower Daniel wondered, "Maybe it's just having a lot more space of every kind that is working on me. Sort of like the space and time when somebody is shipwrecked on an island. Except, my island is well-supplied and it has an orchard... and pies."

After lunch, Daniel decided to deliver his pies to the guys at the marina. He and Henry drove down, finding Luke at home on the houseboat. Luke radioed Pete who was out in the skiff. He would come by for his pie in a while. He sent his thanks.

Luke was surprised and thrilled with his pie.

"Man, I wish I could cook like that! It smells great and looks great. You've got the gift, Daniel. Maybe after we get married you could teach Anna to bake like this!"

"I wouldn't touch that with a ten foot pole," Daniel smiled. "I don't think it is smart to try to teach brides how to get around in the kitchen."

Luke made some coffee and started cutting the pie. Daniel wouldn't take a slice.

"It's for you. I'll just have coffee for now. I have another pie up at the house." But...he was wondering..."You know, I think I owe a pie to someone else around here. Do you know that red-haired girl who lives by that greenhouse on the main road?"

"Sure, that's Ruth. That's the old Sloan place. Mrs. Sloan's been there forever, Ruth's grandmother. Her name is Nan. They have a flower business. You remember Ruth, Daniel. She used to come down here and play 'monopoly' with us all when we were kids in the summer. She was friends with all of us here in the marina...Ruth. We called her Ruthie then."

"I guess so, I just don't remember the 'monopoly days' that much. Maybe I wasn't there for that."

Daniel then told Luke the story of Ruth seeing him floating in the Penguin and rushing down, jumping in the water to help him that day. How embarrassed and ticked off she was. Luke couldn't help laughing.

"What a story! Yeah, I think maybe you owe her a pie." He was still chuckling. Then his face became serious.

Daniel noticed this. "What is it?"

"Ruth is a widow. Her husband got killed in a plane crash less than a year ago last October I think." Luke told him the whole story, at least all that he knew, about Ruth and Kevin.

"Ruth has always lived here on the island," he added. "Her Mom was Nan's daughter. She was kind of a flake. A druggie. After she had Ruth, she and the dad just took off for California. They never came back for Ruth. In fact, I heard they split up soon after that. I don't know what happened to them. Nan raised Ruth. And Ruth has taken over the flower business. She does arrangements too, I think. How did you connect her with the flower farm?"

"I have seen her out working in the flowers when I bike around the roads. Not many people have red hair like that. It's noticeable." Daniel was looking down. "Oh brother, I guess I made her day," he groaned softly. "Well, I better take that pie over and try to make amends. I'm sorry to hear about her troubles."

"Everybody's got'em...troubles that is." Luke slapped his knees and stood up. "Yeah, she and the grandmother would probably be glad to have one of your pies!"

Daniel drove home thinking back about the embarrassing event in the cove that day. What could he say to explain his lying like that in a boat? He was just floating, being still...learning to float in life a little bit. Too bad she had to come along.

He picked up the extra pie in the kitchen and decided to drive on over to the Sloan flower farm at once, before he changed his mind. He and Henry drove with the car windows down, Henry snoozing in the back seat. When they arrived, Daniel left him there and went to knock on the door of the screened-in porch of the big farm house. There was no answer and the place was very still. He saw that there was no doorbell. Daniel stepped back to look over the house. It was a big two-story, white frame house. It was in pretty good shape, though you could tell it was old...probably built in the early 1900's. The house was on a raised foundation sitting high off the ground. He walked around the side and saw that there was an even larger screened-in back porch. Nobody around there either. Behind the house the greenhouse stood, surrounded by a large flower garden blooming with early summer flowers. This was just the beginning of the flower fields, which he could see went on for several acres on either side behind the house. He could see another little house on the other side of the backyard garden, a small cottage. Then a movement in the garden caught his eye. Someone with red hair was bending over some tall purple blooms. It was someone with sort of red hair, faded compared to Ruth's, as he remembered it. The person stood, it wasn't Ruth.

Daniel called out a hello. The red-haired woman straightened up smiling at him.

"Can I help you?" called out a melodious voice. This person was a smaller and much older version of Ruth. Her hair had indeed faded but it was curly the same as Ruth's. This had to be Nan.

"Hello," Daniel called back. "I was looking for Ruth." Nan came forward, still smiling, to introduce herself. Taking off her garden glove she offered Daniel her smooth, freckled hand. She was wearing a plain khaki shirt and wide-legged pants in a Hawaiian print. Her hand was strong, and yes, freckled, with knobby joints, but it looked like the hand of a woman who took care of herself. She looked up at him kindly. She was a small woman with an erect bearing. Her face was as strong as her hand.

"I'm her grandmother, Nan. How, can I help you? What a beautiful pie!"

"I'm Daniel Cross. I'm visiting out at Glass House further out on the coast just off East Island road." He pointed in the direction of Glass House.

"Oh yes, Daniel. We know your house. And, we heard about the death of your father. I remember him here in years gone by. I'm so sorry." She looked like she really meant it, tipping her head to the side in a gesture of sympathy.

"Glad to meet you, Nan. And thank you. I am just spending some time out here at the old vacation place right now. Our cherries are ripe and I thought Ruth, and you of course, might like a pie."

"Well, you missed her. Ruth went to town today to pick up some packages of supplies that came in from the mainland. She's doing our shopping too, so she won't be back for a while. I can take the pie for her if you like. I know she will appreciate it. It's a beauty! Do you and Ruth know each other?" A puzzled look accompanied the question.

"Not really, but we met down at the beach recently. I'm afraid I startled her. She'll explain. Please tell her I'm sorry I troubled her the other day."

Nan did not press him for more. She took the pie, smiling up at Daniel.

"Thanks so much, Daniel. I promise I will not slice this pie until Ruth comes home! But, we have some cherry trees too and I made some cherry jam last night. Would you like to try some on a slice of toast with a cup of tea?"

She seemed sincere. He looked beyond her at the little cottage. It was intriguing, possibly charming inside. Just behind the little house there was a stand of woods, cedar and pine, framing it nicely. He was curious, so he said "yes..." He followed Nan down the row of flowers to the cottage which appeared even smaller up close, almost a doll's house! The windows were sparkling in the light and the white paint was much fresher than the finish on the big main house. They went in and Daniel saw at once that this was truly a very small house. Across the front there were small-paned windows, with a dining nook just under the windows. There was an "L" shaped cushioned bench in the corner and a table. At the other side of the room was Nan's sitting room with an antique settee and a couple of upholstered parlor chairs. The wall behind this furniture was a bookshelf, filled floor to ceiling with books. A round coffee table pulled the seating area together. He saw notebooks and pens; someone here was in the habit of taking notes, lots of notes. Pages of paper were stacked casually on every chair.

Nan drew up a kitchen chair and Daniel was invited to sit at the table on the built-in bench. He could see beyond to a small kitchenette on one side and a door probably leading to the bedroom on the other. That was it. A tiny cabin. Everything was painted white inside, just as it was outside. The floor was dark old planking and there were some braided rugs in bright colors. The furniture was covered in a variety of chintzy prints, light and airy. He was not surprised to see potted plants and flowers tucked in everywhere, on the window ledges, on every shelf and even on the floor.

Nan welcomed him in and went to the kitchen quickly to start some tea. He noticed that the stove was a very old, enameled gas model from the 1930's. It was that mint green with cream colored trim so popular in that day. Nan brought out some cups and plates. When she went back into the kitchen, Daniel sneaked a peek at the china mark. The dishware and cups were Royal Dalton, Arcadia pattern. He had always liked it. White and delicate with a big, blousy, floral design and a deeply fluted rim. The cups were shapely. Nan brought out the jam in a green Depression glass footed dish. This whole thing was making Daniel feel very comfortable.

Nan sat in a kitchen chair and told Daniel about the farm as they sipped their hot black tea and munched toast with the cherry jam. Nan's husband, Walter, had bought the acreage before they were married. He plowed and planted the fields. Then he and Nan came out here and they were married. She had spent most of her life on this flower farm. This little cottage had originally been the farm's work shed. She and Walter had lived for years in the big main house which was old even when he bought the farm land. They had built up a nice wholesale flower business and had just one daughter, Deborah. Nan did not explain about Deborah, but said that she had raised her granddaughter Ruth right there on the flower farm. Walter had died when Ruth was just a little girl, but Nan and Ruth continued there, hiring more helpers to get them through the work of bringing flowers to market. She said that Ruth had gone to a floral design program on the mainland for a while. She had always been interested in putting flowers and wreaths together.

People loved her designs, and now the business was all hers. At the same time, Nan had really longed to move out of the big house and into this little snug place. So, she fixed it up two years ago and made her little place just right for herself. Nan helped

Ruth some, but was happily retired now. Ruth took the big house and made it the center of her floral business. Nan did not mention Kevin or Ruth's widowhood.

How about Daniel, she asked? Would he sell Glass House now? He said no. He too had a little bungalow down on the beach where he was living for the summer, and he planned to keep the Glass House property that had now come to him. He was enjoying the sailing life, and being outdoors this summer. He told her about his little sailboat, the process they had been through in its restoration and the joy that had brought, including his new friendship with Luke, Pete and Peggy.

He told her he had a business back on the mainland, a restaurant, but he would continue to come out to the island and use Glass House for rest and vacation time. He would keep the place. He would sail. Nan was delighted to hear all about that. Her eyes shone as they talked and watching her expressive hands mesmerized Daniel. It was almost like coming unexpectedly onto a fairy tale character in her little house. She was obviously pleased to a have a guest. He was completely charmed. He kept looking over at the paperwork on her chairs and wondering, but she offered no explanation. Finally, Daniel remembered Henry in the car. They walked out to it and Nan was introduced to Henry, who gave a little bow and licked her hand. They laughed and Daniel made his thanks. She declared that she and Ruth would enjoy the pie that very evening. He drove away feeling somewhat shocked at finding Nan. She would be a friend...he knew it. He was also immensely relieved not to have to deal with explanations to Ruth. The pie would be his apology. It had been a perfect afternoon.

Later that afternoon, Ruth finally arrived back home. First she unloaded the boxes of floral supplies from the trunk of the car. They were bulky but not heavy. She stacked them in the screened-in back porch. Then she brought in the groceries. She saw Nan walking over from her house through the flower rows carrying something. Ruth saw that it was a high-domed pie.

"We had a visitor while you were away. He brought a pie." Smiling, Nan held it up like a trophy.

Ruth was frowning and tired. Nan knew that Ruth was perpetually tired these days, and sometimes she exuded bitterness. There was a blanket of grief over this dear girl. Nan had decided some time back not to let this bother her or keep her from treating Ruth just as always, doing all she could to cheer her. She would not allow the tragedy of Kevin, both his life and his death, to harm her relationship with her granddaughter. Kevin was gone now and Ruth would be over this...soon, she thought. She was sure of it. Ruth was looking at the pie blankly.

"A neighbor brought it, Daniel Cross from Glass House. He came by to bring it to you." Nan kept smiling. "He said he had 'troubled' you down at the beach recently. He wanted to make amends I think. You know Mr. Cross died recently. Daniel is here spending the summer and checking out the house, which his father left to him." She was still smiling, holding the pie. Ruth turned away to go back into the house. She didn't offer to take the pie.

"He didn't explain what happened on the beach and I didn't ask. I'll just bring it on into the house for you. We could have some tea and a slice of pie? It's cherry. Actually, he stopped into my place for tea and we visited. He is nice."

Nan followed Ruth up the steps and into the kitchen of the big house. She put the pie down on the kitchen table. Ruth took off her sweater and then leaned over and kissed Nan on her cheek.

"Thanks, Nana. Thanks for taking care of this. I don't feel like pie right now. I need to lie down a while, I'm just worn out. I'll have a sandwich later. Then you can come over and we can have some of this pie. I love you."

Ruth had made "Nana" out of "Nan" as a toddler and called her that still. She didn't look at Nan but hugged her briefly and left the room. Nan stood with hands on hips. She watched Ruth walk away. It was sad to see her like this, so young, so downcast. But Nan was not worried and she went quietly out to her own little house, still smiling peacefully.

CHAPTER THIRTY-ONE

# The Return

SUNLIGHT was shining in through the kitchen window, hitting the sudsy dishwater in the sink and reflecting off everything in the kitchen. Ruth was doing the dishes. She had an automatic dishwasher, but she rarely used it. There was never a big stack to do, and besides, she liked doing dishes. It was meditative and relaxing. She liked doing any kind of work with her hands. She smiled, seeing all the brightness of a summer day coming right in to her sink. She was thinking that this was the first day she had really enjoyed the summer weather this season.

"All the summery things will really start blooming now," she said out loud, her hands swirling in the dishwater.

She pulled Daniel's pie pan out of the water and gave it a final scrub. It had been a good cherry pie, very good. Nan said he was a real chef with his own restaurant. He certainly did make a good pie, she had to admit. She and Nan had eaten slices of it over two days with gusto. Now it was gone, but the pan remained. What a bother to have to return the pan! That was the trouble with taking food to people, then they had to go by and return the pan, visit and chat and make nice. She blushed there in the kitchen hearing her own thoughts in her head. When had she become so harsh and cynical?! There was no need for her to be so ugly, not even just in her mind.

She dried the dishes and immediately walked out the back door with the dish cloth still draped over her shoulder. She wanted to be in the sun, to see the day. The air felt wonderful and she walked out into the flowers, looking lovingly at them all, looking up at the sky too. She remembered the recent day when she had lain in the field looking up, resenting the blue clear sky, finding it empty. It didn't feel empty today and she breathed in the air deeply, realizing that she was getting well in her mind, in her feelings. She was returning to life, just as the fields were. It was a good thing because there was a ton of work to do. She needed the energy to dive into the summer season and especially the wedding season. She had worried about that, about getting through it, but today, she didn't care. These weddings were other people's business, not hers. She needn't live each one with the brides. Let them have their day. She would just provide the flowers. And, she would enjoy the flowers as she always had done. How many people get to grow up in a field of flowers? Not many. She was privileged to be here. She looked over at Nan's house. Surely she was up and doing. She stooped and picked a small bouquet of sweet peas coming up their vine. The fragrance was so deep and happy that it brought tears to her eyes. She wandered through the rows back to Nan's and called in. Nan came out and seeing Ruth's bright face, she grinned.

"Here's something fresh that you need!" Ruth laughed. It was just ridiculous to bring flowers to someone who lived in a flower field.

Nan laughed too, at the irony and with joy to see her girl glowing and happy.

She knew it would happen. "Ruth is young. She is strong," she had always told herself.

The next morning, another sunny one, Ruth came out ready for the day and saw the pie pan still there on the kitchen table. She sighed.

"Might as well get this back to its owner," she thought. "I'll bike over. I need to be outside in the air."

A little later, she pulled the old bike out of the shed. The tires were fine, it appeared. She strapped the pie pan down to the back bumper. Looking at it she remembered Nan's rule of etiquette, that you never return a pan empty to someone who has brought you food...put something in it even if it is just a bag of potato chips! She thought a moment and decided that the sweet peas would be the best offering she could return. She quickly clipped another nice big bouquet and wrapped it up into a cone in some of her green floral paper, sticking it in with the pie pan on the back of the bike. Then she took off south on the road to Glass House.

She had never liked Glass House. It was just so stark, so geometric. She didn't think it fit in with nature there on the coast. As she approached on the driveway she noticed the orchard along the west side of the property. It was an old one and it did soften the look of the property a little. She pulled up to the back door and got off her bike. She knocked softly, then louder when no one answered. Finally, with flowers and pie pan in hand, she walked around to the front terrace. No one there either and it was very quiet. She didn't want to just leave these things on the doorstep. It would seem so rude.

Just then she heard barking down below the terrace. She looked over the terrace edge and saw a large poodle running and barking on the beach to the south. It was the same dog she had seen that day in the cove. She yelled "hello" loudly hoping Daniel would hear her. No response. With a sigh she started down the beach path, taking the flowers and pan with her. She was wearing a lavender baggy tee shirt, khaki pants and just some plain canvas flats. They were not really the right shoes for this path. It was tricky, but she made it to the beach without stumbling. She could see no one in either direction up or down the beach. She saw the beach house and wandered over to it, sinking in the gravely sand, her shoes filling with sand as she went. The beach house door was open. She looked in. It had been fixed up for living, she could see that. Very cute inside! Clean. Everything was neatly arranged, and a red plaid blanket covered the cot. Shells and driftwood pieces decorated the walls. There was a strange wire concoction hanging from the ceiling with bits of blue and green glass attached to them.

As she was peeking in, Daniel came up behind her. He hadn't meant to scare her but she jumped a mile.

Chagrined, he sighed and said, "I think I am destined to be scaring you all the time." He put his hands up, shrugged his shoulders and added, "I'm very sorry." He was smiling now. What else could he do?

Now she shook her head and laughed. "I must seem like a complete nutcase to you! I am so sorry!"

She handed him the pie pan and flowers. "Thank you so much for the really great pie. Let's start again, shall we? I'm Ruth Sloan and I know from my grandmother and from many years past that you are Daniel." She offered him her hand to shake. "Hello Daniel Cross! And you really didn't need to bring a pie to us, but Nan and I are glad you did." She was doing well at making nice.

He had taken the flowers and was holding them to his nose sniffing them.

"Oh, these are so wonderful! Thanks very much. I am missing flowers around here." Then he pointed down the beach. "I was just down at the south end of this stretch of beach chasing a critter who is always hanging around here, an otter. My dog won't stop chasing him either. Did you try to find me up at the big house?"

"I was looking around for you. Then I heard the dog."

"This is Henry. Henry, this is Ruth."

Henry's soft button eyes looked up. His face appeared to be smiling. Ruth really could not help laughing. Then she turned to go. "Well, you can continue your chase. I had better get back to the house and to work. Thanks again for the pie."

"Come around any time. I am here for the summer. I enjoyed very much meeting your grandmother, by the way. She is a very nice woman. We had a good visit together. Her cherry preserves are as good as a pie."

"She liked you too, Daniel. I'm sure she would love a visit from you also, anytime."

"I'll just walk up the hill with you, Ruth. It's a bit narrow and slippery in places."

They walked up single file, Henry running ahead, then Ruth and Daniel. At the top they found her bike and said goodbye, shaking hands again. Daniel was getting ready to try some kind of explanation for the "floating in the boat" incident. Ruth could see that.

She held up her hand. "No need to tell me about that," she said. "I was having a very bad day myself," she said laughing. She walked her bike away waving. "See you around," she said, looking back with a smile. Then she took off down the drive.

Daniel loped back down the trail quickly. He put his bouquet into a nice big coffee can with water. It looked just right on the table. He knew it would soon fill the place with its heady fragrance.

"Well, that's that!" Daniel said to Henry with satisfaction. He was so glad to have a friendly finish to that awkward mess.

As Ruth pedaled home, she was thinking about this meeting and especially about Daniel's beach abode. It was so nicely fixed. He had obviously really worked on it. Why was he down there? Glass House was his, and a prestigious house it was. Very strange. She also realized that she had not offered a word of condolence for his losing his Dad. She felt ashamed. "How could you be so callous?" She berated herself.

"You better straighten up, girl," she said out loud. "It's time to get out of yourself and back into the world!"

Maybe he would interpret the flower bouquet as a gesture of sympathy. Maybe. She decided that she would forgive Daniel for seeing her make a fool of herself in the cove. So... exactly why had she made a fool of herself? What was so foolish that he had seen...exactly?

"Because I was trying to save his life," she answered herself quietly.

"I saw him there and I wanted to save his life."

"Just forget about it," she told herself, beginning to pedal faster.

## CHAPTER THIRTY-TWO

# The Mini Magellan

THE cherries were all fully ripe now. There were four cherry trees in the old orchard. Three bore dark, tart, pie cherries. The fourth was a Bing cherry, a sweet variety. Daniel had been checking them and knew that they needed to be picked right away to be their best. He hated to leave off sailing in the new Time Out, but this had to be done. He thought if he had some help it could be done very quickly. He called Luke and Pete to see if they wanted to come and help, promising them "all you can eat" portions and bushels to take home. They were glad to come up and Peggy too. It was decided that one long afternoon's work should do it. They drove over from the marina, bringing a couple of ladders. Daniel mowed the grass under the cherry trees with the old push mower as it had gotten very long...that way no cherries would escape. He had bushel baskets and long poles too, for shaking the upper branches.

He had more on his mind than cherries. He had been dreaming about the sailing life, thinking of the possibility of sailing around San Juan Island. It was a thought, a dream, an adventure, and then a goal he had cooked up for himself...to sail completely around the island. This had started to brew in him after he had biked over to the American Camp side of the island. He was curious and attracted by that westward and southward feel of things away from the closed channels and bays. It was wilder and highly intriguing. He longed to make this trip, but was afraid that the Time Out was too small, that it was too risky. He thought he would bring it up with Luke and Pete at the cherry picking and get their advice. He would give everyone dinner too, and all the cherries they could haul home, keeping only enough for his own use, some for the freezer and some to send over to Oscar and Trini at The Prow.

As always, Daniel just had to cook, no matter the weather or how tired he was. Cooking was a given and a joy! So, he decided to invite everyone for "Carpaccio di Pesce," a Venetian treat. It was raw fish pounded delicately thin, served without cooking after special marinating. He would use fresh halibut and salmon to create this, steeped in the special marinade and then served with a mustard and citrus dressing on a plate of fresh greens. He would get all the ingredients ready up above, in the Glass House kitchen. Then he would set up a picnic table in the orchard. There were already several old strings of bulb lights hanging from the trees near the house. He could make some fresh cooked corn in the husk on the terrace barbeque pit, too.

He would bring up the idea of "circumnavigation" over dinner. He wanted to hear the advice of his friends, the experts. He called Peggy to make sure she knew that dinner was included in the cherry picking event.

"That would be great." she said. In fact, Anna was arriving for a visit with Luke. Peggy would find out if they all wanted to come. She insisted on making a cole slaw and her "dump cake" peach cobbler.

"O.K.," he agreed, wincing. He hoped for the best. Peaches were beginning to ripen just now too, and the white ones were indescribably sweet.

The four guests arrived in Luke's old blue truck. Anna was with them. Daniel had never met her, having only seen her photograph at Luke's place. As they climbed out of the truck, Daniel was stunned by Anna. She was quite tall, as tall as Luke, gracefully slender with very black skin and short cropped hair. Her eyes were huge and black also.

She had a soft, doe-like look about her face and a gorgeous figure, slim but curvy. Her smile was absolutely dazzling. Daniel could see why Luke was so mad about her. And, she was sweet, too. Daniel was charmed by her immediately, and noticed that she took special pains to get to know him, offering to help with the dinner.

They picked all afternoon in the filtered sunlight, chatting back and forth among the trees. The cherries were very ripe, so bringing them down was easy work. They ate and picked ending up with nine bushel baskets full. A great harvest. As it was getting on towards dinner, Daniel went into the kitchen to start preparing for the "field hands."

When they finished picking and packing up, dinner was served on the outdoor table on a checkered cloth Daniel had found in the kitchen. It was laid out like an Italian picnic with wine and plenty of antipasto dishes. The corn was steaming in its parched, roasted husks. They all enjoyed the Carpaccio. It was something new for everyone, delicate and tasty. Peggy's cobbler was divine even with a "cake mix" topping.

Luke and Pete started telling "sea stories" after dinner. These were tales of adventures, local stories, often passed around the marina and stories of times long ago on the island...some hair-raising, some humorous. Daniel shyly brought up the topic of sailing around the island in a little boat...maybe a little boat such as the Time Out. Pete and Luke turned to look at him with droll questioning looks.

"O.K. buddy, so you're looking for a challenge? You are a little bit crazy!" said Luke.

Pete said, "Umm, Daniel, you cannot sail around San Juan Island in a Penguin, even in a perfectly great Penguin, like the Time Out. Penguins need to stay in protected harbors and bays, having fun skimming around. Penguins are not for open seas!" He looked at Daniel hard.

"Oh, I thought that might be a bit risky," said Daniel sheepishly. "It's just an idea I had. When I went out to the American Camp, I loved the way things look over there, so wild and open."

Luke and Pete looked at each other. "Yeah, it can be wild... it's open water," said Luke. "Actually, you would need to wear scuba gear, because you would very quickly be underwater. The Penguin could not hold up in those seas."

They both laughed and Daniel, embarrassed now, wished he had not mentioned it.

"O.K., I get it," he quickly began. "I was just thinking..."

"Yes, wild, open, free. Just the kind of adventure for a guy like you. Just the kind of adventure for a bunch of guys like us too." It was Pete speaking up with sparkling eyes. "I think it is an adventure that needs to be considered. But...you gotta go in a bigger boat! Peg and I happen to have such a boat," he laughed.

"And...the PegNPete needs to get out more. She is bored sitting in her slip."

Luke and Pete looked at each other. It was a 20 to 30 nautical mile distance around the island, depending on the course taken...a nice little jaunt.

"Let's do it.," said Pete. "By that I mean... let's ALL do it. We'll come with you, or actually you'll come with us."

They all laughed and Daniel looked amazed.

"Wednesday is the slow day at the marina, we can take off and all go sailing next Wednesday for sure," said Luke. "Can you get back over here on the earliest ferry?" Luke asked Anna. "We need to leave early."

"I can do it," she smiled.

They began to plot their trip. Luke and Pete thought they should start from Friday Harbor. They would pick up Anna there early and then begin, heading back south against the lighter morning winds of the inner channel. That way they could sail with the wind at their back later in the day up Haro Strait, avoiding both the aggravating, strong headwinds of morning and opposing tides. They would end up docking for an early dinner back at Friday Harbor and finally sail home in the summer twilight. It was all settled.

That night after all the dishes were done, the cherries packed away, and everyone had gone home, Daniel sat in the lamp light at the beach house. A rare moment of homesickness overcame him. The preparing of food always made him think of The Prow. He wondered how everyone was over there and how things were going in the restaurant. He received a weekly call from Oscar and Trini giving him an update on the business, but tonight he wished he was there, joining in and busy on the dining floor, enjoying the work and the camaraderie. He sighed. This beach life was good, very good...but it was new. Everything he was doing was new. He was nostalgic tonight for the familiar. And, maybe it was the unknown ahead, the challenge of just a little stretch on the sea that was giving him just a little bit of fear, too.

Wednesday morning dawned clear and mild. The threesome, Luke, Pete and Peggy, sailed into the Glass House cove at 6 A.M. From the jetty, Daniel and Henry jumped aboard. They set out for Friday Harbor. The sailing was smooth and under control. The sails were billowed and full, sailing before the wind. They all sipped the coffee that Peggy had made below in the galley. The PegNPete was a homey sloop, broad-beamed, with a solid, full length, lead-weighted keel, and plenty of space in the roomy cabin. Peggy and Luke crewed the mainsail in an easy flow of turns. It was not a racy sailboat but a comfortable island cruiser.

Anna was standing, waving on the dock, in her denim shorts and a red shirt at Friday Harbor. They picked her up and turned around Brown Island to begin their circuit. Pete noted the time and mileage in his log. It would be an adventure they were laughingly calling "The Mini Magellan..."

Henry was slightly disturbed by all this, so he stayed close by Daniel, looking around as if to say, "What's all this!" Now, they were close-hauled, heading back down the eastern coast of the island into a mild breeze. As they sailed, Daniel watched Pete at the tiller. He was beginning to understand Pete's moves and began to anticipate what he would do next in these conditions. He was learning fast.

Pete had already organized the crew positions for the trip. The PegNPete was a mainmasted sloop with simple rigging, nothing fancy. Pete was helmsman at the tiller, Luke and Anna would crew the two mainsail sheets and winches, Daniel was to go to the foremast triangle at the bow to help coordinate the turning of the jib with that of the mainsail. Peg would hang out with Pete as his assistant, bringing him coffee. The girls chatted on deck, ready to move when needed. Luke was trimming and setting the sails.

They were tacking going south, full-sailed, still close-hauled and moving easily. Daniel saw the beach house as they passed and Glass House up above. He had a magnificent view of all from the bow as it smoothly parted the channel waters. Soon they passed the mouth of the marina and were working their way around to the island's southeast tip. This would be the beginning of a more challenging sail. They swung out into the strait, but not too far, just enough to avoid the rocky out-crops at the southern tip of the island. The waters began to be choppy, but manageable. They were still heading into the wind. The view back onto San Juan was spectacular from this vantage point, and Daniel was thrilled to be skimming along full out, with his friends.

They were coming up on the Cattle Point Lighthouse. It looked small from out away from shore, but Daniel could just imagine it casting out its point of light in the night, a real comfort to sailors along all these rocky shores. At the bow, he was looking out to the southwest into the Juan de Fuca Strait. A dark, bluish gray line of clouds was lying on the sea. Luke was pointing to this too. It was sunny and bright when they passed the point, but what they saw now was most certainly a coming squall.

They were not far from shore, off Cattle Point, when Daniel was suddenly overcome by the vastness of the sea all around him. Out in more open water in a craft that he now saw as tiny on the huge sea, he could feel the power of the waters, and the heaving fluidity of the great volume of seas under him and all around him. It was both thrilling and horrifying. He was mesmerized by the feel of the great weight of the water. His smallness on the face of the sea, he could not even consider, it was so fearful. He knew fully that he was an absurdly small speck. The heavy feeling of the cresting of the waves into mounds around him now brought him to a feeling of paralyzing awe as he worked at the bow. The boat cut nicely through the waves, but he was thinking that there was no point of control, such as can be fixed on land. And, he saw that the seas were changing in color from a vivid blue-green to the color and metallic sheen of slate.

The prevailing winds on the Juan de Fuca and on up into the Haro Strait were always rushing up from the southwest, coming straight off the Pacific. They expected this kind of afternoon wind, but Daniel also knew that a squall could mean something more. He was worrying and wondering, straining to see how fast it was moving toward them... whether they would beat it as they swung north into the Haro. He didn't have to wonder long. Luke was shouting, pointing back to the squall line. It was looming higher in the sky and clouds were just beginning come over them, darkening the sky. The roaring of the seas was increasing, and the sails were making a banging sound as they began to luff.

The boat began to heel strongly to starboard, Daniel joined everyone on the port rail, leaning back hard to compensate. The rushing gray seas were right below him now. Luke let the mainsail far out to starboard and began the process of reefing the sail in tight. Better now, they went back to work quickly to balance the sails before the wind and keep on course. They were running before the wind now since the turn north into the Haro. The sea was rolling in dark massive waves.

"This is going to hit us!" Luke yelled. He smiled broadly, loving this moment. "We'll be fine, nothing to worry about." His curly hair was flying in the wind, and his one gold earring shining dully gave him a wild look.

Daniel was very glad for Luke's presence crewing these sails, as they were going to have to gibe up the Haro Strait, before this wind, and so far they did not know how strong it would be. Luke was quick and totally competent for this task. Daniel looked back to see Pete manning the tiller stoically. It was getting colder and the sun was hidden now. Daniel felt a little better since they had come into the Haro, it was huge, but did not feel as infinite as the strait to the south. He could see land on either side, though it was quite a distance to the west. Everyone on board was making preparation for the coming squall. Both girls were good crew members from long practice and were not disturbed. They were putting on their life vests and rain parkas. Peg brought Daniel's gear up to him. She squeezed his arm and gave him the usual pat on his face. Looking back, he saw her take Henry below into the cabin. The wind was now blowing hard and everyone's hair was on end. Daniel put on his gear and covered his head with the hood. It did cut down on the sound of the wild, buffeting wind.

From this point on, there was very little sightseeing, though Daniel did see the American Camp buildings in the meadows up to the east, sodden-looking in the rain, and he recognized the little cove they called "Grandma's." Daniel was crouched in the bow as it rose and fell, trying his best to keep the jib sail properly trimmed and all the lines in order as they moved before the wind. Looking down into the leaden waves was making his heart race. Then the rain began to hit, with more blasting wind behind it.

Luke and Anna gibed the mainsail before the wind, controlling the boom expertly as it swung around on their turns. Daniel did his best in the bow. They were all peppered by rain in the waves of the squall, but it was not a deluge. With the sail tightly drawn in, they did well even in the capricious, gusting wind. Pete kept them off shore to avoid the rocks. At least there were no shoals to worry about in the Haro.

Before long, Henry Island was on the northern horizon. This strong wind was driving them fast, and by now the water was as black as ink. Daniel was a little alarmed to see Pete begin to turn out westward, toward the middle of the strait. He looked questioningly to Luke.

"He doesn't want to take any chances with rocks and kelp in the inner channels," Luke shouted over the wind. "We'll do better going around."

And so as they approached Henry Island, Pete swung around the outside of the island to the northwest. They sailed around Henry Island and then east between Henry and the long, narrow and wild Spieden Island. Suddenly, they were out of the driving wind, but still in a mild rain. The squall continued to run on north up the Haro, but they were coming out of it.

They settled down to sail more calmly around the northern coast, finally arriving at Friday Harbor, a full circle in much shorter time than they could have imagined. They docked at the guest docks, tied down and disembarked, everyone taking a deep breath. The rain had eased up and they began to see sun coming through the clouds. It had all happened so fast. Now they were on land again and for Daniel the whole thing was like a furious fast dream. It was only about three o'clock.

Before they knew it they were eating crab cakes and French fries in a crab shack restaurant, excitedly talking about the trip. They were still wet to the skin, so hot coffee was ordered and a few brandy shots. They toasted the "Mini Magellan" with laughter and excited, nervous chatter. Henry was happily welcomed into the restaurant as was usual in Friday Harbor. But Daniel was still under the thrall of the mighty sea. He was white-faced and a little quiet as he ate.

Pete raised his little Brandy glass toasting Fernando Magellan, the ancient seaman-explorer.

"To Magellan!" he called out. "You know he actually never made the full trip around the world. He was killed along the way in the Philippines. His crew got knocked off by one thing and another too, only 18 out of the 270 finished the voyage. In view of that, we've done very well! All present and accounted for."

"To Magellan," they chimed in.

"And one more for the Crew!" Luke added, laughing.

Then Luke was busy cuddling with Anna across the table, but Pete, sitting next to Daniel, noticed his stricken face and said quietly, "Well sailor, how was that for a ride? Are you all right?"

Daniel looked straight at Pete. "I was scared out there. I'm still freaked out by that storm." He shivered.

"That's good, my friend. That's very good. Only a fool would not fear the ocean. But that was not a storm, that was just a squall."

He took a drink of his coffee, looking at Daniel intently. "The ocean's force, its vastness, has a lot to teach us... about life."

Daniel nodded. "I've lived by the water my whole life. The thing I just saw, that I never really realized before is that it's moving all the time...all the time. There is no stability! And it is so heavy, such weight, so vast! You don't think about that when you're looking at the sea from land." He laughed nervously. "There is no way to be still on it or control yourself on it. It won't let you, all that power and you are completely out of control!"

Pete was still watching him closely. "That's what sailing is all about, my friend. It's a way to learn to get around on that uncontrollable power." His eyes were warm behind his rimless glasses. He put a strong hand on Daniel's shoulder.

"You've had a good lesson for now. You've done well. You've got the knack...it's intuition. Add knowledge to that and you'll see what a great thing it is to sail. You'll be fine." He patted him affectionately.

Daniel was bowled over by this. No adult man had ever expressed any kind of confidence like this in his abilities, with such clean, open affection.

Dry now and full of food, they boarded the PegNPete again. Daniel was still scared, spooked in fact, but he wanted to finish well. Pete directed him to take the starboard mainsail sheet this time so he could learn that task, coordinating with Luke on the mainsail. This was better for him than being up in the swaying, dipping bow. They made their way easily back down the eastern coast of the island. At the Glass House jetty they said good-bye to Daniel and Henry, waving all the way out of the cove. The PegNPete continued south and Daniel was alone again. He checked on the Time Out and made it fast for the night then trudged on up the beach. Wandering around the beach house for a while, he realized he was too restless to settle. Without really thinking about it, he whistled for Henry and they walked up the beach path to Glass House. He stood on the terrace awhile looking out over the sea. He saw it in a new way and his thoughts went back to the rolling and pitching dark time on the other side of the island. He did not like the way he was feeling... the threat!

He made up his mind to spend the night at Glass House. This would be only the second or third night since he had been on the island that he stayed up there. He wanted to get away from the water for just a little while, not have to think about it outside his door. Rather than sleep in his childhood bedroom, he decided to go into his parent's room and sleep in their king-sized bed. It was a spacious room, painted in sea foam green. Bedding down there was a weird idea, but it was fine. There was never a television in the house, so he was lying there just looking around at the bare bedroom walls, thinking a million scattered, flitting thoughts. He tried to read a book for a while, couldn't concentrate and finally turned out the light. Henry was whining on the foot of the bed. Henry did not like changes of routine. Daniel tried to examine his feelings lying in the dark but he was just too tired and drifted off to sleep.

## CHAPTER THIRTY-THREE

# The Fourth

THE fourth of July was coming fast. Celebrations were planned and advertised all over the island for the big day, especially at Friday Harbor. A "Food Faire" was planned on the streets near the docks. Various clubs, churches and enterprises would be hawking food in tents along the streets. Picnic tables were being set up in the middle of town. There would be a pie eating contest and harbor sailboat races would be held during the afternoon. Daniel had promised a pie for the contest. In the evening, a lighted boat parade would take place in the harbor, ending with a fireworks display in the skies over the water.

Daniel had considered entering the harbor sailing races, there was a Penguin class race early in the day, but he decided that he was not ready to enter a competition. He just was not ready to do something like that. He was going to the festivities, though. He wanted to go along with the guys down at the marina. They had invited him to sail up with them to hang out in Friday Harbor for the day.

The day before, Daniel and Henry sailed down to the marina. Over coffee they could discuss the plans for tomorrow, not Henry of course, he had no say in the matter. Daniel found them hard at work hauling out old red, white and blue decorations and flags from a storage shed. Peggy was there too, shaking the dust off of everything they brought out of the boxes. There were miles of triangular pennants...and boxes of white twinkle lights.

"You came just in time to work!" said Luke. "Get over here and get some coffee and help us with this stuff."

They hauled out all the flags, which were plastic, and hosed them off. Daniel painstakingly got all the strings of lights out and untangled them, laying them out in long strands on the dock. There was an air of excitement about tomorrow. The PegNPete would join in the lighted boat parade.

They chatted as they worked. It seemed that Otis and Marion were coming over for the festivities, Anna too. Daniel was thrilled at the idea of seeing Otis. He wanted him to see the Beach House and observe his peaceful state of mind since he had come out to the island.

Daniel helped climb the mast lines to attach the lights and pennants. There would be an outline of the tiny lights around the sails, on the rail of the boat, and everywhere else they could attach them. Pete had a very large American flag that he would hoist later.

They put away boxes and all went down to Luke's houseboat for some lunch. It was there that the plan to take another trip was brought up. Pete made sure Daniel understood that he was invited to be part of the crew again. This time it would be the three guys, Daniel, Luke and Pete. Peggy, Anna and Marion planned a shopping trip to the boutiques in Sidney…girl's stuff. They would take the ferry.

The men could get away from work for several days for a vacation because Otis and Marion were staying on at the marina. Otis could fill in for them, working along with a guy named Jake, a temporary worker living on the island. The sailing party could be gone up to a week, but it might only be four days, all depending upon weather. They were going to cross the Strait of Juan de Fuca.

There was light rain early on the fourth of July, but it cleared quickly and the day promised to be beautiful and warm. Daniel and Henry hiked down to the marina on the cliff path early when the sky was still pearly and the shrubs were giving off a fresh sage-laden aroma. Daniel wore a brand new red t-shirt and faded old navy shorts. And, since he had a boat now and was sailing, he had gone into town one day to the dry-goods store and bought a pair of buff topsiders. Even if his "ship" did not have a deck, he had deck shoes. They were perfect for the PegNPete. His coloring had definitely deepened and his hair was getting a shade lighter than his natural ash brown tone. He still had not had a haircut. He looked healthy and stronger by far than when he arrived on the island weeks before.

Otis and Marion had come in on the ferry the night before. When Otis saw Daniel coming down the docks his face lit up and he was chuckling that deep laugh by the time they met and embraced. He looked him over, turning his face by the chin from side to side. Daniel clung to him a moment, blinking back tears.

"God's doing a good job on you, boy! A good job! You're looking better than ever."

Marion hugged him too. She was a fine woman, sculpted face and caramel skin, like Luke. Her eyes crinkled up with her perpetual smile. She was glad to see him. Anna shyly embraced him and kissed his cheek. She was looking fresh in a red and white checked gingham sundress. She had the longest, most exquisite, dark brown legs and wore red espadrilles on her feet.

They all clamored on board the sailboat and were under way to Friday Harbor by 10 A.M.

The harbor and town were jam-packed. It was a challenge to pick their way among the array of boats of every size. Pete unloaded the rubber dinghy and they all went ashore, leaving the boat anchored in the bay.

It was a perfect, uproarious, busy, food-filled day on shore and in the bay with boat horns going off here and there all day and masses of people milling through the town. Daniel, Luke and Anna saw Nan and Ruth selling snow cones in a tent for their church. They were able to visit briefly and Ruth was introduced to Anna for the first time. The two girls immediately started talking about Anna's upcoming wedding in December, the wedding flowers and all those kind of things. They seemed to hit it off instantly.

Nan hugged Daniel and encouraged him to come see her again. He had been thinking about that. They chatted on happily. He was in the midst telling her about his sailing and biking adventures around the island, when he blurted out that he was crossing the Juan de Fuca soon, sailing with Pete and Luke. He must have said it with some fear because her face changed and became solemn for a moment, her eyes registering that she saw his emotion and understood instantly. He felt very drawn to this little woman and decided he would go to see her again as soon as he could. He would bring another cherry pie from his cherry stash.

This was the first big crowd that Daniel had been in since Paul's death. He was worried about that, as he still had the tendency to withdraw. But now he felt especially protected in the company of his friends. He knew everything was fine. There was only a momentary flickering thought of his nightmare of being lost in a strange crowd, which he dreamed the night of Paul's memorial...a momentary flicker which did not settle on him at all.

Nearing sundown, they got back to the dinghy and scooted out to the PegNPete.

Pete motored the boat out to the staging area for the light parade. As dusk fell, there was much excitement. It was wonderful to see the boats finally all transformed, lit up and slowly circling through the harbor on parade. After the parade, they anchored again and watched the fireworks from the comfort of the boat. There were not only sizzling, bursting lights above, but the whole thing was mirrored and shimmering in the dark waters of the bay. Their lights remained lit up on board as they slowly cruised home to the marina, light spilling onto the water as they went. Pete, Peggy, Daniel and Henry spent the night on the PegNPete. Daniel had been kindly invited to stay so that he didn't have to walk home to Glass House, late in the dark. Peggy had made some sangria and they finished off all the picnic nibbles. Deck chairs were set up on the docks, and there in the dark they talked and watched the natural fireworks of stars in the heavens until late that night.

## CHAPTER THIRTY-FOUR

# *Juan de Fuca*

TWO days later, Daniel emptied his trash, locked the doors (a first since he arrived on the island), loaded up his duffle bag and drove with Henry to the marina. It was still dark out, but the dawn was a pink haze rising quickly over Lopez Island as they checked everything on the PegNPete and started the motor. Everyone was up to see them off. Otis was on the dock with Henry and Luke's dog, George. Henry was whining and straining on a leash beside him. He would be Otis' dog for a few days. Marion and Anna were in their bathrobes, waving from the houseboat. Peggy was wrapped in an old blanket, hugging her coffee mug there on the dock. She had been up even earlier, preparing sandwiches and packing the boat's refrigerator. Pete had been washing the decks, fueling and bringing on water. They were ready.

The plan was to make a big circle around the strait. They would sail toward the mouth of Victoria Bay at the tip of Vancouver Island, then cross the strait and try to get to Clallam Bay on the north shore of Olympia the first night. Next stop would be Neah Bay at the far northwest tip of the continental United States. It was the tip of Washington, and a great camping and hiking area which they would explore. On the return, they would stop over at Port Angeles and have the PegNPete dry-docked for a day so they could work on cleaning up the hull and the keel. Then a straight shot back across to San Juan Island and home.

This time Daniel would be crewing the port sheets, and Luke was on the starboard side. Pete, helmsman as always, had a new digital radar device, which showed any vessel or other target within twenty miles and its position relative to the PegNPete. It even showed the radio call number of the boats. It would come in handy especially in case of fog.

Daniel's stomach was churning. No doubt about it, he was anxious. He had slept fitfully the night before. But he had made up his mind that he would not be controlled by fear of the sea. He would learn to get along, to work the sails and be a part of the adventure, a member of this crew. He would go out onto this larger sea and learn to deal with it the best he could, the threat and the beauty, the good and the bad. This was his intention and pledge to himself.

Once away from the southern tip of San Juan Island, Luke set sail in on a west/northwest course. They would need to skirt around Hein Bank as much as possible. This was a major shoal which rose to only a few fathoms below the surface of the sea. Currents in that area were unpredictable at times. They were set toward Discovery Island on an ebb current, which would help, though the wind would be incoming from the west. They were closed-hauled and sailing the jib, though they might have to drop it later, depending on the wind. Pete was talking and instructing

Daniel as they went, explaining all the details of the PegNPete's rigging and their uses. It was a comfort that he was familiar with all these waters, the winds and the currents. It was another pearly morning, fresh and mild. They could not have set out on a better day. Daniel was beginning to get the hang of the coming about of sails. He was hauling the port sheet and learning to work the winch. Just keeping lines straight and following the coordinated commands was a kind of team work that he was beginning to enjoy.

Off the tip of Discovery Island, they changed course to south/southwest. The waters of the strait were never as smooth the bay waters could be, but the going was easily manageable in the larger boat. They skimmed over the mild chop, heeling slightly to port at times. The sun was rising high in the sky, and glare off the water was blinding as they passed by the mouth of Victoria Harbor. Heavy traffic hit them from this point onward to the tip of the Vancouver Island at Metchosin. In the distance they spotted the Port Angeles to Victoria Ferry chugging along towards them. Pete was calling for more frequent tacks. They had to keep their heads up. They sailed between Bentinck Island and rocks to the east where the Victoria Sound Lighthouse stood, warning of hazardous rocks to the east. Conditions held steady as they rounded Vancouver Island and headed out into the main waters of the Juan de Fuca.

Pete had chosen one of the narrowest and shortest distances to take a run across the strait. He was setting for Clallum Bay on the northern shore of the Olympic Peninsula. The view of the whole panorama of the Olympic was staggering. It was perfectly clear and they could see the snowy peaks of the Olympics as if magnified. In fact the whole view, 360 degrees around them, was exhilarating. Daniel's fears began to melt in the presence of all this beauty. Pete was looking very mellow at the tiller.

"This is why we love sailing!" he shouted, grinning. He was wearing his khaki Friday Harbor baseball cap. His cheeks were already red from wind and sun.

Luke was quietly enjoying the same experience on the starboard side, gazing west. From here it was routine, tacking into the wind on a course which was less than a twenty mile distance. They had entered a slack water current, so the sailing was straight forward and entirely pleasurable. Daniel was getting more and more comfortable on the shifting, moving waters. They were an efficient crew together.

Several huge ships passed them coming up the strait, making for Puget Sound and Seattle. Cargo ships and big fishing trawlers came by as well as smaller fishing craft and one beautiful, 50 foot sailing ketch, heading east in the strait. They were headed for the coast of the Olympic, swinging west a few miles west of Salt Creek. They would be sailing about a mile off shore, hugging the coast the rest of the way west.

Clallum Bay came into view around two in the afternoon. It was a tiny isolated community perched between forest and sea. They cruised into the small array of docks at the far west end of the bay and found a guest slip for the night. It was early, but too far a stretch to sail all the way to the mouth of the Strait out at Neah Bay. They couldn't make it before dark, sailing against ever-stronger prevailing winds. They would take extra days as needed. There was no hurry. Otis was fully capable of handling the marina and Daniel was just along for the ride. There was plenty of time.

The three of them had eaten all the sandwiches Peggy had made and were discussing dinner. First though, came a nice nap, as they had embarked very early that morning, and even though there had been no rough seas on the journey, it was hours of intense work. The three of them spread out in the roomy cabin and slept until nearly dark. Daniel was glad he did not have to worry about Henry now, but could just let go and drift off. He had actually sailed across the Strait of Juan de Fuca, and he was very happy about that.

They took off to explore the small village at Clallum Bay just as the sun was setting. It was that blazing coral orange color over the sea leading out into the strait. They walked the town and found a local fish restaurant on the only main street. Slow smoked salmon prepared by local tribesmen was a melt-in-your-mouth experience. It was served with an herbed, buttery rice dish, green salad and strong coffee. They passed a little T-shirt and hat shop and a marine hardware which was now closed, stretching their legs on the way back to the boat. Daniel was completely relaxed now, having sailed across those waters with his friends. He knew they had sailed an easy passage, but he was grateful.

In the morning when they awoke, fog had descended, covering everything thickly. They couldn't even see the buildings of the little town or the end of the docks. They would have to wait it out...not a good idea to launch back into that main thoroughfare of commercial shipping in their little sailboat in fog.

Daniel loved the fog even if it was slowing down their progress. He had always loved looking at the transformation of everyday objects in fog. Even things of complex form smoothed out and became big soft shapes, colors morphed from clear and strong to muted tones all fitting together as if they were designed by an abstract painter who had added white to every pigment on the palette.

Pete made coffee in the galley. They had a first cup while talking over the situation. Then Daniel jumped into action and started cooking a big substantial breakfast. He grilled bacon in the little oven, and began to prepare an omelet of mushrooms, green peppers and onions. He had brought along some of his favorite Havarti cheese, so he slid a slice of that in, too. French bread sliced thin and toasted in a buttered pan and sliced oranges finished everything off.

"This is a major improvement over the oatmeal I would have made if you weren't here," said Pete, nodding his head in approval.

After breakfast, Pete took a walk to the marina office to see what advice they had about the weather. Daniel and Luke cleaned up. Then they went out on deck and checked all the rigging, straightened everything up and made ready for the last leg to Neah Bay. They sat drinking one more cup of coffee, watching other sailors along the docks, who were also preparing, some gathered in little groups chatting, waiting for the fog to lift.

Soon they saw Pete coming back up the docks. The news was that the fog was localized. It had broken up farther west, according to reports, and was being dissipated eastward by the incoming, prevailing wind. Before long they could see blue sky to the west in patches.

They set sail before noon and slowly wandered through foggy patches, watching to stay away from shore, where rock hazards could lie close to the surface, all the while hugging the coast as best they could to avoid eastward moving traffic.

The wind picked up, blowing straight in from the mouth to the Pacific ahead. They were easily heading into it now, full-sailed and close-hauled, moving swiftly with the consistent lift the sails received from the west. It was smooth sailing. Along the way Daniel was noticing the terrain on shore. It rose steeply and kept rising over layers of foot hills toward the Olympic peaks to the south. The trees were dense and taller than that on San Juan, intensely green. They received much more rain here. This place was all new to him and he was looking forward to the hike they had planned for tomorrow.

At Neah Bay they found a concentration of freighters, fishing boats, commercial rigs of all kinds and the sporting craft of local fishermen and sightseeing vessels, all on the move. They docked the PegNPete at the Neah harbor after skimming past some huge ships mainly headed eastward to the bigger harbors of the Pacific Northwest. The open water beyond was wild and full of strange, tall, chimney rock formations which they could see at a distance, coming near the mouth of the strait. The area was under the control of the Makah People, the tribe indigenous to the area. This point and the surrounding land were all under their governance. Neah was larger than Clallam but still a small marina. From its vantage point, the tiny port watched the parade of maritime vessels of all the world. This was literally the Northwest corner of continental America.

Pete, Daniel and Luke docked the boat at their guest slip, made fast and hopped off to see the harbor and the town. They wanted to rent a tourist jeep for their next adventures. The rest of the day was spent sightseeing and gathering information for the area and its offerings. Pete and Peggy had come here before. It was a first for Luke and Daniel. They did locate a rental jeep. Grabbing the keys they took off around town and along some of the forest roads, Luke at the wheel. It was considerably more lush here than their home base of San Juan. They were truly at the edge of a rain forest.

Today, Daniel wished that he was a photographer. There was so much beauty to be captured. He settled for shots with his digital "point and shoot..." They drove out to find the trailhead of the Cape Flattery Trail about five miles from town. This was to be their adventure for tomorrow. The trail headed off towards the cape through dense forest.

That night they cooked dinner on board. Daniel had bought a piece of a huge fresh halibut from a fishing boat docked near them. It had been caught just hours before and was a beautiful slice. He was getting used to cooking in the tiny galley. First he sautéed the fish in garlic butter and some white wine he had brought. The wilted spinach was an easy fix and there were baked sweet potatoes. He had stashed away a cherry pie secretly from home. It was brought out to Pete and Luke's delight. After dinner they sat on deck watching the parade of ships and boats going by out in the strait. The weather was still mild, and the sea was running its normal high ebb and flow tides. There was powerful energy as the Pacific rushed in and out of the narrow strait. That night as they sat on board, Pete told them the story of Juan de Fuca.

"Who was Juan de Fuca?" Daniel had asked.

"He was the Spaniard who discovered this coast and the San Juan Islands too," said Luke.

"Well, not exactly," Pete added quietly. "He was a Greek, came from a little island off the Greek west coast, there on the Adriatic. His real name was Ioánnis Phokás. They don't know much about him, but apparently he sailed up here exploring for the Spanish in the 1500's. They say he sailed a Caravel, big time choice for coastal explorers since the Portuguese went out, highly maneuverable. They say he used a Latin-rigged sail called a 'Lateen,' a curious rig, a big sail balanced on a diagonal yard off the mast. It was oriented fore and aft, and extended fore of the mast, like a main sail and jib all in one...sort of an 'in-betweener' between the old squared-rigged and our modern main-masted rig. So... they think he was the first European to find this place, but he left after just a brief look around. A couple of hundred years later one of the English seamen-explorers came along and really sailed around the islands, fellow called Barkley. He decided to name a lot of things here Spanish names after those early explorers: Lopez, San Juan, Juan de Fuca, which is what the Spanish made out of 'Phokas'...Long way round to say he was a Greek working for Spain. So it's not the strait of 'Barkley,' it's the 'Juan de Fuca.' " He sat back. That was a lot of talk at once for Pete.

"Pete! I didn't know you were into history," said Luke, grinning. "That was awesome!"

"Well, no I am not into history, I'm into sailing. I've got a few books," he smiled back.

"That was very interesting, Pete. Seriously, I like your story-telling style! Now that was all true, right? No embellishing?" Daniel was teasing him a bit.

"All true," said Pete with just a little twinkle to his eye. "All true."

This was all banter, because Daniel had a growing bond with Pete. He was so honest. He was capable...steady, just like Luke. Daniel was more and more certain that he could trust Pete, just as he trusted Luke. It was funny how he had no particular special attraction to either man. They were simply male friends, handsome, strong guys with whom he could share time in a perfectly relaxed way. When they were together doing their guy stuff Daniel was comfortable. It was good. It felt right.

## CHAPTER THIRTY-FIVE

# Cape Flattery

THAT next morning the three of them bundled up a load of camping gear, including a large canopy shelter, and filled up the back of the jeep. It was not quite a tent, just an overhead canopy, but if they were to trust the weather forecast, no rain was expected for more than twenty-four hours. So, clear skies were expected with a full moon in the evening. They would be staying the night in campgrounds at the south end of the peninsula, a place run by the local tribe. The canopy would do for just a one night stay. It had a plastic floor and they brought sleeping bags. Tent camping was allowed in a big grassy meadow. They could get showers and cook out, too. They had seen pictures in the brochure the tribe gave out. The wide Pacific beach was right there beyond some dunes to the south. They would make a big circle on the forest roads of the peninsula and be back at the boat tomorrow.

Daniel had prepared a pile of burritos for the day, chicken strips in a cilantro sauce rolled in a fresh tortilla, and some imported string cheese with humus he had brought from Glass

House and a jug of mango tea. They could munch on these all day, adding just a few pieces of fruit. He had prepared something special for their campout dinner. They brought along some hickory chips and the dinner fixings in the cooler.

Excitement was in the air as they took off for the Cape Flattery trail. With some hooting and hollering Luke pulled away from the dock for a landward adventure. The brisk air hitting them in the jeep had everyone awake and keyed up for the hike before they even arrived. There were only a couple of cars parked at the trailhead parking lot. The trail would not be crowded. After covering all their gear they set out Indian style, single file, into the dense forest trail.

They were walking through a cool fragrant world, in green dappled light with enormous evergreens above and oversized ferns below. Some of the ferns were as tall as the men. The trail was damp and at intervals there were boardwalks and little bridges over boggy spots. They could hear the sea and the sound of waterfalls as they neared the final point of the trail, where the Pacific Ocean continually slammed into the far reaching westward tip of the peninsula. Coming out of forest at the coast, the view that met them was over-the-top spectacular. There was excited exclamation as the cameras came out.

This was a jagged, rugged coastline where the land and the sea were eternally in a battle. A mist of sea spray lifted all along the coast where small deep inlets had been cut through time with rock formations twisting and fighting against the sea. Some of the dark stone pillars in the waters offshore had been formed by the sea into fantastic shapes which could suggest all kinds of things to the imagination. One huge pillar looked a lot like a totem pole complete with grotesque faces. They wandered back and forth along the trail, looking at the scene from various spots. In the coves, waterfalls fell from the forest down cliffs into the clear, green shallows. Farther out, the waters looked as black as night. The tiny island off shore, Tatoosh, was green and un-forested. there was a prominent lighthouse on the island with no one living there on-site. The high black cliffs and submerged rocks edging the island made an approach by sea near impossible. Daniel was enthralled and took photos from every angle. They stayed for several hours and in the end, hated to leave the spectacular beauty of the place.

All three walked back along the trail in silence, thinking about all that they had seen. This time, Daniel led the way... the sound of his friends trudging behind him felt reassuring. He was thinking that a bond of friendship was forming among them. It was something new for him. It was wonderful. It wasn't like the work camaraderie among the staff at The Prow, and it was nothing like any other male relationships he had ever had. Every day spent with these friends was new and satisfying for a former lone wolf like him. Their obvious acceptance of him, their respect and affection, was like a soothing benediction. There was one thing missing, though, and it was really pressing in on him as he walked the trail back to the parking lot. The missing element was Henry. Right now he missed that hound so much. He wished he had not left him home, but a long sailing trip seemed too risky for a city dog, even for one who had been living on the beach. Next time Henry would be there, a member of the crew.

It was a short drive on a winding gravel road south to the campground. The forest hugged tight to the primitive road. Once they stopped to pick early blackberries. They got a bag full right by the road, then continued on. The view coming out of the trees from above and looking down on the open beach and camp caused them to stop again for photos. Like Cape Flattery, this Pacific scene was spectacular. The ocean was wild, and they could see the surf rolling in for miles along the southern shore.

A convenient campsite was found and the canopy went up fast. There were some other campers there too, families. The kids were running around in the meadow, and some campers were down at the beach playing in the surf. Daniel was delighted with camp work and arranged all his things and the cooking gear with great pleasure. He began thinking to himself nostalgically about Paul. Why couldn't they have done this...at least once in a while? He had no answer and just let it go. He wouldn't spoil a beautiful time with thoughts of what might have been. He was here now and it was wonderful. He vowed to himself that he would start doing this camping thing often.

He had a great dinner planned. He knew the guys were going to love it.

The menu was simple: grilled steak, Luke would handle this. Then foiled vegetable packets, long slices of Japanese eggplant with ginger and green onions all roasted over the camp fire. The salad was already cut up...cucumber slices, cilantro, a bit of red jalapeño, and sprigs of dill... to be served over a bed of cooked rice with soy sauce. The vegetables would take a while, so they sat around the fire talking as the sunlight slowly turned into evening. Luke and Pete had brought some ale that they liked and Daniel had stowed a bottle of wine.

Luke was talking about his upcoming wedding. Having just left Anna on the island, he was excited...he was nervous...he was talking about the plans he and Anna had for redoing the houseboat to be their honeymoon house. He was trying to be cool, but it was clear that he was a full-blown romantic.

"It's going to be great," he said smiling. "I am so ready to have her here with me. I'm tired of living alone. You know, Anna is my best friend as well as the love of my life." He was grinning. "Guy friends are great, but this woman is going to make everything complete for me."

"Yeah, I know what you mean," Pete took a drink of the brown ale. "How about you Daniel? Any woman ever tempted you to walk the aisle?"

Daniel froze for a moment. They knew who he was. However...he realized it was a fair question.

"No, I got off onto another track early on," he smiled. "Girls are nice...but I'm on another track." He looked into the fire. "There was a guy, an older guy who set that going a long, long time ago." His voice was bitter.

Luke looked sad. He knew what was meant.

"Yeah, I know what you mean on that too." Pete was staring into the fire too. "I had a guy like that come into my life too."

Both Daniel and Luke looked up sharply at Pete.

"I was raised in eastern Washington on a little old farm. Had one brother, two years older than me. Our Dad died when we were just little kids. It left our Mom high and dry. So, my Dad's brother took over the farming of our place for Mom. He had a farm just down the road from us. He did the farming for my Mom, and she started up a chicken and egg business there too. She thought she could handle that. We helped, me and my brother."

Pete paused, stirring the fire with a stick. Smiling he said, "We were just a couple of wild and wooly farm boys. I don't know how much help we were but we tried. There were a couple of eggs that got broken. We chased a few roosters around. It was tough though for my Mom and she didn't have much time for us boys after that, always busy, sun up to sun down. When I was about eight, Mom asked her younger brother to come out and help her some. He was a strange one. Kinda pudgy, not much help. Now she had three kids to take care of. His name was Alec, Uncle Alec. After a while, Uncle Alec took me hiking one day near the farm. There were woods back behind us. He promised me a pocket knife to whittle with. We were going along out there in the woods and...he got me and put me up against a tree, pulled down my pants. He did a bad thing there to me. He forced me, and he was laughing and grunting, while he did it."

Pete paused, he looking over at Daniel. Both Daniel and Luke were looking down now, long-faced.

"Hey, Daniel," Pete said. "That's not the end of the story." His face was alive with emotion.

Daniel looked up, watching him closely.

"This thing happened a couple of times. Whenever Uncle Alec could get me alone. I was messed up...started hiding around the farm. I didn't tell anybody. One day, after this crap had happened again, I was up in an old peach tree in our garden, hiding and crying. My brother heard me and came over looking up in the tree. He saw me. He climbed up there with me. I told him. He started crying too. He told me Uncle Alec had done the same to him. We both cried and cried. After a while we stopped crying and started cussing him. We hatched a plan for Uncle Alec." Pete was smiling now, with a faraway look in his eyes.

"We got Uncle Alec out in the woods one day. He thought he was going to have us both. We acted like nothing was wrong, but we had gone out to a spot beforehand and hid our two baseball bats, and some rope. While Uncle Alec was coming after me, my brother got the bats. He walloped Uncle Alec in the head from behind. While he was stunned my brother lassoed his leg tight to a tree. Then we took our bats and beat the living hell out of Uncle Alec. We two kids beat that guy up good. He was knocked out. Then we tied him up good, hog-tied him. We pulled HIS pants down. 'How do you like that, Uncle,' we yelled! I took the pocket knife he had given me and I cut a long line on his face, on his cheek. I wanted him to have a scar to remember us by. We left him there in the woods, pants down and hog tied; now he was the one who was crying." Pete took another quick drink of his beer.

"Wow," said Luke with wide eyes. "Wow..."

Daniel's head was down, crying.

"We went on home to the farm. I took that pocket knife and threw it in the garbage can. Later on, I saved my own money and bought a nice pocket knife for myself."

"After a while everybody was looking for Uncle Alec. It got dark and he didn't show up. My brother and I had made up our minds. If we had to, we would run away from the farm. Maybe we could live down the road at my Dad's brother's place. It wasn't too long until my Dad's brother showed up to help search. He knew something was up. He found our dear uncle out in the woods late that night and brought him home. My mother was screaming...she didn't get it. My Dad's brother did, though. Nothing more was said. He got Uncle Alec cleaned up and put him on a bus out of town. We never saw him again. Finally, our Mom got the picture. She was real sad, but we never saw Alec again." Pete's eyes were gleaming behind his rimless glasses.

Daniel started to sob. "I wish I could have done that. I wish I could have done that." He repeated passionately.

"How old were you when it happened?" Pete asked.

"About five."

"You were a baby," Pete said bitterly. "A baby can't defend itself alone. I couldn't defend myself alone either. I needed a brother, and my brother needed me. Brothers can stick together."

Pete was standing up now. He put a hand on Daniel's shoulder. "Sorry to have hurt your feelings, Daniel. Sometimes though it is good to know you're not alone. As far as I am concerned you are a brother to me." He walked away from the campsite into the dark. "I'll take a walk now down to the beach. Yell for me when the dinner is ready, O.K.?"

Daniel looked up at Luke. His face was serious, calm in the firelight. "I told you that before, Daniel. I told you that, too. I'm your brother... we're brothers now." Then he smiled. "Hey! Let's get this food on the table!"

Luke tended the steaks. Daniel went and washed his face. He took a few deep breaths then came and worked on the vegetables and the rice, getting out the plates and things...it took a while. Daniel was still reeling from all that Pete had said. How strange that he had come out here to get away and had landed with these two guys. Life was so strange.

The moon rose over the Pacific. They all sat down and ate dinner at the picnic table. It was a peaceful time, very little was said, nor were words needed. Other campers nearby were around their fires and getting ready to bed down. After dinner Daniel was rummaging around in their food locker. He came back to the fire with something behind his back.

"Anyone for S'mores?" he smiled.

"OWW, now you're talkin'..." This was Pete.

Daniel had them all wrapped up neatly in foil, a gourmet version of S'mores to be sure...Ghirardelli chocolate. They popped them into the coals and in minutes were eating the warm gooey treat. There was laughter and jokes were cracked as the evening wore on, and finally, crashing into sleeping bags under a moonlight sky.

In the morning, they ate the fresh blackberries they had picked and some granola. The coffee was super strong, made in the camp percolator. After packing up they headed north on a road through a wide river valley, spacious, grassy and flat, the forest off on each side at a distance. There were deer feeding and watering down in the marshes by the meandering river. A very short drive brought them right back to Neah Bay.

From a distance, they could see the PegNPete docked in the marina and were glad to see her. Pete could not conceal his joy... he was ready to sail again. Luke turned in the jeep while Daniel and Pete boarded the boat, gassed up the tank and made ready to leave. Quickly they motored out into the channel and were off. Daniel took up his same port sheet position and Luke was at starboard. Daniel looked back at the little port as it grew smaller and smaller, thinking about Cape Flattery beyond view in the trees. What a twenty-four hours. The whole world can turn in twenty-four hours.

Daniel was watching Pete at the stern, working the tiller, his eyes ranging around, taking in everything about the sea. He saw strength. "He's a whole man," Daniel thought. "He's complete, despite his losses, his dad dying so young, the harm done to him as a kid and by life, he's a whole man. He's steady. He's got peace." Daniel continued watching Pete, watching the boat moving along straight through waves of the sea. "I want to be complete," he thought. "Why couldn't I be a whole man too?" It was a good question, but for now he put it away. He would just enjoy this trip to the utmost.

Now, they were running with the wind, directly east, up the strait. Pete was grinning and letting the boat run full sail. This boat couldn't rig a spinnaker, it was too flat in the water, but the jib was full out and it was a nice breezy day and they were also running with the ingoing tide. They were traveling fast. It was fun sailing a narrow course all the way, trying to stay out of the middle of the channel where the bigger ships were. Their destination was Port Angeles.

## CHAPTER THIRTY-SIX

# The Wicked Way

Entering Port Angeles harbor was like getting stuck in a Seattle traffic jam. It was packed with every kind of ship and boat imaginable. The Victoria Ferry had its berth there. It was also the home of hundreds of yachts and boats as well as commercial fishing rigs of every size. They had decided earlier to get into one of the dry docks and do some work on the hull while they had the chance. The procedure was easy, convenient and soon they found themselves watching as the PegNPete was hauled up and out of the water by heavy equipment and lifted to a dockside work station. They had brought tools and paint for the hull. The facility had a heavy duty power washer on site, so Daniel manned that while Pete and Luke got the rest of the tools and equipment ready.

It was amazing to see the growth on the underbelly of Pete's boat. Most of that could be blasted off with the water, but then the hard work of scraping began. All three of them worked wide scrapers all over the lower hull. Some paint was loose and that came off too, as well as colonies of barnacles and other growth.

The PegNPete was painted Robin's Egg blue below the waterline. They would repaint in the same color. The upper hull was pure white. The boat had a full keel. It wasn't extremely deep but it ranged the full length of the vessel. Pete, with the eye of a craftsman, scraped and sanded the front edge of the keel. Then he carefully filed the fore-edge of the keel where the boat sliced through the water to a smooth even finish ready for paint. He swore that the boat would sail smoother and faster with a knife-edged keel. After an afternoon of scrubbing and scraping they rinsed and left the hull to fully dry.

Time for dinner. His companions so far had not let Daniel pay for anything except the food he brought with him. They had decided to celebrate the last night of their trip by staying at an inn near the harbor, renowned for "fresh catch" King Crab legs. Daniel had called ahead to the inn to let them know he was picking up this bill for dinner and rooms. It was all arranged...he wanted to do his part.

Hoisting their duffle bags, they walked to the inn and cleaned up. After a night in sleeping bags, this would be a good night's sleep for sure. The Crab restaurant and Inn had a wrap-around porch. They found a table outside where all the activity of the harbor could be seen and enjoyed. Daniel did the ordering for them all, and he picked a wonderful wine and some delicate appetizers and oysters. They were stuffed with all the fresh sweet crab that each man could hold. They finished with an extravagant Crème Brûlée dessert. It would have been deadly to go straight to bed with stomachs so full, and so they walked around the shops of Port Angeles a while. Luke bought Anna a set of demitasse coffee cups. Daniel bought the biggest t-shirt he could find for Otis. A graphic of the Olympic mountain range was stenciled on it in bright inks. He got a small one just like it for Marion. Then he bought himself a rustic wooden photo frame. He was going to have one of his Cape Flattery photos printed for it, his souvenir of the trip. Pete found a set of locally carved wooden salad tongs. It was a long way from their Cape Flattery excursion of just a day before. Everyone was tired now and ready to go home to the island.

Very early the next morning, Pete was up and out to the dry docks to get the painting started very early. He also called Peggy for a chat and to tell her they would be sailing back across and home this afternoon.

The hull would only be painted below, under the waterline. By the time Luke and Daniel arrived, he was half finished. They pitched right in, rolled on another coat of the light blue, and it was done. The paint was fast-drying, so by noon they were ready to launch again, saying goodbye to the dry dock and Port Angeles. Pete was hurrying to get out on the water before too late in the afternoon, when seas could be rough. They crossed paths with the Victoria Ferry on the way out of the harbor into the last leg of their journey across the strait, headed for home.

The day had dawned as clear as the days before, but now a dark sky moving overhead indicated some weather coming in. Pete was anxious to get across before treacherous seas built up, so they were hauling very fast. The eastern part of the strait was known for shoals, banks, and a few tiny islands which caused havoc with the currents and tide flow from time to time. The sun was still shining in and out of clouds, but the wind was building up to a howling and capricious level. Their course was north/northwest but they kept getting across the wind in a broad reach and into the trough of the seas. Very quickly the sky was getting darker and the water was darker still. The first thing necessary was to reef the jib sail. This would slow them down, but Luke dropped it and battened it down. Pete was starting to struggle with the tiller due to cross currents. They reefed the mainsail down some too, tight to the wind, a bare minimum of canvas. They were gibing with the wind they best they could.

Daniel was determined not to panic as he looked at the dark heaving seas, but his anxiety was high. Once again he had the sensation of the utter power of the heavy, moving waters. It was like being on the back of a huge, bucking, fluid horse. No land could be seen at all due to low-lying cloud banks coming in all around them. They were sailing now by Pete's new instrumentation. They could not see very far in any direction.

"Get on your life jackets and buckle up to harnesses," Pete shouted over the wind. He looked fine, still concentrating on his steering. Daniel was trying to read his face in this mess, but it was just blankly stoic and determined. He saw that his jaw was set tightly. Luke was adeptly managing the mainsail as Pete called commands. He was riveted on the condition of the sails and sheets.

Daniel was sick. Both sick from motion and sick from fear. He continued to try to do his best without fumbling. He determined again not to panic as he had on their Magellan sail. He would do his job. They were jerked and crashing erratically with heavy seas and heeled over at a precipitous angle to starboard in the troughs. The seas were not yet flowing over them, but it was close. Looking around, Daniel realized that they were in a patch of seas where the waves were not rolling, but were standing up suddenly in triangular peaks all around them, then falling back. This could not be good. Cold piercing rain began to hit them, swirling in from all directions, blurring vision and peppering them hard.

Where had this crazy weather come from?! It was sudden and had caught Daniel completely off guard. Pete knew these waters, though, and he was not surprised. He yelled that the seas were pushing them off course towards Hein Bank, an area they absolutely did not want to sail through. He was trying to right their course but having a struggle at the tiller. This was the Hein Bank they had avoided on the first leg of their trip. It was a long prominence under the sea near the middle of the strait. It was so close to the surface, being only a few fathoms deep, that the sea was totally unpredictable surrounding it. It was far to the west of the channel they wanted to be in, but the violent tide was ebbing and was sucking them out to the west. At times the boat was creaking and seemed as if it was trying to rotate, as if in a whirlpool tide. Daniel just kept trying to concentrate on the commands from Pete and respond immediately to his order. They worked like this for more than an hour, seeming to make no headway. For Daniel, this was now beyond fear, it was survival. He noticed that his hands were bleeding a bit from pulling the sheets to keep them from going slack at an off moment. Surely there were other craft out in this, but for now they could see no one.

Pete called for a drastic eastward gibe. They made the turn and things suddenly began to shift. The waves began to straighten out to a more normal pattern to the east, and Daniel could feel the boat tracking into an easterly current and channel. The sea seemed to have its very own purposes, and soon they were traveling out of the chaos and into a direction which for them meant home. They fought on for another half hour and then they sighted the southern tip of San Juan in the distance! There at the far west end was the tiny speck of a white lighthouse...it was Cattle Point. Now they could clearly see the channel between San Juan and Lopez. Things slowed down on board and the melting of tension was palpable. Daniel was shaking his head. He could not believe all that he had been through in the few days on this trip. Luke with his storm slicker on, his face wet and shining, was grinning at him from ear to ear...never saying a word. Pete was solid as ever, hunkered down at the tiller. He was probably stiff with exhaustion. Daniel suddenly teared up. He was thinking about seeing Henry soon. He hadn't let himself think of Henry much, but he really missed his presence. If there were ever to be a "next time," Henry was going.

They came into the San Juan Marina just at sundown. It had taken them four hours to get through the rough stuff. Pete blew his special boat horn as they were coming in and everybody came out to greet them. Henry spotted Daniel and went into a frenzy of wiggling and barking. Finally, as they approached the dock he leapt into the water, swimming out to the boat. They hauled him on board and he was almost howling with joy. Daniel hugged a very wet dog.

They docked and greeted everyone. Anna was very happy to see Luke and he picked her up and swung her around. There was something very happy going on here.

Everyone was kind of talking at once. They told the tale of their wicked time on the strait just hours before. Pete, now on dry ground, said it was the worst passage he had ever sailed across the strait. He was shaking his head and smiling now.

Otis announced that he had made up some fresh clam chowder, so they washed up and went down to the house boat for a "comfort food" feast. There was crusty bread as well and Marion had made cobbler with some early blackberries. Everyone was talking and laughing and trying to tell everything at once about their trip. The girls had quite a bit to say about their shopping spree to Vancouver Island too. After dinner, Daniel gathered up his gear from the boat and headed to his car. Henry was hugging his legs to the point that he could hardly walk. He said his thank-you's, heart-felt thank-you's, to his captain and his crew mate and headed on out for Glass House. His friends would be around tomorrow, and on through time after that. He could go home now and rest. As he drove towards Glass House he began to laugh and said out loud, to no one but Henry, "I made it across the Juan de Fuca, and back alive! I'm a hell of a newbie sailor!" He tooted the horn a few times. Henry started barking.

Back down in the marina, Pete was hauling gear out of the PegNPete. He heard the distant honking and smiled. He knew what it meant.

## CHAPTER THIRTY-SEVEN

# In the Orchard

Lazy days followed the sailing trip. Daniel stayed on land for a while. The sea venture had been wonderful. He went over it in his mind every day, thinking about every detail of the trip. But now he wanted to roam around his property, reorganize the Glass House kitchen, lie on the beach in the sun and be quiet. At night he listened to his favorite classical station down at the beach house. He would play it loud with all the windows and the door wide open. He could literally feel the music filling the night air. He knew the time was approaching when he should get back to the mainland and to the restaurant. Not yet though. He was enjoying life fully.

He did go out lazily in the Time Out a few times. He was so surprised at how different, how relaxed and confident he felt sailing after his grueling time on the PegNPete. He would cruise up to his favorite cove. There he snorkeled and swam, picking up a few sea urchins and some mussels for a tasty dinner. And, he went down to the marina for coffee with Pete and Luke. He would always take beignets.

He also explored the property behind Glass House, beyond the orchard. It was a narrow, densely forested strip butting up against the National Park property. The forest there had not been cleared out in decades. The place was full of blackberry brambles and their fruit was ripening fast. A couple of weeks and there would be a bumper crop.

His main enjoyment in these days, though, was the time he spent in the orchard. He had taken to spending some afternoons there where it was nice and warm. He loved the filtered sunlight in the orchard and the warmth that lasted all day, away from the breezes and late afternoon shade caused by the cliffs down on the beach. This had been the most wonderful summer. He was comfortable and happy, and he knew he had found a second home. Paul had been right when he recommended the island as a place of renewal. Paul was right...funny how he had understood that.

Light through the leaves of the trees was glowing and fascinating. Today, he had been leaning against a tree trunk with a shaggy Henry lying by his side for hours, just looking at the shifting patches of light, dreaming, reading, sometimes dozing. He was thinking about how he often had the feeling people get out in the woods at times, a feeling that he was really not alone. He was aware of someone watching or some kind of presence at times. He remembered the face he once thought he saw when he first came to the island, a suggestion of a face, up in the trees. A friendly face.

Today, he stood up as the air finally began to chill, brushed himself off and gathered his things. Right then, he thought he heard something stirring just out of view through the trees at the edge of the orchard. Henry was growling low, and Daniel strained to look through the trees. Then he saw her. It was Sheila. He could see her picking her way carefully through the tall grass that grew between the trees. At first he thought she did not see him there as she was walking head down, stepping her way along in some kind of delicate shoes. But she walked right up to him, finally looking up into his face. "I don't want you to hate me," she said. "I don't expect love, but I can't stand hate."

She was wearing silly, little, glittery silver sandals, denim pants and a long girlish pink sweater, a frivolous get-up, but she looked up at him gravely, simply. She had a different look. She looked vulnerable.

Daniel was infuriated by her intrusion. He could not believe that she would just show up like this, without warning. What on earth could she want? At the same time, looking into her face he could not help feeling a small twinge of pity.

He shook his head. "Well, I'm not living in the gray zone any more. It's either love or hate," he said, flatly. "It's late, so I guess you plan to stay. Where is your car?"

She pointed silently back to the road beyond the orchard.

"Give me the keys," he said. He could not conceal his disgust.

"I'm here because I need to talk to you," she said quietly.

Daniel instantly brushed off her explanation. He would deal with that later.

"You stay in Glass House even though it is mine now, it was your and Paul's place first. I'm living down at the beach house. I'll call Luke to come up and see what you need. There is nothing much to eat in this house. He can bring you some dinner from the marina."

He was not going to engage with her in any talk today. She was uninvited. She would have to wait.

She nodded. Then he walked away through the orchard to retrieve her car. Sheila said nothing, but started for the house, head down again, stepping carefully.

Daniel sighed as he walked to her car. He wondered why she had approached the house this way, leaving her car on the main road and walking through the orchard like that? The beautiful late afternoon light was still filtering through the leaves, his favorite time of day in the orchard, but the day was over and ruined for him.

"It's just that she wants something," he thought. "She wants something, and she deserves nothing."

Daniel drove the car the rest of the way up to Glass House, got her bags and took them into the house. Sheila was nowhere to be seen. He called Luke and told him about Sheila's arrival. He laughed, then offered to help! He would bring some dinner and other food over for her soon. He would call her first. Luke was well aware of Daniel's problems with his mother. Daniel had told him recently about the final confrontation with her at the wine tasting event right before he came out to the island.

"Don't freak out," he said, and Daniel could tell he was smiling when he said it, even over the phone. He looked around for Sheila and found her sitting out on the terrace looking out at the sea. The sun was setting and the sea was calm.

"Your bags are in the bedroom," he said. "Luke is coming over...he'll call you first. I am going down to the beach house. I will see you in the morning."

She looked up with a frown. "What happened to the bar? Where are all the glasses?" She was looking at him hard, questioningly.

"They're gone," he said firmly. "I am making some changes. There are glasses in the kitchen and wine glasses in the dining room. Fresh sheets are in the hall closet."

She was searching his face earnestly, and this was something new.

"I'll see you tomorrow," he said and walked away to the beach house path, Henry right behind him."

Just beyond her view, he paused to look back at her.

"What a monumental effort it must have been for her to come out here!" he thought.

As he walked on briskly down the path he also thought, "I've moved on, I am moving on, and I am not going to stop. I'm certainly not stopping for Sheila."

The sun had gone down and it was twilight. Even so, he knew the path ahead well and went down safely to the beach house. Rather than go inside, he and Henry took a good long walk along the shore, wetting their feet in the dark tide. It was a fine, quiet evening when they came back into the beach house and lit the lamps.

## CHAPTER THIRTY-EIGHT

# Sheila's Confession

DANIEL woke up to a brilliantly sunny day. Light was coming in through the south-facing windows of the beach house with force. He opened the door and saw that a perfect summer day had dawned. Just a few white clouds in a periwinkle blue sky. A slight breeze lifted and the waters lapping in with the tide were mild, smelling of sea salt and summer, a day to spend outdoors. Henry looked at him expectantly, tongue hanging out of the side of his mouth. Would there be a swim? A walk? Then Daniel remembered with a groan that Sheila was up above at Glass House! He sighed, the beauty and promise of this morning... suddenly darkened. He walked out onto the beach and paced up and down near the water's edge for a while. Then he made a decision. He was right where he belonged, enjoying life. He would not allow her uninvited intrusion to alter his peace. He took a deep breath. With a grimace, he smiled a smile of irony and shrugged his shoulders.

Daniel looked down at Henry, he said, "Let's just go up and see what the hell she wants."

At the moment, he could not imagine. He certainly did not feel like leaving these present pleasures to worry about the intentions of her visit. He would just throw on his shorts, hoof it up the path and see what came next. He hiked up whistling, Henry at his heels.

Sea birds were diving. He could see Sheila and Luke throwing scraps of bread to the birds from the terrace. They were breakfasting on coffee and rolls that Luke had brought over for them. Luke came over and put an arm around Daniel.

"We have been reminiscing about the old days and the summer vacations. Good times past!" he said heartily, with a gentle pat to Daniel's back. "Would you like some coffee and a roll?"

"I'll just have coffee, black." Daniel said this looking at Sheila with undisguised displeasure.

Luke brought out another mug from the kitchen for Daniel.

Quickly he said, "Well, I need to get going."

Taking Sheila's hand, he said, "It's great to see you, Sheila. Call me if you need anything." He looked at Daniel, then ducked his head and quietly left. Mother and son sat sipping coffee in silence.

Looking hard at her across the terrace, Daniel finally said, "How long do you plan to stay, Mother?" He was immediately shocked at his own rudeness. He then hurriedly added, "Because I'm doing things here, and I really would prefer to be alone..." Not much better.

Her eyes got wide, both from his abruptness and from the surprise of his calling her "Mother..."

Then, some of the hostility that Daniel had hoped he had shed or at least banked down in past weeks came spilling out.

"Yes, you are my mother," he said with sarcasm. "Remember? I was born to you 30 years ago. I was a baby, then a little boy, now I am a man. You brought me into this world. Remember? I was not hatched under a rock! No more of this 'Sheila and Paul' crap. I will call you 'Mother'. You can call me 'Son', if you are able. We'll try for some normalcy in what is left of this family. Can you imagine such a thing? How long do you plan to stay, Mother?"

He had not seen Sheila smile since she arrived, but now she looked across at him smiling.

"I would like to spend the day. I'm leaving on the evening ferry," she said quietly. "I needed to see how you are and how you are living here. And, yes, I agree, I am your mother." She was silent a moment then said, "As your mother, I have some things to say. That's why I am here."

As they continued to drink coffee, Sheila turned to some small talk about the house, and the restaurant. Finally she asked, "How are you feeling now about Paul's death?"

Frowning, he shifted a bit in his seat and said, "It's been strange...but I'm all right." He was guarded, looking at her keenly.

Sheila quickly looked away, out to sea. She continued, "As I said, I came out here to tell you something."

With an effort, she looked back at him. She quickly began. "I came to tell you that Paul was not your father. He was my husband...but not your father." Her face was blandly arranged but her eyes were sharp with fear.

As Daniel heard this, he knew immediately that this was most certainly the truth. Inside he felt a shift and then there was a crack in that very heavy, hard, small stone which had dropped into his midsection the day Paul died. It was completely quiet on the terrace, even the sea birds had flown away. Sheila was sitting there passively, but she had looked away and did not meet his eyes as he stared at her.

"You said you didn't want me to hate you. With that in mind, I think you had better keep talking." His face was a white mask of terrible emotion.

Sheila had expected this. She was waiting for it. But, she was tough and she had come out here determined to complete a task. So, she began to unwind a long tale which she had wanted to tell for a long, long time. It was necessary to go way back in time.

She began to tell him about how she had come back to hometown Seattle after graduating from college, a fact which Daniel already knew. She had rented a little apartment in lower Queen Anne Hill, near where she had grown up. She had gotten a job working as an assistant for Paul Cross at his brokerage.

She told how she had been so pleased with herself, doing whatever she wanted to do, on her own. She also told how lost she had felt there in Seattle, how barren her life was in the small apartment. Not a single college friend had come to Seattle with her. It had been a very long time since she had lived there, so she really didn't have connections with old friends there anymore, no real social life at first. However, she was determined to make her life there, so she hung on. And that is where and when she had begun to live a life of all work. Ambition sparked and sustained her. Friendships came later, all from within the business community. Paul was steadily teaching her the maritime business. She hadn't known a thing about the shipping business, but she was sharp and ready to learn and advance. She and Paul were becoming fast friends, each one appreciating the other's ways and work ethic.

Right about then she had begun to see a young, rugged, interesting man working on the new telephone system installation in their office building every day. She had noticed him, and he noticed her. They exchanged a few words and looks there in the office. She also saw him daily on the park-like grounds of the building, eating his lunch under the shade of a tree. Sheila was not happy eating alone in a restaurant back then so she was also in the habit of taking her lunch. She sat on a nearby bench. After a while she and the telephone man started talking. Soon, they met every day at the lunch hour on the grounds. He was comfortable, appealing and very funny. They laughed and joked through the lunch hours. She invited him over for dinner at her apartment. He was amusing and attractive in an earthy, ruddy sort of way. He gave her a needed distraction from the tension of her new life of loneliness and work. They were miles apart socially. He was a blue collar "techie" guy. She was a college graduate from a wealthy family starting out in the business world. No problem, she did not fall in love with him, but they did become intimate and she was very happy with his attentions.

Sheila repeated that he was so comforting to her. Yes, he was comforting, funny, calm, and now she didn't feel alone. He made her happy in those insecure early days. They didn't meet much outside of her apartment so their affair was quite hidden. Of course, eventually, in a few weeks, he came to tell her that he had been re-assigned to other work, away from Seattle. She could tell he was sad.

They parted friends and she was sorry to see him go. He seemed very sorry also. He said he would be in Seattle from time to time, but she really did not expect much. He had called her a couple of times, just to touch base, but they had drifted easily apart, and it was not a relationship that was going to continue. She told Daniel that she had been fond of him, but her focus went on to other things, especially to the work that absorbed her so fully. She had not expected much from the Telephone Man, but she especially did not expect to find herself pregnant a few weeks later. When she was sure, she began to panic and did not know what to do. Having been raised formally as a Roman Catholic, she abhorred the idea of an abortion. There was no provision in her family makeup for such a situation as she found herself in. It never occurred to her to try to tell her mother or to find and tell the young Telephone Man. No, she would have to work it out some way herself. She went to confession. She prayed.

Then one day, she had blurted out her situation in Paul's office when they were working alone. Paul was a hard-built, tall, dry man and she was just a girl making her way in the world, but they had already become good friends. A great appreciation and respect was growing between them, a bond of wry humor, wit and the recognition of a common work ethic more than anything else. They seemed to understand each other, and though Paul was older, he did not treat her like a kid. They admired one another. Paul had been wide-eyed when she told him the whole story and she had not been able to avoid shedding tears. He had just looked down, patted her back gently and did not say much.

The very next day he had offered to help…"in any way he could." She, however, retained an independent attitude with him and a kind of bravado about the situation. Then, ten days later, Paul asked her to come out to dinner with him. She was surprised, but went. During dinner, Paul proposed to marry her...soon. She was stunned. And, though Sheila was frightened, it just seemed like things were falling into place, into an order that just seemed right. They had a small wedding there in Seattle at the beautiful little Church of San Sebastian, still her favorite. She wore a pale lemon-colored silk suit and carried a bouquet of daffodils. Her mother and other family members were surprised by the marriage, but had let her go with grace and did not probe too much. The whole thing was quiet and somewhat austere. It was the age when women were branching out boldly from tradition and leaving the protective arms of family, so her decision and behavior fit with the times.

The rest of the story of Paul and Sheila's beginnings Daniel knew from what they and Grandmother had always talked about. Sheila added that no one else knew about the Telephone Man, that Willie had never known, and that Paul and Sheila had carried on smoothly, as if nothing was out of the ordinary.

Daniel had arrived "early" of course and the family had raised eyebrows but simply assumed that this explained and was the cause of their rushed wedding. And thus, their "family" had been created. No other children were forthcoming, as neither of them was at all interested in building a house full of offspring. All this, Sheila delivered as a remote story from the past with no wrenching emotion in her voice. But as she wound down her tale, she suddenly burst into tears and covered her face with her hands.

From within this muffled position she said once again, "Paul Cross was not your natural father."

Daniel had no experience with Sheila, no connection which would help him to respond to this astounding story. No natural affection or even his past passionate disdain for her could bridge the distance across that terrace between mother and son that morning. She continued to sit miserably covering her face. Daniel was still sitting there, perched on the edge of the terrace wall, arms and legs crossed.

Finally, he said, "Thank you for telling me the truth. I appreciate it." Tears were welling up now, so he got up and walked to the terrace edge, turning his back on her. He stood there a long time. He felt as if his mind had been shattered. Neither of them spoke.

After a while, he turned, looking at her in incredulity. Incredible! He couldn't believe it. But he did believe it. He knew it was true. He came back and stood across from her. As she looked up at him, he looked down at her feet. As usual, she was wearing totally nonfunctional shoes, some kind of expensive Italian sandals.

"Don't you have any other shoes with you?" he asked. She said yes, that she had some tennis shoes in her bag. "Why don't you go in and get them on," he said. "We need to take a walk." Surprised, she got up and went into the house. "Bring your jacket too," Daniel yelled after her.

## CHAPTER THIRTY-NINE

## Deeper Confessions

WHEN she returned wearing her tennis shoes, they started down the beach path without a word. It was just a rutted dirt path and was narrow in spots. Sheila struggled to keep up behind Daniel, supporting herself at times by grabbing the scrub brush on either side of the path. Daniel did not stop or look back to help her but went straight on at a brisk pace. Henry raced ahead of them. Finally they reached the rocky and sandy beach.

"Let's go north a bit," said Daniel tersely. They passed the beach house, without stopping. They walked a long time in the fresh breeze, finally coming upon white-bleached drift wood and tree trunks strewn all over the pebbly beach, The Bone Yard. The bare wood was shining with intense glare on this bright day. Picking her way through branches, Sheila, who was still struggling to keep up the pace, commented on the wood." Oh, I forgot about all this washed up stuff," she said.

"Yes, I collect it all the time for firewood," replied Daniel. "Henry and I have big bon fires down here and cook. The wood burns hot."

They walked on, gradually slowing until they came to a place where big boulders blocked the way. At low tide you could walk around them, but not now. The sea had come right up among the rocks. Henry walked out a bit into the surf, then came back sniffing around among the rocks quietly. Stopping, Sheila sat down heavily on one of the smaller smooth rocks, away from the surf and spray. Daniel continued standing, tossing a handful of small pebbles that he had picked up out into the water one by one, from time to time. It was a sunny and warm protected spot. Words were not going to come easily to either Sheila or Daniel now. They were just looking out over the sea. Sheila was lost in thought, slumped on her rock seat.

After a while she stood up suddenly and began pacing and talking. "I came here because I have been having problems, waking up at night with my heart pounding, feeling guilty about you, Daniel," she began, swaying slightly on the pebbly shore. "I want to tell you some more about…things." She had been silently crying the whole time as they walked along. She dabbed her eyes. Softly she said, "I've had plenty of time to think."

Now the wind had come up. It lifted the sheer ends of the blue and green scarf she had wrapped around her throat. She began to tug at the fluttering scarf and finally pulled it off with an impatient gesture, tucking the ends into her pocket. She looked away from him then started speaking, words tumbling out rapidly. "I did not want to really consider you and bring you into my life."

"This is not news," Daniel interrupted. He was looking out to sea, not at her.

She continued, undaunted. "Since Paul's death, I have slowed down to think about these things. I came out here to see you because I know I have done wrong and I needed to at least make something right by telling you the truth. Since Paul died, I have problems thinking about you. You are now my only living relative."

At this Daniel snorted and shook his head. His arms were crossed and he was still looking out to sea.

"My mind keeps going back to the beginning. Biology is one thing. I had sex, I had a baby, but I really did not live into that pregnancy. And, there was no connection back to the one who fathered you. I didn't want any." She was intently watching Daniel's face.

"Paul gave me a way out when we married and I thought that just bringing you into the world and us providing well for you was enough...Paul wanted me back then. He wanted a companion in work and life, a partner. And I just wanted his protection, his guidance, and the opportunity to work. I just kept running headlong into that work...back then, before you were born. I just kept running even though I was 'great with child,' as they say. I just kept running straight on, never looking at myself in the mirror, not realizing or admitting that I was a mother."

Daniel turned to watch her face now.

She sighed. "I feel a great deal of guilt about Paul too. You think I was cold and didn't care about him, that after the divorce that I didn't care about him, that when he got sick I didn't care. I did care, but I could not seem to go back to trying to have a relationship. I couldn't go back! Now you can see that Paul helped me so much...in a way he formed me. And then..."

"And then you dumped him. First you used him, and then you dumped him." interrupted Daniel.

Sheila sank further into herself at that. For the moment, she could not meet his eyes. Then she stood, walking up close to Daniel looking him full in the face. "You are right. But, I believe there was more than that. Paul liked me, then he loved me. He loved me very much. I have only realized in recent years that he loved me. It was more than a marriage of like minds and convenience for him, more than a stimulating partnership. He loved me and I know that he kept on loving me, even after I was gone. I know that now. What I don't know is why."

She looked at him, her face desperately tense. "As for me, I liked him too, very much. I admired him. I was grateful to him, very grateful. I just could not love him the way he loved me."

She turned and looked back out at the sea. They stood there side by side for a while, both looking out over the water. Daniel kept pitching rocks.

"I just wanted to work," she continued stubbornly. "I loved work and my dream to create success." Her voice had begun to choke as she spoke, as though her throat was constricting. "And Paul just wanted me. He wanted me in his life."

She began to sob. "This is cruel, more cruel than anything else I have done, but I feel compelled to say it. Who wanted you, Daniel? Who wanted you?" With this she covered her mouth with her hand.

Daniel stepped back from her.

"I can't believe I have said those words. For Paul and me, I see that you were like a guest in our lives." With that her body sagged and she went and sat back down on the smooth boulder.

Daniel was not looking at her anymore. He just stood still there on the beach looking out to sea with his hands on his hips.

He nodded at this last word. "Yes, that is completely true!" he thought. He began to smile. "A guest!" He wanted to sing, to laugh. He knew right then and there that her estimation of him did not make any difference to him at all. Not a "tinker's damn." He was just a "guest." He had an over-whelming desire to laugh out loud, not a bitter laugh, but a joyful laugh! A laugh of freedom, just like a colt, let out of a corral into a huge meadow, kicking and snorting with pleasure.

Behind him, Sheila said, "I have come to tell the truth and say I am sorry. I don't know how I could have done better, being the person I am, but I am sorry. I am very sorry for what I didn't do. All my heart went into my ambition, and believe me," she said passionately, "I don't think I have changed. My ambition is still what drives me and where my heart lies, but I am sorry. I have done you wrong and I did wrong to Paul."

Now, she looked straight at him. "I did wrong to you, Daniel."

Then she straightened her back and stood up again, taking a deep breath. Daniel turned and saw her face smoothen out, harden and recompose into that person he always knew.

"OK...I have ruined your day," she said with an ironic laugh. "Now I need to get along back to the ferry. I will live with my actions and you can sort out this load of crap I have given you." She hastily rewrapped her scarf around her neck. He noticed that her hands were trembling.

Daniel was still silent.

Without a word they walked sullenly back down the beach toward the path up to Glass House. Henry followed slowly behind. As they reached the path, Daniel stopped, and turning spoke at last.

"I do get to say some things, too. Let's go into the beach house and I'll make some tea."

She was surprised and somewhat reluctantly walked with him to the little house.

Inside, he began at once to fiddle with his old metal tea kettle and the gas grill. As he worked, she looked around the tiny cabin and noticed all his things tacked up on the weathered walls. Things collected from the beach...worn, bleached wood, shells, some tumbled sea glass perched in the window sill, reflecting the light, his "faux Calder" mobile. There were his clothes, neatly folded in some orange crate shelves he had put together...and his army bunk with the red plaid blanket.

Then Sheila began to cry hard. Just tears coming down her face soundlessly. She wiped them away with the back of her hand, but more came. The way she saw what lay around her, it was the room of a boy, the loneliness and poverty of a lone boy. A hideout, such as boys construct wanting to get away and make their own boy's world.

Daniel had his back turned to her, but sensed she was crying. He kept stirring and working on the tea, head down. Then he turned and handed her a cup and took up his own cup, stirring in the sugar slowly.

"Sit down," he said, motioning to the neatly made up cot which served as his bed. She sat.

Daniel sat nearby on one of the old kitchen chairs. He looked at her, smiling a grimaced smile. Henry had come in and was shifting around by Daniel's feet. Now he lay down quietly, looking up at both of them.

Sheila was sitting primly on the edge of the bed, with damp eyes and Daniel was watching her. He could not help thinking, "Sheila and the phone man!" Now, he could not help smiling even though she was still wiping away tears. Sheila saw this, her eyes narrowing. Daniel was still absorbing all this new information about her past life and about PAUL! He suddenly felt so bad for Paul. Poor guy. Poor raw-boned, dry, stern Paul... not his dad. NOT HIS DAD!

"Look, I get why you have come out here now, and I know this has been really hard for you. Really hard. I don't know what I think yet. You've given me so much to think about. I wouldn't say that I am shocked about many things you have said. It was evident. But, I never suspected what you have told me about Paul. Now it makes perfect sense. 'The Artificial Family', that's what I would call it, and that is exactly how it felt to me growing up. Something staged, not real. It sure solves a lot of puzzles for me," he said, laughing ironically.

"The thing is, I guess I don't have to point out to you that you don't really know me. You don't know my life and you are pretty much lost in your own feelings, as you have always been. I've got to tell you again that I don't need you in my life. The time for that is long past. I guess I could sit here and work up hostility for you. I could despise you, but I just don't have the energy or inclination to do that anymore. I am most definitely moving on in my life. I can see the agony you've been in. However, let's get it straight that you really do not know me or my life, and you never have."

He took a sip of the strong tea and so did Sheila. Daniel got up and walked to the doorway looking out at the beach and sea. Because of Sheila's distress, he was trying to remain soberly respectful of the great turmoil his mother was obviously experiencing, coming here with this "bombshell," but suddenly, he actually felt like running out of the beach house door onto the beach and hooting and hollering with joy! Why all this was such a relief he did not yet know, but it was. It began to hit him as a tremendous relief!

Looking back at her from the doorway, he smiled, "I will tell you that I am coming to like my life. I am liking it more and more these days. I know what you failed to do, but it doesn't matter anymore." He took another sip of tea. He was calm. He realized that he felt absolutely great. "I'm trying to get really free and really comfortable in my life. Why don't you try doing that too?" He said this hopefully, generously.

With this, he saw her tears spill over and she began to sob. Daniel had brought his mother into his private beach shack world and this, along with his words, was having some kind of deeply emotional effect on her now. He moved over to the cot and sat down beside her, reluctantly, awkwardly putting an arm around her shoulder. This produced a further explosion of crying from Sheila and something like a keening, primitive wail. She leaned against Daniel and sobbed without restraint. He was shocked but just sat there patting her back softly.

It was strange to experience this reversal. Always in their relationship until now, he was the one with the seething, nearly out-of-control emotion when around her, and she was the remote, controlled, cool one. Now Daniel's feelings were subsiding into calm. He felt very little, while she spilled over in anguish.

There were no more words in the beach house that day and after a while Daniel gave Sheila another hot cup of tea which she took and drank. He suggested that they make their way back up the cliff to Glass House. Sheila was clearly exhausted.

Before they climbed up the path, Daniel shyly pointed to the jetty and the Time Out floating there. He told her that he had been restoring the sailboat and using it a lot while there. She just looked and nodded without comprehension. Then they ascended the winding narrow path.

She went directly to her room and after a bit Daniel heard the shower running.

He went out to the kitchen and made tuna sandwiches with some of the store-bought bread Luke had brought up for Sheila. He cut up some apples and carrots, added some pickles and brought it all out on the terrace with some fresh coffee. Sheila appeared, freshly dressed with damp curly hair. She was wearing her delicate shoes again. They ate in the peaceful stillness of the mid-day sun. The capricious, swirling wind had died down now. Daniel noted that he was not feeling the same old hatred toward Sheila. The seething feeling of resentment was gone. It had been neutralized by a sense of amazement and something new... curiosity about this strange woman sitting opposite him.

He did have one question though. He looked at her hard and searchingly.

"Are you sure Willie did not know about Paul, that he was not my father?"

She blinked, surprised. "Oh no, no one ever knew but Paul. I can't imagine that she ever suspected anything. It all went so smoothly. No one knew."

Daniel sat back, satisfied that Willie, his dear one, had not kept something so serious, so important from him. That would have been a bitter pill.

"No, no one knew," she repeated quietly.

After lunch, Daniel helped Sheila to get her luggage into the car. As he snapped the trunk shut, Sheila shyly came up to him and took his hand between her two smaller ones.

"Thank you," she said simply. "Thank you, Daniel for listening to me. Thank you for this time."

Daniel was utterly amazed by this affectionate gesture. He was used to hiding his thoughts from Sheila, but now, he knew he didn't need to hide. "Actually," he said "You have brought me tidings of great joy." He smiled down on her. "I can't tell why yet, but thank you for at last making some sense of things. I will have to rethink my relationship with Paul. He's gone, but I need to think again about how things were, now that you have told me this."

She got in the car and with a choking voice said, "See you soon." And then she drove away and was gone.

Now Daniel felt a rush of nervous energy. He ran back to the terrace, picked up the lunch dishes and threw them into the sink inside. He was wearing shorts, but grabbed a sweatshirt and his sun glasses. He and Henry raced back down the path to the beach. He got a bottle of water from the beach house cooler and launched the Time Out into the bay. Henry beat him into the boat, barking. Daniel raised the sail and headed straight out into Griffin Bay beyond the shore. The day was warm and cloudless now. Daniel set sail away from shore and then north, parallel to the shoreline. He passed the beach with the white bleached driftwood and continued beyond, finally turning out away from shore again where he dropped sail and waited in the midst of the channel, rowing to keep his position steady.

For some reason he wanted to watch Sheila's ferry leaving the island. In a little while he saw the big white ferry round the eastern edge of the island and head toward the mainland. He knew his mother was on that boat streaming towards the far-off shore. He watched it grow smaller and smaller, then finally disappear behind Lopez Island.

Then he set sail, caught the wind, turned his boat and sailed back toward the beach house shore. After a while, near home, he dropped sail and began to row. He wanted to take his time returning home. He felt such a surge of energy, he had to do something to expend it. It was pure relief that he was feeling. He was so glad to have a way of expressing his joy. Rowing was a perfect way, even more perfect today than skimming along under sail.

Henry was installed in the bow intently watching every bird and fish that flashed by, as usual. Looking over the side, Daniel also saw shoals of silvery fish swaying far below in the currents of dark water as he rowed smoothly over the surface of the sea. Then, far below, he saw a long pale form, dully gleaming. He could not tell what animal it might be, but it was traveling along in the same direction as the Time Out.

His mind was flashing through the past, but also taking in everything he was seeing and feeling in the present there on the water. What a day! Finally landing, they climbed out of the boat, walking over warm sand to the beach house. It was cool inside with all the high windows open. Daniel lay down on the cot and in a moment, he was asleep.

In the following days, Daniel resumed his "slow life" schedule, but with one change. In the orchard, at the beach, out on the sea, a thought would come to him which made him grin. "I am the off-spring, the child, of the lonely Sheila and the Telephone Man. Paul Cross was not my father."

And in these days, Daniel began to truly grieve for Paul...an authentic grief, a healthy grief, a grief detangled from mystery and misunderstanding. He grieved for a benefactor, a sponsor, a surrogate father, a departed, distant, but unmistakable friend.

## CHAPTER FORTY

# At San Sebastian

In Seattle, Sheila arrived at San Sebastian on a Saturday morning, a few minutes before 11 A.M. She breathed a sigh of relief when she saw that there were only a handful of people gathered there; they were also waiting to make confession.

She knelt in the pews but was too nervous to really pray. She just knelt there. In just a few minutes she saw a green light over one of the confessionals. She quickly went in. She knelt as usual in the tiny cubicle. It felt especially small today, especially tight. Even so, it smelled wonderful. It smelt of beeswax, books, leather. This was her church; she had been here many times. The grill cover slid aside. She could see the moving form of the priest behind it, a white and black vestment, but of course could not make out who it might be, not even the glint of an eye.

"Bless me father for I have sinned," she began. "It has been six months since my last confession."

"Confess your sins trusting in the mercy and grace of God." The voice was not familiar.

She began haltingly. "It has been shown to me...I have recently realized that... I have a long-time serious sin, Father. I have never confessed it before. In fact, I did not realize that I was sinning." Her throat was so constricted that only a thin sound came out. "I am overwhelmed with my guilt, Father." At this point tears came, hot and steady. There was a movement, as of stirring, behind the grill.

"Confess your sin, trusting in the mercy and grace of Almighty God." The voice was softer yet firmer this time.

"I realize that I have withheld love from someone." She stumbled on. "Actually, from two people. I think it has destroyed...things...many, many things. It is too late to make amends to one; he is dead. The other person is my own child. I have suddenly realized this. I ignored it for years. I thought it was nothing. Now it has crashed down on me. I am sorry. Very sorry."

She rushed on, her voice rising to a high whine, "What can I do, what must I do?" She wanted to continue, to pour out details. The priest's voice stopped her.

"The failure to love and the withholding of love is serious sin. You have made your faithful confession, daughter. The blood of our Savior, Jesus Christ, covers your sin. In its power, it covers all sin. Our omissions and our acts of sin are beyond our power to correct. Turn to your Lord and accept his forgiveness. Allow Him to repair, to redeem. Find the contrition card there on the shelf and read it through."

She fumbled around and found the card. She wiped her eyes, sighed and read silently. She had perfunctorily read it many times before. Now, she read it carefully. Her heart was sinking and her voice was thick as she read out loud:

"My God, I am sorry for my sins with all my heart.

In choosing to do wrong and failing to do good, I have sinned against You whom I should love above all things.

I firmly intend, with Your help, to do penance, to sin no more, And to avoid whatever leads me to sin.

Our Savior Jesus Christ, suffered and died for us.

In His name, my God, have mercy."

There was a time of silence then the voice came low and steady.

"Daughter, here is a worthy penance, for the good of your soul. Go and read the First Letter of John in the New Testament. It is near the back. Meditate upon it. Chapter four, beginning at verse seven to the end of the chapter, especially. You have made your faithful confession. Now, place your whole faith in God. Go and sin no more."

In a louder, firmer voice came this prayer, which seemed to go upward.

"God, the Father of mercies, through the death and resurrection of your son, you have reconciled the world to yourself and sent the Holy Spirit among us for the forgiveness of sins. Through the ministry of the church, may God grant you pardon and peace. And I absolve you of your sins, in the name of the Father, and of the Son and of the Holy Spirit. Amen."

She was looking and could see the movement of a hand making the sign of the cross towards her.

"If you wish to discuss steps for your life, counseling is always available. You may make an appointment in the church office. May the blessing of God rest and remain upon you, daughter."

"Now...Go in peace to love and serve the Lord." There was tenderness in the voice. "The confessional has ended...the reconciliation is complete."

The grill slowly closed.

She went out shaken and sat down again a pew. She scribbled down the verses of the Penance reading. She felt numb. She felt exhausted, twisted. Something in her was leaping up, wanting to keep going, to do something, to work, to continue the "fixing..." Finally, peacefully, she just kept sitting and finally, resting. There was no fixing, no going back. No need to. This must be turned over completely. She would choose to accept this forgiveness. Tears flowed again, softly and peacefully this time. She let them fall.

She was thinking, starting to think about how she was doing things, how she was living... pushing, racing, trying. "I guess I will lay that down too," she said out loud.

The flickering candles were mesmerizing. They were soothing. They were silent. Finally, after she knew not how long, she got up and walked out of the darkened church into the sunlit day.

# PART III

# *Sailing Home*

## CHAPTER FORTY-ONE

# Blackberries

BLACKBERRIES grew all over the island. In fact, locals could find them to be a great nuisance with their thorny brambles encroaching over every other growing thing. Some berries began to ripen in late July, but August was the month when the full bonanza came in. The berries were huge, plump and sweet. No farm-grown berry could compare with their wild, extravagant taste.

Daniel was out in his berry patch in the forest just west of the Glass House orchard. This place was completely overgrown with blackberry brambles. He had decided to venture in and get as much of the ripe berry crop as he possibly could for himself and his friends. He planned to send a box back to the mainland to The Prow. Daniel thought these were just about the best berries he had tasted on the island, maybe because the plants had been undisturbed for years and were strong and thick, or maybe it was just so great to walk out the back door of Glass House and pick as many as he liked. Maybe that made them sweeter to him.

He had dressed for battle before wading into the patch. The thorns were wicked and hidden by leaves. He wore a canvas coat he had found in Paul's closet, his rubbery fishing pants and heavy leather gloves. He was wearing a hat tied on with a bandana, so he could get down low under the brambles where the best and juiciest berries hid. He swathed his neck with a bandana too. He was picking by himself. He wanted to surprise everyone with a few buckets of fresh berries.

As he picked he was thinking of many things. Of course, he was still processing the surprise visit from Sheila and her shattering story. Sometimes he thought this new knowledge about their family was the most bizarre thing that he could ever imagine.

He knew he needed to tell someone, but he was not ready yet. He wanted to call Trini and Oscar and tell them first, and he really needed to know if Otis had been told about this by Paul. All in good time, he had to work this through by himself first. Sometimes it made him extraordinarily sad, thinking about it, sadder than he could even grasp, especially at night when he was in bed down at the beach house. But sometimes, thinking about it, he actually laughed out loud and couldn't stop laughing, just as he had felt like doing that day on the beach...in profound relief that things in life could actually make sense.

Today he slowly picked and thought, going back over memories of key times, especially the times when he was a teenager. He was trying to factor this new truth into the old situations here at Glass House with Paul. How strained and awkward that had been. Why couldn't Paul have broken down and told him he was not his father, now that he and Sheila were divorced? It would have been better than that strange, pretend life! still, he could see what a betrayal that would have been to Sheila. Disclosing this was really up to her. He could see that. He was profoundly thankful that she had finally told him the truth.

He still had so many questions. Was Paul always sorry he had taken on the burden of someone else's son? Did he want to be closer to Daniel, but feel restrained by Sheila? She was the one who was always downplaying the importance of normal family life. It was really Sheila who had shuffled him off to boarding school. Did Paul just do the fatherhood thing without a thought, only going through the motions? Would he have been a different kind of father if he had had his own biological son? Daniel would never know the answers to these things now. He thought back to the dramatic dreams he'd had about Paul since he died. How different Paul was in the dreams. Was that the true reality? The only thing he could feel confident about was that Paul had stepped up and taken responsibility for him back in the beginning. And he had showed himself responsible and caring at the end. His words of love on that last day in the hospital haunted Daniel and at the same time gave him joy. He had to believe those words. Paul was an honest man. Why would he lie as he was dying?

All the buckets he had brought out were now full. Daniel sat down in an open spot and indulged himself in just eating as many blackberries as he wanted, right out of the bucket. What could be better on a summer's day, even if he was sweltering under his heavy garb?

Over the next few days Daniel came and picked every blackberry he could get his hands on. The deeper he went into the brambles the bigger the berries got. After picking, he took the buckets home and washed the berries carefully. Then he stored them in the big Glass House refrigerator in bowls, boxes, sacks, whatever he could find to use.

His solitary thoughts during these days also went back to the recent sailing trips. The Magellan... but much more to the Juan de Fuca trip. He had grown personally on that trip, more than he ever had expected to do in just a few days. He was seeing things differently and his gratitude to his friends was intense. Some of his fears had been put in their place. Some things that he thought were true, he now knew were false, especially about himself. Some things he had hoped for were realized. He had hoped that he was a good friend. He had always tried to be. Now he thought he had proved it, in love and loyalty. Love...this was a new context for the word. Friendship love. These new friends were beyond casual friendship. They had helped him in every way they could. They were for him and they brought out the best in him. They were friends of the "lifelong" variety. It was funny how when friendship blossomed and became real, when he was one of them, he found that the attraction factor diminished. These guys would be the first recipients of his cache of berries. It was something they could get for themselves any time, any day. But these were his own special "Glass House" blackberries. Carefully hand-picked, very special.

He would take some berries to the marina to the guys, then a box to Friday Harbor to be shipped to The Prow. And, he thought he would take some over to Nan and Ruth too. They might grow their own, but it was nice to have somebody do the picking for you! He would take care of all that tomorrow.

Tonight, he would work on a recipe for a Blackberry Trifle. He liked to make it with lemon-flavored pound cake, lemon curd and a drop or two of the limoncello which he had brought over from The Prow. The drink was made fresh every few months in their kitchen from lemon zests, sugar and alcohol. Daniel had put a small bottle of the liqueur in with his supplies as he was leaving The Prow.

Up high in the dining room cabinet, Daniel found a large glass footed bowl. Perfect for a trifle. And, there was another tall square glass dish too. He made a light lemon cake and just enough lemon curd to soak the cake nicely. It was all easy to put together. He made two beautiful trifles...they were picture perfect. He stored them both away in the refrigerator. Then he put a number of plastic cartons of fresh berries together in an old Styrofoam lightweight cooler. These were the ones to be shipped to The Prow. They had already received his care package of ripe cherries from the orchard at the end of June. There were raves of compliments from that shipment. This blackberry bonanza package would blow them away too. He would send his trifle recipe also. Nothing was more fun and invigorating for Daniel than a small scale attempt to feed the world.

At last he and Henry went down to their much more frugal dinner at the beach house. Even though it was August, Daniel felt like making a fire in the fireplace. He was still revved up from his picking and cooking. What could be better for a chef than to take the food out of the field, so to speak, and bring it through every stage until a very special dish was finished off beautifully? He needed to celebrate! So... after dinner he turned on the radio, not to his usual soft classics but to a fifties rock and roll station. He started singing along, loudly, and scooting around the beach house floor in his socks to Buddy Holly and company causing Henry to run around howling.

Before going to bed he put a big handful of the ripe berries on a plate and placed them outside the door by his "refrigerator."

"This is for you, Potter!" he yelled out and went inside. The end of a perfect day.

In the morning, all berries were gone, and the plate was a little smeary with blackberry juice. Daniel looked up and down the beach but saw no one.

It was time to load up the berries, so he went up to Glass House and put the berries and the cold trifle into the car for those down at the marina. He went straight to Peggy and Pete's condo. He knew Peggy had a nice roomy refrigerator, but Luke did not. She could better store the trifle there in her kitchen. The berries needed the refrigerator too. They could do with them as they willed. Probably just eat them fresh.

Peggy was happily surprised, but not shocked at this gift. She knew how Daniel operated, how he loved to concoct special food. And, she was thrilled with the beauty of the luscious layered trifle and all its colors. It was cool to the touch and she knew that it would very soon come out of the refrigerator and be devoured. Daniel was an A-number one cook in her eyes since the beignets. He told her all about his berry picking, and that the trifle was a gift of appreciation to Pete and Luke as well as her.

He excused himself quickly because he wanted to get into town to send off the other cartons of berries and to deliver the other trifle along the way to Ruth and Nan. He decided to call ahead to make sure they were home. He called from Glass House and sure enough, Nan answered the phone. He told her he had something for her, not cherry, something else. She laughed and said she was dying to know, to come on over. Come now, because they were going to a garden show in a little while. Come over now!

On the way he started to get nervous. How could he think that giving these gardeners some blackberries, the most common fruit around the island right now, would be something they would want? It was like "Coals to Newcastle." They were probably trying to get rid of their own blackberries. He blushed thinking about it as he drove, but went on anyway.

Both Nan and Ruth came out to the drive when he pulled in. They were curious. Daniel brought out his trifle first. It was the one in the square bowl. He shyly offered it to them. Both Nan and Ruth gasped. It really was beautiful. Ruth took it and they were turning it around looking at it. While they did that, Daniel reached back in the car and brought out his bags of berries. They smiled at that too.

"We never get blackberries anymore. We've pulled them all out to make way for flowers. They take over so," said Nan. "Believe it or not we have to buy them at the farmer's market!" There are none right around here because all the farmers have dug them out. We usually have to go over around Trout Lake to pick, and it's a prickly job. What is this thing in the glass bowl?"

"I guess you've never had an English trifle? It is a summer weather treat. You've never had one?"

They looked at each other and laughed. "We're just plain old farm girls," said Ruth. "Our cooking runs more to chocolate chip cookies. Nan can bake a good chocolate cake."

"Well, here is your first trifle then. It has to be kept in the refrigerator," Daniel smiled, so relieved. "It's full of whipped cream."

"Refrigerator heck!" said Ruth. "Let's eat it!"

## CHAPTER FORTY-TWO

# At The Garden Club

OF course they did sit right down and eat some of the trifle. Daniel showed them how to serve it, digging straight down through all the layers to get a bit of everything, berries, cake and cream all in one serving. It was a rich mess and they loved it.

"What is the lemony taste?" Nan asked. Daniel told them about the limocello and how they made it back at The Prow. "And, the cake layer is a lemon pound cake too."

Ruth was looking at him now, "How'd you learn to do all this? I know you have a restaurant, but do you do the cooking?"

"I do, sometimes." He hesitantly began to explain his chef's life.

"I've always wanted to cook and serve food. My grandmother sent me to culinary schools. And, I worked in restaurants and traveled in Europe taking classes over there in cooking. My grandmother backed me to start a restaurant in Seattle. It's called The Prow."

Both Ruth and Nan were listening and watching him with interest.

"Just like you love flowers and growing things, I love feeding people." He smiled.

"So eat up!"

They obeyed. As Nan was rinsing the dishes after their feast, she invited Daniel to come with them to town to see the Flower Show at the Garden Club. That's where they were headed when he called.

"Yes, why don't you come?" Ruth added. "We always go to this show. You can pick up some great tips and it is just fun to see all the creations people come up with. I can use all the help I can get in my business," she laughed.

"I'm interested in flowers too. As a matter of fact I do flowers for the restaurant. Visiting the florist every day for fresh flowers is one of the pleasures of my life," Daniel smiled. "Sure, I'll come with you. But, I have to take my own car. I've got another load of blackberries in the car to ship to the mainland on the ferry. They're for my restaurant."

They told him where the flower show was being held and then he went on ahead to get his berries onto the next ferry. As he drove he was thinking about how much better Ruth seemed today. She was bright and healthy-looking. The cloud had moved off from her.

"I guess time heals all wounds," he thought. "That goes for all of us. She is young. She wants to live...that's obvious. It looks like she is getting well."

He was thinking of Nan too. What an interesting woman! He wanted to get to know her. He decided he would visit her at her little house again, soon. She had invited him earlier and he thought she meant it, not just a formal courtesy.

He disposed of the berries at the dock, sending them on their way to Trini and Oscar. They were going to love this package!

Then he drove on to the site of the flower show. It was being held this year in one of the historic homes there in town. He found it quickly. It was a classically Victorian house, white, with all the gingerbread ornamentation of that time. Steep wooden stairs led to the door. He bought his ticket from the garden club ladies and was welcomed in. He was not dressed for the event, having run out in a T-shirt and shorts. No one seemed to mind. Lots of tourists visited the event, and he blended right in. There were some Garden Club ladies acting as hostesses, dressed up in Victorian costumes, hair up in pompadour style. They were directing the visitors and explaining the flower names.

He found Nan and Ruth and tagged along with them. They were whispering comments about the various arrangements. Some were outlandish and tortured into artificial forms. Daniel could tell Ruth didn't like them. Finally, they came to an arrangement of peonies with other spring flowers. It was natural, full and extravagantly beautiful. Ruth was mesmerized. Cameras were not allowed in the event, but Daniel could see that Ruth was trying to memorize this combination of flowers and their placement. This was her passion... her face was glowing. He fully understood how she was feeling. He felt the same.

They went through the entire house including the upstairs suites. One room was devoted to minimalist oriental arrangements, many were lovely. Daniel was thinking that they would have shown better in a simpler environment, away from the Victorian setting.

"These would be so much more meaningful in a simple room with a one color background, maybe a dark painted wall," Ruth commented just then. Daniel smiled.

Nan agreed. "They would look nice on a table in the garden too. I wonder if there are arrangements outside?"

They went out to the house's garden. There were at least a dozen more florals out on the terrace, each one occupying its own table. The contestants had brought their own small round tables and covered them with cloths to complement their arrangements. The charm of this display was wonderful against the green of the outdoor setting. Ruth and Nan were exclaiming. This was right up Ruth's alley, natural... in a natural setting. One display in particular caught her interest. The contestant had created a basket of vines which were still green, as if just plucked.

The flowers were all in tones of blue, Ruth's favorite. Bachelor buttons, delphinium, columbine, blue lavender of course, pincushion flower, all nestled in amongst the green twisting vines. There was only a hint of white, possibly candytuft, among the green and blue for contrast. Ruth was walking round and round it, delighted.

"I'm going to make something like this the first chance I get," she said. "We have plenty of grapevines out along the road. You've got to get fresh green ones for this. I need to plant some pincushions this year." She was sort of chatting with herself, moving around the small table. "I hope this one wins," she smiled.

She was wearing a kind of a long gypsy skirt, of a very filmy print fabric in cinnamon tones. Her blouse was just a plain cream-colored silk shirt, untucked, falling casually from her shoulders. On her feet were those ballet flats with a little cord bow, her favorite ones, in a nude tone. Her hair was twisted up into a bun. It was so curly and wiry that no part of it was smooth. It was just a cloud of curly cinnamon matching her skirt. She wore no jewelry at all. Daniel was watching her. All he could think of was that she needed to be shielded, protected, so she would not be hurt anymore, so she could be herself and make the flower creations that were already dancing around in her head. He had the thought that he would like to stand between her and whatever might try to hinder her.

They went back inside and found Nan sitting in a folding chair drinking a lemonade which the ladies had provided. They had all seen enough.

As they walked to their cars, Daniel thanked them for inviting him to the show.

Ruth murmured thanks for the trifle. Nan looked up at him and clasped both of his hands.

"Come over for coffee tomorrow morning why don't you," she said. "Let's visit."

"I will," he agreed and then drove off for Glass House.

He was pleased. Pleased with his trifles, pleased with his berry-picking, and pleased to be adding a few more friends on the island.

That afternoon down on the beach, he and Henry pushed off from the cove in the Time Out. It was good to be back on the water on this very warm summer day. They drifted along with the northern prevailing wind, only slightly breezy today. They lazily sailed up the coast a ways and then turned back, tacking easily into the wind. Daniel relished the sound of the mainsail snapping to, at the turns. Such a satisfying feeling. The waters beneath them were emerald today with many schools of darting white and silver fish down in the bay below. He saw six dolphins together, jumping out in the middle of the channel, blowing spray and leaping. He decided to continue on past his beach to the marina. He thought he would see how the guys liked the trifle. Maybe by now they had come in and had a taste of it. It was late afternoon.

He docked the Time Out and shouted for Luke. The House Boat was lit up already. Luke, Pete and Peggy came out. They had been in the salon, assessing the remodel job for the future married couple. Everyone was talking at once, excited, with many ideas. Luke and Pete would do the work. It was mainly updating the head and galley with some new appliances, repainting some of the darker areas. The old carpet in the salon would have to go.

"Anna is going to want to pick her own colors for all this," said Peg, arms crossed over her chest.

The men groaned. "There aren't that many choices," Luke said. "It's like stainless steel or white in the appliances."

"Even so, Anna should decide." Peg was still prim and purse-lipped.

"You're right. I'll get her out here to decide colors first." Luke grinned.

"Please leave me out of this." Pete was walking away. "Hey, that was a magnificent dessert! Let's go eat some more of it." He pointed at Daniel and off they all went to Pete's place. George loped along too. He knew the word "eat"...they must be talking about food.

The humans had trifle and iced tea sitting on the dockside. "Thanks, Daniel. We love blackberries. These are from up at your place?" Pete said. Peggy was trying not to lick the spoon, but couldn't help it. Daniel cautioned her not to give any trifle to Henry and George."It makes Henry throw up!" he warned. "George better not eat it either. It is too rich for dogs.

Yeah, I do have a big patch, I've spent several days picking. Stripped the whole place and sent some this morning off to the restaurant. I went to the flower show today with Nan and Ruth in town also. It was very well done, I thought. It's been a great day." He braced himself to change the subject.

"Hey, there's something I want to tell you guys. Something has happened and I've been thinking a lot about it. I'd like to tell you." They looked up at him with interest.

"I guess you all know that my Mother was here last week. Luke knows, anyway.

She came over to tell me something. Something important. Do you want to hear this?"

"Of course," said Luke.

"Tell us," said Peggy, "We're your friends."

Pete was nodding.

Daniel took a deep breath, "Well, she came to tell me that Paul Cross was not my Dad." There was silence. He looked up wincing.

"She came to tell me a long story about me and her, and Paul." At that point Daniel launched into an abbreviated account of what Sheila had told him and the painful visit that had ensued between them. "Since Paul died she has been really tortured about this 'family secret' and she came out here to tell me."

When he was finished with the telling, all was silent for a moment, then Pete exclaimed, "Well I'll be damned!" He took off his baseball cap and rubbed his bald head. "I'll be damned…"

Luke and Peggy were still silent, listening and thinking.

"You are the only people I have told about this," said Daniel. "I needed to tell somebody. Crazy huh? Crazy thing to find out at this point in my life."

"Do you think my Dad knew about this?" Luke asked. "Did Otis know this?"

"I never thought about that," said Daniel, surprised. "I don't know. Sheila, my mother, told me my grandmother and the rest of the family never knew. I never thought about Paul confiding in Otis. Maybe...I guess I'll ask him. Did you know, Luke?" He looked at Luke hard.

"No, no, never. I never heard this until just now." He motioned "no" with his hands.

"So how does this make you feel?" Peggy said, looking at Daniel solemnly.

"I don't know yet. It may sound weird, but at first I felt very relieved. I felt like laughing. It took a big load off of me some way. It made sense. It answered some questions. But...I don't know how I feel yet. It was just last week when she came over."

"Wow," said Luke in a low voice. "I don't know what to think about this. I knew Paul...I knew him pretty well over the years." He was shaking his head. "All I can say is that Paul was a good man, and it would be like him to step up and do something like that. He adopted you from before you were born. Wow. So... where is your natural father? Does Sheila know? What was his name? Does anybody know where he is now?"

"I haven't had a chance to think about that yet. Sheila, my mother, didn't tell me his name. I haven't been thinking about that. I'm still stuck on Paul and all of that. I have been having dreams about Paul out here on the island, before Sheila came out. You know our relationship was odd. I see him very differently in the dreams. Things are beginning to make sense."

Peggy got up and came over and hugged Daniel hard. "I love you, Daniel," she said. "I love you a lot. You're our friend and you can be my son if you want to be."

Pete put a hand out onto Daniel's shoulder. "Yeah, you make a good son," he said.

"Thank you guys!" Daniel was nodding and smiling. "Best friends is probably good enough at this point of my life. It is good to have such friends! And thanks for listening to all this. Crazy, Isn't it?"

Daniel stood up and prepared to go. "I think I am going to leave the Time Out here tonight. It's getting dark. I'll walk down in the morning and get it. Thanks for everything, guys."

"Wait a minute, I feel like stretching my legs too, gotta burn off some trifle. We'll walk half way with you," said Pete.

"We'll all go," Luke said, standing. They trudged up the hill together and onto the sage covered meadow. They were single file with Henry and George out front, and Daniel in the middle, going along the path, not really talking. At the mid-point they stopped and were looking around at the enormous view, nearly 360 degrees of sea and distant island.

"What a wonderful place this is," said Daniel, hands on his hips. "A life-changing summer. You guys go on home now, I'm fine," he said smiling, waving them off. They embraced and the friends reluctantly turned back. Daniel walked on with Henry at his heels.

At Glass House Daniel searched around, looking for his big flashlight lantern to use going down the path to the beach house. It was completely dark now, and there was only a sliver of moon.

He realized he had left the lantern below at the beach. Irritated, he had to decide whether to make his way down the path in the pitch dark or stay up in the big house over night. He wondered if there might be another flashlight in the garage? Rummaging around in there produced nothing. He checked the car's glove compartment. With a sigh of relief he found a small flashlight, it was back behind a bunch of car manuals and things. One of the books was small, thick and leather bound with a flap and snap closure. Looking closely he saw that it was a Bible, one of those small travel copies. He opened it and found an inscription in the first pages. It was Paul's Bible.

"To Paul Cross on the day of his Baptism. With Love, Otis and Marion, with all the saints at Coastal Community Church."

Under the dedication there was a numerical verse reference. It was Jeremiah 31, verse 3. Daniel took the flashlight and the Bible into the house. Fumbling around he finally found Jeremiah, chapter 31, then the verse:

*"The Lord appeared to him from afar, saying, "I have loved you with an everlasting love; Therefore I have drawn you with loving kindness."*

He turned off lights, closed up the house and made his way down the dark path with the flashlight and Paul's Bible tucked under his arm.

## CHAPTER FORTY-THREE

# Nan

NAN had been baking early that morning. She wanted to have something to go with coffee for Daniel when he arrived. So, she made a batch of chocolate chip cookies. Just as Ruth had said the day before, this was their kind of baking. The little house was filled with their chocolate-sugar smell. She brewed the coffee and then sat down waiting on her flowered settee...waiting and thinking. There was something about Daniel, something complex. Some kind of puzzle. It was good that he was coming over this morning for coffee and a visit.

She was looking out the window across the garden to the big house. The big old house really belonged to Nan. Ruth had been living there since she returned home last fall, after Kevin died. Nan had decided then to turn the big house over to her completely and move into the cottage, giving the whole house over to Ruth's floral business. Actually, except for her brief marriage, Ruth had always lived there with Nan, at least as long as Ruth could remember. When Ruth's parents broke up, they just left her there with Nan. It was the best thing that could ever have happened for both Ruth and Nan. Nan had loved raising the darling little red-haired girl and had given her all for her, bringing her up to be healthy and strong. Healthy, strong... and clever she was. Now, the space of the big house was perfect for all the creative things Ruth made in her flower world. For that she did need a lot of space.

As for Nan, she was thrilled to be in her little house. It was all she wanted, all she needed now. She had fixed it up with everything she loved. Everything that brought her joy she had brought here out of the big house and re-installed in her cottage. Yet there she was, really still right in the same place, right in the middle of the flower fields where she had worked and spent nearly her whole life.

She loved watching her granddaughter work and live across the garden. She knew how grieved she had been. They always shared the evening meal together, and Ruth shopped for Nan and looked out for her now. The only dark spot in their lives had been Kevin, that wild, handsome, destructive man who had swept Ruth up and away. Nan had never understood what Kevin wanted with Ruth, but she guessed that Ruth's freshness and natural ways were a balm to Kevin, some kind of anchor for him. In just two years he was dead and Ruth came home from their little apartment down at the harbor, torn up and grieving. When she came home she changed her name back to Sloan. It appeared that the flower farm was where she wanted to be, to settle down and stay. Nan prayed every day that she would soon be healed and restored to her joy in life and in work. Thankfully, just since summer began Nan could see that this was happening for Ruth.

Right now, though, Nan was thinking of Daniel. Her radar was up about him. Since the day he showed up in the garden with his cherry pie, she had been thinking about him. She had it in her mind that she might be able to help him somehow. There was an openness, a "searching" in him. He had recently lost his father, she knew that. She remembered Paul Cross from his years of visiting the island. They had met a few times, a man of military bearing. She knew that Otis down at the marina deeply respected him. A very quiet man, very reserved. Now...gone. She could not seem to remember the rest of the family... the mother. They had probably never met.

As for Daniel, he had an angelic look about him. He was boyish, yet he was a poised man. A man...with a beautiful face and form...and fine coloring. Her feeling for him was not quite protective, or even grandmotherly. She sensed that she was something more like a "watcher." "Even an angel needs an angel," she thought.

He pulled up into the Sloan driveway about 9:30 that morning. He could see Ruth in the greenhouse. Her red hair was a marker no one could miss. She came to the greenhouse door and leaned out smiling, wearing bright blue rubber gloves.

"Good morning! Nan's got coffee on...and cookies too. I can smell it. Come back around when your visit is over. I'll show you the greenhouse." She waved and ducked back into the greenhouse.

Daniel could see she was very chipper this morning. She was in her element. He just waved and smiled back, then went on to the little cottage. Nan had seen him drive up and was standing at the open door.

"Welcome," she smiled. She wore jeans and a kind of peasant blouse, in a dusty rose color, embroidered profusely. She was wearing green malachite jewelry and leather sandals. The whole thing gave her an "ethnic" look today.

Daniel stood in the doorway looking around again in wonder as she ushered him in. "This is the very smallest house I have ever been in. I hope it doesn't offend you, me saying that!"

"Of course not," Nan was laughing. "This house is intended to surprise and hopefully, delight. There's a movement afoot to find and live in tiny spaces. I'm avant guard!"

"I'm sure you are! It's a mixture of avant guard and Little Red Riding Hood's grandma's place!"

"That little grandma was sickly and in bed. I'm fit as a fiddle!" she declared. "Why don't you just sit back in my wingback chair and I'll get the coffee?"

Daniel settled into the high-backed chair on the "parlor" side of the tiny room. The chair was covered in a brilliant yellow canvas duck, cheery and comfortable. He noticed immediately that the sheaves of paper he had seen scattered about on his last visit were gathered and stacked high on another chair nearby. Books were tossed and stacked there too. The round low table was cleared and wiped to a shine, ready for the coffee service which was being set up.

Nan brought in her coffee service on a dark wooden tray. The big china coffee pot looked like an old Bavarian pattern he knew. The Sugar and Creamer were probably Wedgewood, cream-colored, ribbed and over-sized... so accommodating for coffee and a nice long visit. So, they sat and sipped. There was a huge stack of cookies on a matching Wedgwood platter.

"Very nice of you to have me over again. I confess, I am envious of your place here. Your stove reminds me of something, of a memory, but I can't quite remember where it fits into the past. I love that design with the high side oven."

"We've always had it. It came with the big house. We bought a new electric range back in the 60's so this stove went into the storage shed, which actually was this building where we sit. So it has been here a long time. I cleaned it up and it works just fine," she smiled back.

"I'm cooking on a two-burner Coleman down at the beach, and in the fire pit sometimes," he laughed. They began to talk about Daniel's place and his summer visit so far. He told her about the Time Out and its restoration, about sailing and about the trip across the strait with Luke and Pete. Nan's eyes were big at the story of the storm on the return trip.

"I've lived here most of my life and have never been across to Cape Flattery," she said wistfully. "It sounds so beautiful, so wild!" Both she and Daniel were now on their second cookie. She poured more coffee for them both. Their cups and saucers were Wedgwood, "Flying Cloud" in a rust tone. This pattern had a multi-masted Tall Ship schooner as its central design.

"Your china makes me think of my restaurant on the mainland. It's called The Prow. Our dishware has a ship design too, in black."

He began to describe the restaurant to her, telling her about its conception and his grandmother's part in it, the décor and the menus, Trini and Oscar, the wonderful kitchen and their specialty, Prow Chow. She was a good listener, sitting poised with her eyes searching his face the whole time. Just talking about The Prow made him feel homesick for the place immediately. He knew the time to go back and pick up his life there was coming soon. He was ready and he told her so.

"I just want to tell you how welcomed and happy I have been out here this summer, how wonderful it has been to take this time since my father's death and be picked up and helped here by people, people who are now good friends to me."

"That is a great testimony to the island's hospitality, Daniel. I am proud to hear it. I'm so glad that you have found comfort here after the loss of your father." Her voice was gentle as she said this.

"Yeah, a lot has happened out here...things about my father." He paused. He wasn't quite sure what to say to her, but he felt he wanted to tell her about things going on in his life. He had an idea that she cared, just as his other friends had cared. On the other hand, he hardly knew her. They were brand new acquaintances. Something told him to just keep talking, to trust.

"Actually, I have lost my father twice. Once at his death and again since I have been out here this summer."

Nan's face registered a trace of understanding. She nodded.

"My mother, Sheila Cross, I don't know if you ever met her?"

"No, I don't remember your mother at all. Somehow, we never met."

"She was never as keen on vacationing here as Paul was. And then they were divorced. My mother visited me a little over a week ago. She just showed up in my orchard one day. I wasn't expecting her. The truth is we don't get along. I was not happy to see her." He waited to let this sink in with Nan. She was still listening, nodding.

"My mother came out here very anguished. She came to tell me something that was a complete surprise to me, something that was weighing on her. She came to tell me that Paul Cross was not my father." As he said all this, he felt his mouth and throat become dry and tight. He stopped and took a drink of coffee. Nan poured more into his cup without a word. She was still listening, her face looked kind, and soft, not shocked. He sighed.

Then he launched into the story of his mother and Paul, of their "arranged" family and his birth, and of another man with whom his mother had had a quiet and brief affair. He didn't say too much about the lack of affection or connection in this family, somehow he saw that she knew. He did tell her about the two dreams he had dreamed since being on the island, dreams of a different kind of Paul.

"I guess I was shown the 'island' Paul," he said. "Somebody I never knew in this life."

Nan was slowly shaking her head. "What a devastating thing, Daniel, to hear this brutal piece of news! I have to tell you that I have felt that there was a puzzle of some kind in your life. This makes it clearer to me. I feel so honored that you would tell me these things about your life. Thank you for your trust, your openness. You are somebody I am very glad to know." Her face was open too, honest and full of compassion. She took another drink of coffee, looking at him over the top of her cup. "This is quite fresh in your life and I would have to imagine... disorienting. How are you are handling it?"

Daniel was not sure how to respond to her comment. He said nothing at first. He too silently drank more coffee from his beautiful, voluminous cup. It felt so good to be here in Nan's house. He had told his tale. It was a story that burned in him. He saw that he would be telling it often. It felt good.

Finally he said, "As you say, it makes things clearer to me too. And even though it was a 'brutal piece of news' as you put it, for various reasons I feel a sense of freedom now." He smiled and picked up another cookie. "It sort of feels like the relief you feel from unraveling a very tangled knot."

"I always thought Paul seemed to be a good, honorable man. Perhaps he was not your biological father, but from what you have said, I think he stepped in...just at the right time."

Nan stood up. "Let's go walk around the property a little bit. We've been sitting so long. I want to show you our place and the flower fields." She took his hand, and they went out of the little house into a fine summer morning.

First they wandered into the dark evergreen forest directly behind the cottage. Unlike the natural woods on the island which were usually so dense as to be impenetrable, these woods had been thinned through the years. This allowed some trees to grow very large with thick trunks. They had been given plenty of room for growth through the years. The shade there was heavy...branches had been trimmed up year by year so that the lowest branches were higher than a man's head. Walking among and under the trees was easy and the forest felt park-like and spacious. There were two wrought iron benches there, and short grass grew among the trees.

Nan said, "This is our park. It is not very big, but big enough for us to walk around in the shade when we want to."

Behind that were rows of smaller evergreens, firs, blue spruce, pines. They were growing in neat rows. The tallest were about nine feet high. "These are our Christmas trees," Nan said happily. "We cut a few every year and plant a few every year to keep the supply going. People around here order their trees from us, and pick them up fresh cut. They're prized by people around here."

To the north of the trees, several flower fields grew. The flower rows were arranged according to season and water needs. Those needing irrigation were closest to the house and barn.

"We have a good well, and we water as needed." She pointed to a large pump system at the edge of the fields. "We grow bulbs... iris, Dutch iris, and we sell a ton of daffodils every year. We have three good workers who come in up to three days a week as we need them. They cultivate, feed, pick and wrap the flowers for market. One of the men has a truck. He picks everything up and gets it onto the ferry for our customers on the mainland. It's a good arrangement and we do profit-sharing with our workers. Ruth and I don't do this work anymore. I'm too old and she's got her hands full with the floral design business."

The rest of the fields were the cut flowers. Now at the very height of summer, the rows were burgeoning with flowers. Nan stopped and picked some gerbera daisies and white marguerite daisies. They made their way east, through open grassland toward the cliffs overlooking the cove below. This was where Ruth had gone the day she saw Daniel in the sailboat below. They walked far enough to peek over the edge at the green waters. Daniel wondered what on earth Ruth had thought when she first saw him below. Nan said nothing and evidently did not know the details of what had happened that day.

"We live in a blessed place," she remarked, holding her bouquet close to her chest, looking back at all the myriad fields of flowers. "This is our life," she added quietly. "You are always welcome here, Daniel."

As they approached the houses again, they saw Ruth coming towards them. She was holding up a basket.

"Hey you guys! It's lunchtime already. I made up some sandwiches. Let's eat!"

Daniel laughed. "Well, I seem to be spending the entire day here today! I hope I'm not in the way."

"Come on, don't be difficult!" said Ruth. They sat around in the sun on the benches of the long outdoor worktable and ate the chicken salad sandwiches which Ruth had made. There were bread and butter pickles too, home-made from their own cucumbers.

Daniel commented on all the flowers he could see from where he sat. He knew the names of most. They were impressed.

"I love flowers. At my restaurant, we have a big fresh bouquet in the foyer... fresh every day. I get the flowers on the way to work and do the arrangement first thing every morning. You must come over when you can and be my guest at The Prow for dinner. I would love for you to see the place for yourselves."

"We get to town once or twice a year. We'd love to come to your place." With this Nan got up. "You and Ruth can look at the greenhouse while I go and straighten up the coffee things." She smiled and left.

"O.K. Come on, let's tour the greenhouse. It's not that big but is chock full of plants!" Ruth grabbed up the lunch leftovers, stuffing them in her basket, and led the way.

Walking through the greenhouse door, Daniel was overwhelmed with the fragrances of gardenia, rose, jasmine, carnation and many other flowers.

The Oriental lilies blooming there were enormous. He was delighted to see and smell the heady fragrance of the small, rubbery and brilliant white plumeria blossoms there too. She had everything organized and well groomed. The whole array was jungle rich, the damp environment causing the fragrance of blooms to be magnified. It was exquisite, and Daniel said so. Ruth was abashed by his compliments and he saw her blush.

"I do work hard at it," she said. "I love these flowers and I love this work. I guess I was born for it."

"I guess you were," Daniel agreed.

"Since I came back to the farm, business has grown and I have become established here on the island as a floral designer now. People know my work. I'm very grateful for this life." She said this quietly but with pride.

"I'm very happy for you, Ruth," said Daniel gently. "It is wonderful to be able to do work that you truly love. I know... that's the way I feel about cooking. That's the way I feel about being a chef. Even though I have moved on more to management, the food comes from me."

After looking all through the greenhouse and hearing Ruth's narrative about each and every flower as if they were her children, Daniel took his leave, walking back to Nan's to say thank you and good-bye. She was in the kitchen washing up china. He helped her do the drying. Then it was time to go. He hugged her and she held him tight.

She looked up at him. "Why don't you come back tomorrow afternoon and take me to church?"

Daniel was dumbfounded by this. "I'm not really a church guy," he quickly said. "I don't attend church." Frowning he added, "But why would you be going tomorrow? It's not Sunday, it's Wednesday." He was suddenly extremely uncomfortable.

"I didn't think you were a church-goer," Nan said matter-of-factly. "I need a ride. Ruth has to use the car to go into Friday Harbor for a wedding consultation tomorrow afternoon. She was drying her hands and walked out now to the parlor area. Looking down at the stack of papers and books on the chair, she said, "I'm a teacher at the church. I teach a weekday Bible study on Wednesday afternoon. You can take me and wait in the back of the church for me. You don't have to participate in the class. It's a bunch of ladies and we'll be up front." She looked up at him boldly. "I could ask one of the ladies to pick me up, but I am presenting a lesson tomorrow that I think you need to hear. You can just sit in the back and listen. We're real friends now, Daniel. Will you come for me here at two o'clock, please? It only lasts an hour."

## CHAPTER FORTY-FOUR

# Calling Otis

THIS day was not over. When Daniel arrived home from the Sloan Farm he sat down at the kitchen table in Glass House. Henry had been waiting there for him, snoozing in his kitchen dog bed. Daniel was thinking over the events of the day; it was now early afternoon.

The day was hot and he was tired. He wanted to head out in the Time Out and find a place to take a dip in the sea. But he knew he needed to make a call first. He would do it now, today. He had told his tale to Nan. But there was another connection to be made, an answer which he had to seek. He dreaded it. Finally, he took a deep breath and picked up the phone. He called Otis.

Otis was surprised but pleased to hear Daniel's voice. They had spent some good times together at the marina during the Fourth of July holiday. Otis was relieved and happy to see Daniel healthy and doing well among friends. He had gone down to the beach house with him and seen his hideaway. It was good.

"What's up, my man?"

Daniel could hear the smile in Otis' voice…such a rich and warm voice. It made Daniel feel good just to hear it. Otis always made people feel safe and sound.

"I've got some news for you I think," Daniel said. "Actually, I'm calling you to find out if it is really going to be news for you."

"What is it?" Otis was chuckling now, intrigued.

"My mother was here about a week ago. She came out to tell me something important. Did you know she was coming?"

"No!" Otis' antennas were up now. "What on earth?"

"She came out here all upset, because she needed to tell me that Paul was not my father."

Silence on the other end of the line. Then a deep sigh. "Ummm."

"Did you know that Otis? Did Paul ever tell you?" Daniel had to know.

"No son, I did not know that. He never said a word to me. Not a word. I have to say though that now that you tell me this, I am not surprised… I am not surprised." His voice was serious now.

Daniel told Otis the whole story, start to finish about his day with Sheila and all that had happened, all that she had told him. Everything. Otis was silent on the other end, but Daniel could hear him breathing as he took in this painful tale.

When he at last had finished telling everything, Otis was still quiet. Then he said, "Well boy, there is your answer to some of the things which have bothered you for so long." It was a matter-of-fact statement. "I hope you believe me. I never knew about this."

"I believe you, Otis. I just had to know if you knew."

Daniel was listening closely, wanting to pick up whatever clues he could from the way Otis responded. Of course he believed him. He just wished he was there with Otis to see his face, to see what this meant to him.

In a moment, Otis answered that question. "What an incredible guy Paul was! Incredible." Otis had bounced back to his ever-joyful attitude. "O.K., Daniel, so how do you feel about this now? How does this make you feel?"

Daniel laughed, "That's the same thing that Peggy said when I told them yesterday down at the marina. I feel..." Daniel spoke haltingly. He wanted to get this right. "I feel like a deep running sore is finally closing up in me. Something that has been long-time painful is drying up and healing up. There will be a scar, but it will be all right. When my Mother first told me, I felt like leaping around for joy, actually. It came as a tremendous relief. I don't know why. It made me feel free...and it made me care more for Paul, not resent him. I think I can love him now...for what he did for me."

"That's so right, Daniel. So right! I wish I was there with you right now...I wish I was. Do you want me to come over? I can get on the ferry..."

"Thank you, Otis. Thank you for everything. I want to see you too. You don't need to come right now. I'm fine. We are going to have a picnic in a week or so out here...an end of summer celebration. I guess Luke has already told you about that plan. We're all going out to Cattle Point. I hope you are coming for that?"

"I'll be there. Marion and I will both be there. Wouldn't miss it. Let me ask you now, how are you and Sheila? How was that left?"

"Umm, I don't know. I really don't. She was so different. She put herself in a very vulnerable position coming out here like that, certainly not the way I have always known her. She was stricken. That's the word I would use to describe her. She was sorry...she was emotional. We parted on good terms. I thanked her for telling me the truth. Who knows how things will be now between us? You are probably wondering who my natural father is. I don't know. She didn't tell me his name, just the story of their relationship...I didn't ask. I guess I had enough to chew on with what she told me. She did say that my grandmother, Willie, never knew either. The whole thing is hard to believe, but I do believe it. Sure makes sense, doesn't it? I have no idea how this will affect my relationship with Sheila. I call her "Mother" now though. I got tired of this first names crap. It's ridiculous. I told her we needed to at least try to be normal with what is left of our family. No more 'Sheila!'." He said it with passion.

"I am so happy for this truth coming out, Daniel. You know, the Bible says 'you will know the truth and the truth will set you free'. Did you know that? It's a great truth about truth."

"No, I didn't know that. By the way, I found a Bible that was Paul's. It was in his car. It's the one you guys gave him when he was baptized at your church, I guess."

"Yeah, that was a little travel Bible. I remember it. Glad you have it."

"A lot has happened to me out here this summer, Otis. I'm trying to turn things around, to make peace a primary factor in my life."

"That's good news, Daniel....very good news."

Now Daniel was chuckling a little bit, it was ironic laughter. "My dear Mother did leave me with one disturbing and unanswered question though. 'Who wanted you, Daniel?' she said. She delivered this at the end of her 'confessions.' That's been rattling around in my head. But, by the time she said it I was already thinking... who cares about her assessment of me. I felt free of her stuff. However, it is a very important question, I guess."

"Oh yes, it's a very important question for all of us...for all of us. I have some answers for that one! Yeah, man, I have some answers! I think you know where I am going with that. I want to talk to you about it...when I come out there to see you. Until then, let me just say...somebody planned you!" Otis' laugh was a deep one now.

They drifted into small talk, Otis piled on the love and reassurances which rolled so easily out of him. Daniel could feel it coming in to him even over the phone.

Daniel told him about the bumper crop of blackberries. He promised to send Otis a packet of his blackberries. He would send them tomorrow on the ferry.

"I spent the morning with the Sloans today. Nan invited me for coffee. She showed me all around the farm. We talked about Paul. She knew him a little. I told her about Sheila... Mother's... visit. She wants me to take her to church tomorrow, to hear her Bible study lesson with some ladies."

"Oh my, Daniel. That Nan..." look out for her! She's incredible." he laughed. "You are the incredible one, Otis. You are the one. Thank you for all you do and have done for me and my family. Your strength helps me. It steadies me."

There was the chuckling laughter again, then there were good-byes. Daniel was alone again in the kitchen. He didn't feel alone, though. He felt great, even better and more relaxed than he had down at the marina yesterday, more than he had felt with Nan all day. Something good was happening…connecting with people was good. Life was good. He and Henry went down and launched the Time Out.

CHAPTER FORTY-FIVE

# At Nan's Church

FIRST thing the next morning, Daniel loaded a big box into his car and rushed down to the harbor. He wanted to get two gallons of blackberries onto the ferry for Otis and Marion as early as possible. They had been partially frozen and wrapped up in Styrofoam the night before. The package was loaded onto the ferry just in time before it took off. Daniel had told Otis when to get out to Anacortes to retrieve them and he would have to drive some distance to get there. As the ferry moved away from the dock, Daniel was satisfied. He wanted Otis to have those beautiful blackberries today. They would be nice and fresh.

He had not slept well the night before. He planned to stop off on the way back from the harbor and tell Nan at Sloan Farm that he simply could not go to church with her today, that he would be happy to drive her and just drop her off. One of the ladies could bring her home. He didn't want to go. It was too foreign for him, way out of his comfort zone. But...when he reached the driveway of the farm he just drove on past without stopping. Sighing, he was thinking that she had listened to him and his story yesterday. He would just have to just pick her up, go with her and listen to whatever she had to say. He would sit in the back and listen the best he could. They were friends now. Real friendship is always a two-way street.

So, he drove on back to Glass House. He wanted to keep busy up there today. He would work on a plan for the living room remodel. Before long he would be going back to the mainland. Since taking out the bar and re-surfacing the wall behind it he had done nothing, and hadn't cared. All summer the living room had been nearly empty of furniture since he had sold the old red sofa. Now, he had some ideas and wanted to get them firmed up before he went back to the mainland. Today, he would take some measurements and make some photos of the place. He had an idea in mind for changing the space. It would be wonderful to make a library wall where the bar and mirrors had been. That whole south side of the room could be wood library shelving for books and things. He might even put a fireplace right in the center of that wall. There was no fireplace in the house now. It was not fashionable when the severely contemporary house was first designed, but this could be changed. It wouldn't even be a difficult thing to do since it was an outside wall. He would change it. Yes, an idea about Glass House was forming, a radical idea. He tried to keep busy and not think about the afternoon ahead.

Finally, he took a long hot shower there at Glass House and found some khaki pants to wear and a shirt. He had always enjoyed dressing well but since coming to the island, he didn't care what he wore...this was freeing. Nan had said come as you are, but he couldn't go to church in shorts, he just couldn't. So he sat around after lunch looking like a kid waiting to be picked up by the Sunday School bus. He had shaved carefully.

Nan was perky when he arrived, smiling in her summery cotton print pant suit.

She was still wearing her clunky sandals, but he noticed that her nails were freshly done and she had a bit of lipstick on. This was going to be a ladies' thing. Why on earth had she asked him to go! Dutifully, he helped her load up her book bag, which he noticed was very heavy.

It was full of books and a stack of some kind of booklets she said were for the students. Then off they went. She thanked him for coming and patted his hand a couple of times as he drove. He had to admit that this woman had treated him more like a mother already than Sheila had ever done. Maybe this was some mysterious part of mothering that he did not know about. They drove up the main road, then west on small country lanes for several miles.

The church was plain, nothing like the Catholic churches he had visited with his mother in childhood. The white frame building was unadorned except for a modest spire topped with a cross. There were a couple of out buildings, offices he guessed, but the whole compound was small...and plain. The white wooden sign in the grass in front of the church read, "Beulah Land Christian Fellowship," and in smaller letters below, "Non-Denominational." Nan opened the front door with a key and they went in. It was plain inside too. There were pews. The clear glass windows all along the sides of the narrow church let in daylight, no stained glass. The floor was wood planking which echoed as they walked down along the center aisle.

Daniel felt an inexplicable anxiety as they neared the altar and the pulpit area. He felt as if something was being pulled out of him the closer they got to the front. The altar was a simple thing: a long wood table with only a white cloth runner on it and two white candles in brass candleholders. Nan put her things down and bustled around, setting up some folding chairs in the open area in front, between the pews and the altar. She handed him a booklet from her book bag.

"This is the material we're studying," she said. "You can have this copy. I have plenty." She was arranging the chairs and her books and papers.

Daniel withdrew to the back of the church. This felt better. Looking up, he saw that there was a wooden cross on the wall behind the altar. There was no man hanging on it. That was a slight relief. He looked around at the pamphlets arranged in racks at the back of the church and picked up a couple to have something else to read. He sat down in the back, settling in to see what was going to happen. Nan waved at him with a smile, and asked loudly if he could hear her back there. He could... it really was a small church and sound was amplified in this empty space. He waved back...so uncomfortable, he felt stupid. He was rolling and unrolling the thin booklet she had given him. The title in blue letters read, "The Letter to the Romans, edited by Thomas Mc Adams, A New Testament Study." It was large, the size of a page of notebook paper, probably thirty pages. He didn't look through it.

Women of differing ages began coming in. They carried Bibles. They didn't seem to notice him, but went straight on, greeting Nan up front. There was loud chatter as these women all greeted each other. They sat down in the circle of chairs. Then they quieted down as Nan stood and put her things on the little podium in front of them.

She started talking in a strong voice, but Daniel couldn't pay attention. He was thinking back to childhood days and her voice just trailed off as he got lost in memories. He was remembering being in church with his mother. Sheila would kneel on the kneelers. Daniel would kneel too, even though she didn't tell him to. He just wanted to do what everyone else was doing. She was looking forward at the cross, and the man on the cross, and Daniel would look at Sheila's face, then back to the man on the cross. He could see that this meant something important to his mother. He couldn't figure out why that man was there, why he had been treated like that. It was so terribly threatening. "Could that ever happen to me?" Daniel had thought. He never asked questions like that out loud to his mother. Never.

Later, in school and in life, he had learned that the answer to the cross thing is: "Christ died for us." He still wondered, why?

Nan was talking away up in front. She stopped and went around behind the altar. She reached up and touched the cross. Daniel involuntarily shivered.

"What this letter from Saint Paul is trying to say is that Christ is no longer on the cross. He finished that work. He died… they took him down and buried him. And…the thing that he took with him onto the cross died too. That was 'sin.' This is the word we use to mean separation from God, or rebellion. Sin was nailed up too. The power of sin died with Jesus. They buried him…but he rose again, in his body. He lives, even today."

She paused to let that sink in. She was a good teacher, Daniel could see that. The women were looking up at her. You could hear a pin drop.

"We've been studying this letter for a while. Now we come to the bottom line." She walked back around to her podium. She adjusted her Bible, and then looked up directly at Daniel sitting in back.

"Let me read this section of the letter in a more modern version. I think it fits the bill for today." She smiled. "This is from letter to the Romans, chapter six." She began reading...

*"Could it be any clearer? Our old way of life was nailed to the cross with Christ...a decisive end to that sin-miserable life- no longer at sin's every beck and call! What we believe is this. If we get included in Christ's sin-conquering death, we also get included in his life-saving resurrection. We know that when Jesus was raised from the dead it was a signal of the end of 'death-as-the-end'...When Jesus died...he took sin down with him, but alive he brings God down to us."*

"This message applies to us today. It's ours, when we ask Christ to be Lord of our life," she added.

Nan kept reading other passages and talking on, but Daniel couldn't grasp most of the rest of what she said. By the end of the hour it was all a blur of words. Finally, he could see that she was wrapping it up.

"Ladies, this has been a wonderful study these past weeks. Thank you for participating. You can never come to the end of the treasures in this letter. We know from what Saint Paul has written here, that we have been 'adopted.' We were adopted by God himself when we believed. Believers can now call God 'Father.' We are, every one of us...adopted. Not one of us was naturally born into God's family. We all need to be adopted." She paused to let them think about that. She was looking directly back at Daniel.

"Here's something I once heard said about the Letter to the Romans. It regards chapter eight. I think it sums everything up." She was reading now from her notes.

"We enter this chapter with 'no condemnation,' we close it with 'no separation'...in between 'all things work together for good to those who love God.' Let me close by reading these words from the end of Romans...chapter eight."

*"The One who died for us---who was raised to life for us!--- is in the presence of God the Father at this very moment sticking up for us. Do you think anyone is going to be able to drive a wedge between us and Christ's love for us? There is no way! Not trouble, not hard times, not hatred, not hunger, hot homelessness, not bullying threats, not backstabbing...none of this fazes us... because Jesus loves us..."*

Then Nan asked one of the women to pray a prayer and she did. It was quietly spoken so Daniel could not hear it. After that they all stood up, embracing and laughing. He saw that Nan was laughing too. They filed out down the aisle still laughing and talking. Nan stopped them and introduced Daniel to them all as they passed by.

One woman blurted out, "Oh! When I came in, I thought he was the gardener!"

At that they all laughed even more. He smiled back somewhat sheepishly. They looked at him with affection, some shook his hand, and all trouped out.

Daniel went up to the front again with Nan and helped her put up the chairs and get her things together.

"Why were they laughing like that about me being the gardener?" Daniel asked.

"Oh! It says in the gospels, in the New Testament that the first person to see Jesus alive after his resurrection was a woman and she thought he was the gardener there in the tombs!" Nan was smiling broadly. "So it's like a double-meaning Bible joke!"

Daniel drove home slowly to Nan's down the country roads. He was glad that was over. It had been strange, but not too bad, not terrible. He was proud of Nan, proud of how well she did up in front of the women. She had dignity and he saw another side of her, an intellectual side. He saw her as someone who could think and deal with heavy questions very well. He had a couple of more questions for her.

In the church he had started thinking back about stealing those chocolate bars long ago as a boy. He was thinking about his childish idea that maybe Jesus had stolen something like that, and that was why he was killed. He remembered that he had worked out over time that it needed to be something more serious than stealing chocolate bars.

"When I was a young boy I stole some chocolate candy at the house of my parent's friends." Driving along Daniel began to tell Nan the whole tale of his stealing and how Paul had shamed him and made him go to the door to return the candy…how Paul had told him about the Ten Commandments which he had never heard of before. He told about his thinking that maybe Jesus had stolen something too, and had been killed for it. He laughed a little, telling his story.

Nan just smiled.

"So let me ask you this, Nan. I want to get this straight. What you were saying today is that Christ was not killed, did not die, because he stole something, not candy bars, not gold bars or anything else, not for any kind of fault of his own."

He breathed in sharply and then breathed out.

"You were saying... today... that Jesus died because I... and others stole things and...did things. We stole the candy...he took the punishment for it."

"That's right, Daniel. That's right." Nan was calm and quiet.

He was silent for a while. "I'll have to think about that."

"I hope you do, Daniel."

They arrived at the flower farm. Daniel helped Nan get her things into her little house. She was clearly tired now. He refused her offer of a cup of tea.

"No, I'm going. Thanks for everything today. You are a good teacher. I know those ladies really got a lot out of it. I appreciate you including me...these are new concepts for me. One other thing...what does 'Beulah Land' mean?"

"Oh! In Old Testament Hebrew, 'Beulah' means 'married.' It is used to describe the land of promise, sort of a metaphor for a happy, settled life. San Juan Island appears like a 'Beulah Land' to many here. That's why they gave that name to the church."

He bent and kissed her cheek. Surprisingly, she put her arms around him, holding him tightly. She leaned her head against him for a moment. "Thank you for taking me. You have my love, Daniel. You have all my love."

## CHAPTER FORTY-SIX

# Last Days

MELLOW days had come. The full fruit of summertime, just about to wane. It was the second half of August now. There was nothing more to plan, build or make. Just time to live and enjoy the days and also the nights, with stars seeming to come right down to earth some nights, they were so bright. Every evening was a fireside night on the beach. Every day was a sailing day.

It had become as automatic as breathing to get in the Time Out and shove off with Henry onto the waters. Daniel was a proficient sailor now. He was relaxed at the tiller and knew all of the rigging and what it would do, and not do. The sea would certainly not be conquered... it was ever changing and unpredictable. But, his boat he knew. The little thing had brought him so much joy this summer.

The time for return to The Prow and his mainland life loomed ahead. Probably "loomed" was not a good description, he had to admit. He was going back with many things cleared up. He had rested, he had grieved. The old family tensions had disappeared like a gust of smoke from his camp fire. He had no idea what the future would hold, but things certainly would not be as they had been. He looked forward to it. Since he knew he could return here really anytime he wanted to, any time he needed to, he was happy, he was grateful.

The plan was to close up the houses and take the Time Out down to the marina for winter docking right after Labor Day. There was the end of summer picnic ahead that he was looking forward to, a culmination, a gathering of friends to mark the time, to cook and eat outdoors again. It would be one last picnic, and a time to reminisce about this summer and its adventures. They were all going out to Cattle Point.

Potter had been visiting the beach house frequently. He and Daniel had an established routine of sharing now. Potter seemed to like both ham and raw eggs so he often found those things on his special plate by the beach house door. In return, he usually brought a nice plate of fresh crabs, or even a few sea urchins, which Daniel savored. They seldom saw each other, but there was a bond. It was a trader's bond, operating "fair and square." Potter had stopped trying to pry open the "refrigerator." There was respect. He would miss Potter.

For a few more days Daniel went out in the Time Out every day. The weather was glorious. He encountered many others in sail and motor craft everywhere in the bay during the final filling up of summer days. Boaters and tourists were friendly on the water and the dolphins even leapt obligingly for the tour boats, showing off in one last fling, it seemed. You could hear laughter across the water on still days. Afternoons, the breeze worked up and it was good sailing. The joy he felt out on the water was unlike anything he had ever experienced. There was big space, motion, beauty and the slight but real element of risk that thrilled him. Henry was a boat dog now. Daniel was wondering how he was going to ever readjust to the life of a city dog. Henry had a sixth sense about fishing. He seemed to know just where the schools of fish would be hanging out and pointed to the spots, rushing to the bow and looking over the gunwales at certain places. He didn't bark, but would whine and wag his tail when he caught scent of a good fishing spot. By now, unclipped all summer, he looked like a wooly Flemish Water Dog. He was right about the fish every time and Daniel brought home the catch for pan-fried dinners.

He hadn't seen Nan and Ruth for a few days, not since the church visit, but he had been down to the marina for coffee with the guys and Peggy. They were busy with tourists and helping folks get their boats launched for end of summer vacation jaunts. They just had time for morning coffee and then Daniel went on in the Time Out.

He had asked Peggy to come up and do an end of summer housecleaning at Glass House at the end of his stay. She would come and do that soon, while he attacked the beach house for a last scouring. He bought a nice, heavier padlock for the beach house. He wanted to protect it well now that he had fixed it up and furnished it. Not that anyone around there would bother anything, but it seemed like the right thing to do with a place right on the water, accessible to all.

Then one night when he returned from sailing up the coast, he was too tired from a warm day in the sun to cook outside at the fire pit. So, he just sliced some of his favorite cheeses and an apple. He opened a can of soup and sat at his table in the lantern light for a simple dinner. Looking up at the mantel, he noticed

Paul's little travel Bible lying there. After supper, he pulled it down and decided to look up the part that Nan had been teaching from at the church that day.

"I guess I could learn something from the Bible," he thought.

He got the study booklet out of a drawer too so he could try to understand it all. The print of the little Bible was very small, but after searching around, he found the book of Romans or Paul's Letter to the Romans as it was called, near the back. He started right in reading at chapter one. By the end of that first chapter, his heart was frozen ...frozen and yet beating fast, beating out of his chest. He felt tears welling up, tears of betrayal.

"Why do I keep trying to trust women!" he said out loud. He could not believe that Nan, sweet understanding Nan, had directed him to read this stuff. He read the chapter again, and then again. He went on reading... chapter two, chapter three. He was hoping that he had misinterpreted what was written there, but he had not misinterpreted it. It was clear. The writer was pronouncing a sentence of doom on the kind of life he had been leading with men since adolescence. And the doom was not just for him, but also for everybody who failed to acknowledge what the writer called the "invisible qualities- eternal power and divine nature of God." It seemed by the third chapter that not just he, but everyone, was under some kind of blanket judgment. Nobody was O.K.

He thought back to the things Nan had read and talked about at the church and he was confused. This was not the impression he had from all that she had said that day! He thought she had said that everything was taken care of, that a price was paid by "the man on the cross" for everything ...everything, according to the Bible. She knew all this was written in this book, yet she had told him that she loved him so tenderly as he left her that day, so motherly. He suddenly realized that Otis probably believed this too! He probably looked at him through this filter. Otis was a church guy, a Bible guy. Dear, kind Otis. What a load of hypocrisy!

Who wrote this!? Who sat down and concocted these words? Was this stuff still believed and accepted as from God, or was this something embarrassing to believers, to be skipped over, something from primitive times? The letter was written by someone called "Saint Paul." Big time irony with the name, "Paul" and he laughed out loud bitterly.

A feeling of despair was building in him. He chucked the little Bible across the room where it lay, open and face-up. How terrible to have a sentence like this laid on him from a little leather-bound book with miniscule print! Yet the whole thing was powerfully dragging him down to a place where he did not want to be. He lay down on his bed, looking up at the ceiling. He lay there all night, still in his clothes, dishes scattered on the table. Henry was mournfully watching him from the foot of the bed.

The next morning he got up and picked up the little Bible off the floor. He shut it and snapped the cover closed forcefully. Enough of that! Forget it! He cleaned up his kitchen mess, washing up all the dishes in his old-fashioned dish pan. Coffee would clear his head of the thoughts from last night. He made some, then irresistibly opened the Bible again to Romans chapter one. Some of the phrases chilled him to the bone... "God gave them over in the lusts... exchanging the Truth of God for a lie... abandoned the natural function." Then the whole thing was ended up with a glut of denunciation… "evil, murder, disobedient to parents, unloving, unmerciful." All he could think of was that Nan was teaching all these things in her class, in church!

Daniel could not let this go. She had deliberately, pointedly, brought this stuff to his attention. He threw on some clothes and with energy fueled by rage, he hurried up the path to Glass House, gripping the little Bible in his hand. He was boiling over with rage. Anger, a sense of betrayal and something else…a tinge of fear propelled him up the hill. It was the first time he had felt this kind of fear since coming to the island. Out on the water, sailing, there had been the fear, even the terror, of natural forces, but this was different. This was that old uncertainty, that insecurity that always plagued him about where he stood with the people in his life. He was going to do something about it!

He phoned the Sloan Farm from the Glass House kitchen phone. He hated to call the big house, but he knew Nan did not have a phone out in her little house. Ruth answered, as he feared she would. He was abrupt.

"I need to talk to Nan, please," was all he said. Ruth was surprised but didn't ask any questions. She just went to find Nan.

"Hello," said Nan's quiet voice.

"Nan, I need you to come over here, please. I have something to ask you." His voice was cold and she picked that up immediately.

"Sure, Daniel, I'll be over in a few minutes," she said gently.

"Good," he said abruptly, but was already regretting calling her. Her voice was so kind, and she was old, and what difference would it make what crazy stuff she believes? He was trying to talk himself out of his position on this, but anger welled up again as he hung up the phone.

Nan came to the back door and into the kitchen meekly, but Daniel could see that she was not upset, not worried. Her face was calm and she looked Daniel straight in the eyes.

"Nan, I am so mad at you! I feel so betrayed by you!" He was exasperated and held up the little Bible, shaking it. He was shaking too. "You gave me this...'Romans'... to read. It's terrible. It's hateful. I am so disappointed in you! Why would you do this? I thought you were my friend! You do realize that I live my life in relationships with men, don't you!"

She looked at him gravely. She sat down on a kitchen chair. "No, I don't know anything about your sexual experience. One can surmise, but I don't know that. If you say so, that makes a lot of sense."

"Nan! I've got a lot going on in my life and I don't need somebody suggesting to me that I have some kind of clinging black disease on me or in me as your man 'Saint Paul' here insists! ...sin!" He said it with venom.

"Yeah, Paul pretty much lays out all the faults of humankind, right there in one short chapter. Powerful, isn't it?" Nan was sitting flat-footed on a kitchen chair with an impassive face. She held her purse on her lap. Her hair was like a cinnamon cloud shining there in the sunny, bright, sterile kitchen, still slightly damp from a shower, Daniel thought. She had probably dressed quickly and jumped in her car to come over. Nan was watching him too. He was aglow with emotion and the health of youth. He was wearing a neon orange T-shirt and shorts. All around them ...something else was swirling in the kitchen... a great struggle.

"What I know is that you have been coming out here since you were a boy. I know you used to bicycle around these roads. You were always alone. I know your father hiked alone, not with you. I saw him. I know that you've lost your father, and that now you know that he wasn't your father. I know that you've come out here this time wanting to live, to breathe free. I see that you are not free. You are actually...bound. I know that even though you have had a wonderful time and lively things have happened this summer, God is not finished with you. That's all I know, except that I love you, and I have wanted you to be free from the first time you came to bring us a cherry pie. And, I do know the way for you to have the life you are wanting. That's why I invited you to hear the 'Romans' message at our church. Despite what you think of it, it is about freedom."

Daniel's mouth had fallen open and his expression was sheer incredulity. He was shaking his head. "I cannot believe that you are saying these things to me, Nan!"

"Do you know the story in the Bible about Lazarus, Daniel?"

"I'm afraid not," Daniel answered sarcastically. "My Bible knowledge is thankfully small."

Nan was undeterred. "There is a story in the gospel of John about some girls called Mary and Martha. They had a brother, Lazarus, and all of them lived together. One day Lazarus got sick. He was very sick. All three of them were friends of Jesus so the girls sent someone to tell Jesus, to get him to come and help. They knew he performed miracles of healing. But he didn't come. He waited. In the meantime, Lazarus died and they buried him. There was overwhelming sorrow in the family."

At this Daniel snorted. "That sounds about right. Help... just out of reach."

"Well, help did come. Jesus did arrive even though they thought he was late. He called for the opening up of the grave and told Lazarus to 'come out.' He did come out, they unwrapped him from his tight grave wrappings and he was perfectly healthy and fine. He was made alive again by Jesus after 4 days of lying dead. Sometimes, people are wrapped up tight in a shroud and they don't even know it. They think they are O.K. but they are bound. They are dead. They are not free... because of sin, because of lack of faith."

"Are you saying that is me, Nan?"

"Yes, that's what I am saying. That is what the Bible is saying. That's what the letter to the Romans is saying. It's what God is saying, and has been saying all along."

"How can you say that to me Nan! You've only known me a very short time! You don't know my life! I consider myself to be a decent man and I lead a decent life! I work very hard at what I do. I don't hurt anyone and I try to be helpful to everyone I know! I've tried to be a good friend to you!"

"Being a good person and being free are not the same things, Daniel. Lazarus was a good man, a good brother, a good friend... but he was dead, he was bound and nobody but Jesus could do anything about it." Nan was looking at him with great sympathy.

"I can't help who I am!!" Daniel shouted, his face was red now. He couldn't believe that he was shouting at this little lady. He began to tear up. "I was pushed into my sexual orientation! I was formed to go this way very early." Now, his voice became cold, his face was set. Bitterly he continued, "and then... I agreed...and chose it for myself...and why not? I won't say I was born this way, but pretty damned near! Where was God! Where was a parent who cared? The path of a 'straight man' was not laid out for me. It was impossible!"

Nan was still sitting calmly, looking at him intently. "Sit down Daniel, will you please?" She was not smiling. "I want to tell you a story that's not in the Bible. It's a story about me."

Daniel reluctantly sat down, but he was partially turned away from her, he didn't look at her. He was still seething. There was no mistaking his disappointment with her.

Nan sat up a little straighter on her straight-backed chair and began. "I was raised in Seattle. My parents were both alcoholics, and my raising at home was chaotic to say the least. We kids lived catch-as-catch-can. I guess there was some kind of love, but it was terribly twisted. There was no order, no beauty, no cleanliness really, in that house. I remember we would just wash the clothes all together, my sister and I. We would dump everybody's clothes in the middle of the floor and everyone just grabbed things to wear without any sense of ownership, just something to put on. There were few boundaries. When my father was drinking we all hid, especially as we got older because he would 'take liberties' with us girls, if you know what I mean. We were not raped, but it was pretty bad. There were two of us girls and one brother. My mother was useless and drunk much of the time. She was victimized by my father, beaten at times and just went right back into drinking as her solution to her life problems. The school knew that we were 'rag tag' kids, probably abused, but nothing was done about it. I used to go to the library after school, just to stay away from home a little longer. The library was open late into the afternoon. I started reading there, seeing, through books and magazines, that there could be another way to live. I loved the house and garden magazines and the books about flowers. I could never grow flowers at our place, but I dreamed about having a garden, maybe growing some flowers, and I saw beauty. I dreamed of having such a life one day."

She had been sitting very still with her feet flat on the floor looking straight ahead as she spoke. Daniel had turned to watch her, mesmerized. Now her eyes filled with tears. She reached down into her purse for a couple of tissues.

"When I was fifteen, there was a terrible fight between my parents one night. My brother tried to break it up, but that only made things worse. My mother just lost it and was screaming and cursing at the top of her lungs. My father grabbed her by the throat and wouldn't let go. He kept squeezing her throat and striking her with the other hand. We kids ran out the door for help. The neighbors had already called the police. When they got there, my mother was dead. My father had strangled her. She was gone. We were just shivering out in the yard. My father was taken away. He was convicted of second degree murder and went to prison. Our mother and our home, such as it was, were obliterated. I have no memory of my mother's funeral. I guess I just blocked it out. We kids were divided up among foster homes and we tried to keep going in school. Our father was in prison. Not exactly a reference with other kids to make you a desirable friend. At least the fighting and drinking had ended."

She stopped for a minute and took a deep shuddering breath, wiping her eyes and face.

"I'm so sorry, Nan." Daniel said it quietly from his chair.

She smiled, looking at him. "I promise you that this terrible story has a good ending and has something to do with the Bible and all we have talked about, but not yet, Daniel."

"I was so messed up and so lonely. Our brother was the oldest. He just took off, disappeared. My sister and I were put into a large foster care home with about a dozen other kids just as bad off as we were. It was O.K., but even in that bigger home, I was so lonely. A boy at my high school liked me. I grabbed onto him with a passion. I was like somebody sinking without a life saver. I wanted love and he was sweet. We got too close and pretty soon I was pregnant. I was only sixteen. The boy's parents were determined to dislodge their son from this situation so they arranged an abortion. I was not an ideal match for their son, and we were way too young for anything permanent. My foster care family agreed. Actually, I agreed too. I wanted out of the situation as much as they did. My guilt and despair only multiplied after the abortion. I felt like a dead person, a 'dead girl walking.' I still had my sister. We tried to hang on to each other, to cling to each other for a while, but life just kept going and she married very young and moved away."

She stopped and blew her nose again. "I kept going to school. Somehow, I just kept going. I studied. I tried to do well. I just kept going, stubbornly. I didn't know what else to do. I graduated from high school. I wanted to go to college to get a degree in botany."

She looked over at Daniel with a smile. "Flowers were always my goal. I searched around for help. I found out that there was a Christian Home for Girls in Seattle. I had to have a place to live. I was a little old for it, but they took me in and I got a part time job." She looked at him again, bright-eyed. "A part-time job at a florist shop!" She shook her head. "I was so happy. At the 'home,' I learned about Christ, about his life, his death, who he was, his promises. We had Bible studies. I was intrigued but cautious.

Frankly, it sounded way too good to be true!" She laughed. Daniel was teary now, but he smiled too.

"There was a guy who came to the home to help out. He did some cooking and paid for a lot of the needs of the house. His whole family was involved in Christian ministry and his sister was our Bible study teacher. They all volunteered when they could. The guy's name was Walter Sloan. He was handsome in a steady, strong way...wonderfully strong. Their family owned a farm and Walter had grown up on it on the outskirts of Seattle. Walter was older than me by about eight years. He was a Christian man. The things that I had heard about Jesus, I saw in Walter. He acted it out...effortlessly. At least it seemed that way to me. I loved him. He loved me too."

Nan was looking at Daniel now. "They let me stay in that home all through college. I wanted Jesus. I wanted him to heal me, to help me, to give me life. I wanted him to forgive me. I wanted to finish school, I wanted to marry Walter." Her eyes were bright. There were no more tears.

"All I can tell you, Daniel, is that Jesus did love me. He helped me, he changed me. He gave me all those good things that I wanted and prayed for. He sent Walter to love me back to life, to give me freedom from the past. Walter and Jesus both knew my upbringing. I hid nothing. They both knew about my parents. They both knew about the abortion. Jesus forgave my rebellion, my sin, my murderous abortion." She shivered. "Walter did too. He valued me. He loved me. He took me the way I was and made me his wife. Walter rescued me, and Jesus saved me...So, Daniel, I am pointing all this out to you, because Jesus is able to help you too. Nothing is impossible with God."

Matter-of-factly she added, "The Bible is God's Word. It's true, no matter how we feel about it."

Daniel's head was down now. He did not look up. This was really more than he could handle just now. Hearing all this, he loved Nan again greatly, more actually, than before. His anger against her was gone. But even through her shattering story, he was still thinking about himself, about last night. He did not know what to do with the things he had read in the "Book of Romans." He couldn't shake it, or the things Nan had just now said about him.

"While I was going to school, Walter took some business classes with me. We plotted, we planned, we prayed. Walter started looking around at property. He found the old farm that is now our flower farm. He had been saving and he could get a loan. His parents helped us. That's how we got out here. I got my botany degree, and we got married, and we came out here. We joined the Beulah Land Christian Church. We were married, the land we bought was a 'married' land. She smiled. "It produced flowers and supported us, and we have lived here ever since."

Quickly she added, "Walter died too soon. It was when Ruth was still just a little girl. I miss him every day, and I think you would have liked him!" She sighed and leaned back in her chair, relaxed now. Her story was told.

There was quiet in the kitchen for a while, then Daniel spoke. He was looking hard at Nan. "You know, you can never tell about a person by just looking at them and being with them. You meet someone. You think you have some idea of what kind of person they are. Maybe you concoct a little story in your head about how they probably grew up, just from the way they act. You meet them and do things with them...but you don't know them. You just don't know them. I didn't know about your life. Thank you for coming here and for telling me about yourself. I will think over what you have told me. But Nan... you don't know me either. You don't know very much about my life."

He began to tell her about himself as a five year old, about his life in the condo in Seattle, about the trip to the park, the ice cream man, the leafy place where the "Gentleman" took him, about the multi-layered pain of his experience. And, about the confusion of who he was in his parent's life, about being booted abruptly out of that life with them, about the jumble of life in boarding school, about Willie. She listened intently, her eyes glistening. He told his story briefly. These days he was just sick and tired of talking about it. He breathed deeply, anger gone now. He looked out the big window over the sink to the south at the sunny sky.

The two of them sat peacefully together in the bright kitchen. Nan had very little comment about his life story. She just obviously accepted and took in all that he had said, nodding.

He continued on, drawing out his words slowly with a sigh. "Nearly everyone I have met out here harbors some kind of horrendous story. Life has done its best to bring some people down, but I am beginning to see that life doesn't work like that. We don't go down...we just go on. Sometimes the road is good, sometimes it is not good. I am doing the best I can with the road I am on."

Emotion was gone. It was just a statement of fact. He had traveled as far as he was going to go today and Nan knew it.

"Would you like some coffee? I'll make us some." He smiled. Nan smiled too. She picked up her big purse and opened it. She brought out a paper bag filled with recently baked chocolate chip cookies.

## CHAPTER FORTY-SEVEN

# Picnic at the Lighthouse

MIGHTY were the preparations for this Labor Day picnic. It seemed like the whole southern end of the island would be there, and a bunch from the mainland too. Daniel had called Oscar and Trini and told them to shut down the restaurant both Sunday and Monday and come on out to the island for the end of summer celebration. Any of the kitchen staff who wanted to come were also welcome. They could bring their sleeping bags and camp out.

Otis and Marion would be there. They were bringing several people over from their church. Anna of course was coming with them and also her brother, Glenn, with his wife, Dotty.

Ruth and Nan were to be Daniel's kitchen helpers. He had conscripted them a week before. They were interested in seeing him cook and willing to help with the preparations. They wanted to see him at work in the kitchen first hand! Maybe they could pick up some tips, maybe some recipes, they thought. He had a stupendous feast planned which would be produced out of the

Glass House kitchen. Of course, others would be bringing food too. It was a community thing. Some of the Beulah Land Church ladies were coming to the picnic with their families. They were in charge of cookies, cakes and other sweets, and Daniel planned to finish off all his frozen blackberry stash with several huge cobblers.

Luke, Pete and Peggy would be the setup committee out at Cattle Point. They would get the seafood too. Plenty of crab, oysters and shrimp had been ordered for the event. Their local fishing friends would haul it all in for them to the marina.

The three guys had gone out one day and staked out their preferred picnic site, as close to the lighthouse and southern tip of the island as possible, a grassy place right down by the beach. It was going to be a big deal. The final summer fling before back to town, back to school, back to work.

It was going to take two days to get the picnic food prepared in the Glass House kitchen. Daniel had shopped days before so everything was ready when the girls arrived. To their delight, he had made beignets to start the day! Soon they were eating and laughing at all the sugar spread all over the place, including their faces, a delicate treat with their coffee.

Daniel was easy to work for. He told everyone exactly what he wanted them to do. They started with the crabs, which Luke had delivered on ice earlier that morning right to the kitchen door. Daniel gave Ruth and Nan big white aprons, which he had bought in town. After steaming the crabs, they all sat around the kitchen table and cracked and picked the crabs, piling the crab meat into bowls and chatting as they worked. Of course, they had all cracked and picked crabs many times before, so this was easy for them. They had to watch out for Henry. He kept trying to run off with crab shells and pieces. Shells are not good for dogs.

As they worked, Ruth wanted to know about The Prow, so Daniel began the story of how it all came about. "I wish you could have known Willie," he said wistfully. "She was my partner throughout the whole process. She owned the building where The Prow came into being, and I got an education in culinary schools because of her."

He went on to describe the layout and theme of The Prow to them. The beautiful sculpted ship's piece in the foyer, the colors, the dishware, the kitchen with its high ceiling. His face was shining talking about it. He described Oscar and Trini. They would meet them soon.

Ruth's eyes were soft looking at him as he described all this.

"He loves this stuff," she thought. She was thinking too, how like herself he was in this way...in his passion for the work he had chosen, developed from nothing, but supported by family.

"I hope you will come over to the mainland and visit my place," he said shyly. "I want to show you around and give you a bowl of the best chowder in the Northwest." They said they would come.

The crabmeat was stored away to chill in the big refrigerator. Tomorrow they would mix up a crab salad from the chilled crabmeat. Next on the list was the "Andalusian Potato Salad." Red potatoes were scrubbed, boiled and cut into pieces. When the potatoes were cool, raw red onion shreds, green olives and capers were added. Green beans were blanched, and cut thin, left crispy, then added to the salad. The dressing would be simple olive oil and vinegar. This potato salad could be served at room temperature on the day of the picnic. The corn was shucked and cleaned, ready for cooking down on the beach. Gourmet pickles were sliced.

The shrimp had to be shelled and cooked, then cut into bite sized pieces for shrimp tacos. Loads of cabbage was shredded as an accompaniment. The girls were efficient...it was all done by noon on the first day. They buzzed around cleaning up and then took off until the next day. Daniel waved them out the kitchen door, smiling. Then he sat down for a bit. He was thinking that the Glass House kitchen had never known such activity, such life and such fun.

Day two was the "put together day." Daniel showed them how to mix up the dressing for the crab salad and chop the vegetables for it. He used red and green bell peppers, celery and jicama. It was a beautiful, colorful mix. They mixed up the potato salad too, tossing it all with the oil and vinegar dressing to marinate and flavor the bland potatoes. Daniel showed them how the potatoes should be in chunks, but not too big, not too firm. The potato should "melt" a little around the edges into the dressing.

Taco shells had to be made ahead. Daniel showed them how he dipped the corn tortillas in a heavy, spicy, powdered seasoning then quickly deep-fried them folded over. The girls drained and stacked them in boxes ready to fill down at the picnic site. Then he made his cobbler while they watched. He just sugared and cooked the fruit through lightly first, then poured a batter crust over it and baked to a golden brown. They made two big pans, and that just about finished the kitchen work. The rest would be done on site down at the beach. The three of them commented on how satisfying it was working like this together. Now they were getting excited for the event the next day.

That afternoon people started coming in from the ferries. Trini and Oscar were first, bringing a couple of kids, David and Wes, who worked in The Prow kitchen as bus boys. More from the restaurant were expected the next day. Later, Otis and Marion showed up with Anna and her brother and sister-in-law. Glenn Babineaux could have been Anna's twin. He was tall, elegant, and very black. Dottie was little but buxom with long tiny braids and huge brown eyes. Their smiles were all gorgeous, just like Anna's. They dropped in just for a moment, said hi, then went on down the road to the marina.

Trini and Oscar with the two boys climbed down to the beach house. They spent the afternoon trying out the Time Out, just along the shore of the cove. Daniel took them all for rides. Trini had been afraid to go out on the water, but they finally convinced her to get into the boat. She was thrilled, yelping a little as spray hit her. David and Wes ran around the beach tossing the Frisbee for Henry until sundown. Potter was nowhere to be seen. Too many people, too much noise. Just plain hot dogs over the fire pit grill and chips was dinner tonight, with some nice red wine. They would feast tomorrow. Everyone sat around on the beach until late. There was so much catching up to do, everyone talking at once. Finally, the four guests made their way up the path with flashlights. Trini and Oscar would sleep in Paul and Sheila's old room. Wes and David wanted to sleep out on the terrace in their sleeping bags under the stars. It was a balmy evening, not a cloud, and none expected. Daniel stayed below and lay in his bed, marveling at how different things were at the house and on the beach with people... people all around and working with people. It was like The Prow, relocated.

Morning dawned with a frenzy of doing. Daniel was up with the dawn and working away in the Glass House kitchen. He made more beignets for them all, and coffee. He had the thought that he could open a French bakery, he was getting so organized with the beignets. They started by icing and loading up the food, then hauled everything down to Cattle Point, taking both cars, trunks packed tight. Of course, Oscar and Trini had brought some special things from The Prow. They were keeping them under wraps for now. The marina crowd was already at the picnic site setting everything up when they arrived. Nan and Ruth arrived and there were introductions and greetings all around. The men dug a pit in the sand on the beach while folding tables and some chairs were set up on the grass higher up. Portable barbeque pits were brought in. All the food was carried onto the site and cooking got underway. People were continuing to arrive, the kids running directly down to the beach and into the water. Peggy, Anna and Marion worked on the tables. Daniel's crew, including Ruth and Nan, were preparing to stuff the tacos and cook the corn. Some boys and men were down on the beach getting the seafood going. Otis was just walking around, sort of bellowing about how wonderful it was to be back on the island, and how great God is. There were many dogs to keep Henry company. They were running and barking up and down the beach, sniffing around the food and being shooed away. Right then, a few more staff members from The Prow came driving up... it was Sarah, Dora and Janus! Daniel was thrilled and welcomed them with hugs all around. The church folks drifted in and the marina workers and guests too. It was a zoo...a wonderful picnic zoo.

A little after noon, things were readied and it all came together. The food was all produced and laid out for consuming.

It looked like a cross between a medieval feast and a pot luck dinner. The Prow staff brought out their special dishes. Trini had brought her coconut flan on ice. Sarah had brought some very delicate, light rolls and Scandinavian herbed butter. There was also a big dish of marinated mushrooms and pearl onions. The only thing missing was a roasted suckling pig... but, that was truly the only thing missing. There was food everywhere. Suddenly, Otis' booming voice was heard over the murmuring and the church folks all joined in. It was the ancient Doxology sung acapella ... "Praise God from whom all blessings flow... Praise him all creatures here below..." The harmonies were beautiful. Daniel could feel the hair on the back of his neck standing up. Nan was beside him, Ruth too. They took his hands softly, one on each side.

The afternoon was spent grazing on the food, walking the beach and wading in the surf. Daniel spent time with his Prow friends and walked them down to the lighthouse for a tour. He told them about his sea adventures sailing the straits. They were wide-eyed and amazed. After a while everyone grouped around on the grass, resting and talking, looking out to sea. Daniel sat with Nan and Ruth for a while. After a bit, Ruth went to play with the kids and dogs down on the beach. Daniel took the opportunity to ask Nan for a favor.

"Have you told Ruth about Paul not being my dad?" he asked.

Nan looked up at him sharply. "No, Daniel. That's a private matter. That's not for me to be talking about."

"Thanks...that's very nice of you. But, I wonder if you would do me a favor. Would you tell Ruth about this for me? All my other friends here know about it. I've told them myself. I'll be leaving soon. I'd like Ruth to know what happened...what has happened to me out here. O.K.? But, I'm just tired of talking about it. I would like her to know, but I just don't want to go over it anymore."

"O.K., Daniel. I'll tell her if you like. I understand. I think it would mean something for her to know this." She looked grave.

"I would really appreciate that, Nan. I just don't have it in me to go over all that again. And, I want her to know."

"I'll tell her soon."

"Good, it is almost time for me to head on out of here and back to my life on the mainland. You've been a great friend to me, Nan."

Nan smiled. "There will be many more times and days like this. You are an islander now. It has seeped into your blood!"

"I think you're right." He looked far out over the strait.

They all stayed into the evening, going back finally and finishing off all the remnants of the picnic food, acting as if they hadn't eaten a thing all day.

Some people began leaving, sleepy children had to go. The Prow staff said their goodbyes…they needed to catch the ferry. But many others stayed, quietly enjoying the dark beach and the star-filled sky. Anna and Luke came to sit down by Daniel and Ruth.

"We wanted to talk to you guys about the wedding this December." Anna began.

"Oh, what wedding is that?" Daniel kidded. "Oh yeah! You two are getting married! That's right!"

Anna punched his arm. "We want to see if Ruth will do the flowers. We thought maybe you could help her too? You know we are getting married over here, right?"

"They are being married at Beulah Land, Daniel," Ruth said. "I was hoping you would ask me to do flowers, Anna! I want to be part of this event. Daniel can help me, if he will."

"We are having a tent too, on the church grounds...for the reception." Anna was smiling about it. It was clear her dreams were coming closer and closer to reality.

Daniel looked at Ruth. "Would you trust me to do this with you? I'm a cook, not a florist."

They all looked at him. "You're an artist, Daniel. With food and everything else," said Luke, matter-of-factly.

"You will be good help," smiled Ruth. It was all settled.

"If you like, I could have Trini and Sarah make your wedding cake. It would be my gift."

"Wow! That would be great. Thank you, Daniel. We accept!" Anna was thrilled.

"Two things settled then," said Daniel, pleased.

They sat on in the dark, with Otis and Marion too, talking about this time and place, this beautiful summer and beyond, into the future, the plans for the wedding coming in just a few months. It would be winter. It might be cold and frosty, a different season on the island. It seldom snowed...but it might!

Tonight though, the balmy evening wore on and on, under the stars. Finally, reluctantly, they all cleaned up and packed up slowly, driving off through the dark, one by one, leaving the little lighthouse alone shining its light on the dark coast.

## CHAPTER FORTY-EIGHT

# The Lighthouse Dream

THE night after the picnic, Daniel dreamed of Cattle Point. The circumstances of the dream were clear...they were picnicking there again. Everyone was there just as it had been the day before, plus a few more people milling around in the background. Trini and Oscar were there, and others from The Prow staff. Sheila was there! And Willie! Jim, Paul's housekeeper was there. Otis and Marion were there, and all their families from the mainland. Luke and Anna appeared, and Anna's brother Glenn, Pete and Peggy, Ruth and Nan, some of the families from the church. He couldn't be sure, but it seemed that Thomas was also somewhere in the crowd! Everyone was eating and drinking and looking out over the point to the west, toward the open waters of the strait. It was a big crowd.

Then they all sighted a sailboat approaching, coming around from the east. As it came nearer, Daniel saw that it was full of people too. On shore, the sound of singing could be faintly heard coming from the boat. It was an odd craft, antiquated in design, square-rigged and rough. It did not come to shore, but sailed right past them all as they watched.

Someone in the boat was waving to them, both hands over his head. It was Paul. He was wearing his white casual shirt again, shirttails untucked. He looked tanned as before and wonderfully healthy. He was standing up in the stern of the boat, near the tiller. They could all see him well enough to see that he was smiling broadly, smiling and waving. He was talking to the man at the tiller. Then the helmsman waved too, smiling a dazzling smile. He was that One, the Man on the Cross. The picnickers were shouting happily towards the boat. Daniel heard Otis' booming voice. While they watched from shore, Daniel saw Sheila move forward. She walked right down to the edge of the water, waving too. Sheila was wearing a long, dark, full skirt, something Daniel had never seen her wear in his life. It was flowing all around her ankles. He noticed that she was barefooted. She seemed to be straining forward to hear the singers on the boat. It looked like she wanted to say something, to shout something to them, but she didn't. At least he couldn't hear her. She waved vigorously. The boat sailed on, heading out west towards the straits, towards the open sea. They watched and waved until the boat disappeared in the afternoon haze.

Daniel saw Sheila turn and start walking back up the slope towards him. Now she was smiling too and had something in her hands. It was something black. In fact, as she got closer he could see that it was the same black marble urn that had contained Paul's ashes. She walked right up to him with a beaming smile, handing him the urn. He took it from her and saw that the top was off the urn. It was empty and clean inside.

He woke up sleepily after this dream. It was still dark, morning was hours away. He had left all the windows open and he could hear the sea outside, and the breeze. He was so comfortable down under his blanket, sort of curled up, so drowsy, listening to the sound of the water. Henry was on the foot of the bed. He moaned and stretched out, turning over with a lazy "huff." Daniel didn't open his eyes. He didn't need to. He knew where everything was, what all the sounds were and so he just lay there, feeling the comfort of his place, the smells of wood and sea, the sound of water moving, the softness of his blanket up under his chin.

"Someone loves me," he mumbled. "Someone loves me. I feel it." He drowsily cuddled down deeper in the bed, covering himself right up over his head. He was soon asleep again.

## CHAPTER FORTY-NINE

# The Sunflower Sail

DANIEL was getting Glass House ready for his departure. Peggy would be coming up tomorrow to help him do a housecleaning day. There wasn't a lot to do but he wanted to leave the stove clean. He had made good use of the oven in recent days. The refrigerator definitely needed to be cleaned out and scrubbed down too. He would tell Peg to take the food home with her. Better to leave it nearly empty...he wasn't sure when he would be back.

Luke would come up later, after the marina quieted down, to do the high windows with his "pro" tools, wrap things up and close down for the winter. Daniel knew he had to go, but he felt so heavy about it, so...heavy.

It was odd, thinking of the place lying there alone on the coast all during winter. The orchard would go back to its silent days. He and Henry would be far away. He could imagine the empty rooms, the wind hitting the big windows in its banging way, the creaking limbs of the orchard trees. There would be damp foggy days and rain on the slate terrace. He could think about that, but could not bear to think about the beach house all alone. It was his home now...his main home. He would lock it up tight. Potter would be the only sentry. Daniel had been clearing out his beach refrigerator bit by bit, and Potter was getting a steady supply of goodies on his beach plate. Maybe he too knew that summer was over.

He folded the two white chef aprons he had bought for Nan and Ruth and put them in the car. There was a pile of beignets he had made earlier. They would be the last batch before leaving... no more frying in the kitchen if Peg was coming to clean up. He packed the beignets up too. He called Henry to get in the car and drove over to the Sloan Farm.

Ruth was working in the greenhouse. She could see him coming, but even so he dangled the bag of beignets through the door frame as if she could not see him. She was giggling.

"This is the stuff that makes you fat," she said.

"I know, but I just can't stop making them. Actually, the truth is this is the last batch before I head out to resume my life as a restaurateur. What are you working on?"

She held her old-fashioned galvanized watering can in her hands. "I am finishing up here, getting the watering done for the day. We are going over to Lopez Island this morning!" She was wearing a celery green knit top and another of her long flowered skirts, a softly colored print, also celery green with other pastels. He could see now that she was dressed up to go out. He noticed for the first time that her brilliant hair was getting longer. He had the thought that she had probably not cut it since he had been on the island. It was a mass of curls framing her bright, childlike face. No makeup, no guile.

"Wow, what's going on?" He was interested, intrigued about Lopez. He had only briefly visited Fisherman's Bay. He had never explored the island.

She put down the watering can and came over to take a beignet from him. She was grinning. "Come outside with me. I want to show you something. It's a new flower for us."

She led the way behind the greenhouse to a patch of flowers he had not noticed before. They were all sunflowers...every kind of sunflower. "This is our experimental sunflower garden," she said. "We want to grow some sunflower fields next season. They are super popular as a cut flower these days. Ours are all blooming now. Look at this one! Isn't it cute?" She handed him back the half-eaten beignet and cupped one of the flowers in her gloved hands.

It was cute. It was a smaller-headed frilly variety, which looked like a chrysanthemum on steroids. "This is a Teddy Bear Sunflower!" Ruth was clearly in love with this new flower. "We're going over to Lopez to buy some seeds in bulk so we can grow these little honeys. We are putting in several varieties, but this Teddy Bear is my favorite." Her face was beaming. "Hey, why don't you come with us? We're going down to catch the ferry in just a few minutes."

He only thought for a about a minute before agreeing to tag along to Lopez Island...as long as Henry could go too, of course. He was glad to do anything to delay the pain of preparing to leave the island. He offered to take his car on the ferry, since there was plenty of room for the three of them and the dog, too. It had a huge trunk for the bags of seeds they would be carrying home. Ruth agreed and went to round up Nan.

Nan had been fixing a lunch in the big house. They planned to picnic there on Lopez along the way to the seed place. She greeted Daniel heartily and said there was plenty of food for three. The two women busied around finishing up and then they climbed into Daniel's sedan and were off.

The ferry was waiting at the dock when they arrived, and they drove right on board. This was Daniel's first ferry ride since he had arrived on the island. He was thinking somberly that he would be taking it all the way back to the mainland in just a couple of days. It was still morning, only about 10 o'clock, so not a crowded time on the inbound route. They sat in the sun on the deck, and Ruth told him all about the sunflowers. This time, Henry was out on deck too, though he was required to have a leash. He was serenely looking out on the water...by now, he was a well-seasoned sailing dog.

Apparently these sunflowers were all the rage on the flower market now, and Ruth and Nan hoped to raise a big crop for next year. They had a field specially prepared already and expected to do well come next summer. The only drawbacks to the crop were that the plants required a great deal of water to grow nice and big with heavy blooms, and they were slightly more work to harvest. These would be the biggest flowers the farm had ever raised! Ruth was in a flurry of excitement over this new turn in the business. The grower on Lopez was into the production of seed, even more than the flower crop. Their seeds were shipped all over the country. Ruth was excited to see them actually growing in the fields in person, and to ask the grower probably a million questions! She was chattering on and on about these seeds.

Nan got up to go in and buy them each a drink at the concession inside. Ruth stopped her stream of talk about the flowers and turned to look seriously at Daniel.

"Nan told me about the situation with your father," she said. "She said you wanted me to know about Paul and about your mother coming out here this summer." She was looking at him directly. "Why didn't you just tell me yourself? Why did you ask Nan to tell me this?"

"I don't know, Ruth. I guess I am just tired of talking about it. It's been a very explosive thing this summer for me." He was looking away and was a little uncomfortable with her directness. "I just wanted you to know." He kept looking away.

"We are friends, Daniel," Ruth said evenly. "You can tell me anything. I'm glad to know about this. I'll bet it is a big deal in your life. A big deal. I just want you to know that you can talk to me. We don't have the most perfect family out here either, you know."

"I know, Ruth. I know all that. I just really didn't feel like repeating and repeating this tale about my family. But, because we have become friends, I thought you should know. It IS a really big deal in my life." He smiled grimly, shading his eyes from the sun with both hands as he now looked at her. "It's a big deal to me, and I wanted you to know."

"Good," she said. "I just wanted to tell you that Nan had told me. We can talk some other time about it." She pulled her big brimmed sun hat down further to cover her eyes, partly to escape the sun. But, it was a gesture of finality. Nan was returning with the three drinks balanced in her hands. They went back to the topic of sunflowers.

Lopez Island was a grower's paradise. Daniel could see that immediately as they left the ferry dock. There were fields all over the island. Vegetables, orchards and yes, flowers flourished around every turn of the country road. They stopped at a picnic spot which Ruth and Nan knew of along the way and opened up their container of goodies. Nan had done well. There was a very tender fried chicken, and a cole slaw which Daniel wanted to copy, red and green fresh cabbage, broccoli, red onion, and a dressing that was new to him, some kind of homemade French. Rolls and her chocolate chip cookies finished things off.

The seed farm was just around the bend. As they approached, an astonishing, huge array of sunflowers of every possible kind was there before them. The fields were enormous and everything was in final bloom here at the end of the season. Ruth told him that these flowers would be allowed to dry in the fields, and then the seed would be collected from them.

The owner met them as they pulled in and took them on a tour of the fields in a golf cart. Many of the flowers were way over their heads. Daniel had never seen anything like it. He wished he had his camera with him, but Nan had hers and was snapping away. They bought small bags of at least ten varieties of flower seed and four big burlap bags of the "top of the list" flowers, the Teddy Bears. They also bought some multi-colored and variegated stock and the traditional giants. Daniel bought a small bag of the Teddy Bear seeds to plant along his barren driveway. Everything fit into the trunk and Ruth was murmuring thanks and chattering up until the moment they drove away.

She sighed a long sigh as they drove to the ferry and looked at Daniel with a big grin. "This is going to be so much fun! I can't wait to see them come up!" The grower had warned her to plant directly in the fields around the last week of April, depending on weather.

When they arrived home on San Juan and pulled in to the farm driveway, the women were clearly worn out. Daniel helped them unload the seeds. Then he had an invitation for them. He figured they would probably decline. Time was running out for him, and they were very busy.

"We are so glad you came with us, Daniel. I don't know how we could have muscled these big bags by ourselves!" said Nan.

"I'm glad I got to come with you. Those fields were a sight. By the way, I'm taking the Time Out on one last sail before I take it down to the marina for storage.

Would you two like to sail with me, just for a ride along the coast? You've never been in my sailboat. Tomorrow is cleaning day, but I plan to go the day after that. It will be my last day on the island."

Nan and Ruth looked at each other. Nan shook her head. "I don't think I can do that, Daniel," she smiled. "I would like to, but my old bones would have a hard time getting up and down that path much less riding in a boat. Thank you for the invitation though, how nice of you!"

Ruth had perked up at the suggestion though. She smiled widely and said she would love to go!

"I've got finishing up work to do...cleaning and packing tomorrow," said Daniel. "Come down after lunch, day after tomorrow. The wind is much better for sailing in the afternoon."

Ruth just grinned. She was looking forward to it.

## CHAPTER FIFTY

# The Final

It was time to close up the place and leave. This was his last full day on the island. The pressure to leave was strong, but Daniel still had that yearning to go out on the water for one more sail. He wanted to finish off his time on the island with sailing memories…just one more time of open air, wind and cutting through the water. He wanted to go somewhere nearby, along the coast, not a far-flung journey. This would be his last chance before fall set in and his boat was brought up out of the water.

Ruth arrived in the afternoon. He had been working all morning, hauling everything that needed to go up to Glass House for storage. He had dug up the beach refrigerator, washed it down and filled in the hole. He brought the barrel into the house, storing it in his closet alcove. There was just enough food to finish off the day, so he had made some sandwiches and things for the time on the water.

Ruth was looking perky and ready to go. She had her hair up in a bushy ponytail, wearing a baseball cap, shorts and camp shirt, and dark glasses. She was so fair...Daniel asked her if she wanted to put on sunscreen. She said she already done so at home. Daniel had progressively turned a golden tan, the result of being outside all summer. His hair was a shaggy mess, slightly bleached out, since he had not gotten a hair cut the whole time on the island. Henry was shaggy too for the same reason. It was doubtful that Daniel had looked in the mirror much to see how he looked. He just bathed and shaved regularly and that was it.

They launched into the bay and set sail north up the coast. Henry was in his patrol position in the bow. This made Ruth grin. Henry looked so serious, so vigilant.

"He has gotten to love his job as boat guard or whatever he thinks he is." Daniel was grinning too. "You know, he is a tremendous fishing guide. He knows right where to cast to catch a load of fish. I don't know how he knows it. I can't imagine that he smells the fish, but maybe he does." He shrugged his shoulders. "We'll go up the coast and then tack further out and see if we can catch the wind for a little speed."

Ruth's eyes were bright. "I've lived here my whole life and have never been out like this in a small sailboat. We used to go fishing with some friends in a motor boat, but never in a sailboat. I have to tell you this is a thrill for me!"

They sailed north. The water was perfect, with just a slight ruffle to the surface and the afternoon wind was coming up the channel now from the strait to the south. Daniel did some zigzagging just to show her how the sail and the boom worked. Then he let her manage the sheet while he manned the tiller. He directed her as they turned. He could see that she was loving it. She was not afraid of the water, he could see that, too.

He was watching her closely. She was such a practical girl, so savvy, and yet there was an element of incredible innocence, bordering on naiveté. Probably the best description for her would be "focused," he decided. She was focused on her flowers and her business. The rest of the world could "go to hell in a hand basket." That's what it looked like any way. It was a rare combination. Actually, he thought, "focused" would be a good word to describe him also. "Focused" was the way he had always been, until this summer.

They were on a long straight run up the coast. The sail was taut and close-hauled with the southwesterly wind for speed. They were both taking in the sensation of the neat speed and the slight tilt of the boat. It was beautiful. He started to smile, then laugh.

"Do you remember when we first met?" he said.

"Sure, you were pretending to be dead in this boat up in the cove below our farm," she said, smiling alongside him.

He couldn't see her eyes behind the dark glasses.

"Although, I do remember you biking around the roads when you were just a boy in the summer. You had skinny legs...a skinny-legged boy."

"And you thought you were going to save my life that day at the cove!" He was grinning. "What made you think you could save my life, all by yourself!" He was laughing at her.

She was perfectly serious, tightening her grip on the line. "I don't know. I had been writhing around that day, grieving for a dead husband. I didn't want to see anyone else die, if I could help it." She looked over at him with an open face.

"We'll go through that cove on the way back," he said. "Just for old time's sake, even though it was really only a couple of months ago," he laughed.

They tacked and gibed for a long while back and forth in the bay. The wind grew stronger out in the middle, so they let it all out, the billowing sail filling with air and as they were pulled over they hung out over the opposite gunwale to balance against the wind. They were moving fast and Ruth was delighted, shrieking from time to time with joy.

Daniel gave her a pair of gloves to protect her hands after a while. He didn't want to be responsible for blisters. The gloves were huge on her, but she wore them.

Soon, he headed the Time Out southward, down towards the little cove below the Sloan Farm. They turned in and dropped sail in the middle.

"Here we are, right back where we started from!" Daniel laughed. He could laugh now. It had not been a laughing matter that day back in May. Ruth smiled sheepishly, she could still feel the smart of the pain of that day, but she was happy to be here too.

"This cove, we call Scimitar Cove," she said. "From above it is shaped like a scimitar with the blade being the thin width of gray sand at the edge of the water. Very exotic, no?" she grinned. "We don't USUALLY swim here! Too many rocks to dodge."

"I've brought the Time Out here many times this summer. I usually take a dip right out here in the middle. As if on cue, Henry leapt into the water, barking. He knew the drill. Daniel looked at Ruth. She sighed, took off her hat and glasses and dove over the side into the water. Daniel was quick to follow. They just dog-paddled around a while, splashing and swimming underwater. Daniel could see some fish and other creatures down below. The water was dark and surprisingly cold. It was early September, so the temperature was changing. In a few minutes they were back in the boat shivering. Daniel hauled Henry up, and now they were all cold. There were a couple of towels on board, so they dried off as best they could.

"Now we will be all sticky until we get home. Oh well," said Ruth. It was clear she didn't care.

Daniel lifted the sail and rigged it to get out of there. He was glad they had done this. It was a happy closure to the cove event. They dried in the sun and wind as they began the way home.

Suddenly, just as they were passing the "Bone Yard" of bleached out driftwood tree trunks, there was a jolt and a loud thump at the hull. Daniel knew immediately what it was. The keel had been hit by a submerged incoming tree trunk. Something about the currents in that area caused fallen tree trunks to drift ashore right at this spot. They had obviously been rammed by one. He tested the keel by trying some sharp turns. He could tell the keel was damaged some way. He thought about going over the side to look at it from below, but they were now in a swift current and tacking into a stiff breeze. He would have to wait. Ruth looked at him questioningly. He was thinking.

The best thing to do would be to raise the keel as far up he could to try to save it. They would have to drop sail and row. He had planned to take the Time Out all the way into the marina at the end of their sail. It was to be the final sail before handing his boat over to Luke and Pete to take care of and dock for the winter at the marina. He wasn't sure if they could row all the way. Maybe with two people they could.

"It's the keel," he said. "I've got to bring it up. We'll have to drop sail. Can you row?"

She smiled. "Oh yeah, I can row. I was on the sculling team in high school. We practiced at Friday Harbor. I can row. It's been a while."

He looked at her lean arms. "O.K., we'll try it. Do you think you can go all the way to the marina?"

She nodded her head, "yes." There was a gleam in her eyes. It was clear that she liked the idea of a challenge.

Daniel lifted the keel in its slot. It could not be brought all the way up, but he managed to get it mostly out of the water. He could tell it was cracked. He stabilized it the best he could with some duct tape from his tool kit. They took up the oars and started rowing, one on each side to start with, two-handed.

"Put those gloves back on. I don't want those hands ruined doing this!"

She obeyed, but with a look that said, "Who do you think you're talking to?"

They were rowing against the tide at first. It was hard going, but within a half an hour they could feel the tide begin to turn the other direction. It was ebbing, making things much easier. The sun was about to set as they passed by Glass House and the beach house. Daniel took a break and let Ruth row a bit at that point. They had both been nibbling on the sandwiches he had brought. They had some water bottles. He planned to finish, rounding the point into the marina on his own.

Their pace was steady now, with Ruth at the oars, rowing smoothly down the coast. Daniel was watching her, looking at her smooth delicate arms, seeing the bicep muscles work the oars. She was so small, but strong. She wasn't very tall, he guessed five foot two, so she had braced her bare feet against their picnic box for leverage. Her toes were neat, unpainted, but with pink, pearly nails. She paused to hand him her sunglasses, as the sky was darkening towards dusk. Now he could see her amber green eyes in her calm face. She looked like she could row like this for hours.

Daniel wasn't about to let that happen, so he came over and took the oars from her with a smile. He wrapped her up in the now-dry towel, as the air chilled. They were both completely dry now from wind and sun. Ruth and Henry sat huddled in the bow as Daniel rowed the last stretch, coming into the marina just as darkness fell.

They met Luke and Pete in the skiff, just coming out the entrance of the marina. Luke's dog, George, was in the boat barking. It was clear that they were all alarmed. "We were just coming to look for you," said Luke. "What happened? We expected you a couple of hours ago."

"I'll show you when we dock," Daniel said grimly.

They tethered the Time Out to the skiff and towed it in to the docks.

"We were broadsided by an underwater tree trunk, up by the Bone Yard," Daniel shouted over the boat motor.

Pete groaned. "This happens. Is it the keel?"

Daniel nodded. "I pulled it up and we rowed most of the way. Ruth was on the oars too." He smiled big and hugged Ruth, patting her back, to her surprise.

"All right Ruthie!" Luke gave the thumbs up sign. For some reason, Ruth was not thrilled with this praise. It embarrassed her. She smiled tightly.

Peg had come out and as Ruth left the boat, the two women walked off together to the condo. Dinner had been waiting for them. The two dogs romped around outside while Luke, Pete and Daniel worked on the Time Out, trying to pull the keel out carefully. The blade was now sheared off right through the middle. The working mechanism was fine, it just needed a new blade. Pete said it would be no problem to replace.

"I wanted to get it on down here tonight. I really need to leave in the morning. Can you guys take it from here? I hate to leave it like this."

"That's not a problem, Daniel. It's easy to replace. We'll order it tomorrow and while we are waiting on it, we will give the Time Out a once over check-up. I'm sure that there is not much to do." Pete was calmly looking at the broken piece. "This is an old craft, but these keels are available. Don't worry. This one was fiberglass. We'll replace it with one in a new material, sort of like nylon." They took the Time Out to the dock where it would be spending the winter, then followed the girls in to dinner.

Ruth was already in the shower at Peg's invitation. Her clothes were in the washer. She came out in a minute wearing Peggy's bathrobe, and with wet ringlets piled on top of her head. This gave her an Asian look, as if she were in a kimono, they said, kidding her. Her face was already ruddy especially across the nose as a result of a day in sun and salt water, not to mention wind.

"I'm clean," she said, "unlike some others around here."

Daniel waved off the offer of a shower. "You'll just have to put up with me, as is, Henry too." He had simply smoothed down his longish hair and washed his hands and face. There was no doubting Daniel's scruffiness, but he looked very handsome in a working man's way. He was brown and his hands had become hardened from working and sailing.

They ate and drank while Ruth told the story of their adventure with enthusiasm. Dinner was a normal "Peggy affair," meatloaf with a catsup topping, mashed potatoes and green beans. They wolfed it down. There was a nice red wine, and they hit that hard too. A review of summer sailing stories was given by the guys, with the waves on the strait now described as higher than a house. The laughter was boisterous, feelings were high.

Finally though, it was time to go. Ruth watched the men do their awkward goodbyes, but she saw the tears in their eyes. Daniel embraced Peggy with tenderness. For her, the words "I love you" came easily. Daniel mumbled something back. Ruth went and dressed again in her own clothes. They were ready to go. They had planned to walk back to Glass House on the cliff path. Pete and Luke objected loudly and said they would drive them, but Daniel put up a hand and said, no.

"I want to walk this one last time in the dark," he said. "Ruth will bring the flashlight just in case."

"We will be fine," Ruth agreed. "Henry will be our guide."

There were last hugs and thick voices, extra hard backslaps and handshakes from the men. Their feelings were deep. It had been an incredible summer.

As they left, Daniel detoured over to the place where the Time Out was to be kept. He got in and placed a kiss on the bow. Then he quickly started off down the dock without a word. Ruth was following behind. He reached back without looking and took her hand, squeezing it hard.

"Thanks for spending this last day with me, Ruth," he said with a thick voice. "Thank you."

They trudged up the hill and into the cliff path. It was not a full moon night, but there was a piece of moon, and it was bright enough for them to see well. Henry was up front, then came Ruth, Daniel followed. He was watching her up there. It was a path fit for only one walker at a time, single file. He could see her slender white legs, shining in the moon light. "She is so little, but strong," he thought for the second time today. This was a night of tears and he let them fall in the dark. Another strong emotion swept over him as he watched her up ahead, trudging with her bare legs and her curly, curly hair in the dark. He both wanted to crush her against himself and to protect her from any such a thing at the same time...to protect her and keep her as she was, forever.

"Hey you Sloan woman!" he suddenly shouted at her. "Stop!"

She did stop, and she turned around.

"Are you Sloan women trying to kill me? Are you trying to bewitch me?" He was not drunk, but a little wine and a lot of emotion was fueling him.

"That's a funny thing to say from a guy who has dragged me into his little boat and made me row like a galley slave the whole length of the island." Her eyes were narrow and sparkling in the moonlight, but then she grinned...then she laughed. She turned around and kept walking along the path, throwing her head back and laughing out loud from time to time as she walked on. She didn't care what he said, what he thought. He saw that this whole day had given her joy.

He put Henry in through the kitchen door at Glass House. They stowed her bike, which she had ridden over, in the trunk of his car, then drove home to Sloan Farm. He went in to say goodbye to Nan. She was sitting up in her little house reading.

He had never been over there at night so he had never seen the little house lit up. It was utterly charming by lamp light. Ruth and Daniel told the tale of their day of adventures briefly. They were both so tired. Daniel was standing. He didn't want to sit down, because if he did he might never leave this little homey place. They said their good-byes. They said their thank-yous. They promised to see one another before Christmas when he would return for the wedding and its preparations. Nan pressed a book into his hands. Of course, it was another Bible, a larger one.

"You need something better than that travel Bible," she said. "This is a real Bible."

He thanked her. He kissed her cheek and left.

Ruth walked him to his car. "We need to talk...about the wedding flowers...about the design. And Daniel, Nan isn't the only one who prays. I will pray for you too." She patted him on the back sweetly. She hugged him and sort of nuzzled his neck softly. It made his hair stand on end. Then she left him to go into her house.

That night, at the beach house, Daniel dreamed again. He dreamed he was right there in the beach house asleep. He felt something rattling in his chest, something fluttering. In the dream, he woke up and threw off the covers, looking down at his chest in fear. He stood up. It was dark, but there was still enough light to see that his chest was not a normal chest, but a cage, like a birdcage. In fact, it WAS a bird cage and there was a white bird in it, fluttering around wildly. He was staring down at this in alarm when the door opened. Ruth walked in. Since it was a dream, her movements were dreamlike, slow. She was wearing a long white linen shift. It covered her completely but he could make out the movement of her slender form beneath the linen. She was not smiling. Her face was very serious, determined. She walked up to him with a big, old-fashioned key in her hand, a brass key. She fitted the key into the slot in the birdcage door and opened it. In his sleep he was feeling the discomfort of the bird, as if flying around in his chest. When she opened the door, the bird rushed out of the cage and flew out the open door. Ruth was standing there with him. Her hair had brushed his face as she worked to open the door of the cage. He could smell the scent of her soap, a plain, lavender scent.

He woke up. Henry had jumped down off the bed and was looking up at him expectantly. He realized he had been struggling and flailing around in bed during the dream. He got up and looked at his watch on the table. It was five in the morning.

"It's time to go, Henry. It's time to go."

Everything was cleaned up and ready. He just made a last pot of coffee and sipped it as he bustled around putting things in order, making the bed and grabbing the last bag of trash. No shaving, no shower. He had showered the salt water off last night. Everything except his duffle bag had already been taken up the path, yesterday. Henry knew, as dogs do, that they were leaving. He ran outside ahead of Daniel, running around excitedly on the beach, wetting his feet in the surf. Daniel drank his coffee standing in the doorway, looking out over the bay. In the dawning light, he saw something out in the middle of the cove on the surface of the water. It was Potter... floating on his back.

Daniel went back into the beach house, rinsed the coffee pot and threw the grounds into his trash bag. Reluctantly, he walked out and closed the new padlock on the door. Stepping back he looked up at his house, his retreat, his home, one last time. The house looked dark, as if it were already going to sleep for the season.

He was soon up the path and onto the terrace where he looked down one last time onto the waters of the bay. Potter was still floating. Daniel could faintly hear his chatter echoing up the cliff.

Glass House was already locked up, so he just circled the house outside one last time, walking through the orchard in the pale light. He paused a moment in the middle of the orchard looking around just to imprint the scene in his mind. The apples were ripe and fragrant above him in the trees. He had arranged for pickers to come soon and harvest them. They would be boxed and shipped to The Prow, with just a few sent down to the marina for his friends. For some reason he said, "Thank you," out loud, "Thank you." Then he and Henry got into the car, and he drove away as the sun just began to lighten things all around.

They passed the Sloan Farm in the dawning light. All was dark there...they were still sleeping. He wound his way down to the harbor and was soon on the ferry. The big chugging boat pulled away from the dock and they were off. He would be back at The Prow in time for lunch.

## CHAPTER FIFTY-ONE

# Back In Town

THEY didn't go first to The Prow for lunch. Daniel dropped his bag and took a long shower at the condo. He wanted to shave and clean up. Then both he and Henry went out for some work on their hair. Henry was taken to the dog grooming shop. The groomers were amazed at Henry's island "shag." Daniel headed over to the salon for a haircut. This time, he told them to leave it somewhat longer. He didn't need a clipped city look any more.

The condo was immaculately clean when he arrived. The housekeeper had been there every week, watering the one single plant, dusting and giving the floors a once-over. She had obviously just cleaned the day before. Even so, it felt like an empty shell compared to his home on the beach. The only sign of life in the place was the big, shiny, green philodendron, now so big that it had finally touched the ceiling. He had sighed as he hung up his clothes in the silent house. He wondered how he would feel at the restaurant…how would it be there now?

Actually, he realized that he had been mentally holding his breath, afraid to see how things had changed at The Prow in his absence. He was afraid that Oscar and Trini would have done things, or not done things, to compromise the way he always wanted things maintained. He need not have worried. Everything was fine.

As he walked through the front doors, he saw that the shine was on everything, from the beveled windows to the beautiful ship's prow gleaming there as always. He was happy to see it. He saw the serene expression on the face of the classic wooden lady as she lit the way with her lantern... perpetually lighting the way. Her little carved child was safe against her body, cradled in her other arm, as always. He had missed her, but...he noticed immediately that though he saw her with love, with affection, it was not with that yearning need that had always drawn him in before. It was beautiful, it was delightful, it was right, but that was it. There was a big bouquet of yellow sunflowers on the Maitre 'D's station.

Everyone heard him come in and came rushing around, hugging and greeting him. High fives and low fives from Oscar. They all murmured that he was looking good, all tan and everything. He checked out the kitchen. Prow chowder was hot on the stove. What more could be asked for? He went to the office with Trini and Oscar for a good long talk over coffee. Trini showed him the books. She had done well. Then he hung out with everyone in the kitchen, hearing all their news. He would tell about his adventures later.

There was not much for him to do at first. He called the bank and told them he was back. He called the main suppliers and thanked them for their cooperation with the staff while he was away. Trini had prepared a special table for him and a fine dinner. They did not want him to have to jump right back into the middle of work. They didn't want him to stress. They wanted to show him the same hospitality they had been keeping up for everyone who came through the doors.

The bottom line was that The Prow had not changed. They had made a few changes in staff organization, firing one bus boy who just could not stop breaking dishes. A little blond girl had been hired in his place, Trudy. He noticed some rather more flamboyant garnishes on the plates, the expressive product of his colorful head chef.

The first week he was back, they held a staff dinner after hours. Everyone was there. A long table had been prepared beautifully, so everyone could sit together. Daniel raised a toast to Oscar and Trini and then to all of them. Then they "roasted" him. They called him "slacker," "beach boy," "Popeye the Sailor" and other less savory names for being gone so long. He paid them back by telling the hair-raising tale of his Juan de Fuca trip. They were mesmerized. Daniel could tell that they really had missed him.

October arrived, and he was fully immersed in work. He was in the dining room on a Tuesday afternoon, that golden, apricot light of a fall day was shining in through the west-facing windows as he walked by, checking every table. He sat down to his routine with a damp polishing cloth, carefully buffing the extra flatware and folding napkins at a back table.

He was thinking and enjoying the aromas coming from the kitchen. He had been experiencing a new feeling at The Prow. Before, it had been a tense, every day stretch to make things conform to his vision of perfection. Now, he was relaxed, trusting that he and the staff would give their best for everyone coming through these doors, one day at a time. This was new for him...strange.

He was remembering island days. It was unbelievable to him now, that he had been out in the islands since May. The months out there had seemed like only weeks. He was thinking about freedom, the freedom he had gained out there, the space. He remembered his first days on the island, how he had almost turned around and headed right back for the ferry in despair. Now the island was a haven, more than a haven, a home for him where once it had been an empty and miserable place. Life had turned around...every aspect. He was polishing and thinking. He had a feeling that he was moving into something new. Something was coming, that much he knew. He had some ideas, but he couldn't put it all together, yet.

He had not seen Sheila since her mid-summer bombshell visit to the island. She had written him a letter which arrived at Glass House two weeks after her visit, saying again that she was sorry, telling him that she appreciated the way he had received her and her story. He had responded to her with a terse little note after that, non-committal but polite, thanking her again for the truth. In it he had addressed her, "Dear Mother."

There were many more things he wanted to say to her now. He had questions. He had been thinking hard about Paul. He wondered how much influence she had on how Paul had treated him, whether or not Paul had agreed with the things Sheila had done to keep him out of her life. This was only natural curiosity now that the truth was out in the open. Did he really want to be called "Paul," or was he just deferring to Sheila's over-bearing ways when that was decided? Did he become a "hands off" dad as a result of Sheila's attitude toward Daniel? A lot of questions. He wanted to think things through and not be carried along by those strong old emotions anymore. He wanted to know the truth, but...it might be better just to let it go. Probably only Paul knew the answers to these questions and he was gone. Daniel had already demonstrated to Sheila that he was moving on. That old dynamic was over. It was a tremendous relief for Daniel.

That very evening, Sheila called him there on his office phone. She said "Welcome Back," but she had other agendas on her mind, as usual. She told him that Paul's two top agents were moving along in the process to buy out Paul's insurance firm. Could Daniel come to the lawyer's office to discuss the plan? It was time to consider their offer. He was glad to hear that it was getting settled and he had some other things he wanted to talk over as well. They agreed to meet at Sam Ellis' office the next morning.

Daniel dressed up a bit for the meeting. He put on a nice pair of slacks and a light tweed coat with a blue shirt. He wanted to appear business-like for this conference. He was going to have to trust Sheila on the terms as he knew nothing of the value of Paul's business. He was pretty sure she would be working a sharp deal. When he walked into the office, Sheila was visibly stunned by Daniel's appearance. He had not realized how much strength he had gained sailing, how healthy and brown he had become. He had not gained any weight, he was more sinewy and lean, despite the beignets! His hair was trimmed, but his high color gave a striking look to his eyes and hair.

Her face registered delight and she came and put an arm around him, looking up at his face. Now he was stunned. She was acting like a mother, a doting mother at that.

"You look wonderful, Daniel. The island life has helped you."

"Thanks, Mother," he said, tight-lipped.

Sam looked at both of them curiously. Something was going on. He gave them coffee and then began explaining the sale. It seemed that Andy and Bill, the two managing agents, had gathered up some of their monies and had matching funds from a bank, enough for a twenty-five percent down payment on the business. The down payment alone would be in the millions.

They wanted Sheila and Daniel to carry a note on the rest for a few years. Sam agreed with Sheila that they were being offered a fair price for the business which was solid, employing twenty people and with annual revenues in the millions. Sheila was fine with the price, but she wanted good terms. They were fortunate that these two men could step in and take this business so soon after Paul's death. It was perfect. She told Sam that they needed to get out, but then paused and looked at Daniel.

"I hope this is your wish too, Daniel. I had thought that you have no interest in working this company. Is that right?" She was trying to be respectful and not run over him the way she was used to doing.

"No, I have no interest in jumping in to an insurance agency. I am just grateful for all that Paul has created here."

Sheila looked at him sideways with an amazed expression. She was happy he recognized that, but was surprised.

Sam spoke up. "Your income from this note will be considerable for both of you for the next ten years. The business is solid. I think they will be able to comfortably make the note payments. If you don't want to work, you won't have to anymore." He smiled at them both.

Sheila and Daniel looked at each other. "That's never going to happen," Daniel said in reply. "Sheila...my mother, is a workaholic and I have some plans of my own for the future."

They signed some preliminary paperwork, shook hands all around and were done.

"May I take you to lunch, Daniel?" Sheila was looking up at him and she saw him stiffen a little. She hurriedly said, "I was thinking of something casual. How about the little fish and chips place over at Pike's Place that you used to like?" He was willing to do that.

"I'll meet you there. I need to take my own car." He wasn't going to let her drive him.

The "fish fry" place in the Pike's Place Market was actually a little pub, the sort of place with a string of beers on tap and casual food... sandwiches, oysters and fish and chips. It was on the harbor side, overlooking the bay with all its shipping and sailing craft passing by the windows. There was plenty of activity on the water and the market too was noisy, with people coming and going through the narrow corridors, tourists shopping and the fish mongers shouting off to the side. Fresh fish and shellfish were continually being brought in, which gave an atmosphere of pervasive dampness to the place. Sheila and Daniel met at the pub and were seated in a quiet corner at an old-fashioned, high-backed booth right by the window overlooking the bay, away from noise and market activity. They both ordered the fish and chips.

Daniel began the talking as he had further business on his mind. "I am planning to make some changes," he began. "I have decided to move my residence. I want to sell the Graystone

Arms. I thought maybe you could help me with that. Would you sell it for me?"

She was surprised and pleased. This was a great property in an even greater location. The wheels were immediately turning in her head. Then she paused, looking at him carefully. "What's going on? You renovated that place yourself. It belonged to Willie. Where do you plan to go? What's happened?"

"I want to be nearer the water, nearer to the harbor. He nodded towards the water out the window. If you think about it, you'll know where I want to be."

She was quiet a moment. "You want Paul's condo, don't you? Did you know that it has not sold yet?"

"Yes, I know. Can we work something out? I'd like to be down on the water. Being on the island, I have gotten used to it. I also plan to buy another boat, a sailboat, and Paul's place has its own boat slip right outside the deck. I spent the whole summer sailing out on the island. My little sailboat is great for cruising around in the bay, I love it. But, I would like a boat I can take off in, to go further away from shore, something with a cabin. I haven't looked for one yet, but since we are really rich now, I should be able to get something fantastic. Not too big though," he smiled. "What do you think you can get for the Graystone?"

They talked on comfortably for some time. Sheila said she would think about the condo sale and about Paul's place. She wanted to look at numbers about all that. They talked about the pending sale of Paul's business. It seemed they were truly in agreement about that. They did not discuss Sheila's trip out to the island or her confessions, though that hung in the air. Finally, Daniel looked up from his lunch and bluntly asked her, "I would like to know my father's name. Will you tell me?"

She looked as if a blow had hit her. She now avoided his eyes. "I can see that you would like to know that, especially now." She paused. "His name was Matthew. Matthew Fleming. He was from here in Washington, but not Seattle." She brought her napkin up from her lap and laid it on the table. Lunch was over for her. "You probably would like to know where he is. I really do not know. We lost touch and that was it. He certainly never knew about you." There was resignation in her face, in her voice.

"Fleming...that's a nice name," Daniel said softly. "Matthew." He was looking away, thinking. "Are you sure you don't know anything else about him? Where he went to school or anything?" He looked back at her, searching.

She was thinking, remembering. "We really never talked about our lives that much. We were living in the present... it was a brief thing. He was a very nice guy. We had fun." She smiled a rather sweet smile. "I'm sorry I don't know more. Paul and I just wanted to put that behind us. You looked a lot like me as a child, so I didn't have that remembrance." She put her hands over her face for a moment. Something was coming, he could tell that.

"There is one thing I do want to say to you about all that. Since I have come home from the island, from telling you about all this, I keep thinking about that terrible thing I blurted out to you when we were on the beach that day. I said, 'Who wanted you, Daniel.' I am very sorry I said that brutal thing. It just came out. I think it had been on my mind for years, but I had not admitted it to myself. It finally came out in the passion of that day. I am very sorry that I said that to you. But...I have been thinking about it on and on."

There was more, he could see but she was taking her time, wandering through her own thoughts.

"You know that I am Roman Catholic, Daniel, as was Willie. I continue in that faith. Since I came out to see you, I have been to confession over the many things I did wrong through the years, to you and to Paul. I have made my peace with God." She drew in a shuddering breath. "God is very great, Daniel. He is so much bigger than our problems. I have committed myself to receiving his forgiveness...and that's a difficult thing for me." She took a swallow from her water glass on the table. Her face was calm. "Since then, I am going to mass more, I am praying. And...God is showing me...that he is the one who wanted you. He is the One." With that she looked him straight in the eye.

"Well...good, Mother. Thank you. I'm glad to hear it." He said quietly. "I'll have to think that over. I have something more to say to you too. I am sorry for the things I said to you at the restaurant that day last May. I should not have blown up like that. It was bad for you and it was bad for me too. I apologize. And...I don't hate you. I can't hate you anymore. I have some sympathy for you and for Paul too. That was a tough thing you went through. The decisions you both made and the life you chose probably were not your first choice. You probably had other plans, other goals. I know that now. I understand many things better now, putting our lives in perspective. I have a few questions about Paul, about the way things were, but I have decided just to let all that go. In any case, your choice was of benefit to me. I see that now."

He paused. "Please come back to my restaurant any time you want. I will treat you with respect and with hospitality. That's what my place is all about."

Her eyes were full of tears. He could feel the release of something in her from across the table.

"Thank you, Daniel," she whispered. "Thank you."

## CHAPTER FIFTY-TWO

# Flower Power

MUCH later that night, after the meeting and lunch with Sheila, Daniel and Henry were lounging on the sofa at the condo. Daniel had a magazine that he was leafing through, but his mind was on the events of the day. He could not help feeling a certain rising emotion, a wonderful feeling, a satisfaction. It was joy. He felt like laughing.

"My father's name is Matthew Fleming," he told Henry out loud.

"Matthew...Fleming." He enunciated it again slowly for Henry's benefit. "I just thought you might like to know." He continued to pretend to read. Then he sat up. "I think I need to tell somebody else. Somebody who can talk back to me."

He picked up the phone and called Ruth, even though it was ten o'clock. Surely she would still be up. She answered, but with an alarmed voice. It was the first time he had called since he left the island.

"Nothing is wrong," he said. "I was hoping you would still be up. Everything is fine. I have been meaning to call you. We need to talk about the wedding flowers."

"Oh, yes, we do," she said in a lively tone. "We do need to talk. I have all these ideas running around in my brain and I need to unload them. You need to help me settle down and pick the best ones! Actually, I don't know how to describe what I am imagining, in words. They are just pictures in my head, though I have drawn a few out on paper. I even colored them." She was instantly on a roll.

"Wait. We can talk about that, but I have something else to tell you. You are the first person I have told."

Now she was quiet on the other end.

"I found out my natural father's name today. His name is Matthew Fleming."

"Matthew Fleming! Wow that's a great name. Who told you? Where is he now?"

"I had lunch with my mother today. I decided to ask her and she told me his name. That's all she knows. There has been no contact between them since before I was born."

"Wow, Daniel! So what do you think about that. How did you feel when she told you?"

"That's why I am calling you. I had to tell somebody. I told Henry, but he said nothing. I needed to pass this news on to a living human. I am very pleased to know the name, but otherwise I don't know how I feel."

"Well thank you, Daniel. I am glad to know that I rate a higher position than your dog."

She wasn't really indignant. He knew her now. She was just handing him one of her joking, teasing replies...she was a very playful girl.

"Yeah, I told Henry you would have something to say, some kind of profound reply." He was chuckling into the phone. "No, honestly, I don't know how I feel. I guess it is a relief. I think I may have had the idea for a while that I was just hatched or something. Now I know that I had a real physical father. He just doesn't know about me. For all I know he could be dead. But, we've put a name to him."

Then he told her he was probably going to move...that he wanted Paul's old place and would probably be looking for a sailboat too. She was quiet on the other end of the line. Then she spoke in her direct way.

"You're in a transition."

"Yeah, you're right, I am transitioning. It's obvious. How about you? What's happening in your life?"

"I'm flowering." She started giggling at her own wittiness. "Yes, I am flowering and blooming. The growing season is over, but you should see my greenhouse! It is full and the stuff I have blooming is awesome, gorgeous. I wish you were here to see. By Christmas it will be coming out the door over here! I'm going to have bales of stephanotis!"

Daniel was thinking. "I would love to see the greenhouse, but I can't get away to go over there now. Why don't you come over here for a day trip? Bring your 'pretty pictures' for the wedding and we can work together and then go to the wholesalers and settle the designs for the wedding. I think you are going to need some extra flowers from a wholesale supplier for the church and the tent decoration. I'm guessing your greenhouse specialties, the stephanotis and all that will be for the bouquets and stuff, for the special things, not for the tables. We can plan and then order while you are here. They will deliver at the right time on the ferry in December, so you can have what you need. I'll come extra early to help with the work. If you come over, you can visit the restaurant and have lunch with us. Why don't you come on over?"

"I could do that," she said.

He could tell she was thinking, considering.

"Come next week, come on Monday. It's our slow day, but we're open. I can work with you, we can have lunch and then go to the floral place."

"I need to check with Nan and I'll let you know. It sounds right...and fun. I haven't been to the mainland in a long time and you know where everything is."

There was a long pause.

"I hope you can come. Henry and I miss all of you very much."

"Yeah...we miss you over here too. I'll let you know. And thanks for telling me about your father. Can I tell Nan?"

"Yeah, go ahead and tell her. I'd like to know what she thinks too."

"Yeah, well, I'll call you about Monday."

"O.K., thanks for listening...I'm glad I called even if it is late."

"It's not too late."

Ruth took the earliest ferry on Monday morning. She had her roll of designs and pictures and her box of special markers with her and some notebooks. The traffic was crazy and a little disconcerting to a country girl, but she made it through the madness and pulled up at The Prow at 10 A.M.

Daniel had been waiting, looking out the window, watching for her. He met her at the doors. She was wearing town clothes, a black turtleneck knit top and a blazer, tan wool slacks, with black leather boots. Daniel was amazed. He had pictured her coming in one of her tea-length skirts. When he told her that, she just tilted her head and frowned at him, shaking her head.

Once inside, Ruth was amazed by the ship's prow looming over them in the foyer like that. She loved it. Daniel explained about finding it. Then they went on a tour of the restaurant. She knew Trini, Oscar and a few others from the picnic. They toured through the restaurant and she met everyone else.

"Your kitchen is awesome!" she told Oscar and Trini, looking up at all the growing potted herbs in hanging baskets. "I need to try this at my house!"

She and Daniel went to a front table near a window where they would have natural light, and Ruth laid out her plans and sketches. They worked until noon when people started coming in. Then they wrapped it up for a while, and Daniel ordered lunch for them. He wanted her to try the Prow Chowder and then they had a salad of spring greens, blueberries, walnuts and very thinly sliced, crisp apples, which he pointed out to her were from the orchard of Glass House. The dressing was a special, "Prow" vinaigrette." The fish was trout cooked in butter with shallots. Ruth declined dessert, saying it would be way too much for her.

Daniel suggested a walk after lunch. He wanted to show her the waterfront. It was a nice day, a sweater day, a little crisp, but sunny. They walked the short way to the waterfront walk. He wanted to show her Paul's condo too. They found it and walked around looking at the white, geometric building from different angles. You could see inside a bit through the big picture window.

Looking up, he said, "I think I would like it here. I would want to paint, but don't have any ideas yet about the colors. It is hard to pick colors when the water reflects right into the place. The water changes how everything looks."

"It may take time. Why don't you just move in and live here a while?" Ruth suggested.

"Maybe so, maybe so. I'm waiting to see what kind of deal my mother comes up with," he smiled. "Let's get back to the restaurant and work some more."

Ruth's design ideas were completely charming. Daniel could not think of one thing to add to what she had brought. He would just come over in December and help her put it together. She had "carte blanche" from Anna. The only instructions she had given was that "red" should dominate and that she was not wearing a veil due to the kind of wedding dress she had picked out, which so far was a well-kept mystery. Anna requested a coronet or wreath of flowers for her hair. Everything was tending toward an "English Christmas" look. They would not use poinsettias, the usual Christmas flower. The main flower would be ordinary red carnations. They were small enough and brilliant enough to make clustered designs of an infinite variety, and the fragrance was so nice and spicy. Ruth was planning a bridal bouquet of traditional white stephanotis in a domed, tight, round configuration. The bouquet would trail green leaves, probably ivy and red silk ribbons. She thought a coronet of stephanotis, that beautiful waxy white wedding flower, with just a little ivy, would be beautiful on Anna and would match her bouquet.

This was girl stuff, but Daniel always loved any kind of designing and he loved working with flowers, so he was right in the thick of her planning. He wanted to help Ruth and would be a right hand man for her getting all this put together when the date rolled around. She was stirred up about this work, which was a real labor of love.

They took a ride in Daniel's car over to the floral warehouse. All the spots for flowers and the number of arrangements needed for the reception tables had been carefully laid out and accounted for. The order was placed. They needed some shiny greens, some ivy, holly and fir, even though the island was covered in them. These would be clean and cut to size. Ruth ordered a dozen readymade green garlands, too.

That would save some time and work. Buckets of carnations were needed in red and white, white trailing jasmine, forget-me-nots, white yarrow and miniature white and red roses were on the list. Then they took some time to wander around the flower warehouse and greenhouses just for the pleasure of it. Walking through the rows of fragrant plants and blooms was like heaven for both of them, as they quietly took it all in.

"This is our dessert! So much less fattening than Trini's flan," Daniel laughed.

By late afternoon they had seen and done it all. The plans were in place, and Ruth felt so much more confident, having Daniel there to say "yes" or "no" to her myriad ideas. She was happy and tired. Daniel was happy that she had come and seen his restaurant, his world. Her presence had filled in something that he needed: someone special from the island to enter his mainland world, to see and appreciate.

He said good-bye at the street as she got back into her car. First she gave him a big hug and reached for his hand. She held it tightly in her little hand, then patted his cheek softly with her other hand. She grinned and he blushed. He stood watching her red taillights disappear through the dusk and traffic.

The next morning, he and Henry stopped at the hole–in-the-wall flower shop on the way to the restaurant. They had resumed their in-town routine each morning. Today, Daniel bought three full bunches of red carnations. At the Prow, he arranged them in a profuse, glorious bouquet, leaving the stems very long, in a tall clear glass vase, placing them in their prominent spot in the foyer. Now he was ready to start the day.

As he walked away, he said out loud, "Flower Power."

## CHAPTER FIFTY-THREE

# The Trade

SHEILA called one morning a week after their meeting and lunch at Pike's Place. She wondered if she could come over to see the Graystone Arms. She had an idea and she wanted to see the property. Daniel left his key under the mat before going to work.

Later that day she called. She wanted to meet him at the attorney's office. More paperwork was ready to sign on the insurance agency sale. He went over right after the lunch crowd.

After cordial greetings and some small talk, they looked over the final terms of the sale. Everything was fine. The needed signatures were finalized, and then Sheila said she wanted to discuss something else.

"I looked at your property, the Graystone today, Daniel. I walked around and have been checking values. I only vaguely remember the condition of the old building before you took over. I could see that you've done a top notch job there with the renovation. I love the colors…and the floors! I would like to take the Graystone Arms for myself. I would like to own it, as an investment property. It originally belonged to my grandfather... you know that. Then Willie had it...now you. I think it ought to stay in the family. I would like to buy it from you. Actually, I want to propose a trade."

Sam nodded in agreement. "Your mother has been talking to me about all this. We can affect a trade within the workings of Paul's estate. Monies are coming, to be portioned to both of you from the sale of Paul's asset, the insurance agency. We will just re-apportion the amounts so that the amount due you for Graystone, beyond the trade, will come over to you from the down payment on the agency. It will be in the estate and you can take it out as you wish. You will exchange deeds on the two properties. Paul's condo and boat dock will be yours."

Sheila was smiling. She was sitting on Sam's sofa wearing a very attractive silk dress in her favorite, lemon yellow, with a multi colored silk tweed jacket and faceted citrine jewelry. Her eyes were sparkling and she seemed relaxed. This whole thing obviously pleased her immensely. This was her realm, her area of expertise. She had been working on this, Daniel could see. It was the right thing to do, and she had done it well.

"I had never thought about you wanting to take Paul's place before. It makes sense for you." He could see she was happy about that. Daniel got up and went over and took her hand. He gave her a kiss on the cheek. She was thrilled.

Sam was grinning and shaking his head. "So happy for you both," he said. "The sale of the agency asset will close before the holidays. You will have a new home in the new year, Daniel."

"You can move in whenever you like." Sheila handed him the keys.

Daniel left Sam's office walking fast towards Paul's place. He was thinking about how much had changed in less than a year. Last year at this time Paul didn't even realize he was sick. Now he was gone. Staggering changes had been made since then, in everyone around Daniel, and if he would admit it, in himself. He put the key in the lock and went in. The place was empty...all furniture was gone now. It was just blue gray walls and off-white carpet. The view out onto the harbor was stunning with nothing in the room to distract. He checked the kitchen. It was a galley-styled space...he liked that. White expensive cabinets. Black tile counters. Stainless double refrigerator. Perfect. There was a deck outside, gray stained, hanging right over the docks. He saw the empty slip. He laughed, thinking he could leap right over the rail into his boat when he found it and brought it here...like Captain Hook...like Peter Pan. He was giddy with excitement. He hurried upstairs. The bedrooms were nice. The master bedroom had the same huge picture window as below, overlooking the bay, natural light everywhere.

Ruth was right. He should move in and live there a while before making changes. His neutral tweed furniture would be fine in there. He had no particular bad memories about Paul being there sick. It was O.K. They'd had some good talks there, before he died, real father to son talks. It was going to be Daniel's place now.

## CHAPTER FIFTY-FOUR

# On Friday Night

It was already November. Daniel was having some maintenance done on his new condo, getting it ready. He planned to move in right after Christmas, after Luke and Anna's wedding. Right now all he could think about was returning to the island for Christmas, to be with his friends. They were going to close the restaurant for three days for the holiday this year. Trini and Oscar would come out to the wedding and bring Anna's cake. Ruth and Nan had invited Daniel, Trini and Oscar to stay at the farmhouse. Sheila had been invited to the wedding. Otis wanted her to be there, and she was planning to come. She was staying at an inn at Friday Harbor. Glass House would be too cold and empty for a Christmas stay. Christmas on the island was a first for Daniel, and he hadn't spent Christmas with Sheila in many years.

That Friday night the unthinkable happened, the dishwasher broke down at the restaurant. It couldn't have been at a worse time as there was a very busy dinner crowd that night. Daniel looked in and saw what had happened, some crockery had broken in the washer as they were at the height of the dinner hour. The jammed up pieces sticking in the washer brought the run to a stop but the motor was still turning and it burned right out. They tried a cleanout and restart but the motor was gone. Hurriedly, Daniel organized a hand washing line and they carried on, but it was really stacking up by the end of the evening. At ten thirty he let the kitchen workers go on home. He and Oscar and Trini stayed to finish.

Daniel was tired, but he didn't really mind. Hands-on work always gave him pleasure and he took the washing station while Oscar and Trini dried and put things away. There was not much left. They slowed down and chatted as they worked.

"I'll call first thing in the morning to get a replacement," Daniel said. "Hopefully they will have one in stock in town. Otherwise we could be doing this for days!"

They were almost finished. Trini and Oscar went out to check everything in the kitchen and dining room one last time. By now the wash water had become too dirty so Daniel drained the sink and began filling with clean water. He renewed the rinse sink too. He was relaxed and feeling mellow, dreamily working at the sink. As he washed dish after dish, a thought came to him. It was the kind of startling thought that shakes up the mind, sort of like a premonition, a forewarning.

"The dish goes in covered with junk, then it comes up out of the water clean." It was so obvious as to be ridiculous to even think it. So obvious that it was amazing.

"This dish is now ready to be used again." Also obvious. He used the sprayer which hung down from overhead for the final rinsing. The dishes had a beautiful shine as they emerged all clean. His chest began to swell with emotion. At first he didn't know where this was coming from. Tears were forming but he held them back. Then he started remembering.

In his mind he had now gone back to the day when he drove Nan to her church group meeting. He saw himself there with her in the back of the little church, out of the way, trying to be invisible. He recalled the plainness of the church house, a place with very little ornamentation. He had been sitting, leafing through some brochure they had put there in the back of the church. Nan was talking about the Man on the Cross. She said his name, "Jesus." Daniel did not like to speak his name. It embarrassed him. So he referred to him as "the Man on the Cross." Nan had been standing in front of her ladies' group in her straight, vigorous posture. He watched her. It was strange, she was not very tall, but she seemed so tall. His attention was brought back to the words she had said.

"Jesus was and is the Messiah, the Anointed One. The one from heaven meant to die to take away our sin. His blood is the cleansing power for all of us. When we believe, it covers us. It cleanses us." She had smiled and thrown up her hands, as if to say, "How obvious."

"Sin is the condition of being broken away from our God, our Creator. The separation comes from our walking away from Him, turning away and not doing what we really know in our hearts is right, what He has shown us is right. The book of Genesis tells us that it started from the beginning. It's serious, so serious we don't really get it."

She spoke with strength and he could tell she believed it utterly. He remembered her walking around the table, which was an altar. She had touched the plain cross on the wall.

"The thing is, He's not on the cross anymore. He's finished with that ordeal. Now He is available to each of us by His spirit... and we need him... to do life in the way our Father intends for us to live."

She had said a lot of other things standing there that he couldn't remember. He just remembered her standing there for a long time looking at everyone, not moving. And everyone in the room was still too, thinking about what she had just said.

He remembered rolling and unrolling the magazine he had been holding in his hands, rolling and unrolling it tightly in a nervous gesture at the back of the church.

Then...he was remembering the terrible night after that on the beach when he had opened Paul's little Bible to the book she had suggested...Romans. The shocking words he had read there, the anger he felt. Of course, he remembered his morning in the kitchen with Nan and her story. It was only a few months ago. It was clear that she accepted those terrible words in the Bible, and then she told her heart-rending story... about her father, her mother and all that loss...about how she had found peace later, and Walter. He knew what she had done to get that peace. He knew she still had it, that she would always have it. He had been so mad at her over all this, but she was not disturbed at all by his anger, and he had gotten over it. He loved Nan.

He looked down and realized he was holding a clean dish in his hands. He wasn't sure how long he had been standing there like that. "I'd like to be like this dish, all shiny...clean." He thought. He set it aside, swirling the water now with his hands. It felt good to have his hands in the scalding hot water.

He was thinking about the way he used to look at the crucifix on the wall in the church when he went as a little boy with Sheila. He was thinking about how he wondered then what the Man on the Cross had done to deserve such gruesome punishment. He smiled grimly remembering once again his thoughts as a boy that it was something worse than stealing chocolate candy bars. It had to be something worse. He was feeling again his own terrible confusion, embarrassment and shame about the chocolate bars...way back then.

Nan had said that day that Jesus Christ didn't do anything wrong, nothing at all to deserve to be nailed up. She said He did it for us...because we needed to get back to God. He made Himself into the "Way Back." Daniel had been stunned by her statement. He could barely stand to think about it at the time, but he was thinking about it calmly now.

He continued to swirl the water with both hands. Then he brought his hands out of the water, scrutinizing them. No nail holes here. No blood. These hands had not been subject to punishment.

He began to speak out loud in the lowest possible voice. "I don't know you, Man on the Cross. I need your help." He was looking at his hands.

"My life is good; I'm thankful for all I have and have been given. I have so much... money, two great houses, and now I can buy whatever I want. I have this restaurant. I had Willie. I have the best friends in the whole world." He put his hands back into the water. "It is not enough. I want to get connected like Paul did. I know he is with you now. I saw him in that boat with you... out at Cattle Point." His eyes were closed now.

"I think, somehow, I'm lost...just like I was in that terrible nightmare I had right after Paul died." His voice dropped to a whisper. "I know I need to make changes. I would like to get cleaned up, like these dishes. Your book... Romans... says I am not living right...I guess you know everything, so you know how I have been...with boys, with men. I admit I have accepted their attentions, their affection, their... adoration. I can see that this is not right. I'm sorry. I'd like to be...regular. There's a girl..." He rushed on. "I haven't been looking for you, I'm sorry about that too. I see that you have been looking for me. I would like...to belong to you. Please accept me."

He continued to swirl the water with his hands.

In that moment, he felt like he was being held, almost like being held like a baby. He sighed deeply. His whole body relaxed. He knew that he had been heard. He knew that things had changed, that things could change more and for the good, that the connection would grow. He would not be alone any more. He knew it. The tears finally stopped burning his eyelids and came out softly and flowed down his face. It was O.K... He didn't mind. His whole mind had been engaged like a child during this time. He didn't know how long he had been standing there like that at the sink.

It was almost midnight. Oscar and Trini came back in after stowing everything away for the night. They saw his tears. Trini came and embraced Daniel, who still had his hands in the water.

"Come on, *Mijo*. We're finished. Come and sit down with us. *Que paso?*

What happened? Everything is alright. Are you sad?"

He did as she said. He dried his hands and came out to the kitchen, sitting on one of the stools there. They stood by him and Trini put her arms around him. Oscar was looking down at him silently.

"No, I don't think I am sad. I feel fine. I've just made a decision. I just had something happen." He looked up at them, relaxed.

"What do you guys think of the man who died on the cross?"

"*Jesu Cristo?!*" said Trini. There was surprise on her face. "*Pues, es el Salvador!* Our Savior."

"Yeah, man. He is the guy. He's the one. The whole world is in his hands." He laughed, "What's going on? Why are you talking about Jesus?" This was from Oscar.

Daniel turned and looked up hard at him. "Do you really believe all that?"

Oscar inhaled sharply, avoiding Daniel's eyes. He looked up at the ceiling. Then he looked back at Daniel with a smile.

"Yes, I believe all that. We grew up Catholic, in Mexico. Jesus on the cross is... everywhere and is looked up to in Mexico. I went to catechism. We all went. It's our way." He put his hand on Daniel's shoulder.

"Later, things happened in my life, Daniel. Big problems, people wanted me to do some bad things, some illegal things. It put me in a corner. I had my problems. Trini can tell you about it. That sent me back to the Christ again, for real, not just a religion. Not just going through the motions. He helped me. He moved me out of a bad place. Many of my prayers have been answered by Jesus... I love him," he said simply. "I guess we've never talked about it. We should have."

"That's the same for me, Daniel," said Trini somberly. "Pretty much the same. We know Jesus. We love Jesus." Her black eyes were riveted on him.

"Well, I'm talking about him now because I need him. My life is great these days, but I don't want to be alone anymore. I see that I don't have to be alone anymore. And, now I am going to be talking to him. He visited me tonight. I think he has been trying to get through for a while, even out on the island. I have decided to trust him."

Daniel looked up at them both. His face was calm.

They looked at him in wonder. There were no words to say. Nothing else was needed.

They drove Daniel and Henry home to the Graystone Arms as usual. On the way home Trini got teary, "You make me happy, Daniel, very happy."

He let himself in to the dark condominium, turning on just one lamp. It was really late. He was still thinking hard about all that had happened. He took a long shower then fell into bed. Physically and emotionally he had been wrung out, but he was feeling a sense of peace that he had never experienced before. He realized that he felt cherished. At last he knew that he was somebody's beloved child. So much had happened from every angle. It was astounding. His down cover felt so good... he snuggled down into it. Face down in the covers, he was soon asleep. It was a deep sleep, with no dreams.

In the darkness of early morning, he awoke enough to realize that someone had quietly come into the room. He was still drowsy, but he heard the creaking of someone moving up to the bed in the darkness. In his sleepiness he couldn't think through who it might be. Someone was there though. Daniel was lying flat on his stomach. He drowsily tried to rouse himself to sit up, but he couldn't seem to move. Something very heavy began to lie down on his back, covering him. He was awake now! It was something of shocking weight. It started pressing down at his legs and slowly, powerfully covered his whole body moving from his feet up to his neck. It engulfed him, pressing him down into the bed with a force that was beyond human strength. His eyes were not open, but he knew it was something very dark, black in fact. It was sinuous, muscularly powerful, twisting, coiling... it was on him, like some kind of animal. The breath was being pressed right out of him. He couldn't move. It moved close to the back of his head, sniffing at his neck and through his hair, just as an animal would do. It was drawing in breaths from his skin and hair. He was completely paralyzed as his own breath was being inexorably pressed out of him.

At last he began to struggle. He was being smothered and he could barely resist, but he did resist, pushing back and trying to sit up. Maybe he was praying, because anger rose in him...and strength. He began to try to breathe deeply, to rise up pushing this presence off him. In slow motion he turned his head to the side and with a supreme effort, sat up. In that moment, it was over. The thing was gone without a trace. He should have been terrified, there in the dark, but he was not. He felt strong. He sat on the edge of the bed and turned on a lamp.

"You can't have me," he said calmly. "You can't have me anymore. I'm not alone anymore. I belong to God. I'm free."

## CHAPTER FIFTY-FIVE

# A Christmas Wedding

DANIEL had heard some shocking news. Anna would be married in a red velvet wedding dress. He had heard this from Ruth, who called him all thrilled and excited about it. It was surprising but it did make sense, actually. It was a Christmas wedding after all. The gown was strapless... a pencil slim sheath, with a fishtail flounce at the bottom. Ruth had not seen it but she described it. She had heard about it from Peg. The color was a "rich Christmas scarlet...Velvet!" she told him. Of course, Luke did not know and would not know until she came down the aisle. Daniel grinned thinking about that moment.

Ruth and Daniel had their plan ready for the wedding flowers and bouquets. It was all set. Since it was Christmas, there would be greens to add at the church. They were planning to use some small natural fir trees of different heights in the front, dressed only in white twinkle lights on either side of the plain altar. Ruth would bring these from her own Christmas tree orchard. Her farm crew would cut some of the best formed little trees and put them in place at the church before the wedding so everyone could enjoy them. She would bring in a few of the swagged garlands early too. Their recommendation to Anna for lots of red carnations had been eagerly accepted. So much could be done with the small fragrant flowers. A lot of this was to be a surprise, to everyone. Daniel and Ruth, with the help of Nan, would assemble all the flowers the day before the wedding at Sloan Farm. Everything remaining would be put up at the church the day of the wedding.

The ceremony was to be at the Beulah Land Church. The couple could have decided to be married on the mainland at Otis and Marion's church, where they had met. But Anna wanted to be married on the island, in the quaint church, near her new home where so many lovely things had already happened for them both. The Beulah Land pastor had agreed to allow Otis to perform the ceremony. This would happen on December twenty-third, just two days before Christmas, in the evening. That meant candles. The little church would be glowing and beautiful.

It would not be a huge wedding. Only about a hundred people were invited. They had decided to rent a big, white, weather-proof tent and have the reception on the church grounds. They were hoping for a quiet, windless night. Space heaters would be brought in. Daniel could have done the food, but they did not want him to work. They wanted him to enjoy and be with them. Someone else from Friday Harbor would cater the dinner. How much fun it would be to celebrate in a tent! And then, Luke would take his new bride to the houseboat and carry her over the threshold. They did not want to take a honeymoon immediately. They wanted to settle in and keep visiting with friends and family the next day, and enjoy their first Christmas on the island. If it was nice weather, they might even go for a sail on Pete and Peggy's boat.

Luke and Pete had been working hard all fall on Luke's houseboat. It was almost finished. It would be ready for the newlyweds. There was a new sink, stove and refrigerator, all in stainless steel by Anna's request. Luke had told Anna he wanted her "in the galley cooking right away." This was met with threats from her of a "whoopin' with a cast iron pan."

Anna had said good-bye to her class of school children at Thanksgiving. They had put on a Pilgrim's feast in the classroom and one of the mothers made a little wedding cake for Anna with a plastic bride and groom on top. The whole class had shared in it and then Anna kissed them all good-bye. Her life was now a whirl of preparations. He heard all this in regular reports from Ruth, who said she thought this was going to be the "coolest" wedding she had ever done. She was ready to start working and they were counting down the days.

Daniel called Luke one day, just to see what his condition was, to see if he was ready, or nervous, or what. Pete and Peg were there with him. They were all working, putting the finishing touches on some things in the houseboat. Pete, the perfectionist, was closely inspecting everything, tightening screws. Peg had a paint brush and was varnishing a couple of doors. They all got on the phone, one by one.

"When are you going to get on over here? There's not a damned beignet to be found on the whole island. We're starving to death." Pete was always the same.

Peggy was talking silly about some kind of "trousseau" stuff that he did not understand, "something borrowed, something blue."

Luke got on the line. "How are you doing? Are you gonna make it?" Daniel said, just to kid him a bit.

"I cannot wait for this woman to get on over here so we can start this life. We're not teenagers you know. We need to get on with this! Let's go!" They both laughed.

Daniel told him he would be there soon. "If you change your mind, I'll have the Time Out waiting in the cove so you can make your escape."

"Not in a million years," said Luke. "What on earth would I do then!"

Daniel arrived on the ferry two days before the wedding. He was bringing his clothes for the wedding and some for the wedding party. He would wear a new black cashmere jacket for the occasion, and his gray flannel slacks, and he was bringing two tuxedos, one for Luke and one for the best man, Pete. He also brought a special item. Anna had insisted that Luke wear a red cummerbund to match her dress, though she didn't tell him why just yet. He thought it was just a "Christmas" thing of hers.

Daniel took his time driving down the road to Sloan Farm. He wanted to enjoy the ride, noticing the way the fields and trees looked in December in a cooler light. The air was clear, cold and seemed thinner somehow. There was a cloudbank to the northeast, not unusual during these months. They could get storms from that direction on occasion. For now, it was far off, piled up over the mainland. The fields were brown, but the dark, evergreen forests stood out sharply against the empty fields. He was so happy to be here that he could burst.

Ruth and Nan came right out to meet him and Henry. They were all smiles. Ruth had even cooked a meal, a nice hot lunch for them. It was cold and getting colder. She said the weather report was forecasting a heavy freeze overnight. They ate a homemade chicken pot pie casserole with a lettuce salad. Even though it was a cold day, they had some chocolate ice cream. Then Nan brought out a pot of coffee.

Ruth showed him his room upstairs. She showed him Trini and Oscar's room too. The second story of the old farm house was barn-like with huge rooms, very old-fashioned high ceilings and ancient farm furniture. His bed had a walnut bedstead with the headboard nearly reaching the ceiling. Wooden plank floors creaked a little and the two tall windows were hung with the standard white lace curtains. The hall bathroom had wooden floors too and a claw-foot bathtub.

"I hope you don't get too cold up here. We've got the heaters all on, but it is hard to heat this old place. There are piles of quilts though. You'll just have to cover up."

They went to the workroom and the three of them started right in. Nan was making all the men's boutonnieres. They were red carnations adorned with smooth, shiny holly leaves. Daniel joined in and helped her. Ruth was working on some kind of vine basket she was weaving. It would be the main centerpiece on the altar. It was a loosely formed, natural looking thing of fresh vines, with tendrils arching across the free-formed handle and spinning around the base. While they sat and worked, Ruth and Nan filled him in with details of the wedding party.

Pete would be Luke's best man. Anna's brother Glenn would also stand up with Luke. Dottie, Anna's sister-in-law, would be matron of honor. There were two other maids of honor, Anna's best friend from high school and one of her fellow teachers from Anacortes. Peg had declined a position, saying that she was way too old for this group. She would be the guest book hostess and general helper at the reception. She had a beautiful new dress for the evening, periwinkle blue. Anna's parents were coming a long way from Louisiana to see their only daughter married. Mr. and Mrs. Babineaux had never before been to the islands. Mr. Babineaux would give away the bride, of course. Otis would officiate. Luke's three sisters would be present to sit with their mother, Marion. With assorted guests, neighbors and friends the little church would be full.

Later on, Peg dropped by to pick up the two tuxedos and visit for just a moment. She pecked Daniel's cheek absently. She was so preoccupied with details of the wedding that she was spinning. She chatted a minute, sniffed the flowers and then ran on.

Nan was ready to nap, but Ruth and Daniel worked on, preparing the round balls of carnations that would decorate the ends of the church aisles. They were made by attaching the flowers with pins to soaked floral balls. Tomorrow they would be placed on ribbon decked dowels with greenery and silk ribbon. They would look like floral "lollipops" when in place. The same design would be the centerpiece of the reception tables. It was a very contemporary look, not anything like what would be seen at frilly spring weddings. Ruth was pleased with the way they were shaping up. They had a quick dinner there in the kitchen, then talked and worked until every last one of the pom-poms was finished and stowed away.

Daniel wanted to go out to the little house, to sit and visit with Nan. He wanted to tell her about his decision that Friday night at the restaurant, and about what happened later, in the early morning hours. He saw that her lights were still on. Somehow the time was not right though. These days were about

Anna and Luke and the celebration they were all preparing. He would wait. He had been reading the Bible she gave him. He read every night before he went to sleep. He had brought his Bible with him on this trip. It was by his bed upstairs.

His life was changing, on the inside. Actually, he realized now that he had been slowly changing ever since he came out to the island. It had been a process of change and it was still going on. The corner was turned that Friday night, though. He had come face to face with the One. Trini was right, he thought. He is El Salvador, the Savior, and The Christ. There had been a turn, a shedding and the connection was forged with a passion.

He went on up to his room for the night. Something strange, had happened coming over on the ferry this time, something striking. He wanted to think about it. He wanted to try to pray. He wanted to look into his Bible.

Aboard the ferry, bound for San Juan, he had been standing by the railing at the stern, watching the waters as the ferry pulled away from the docks. It was chilly, frosty outside in fact, but he loved being out on the sea again. He stood watching the buildings of Anacortes as they diminished in view, becoming a low stack of blocks on the horizon. Looking down into the churn, his eye caught a movement in the water. It was a stray mooring rope which had apparently been missed at departure. It was twirling violently underwater in the wake. Then suddenly it broke loose and was flung high up into the air and free of the ferry. He saw the rope slowly fall back into the sea. It did not rise again from the wake. He was thinking about this. He couldn't help thinking of what his counselor, Charlotte, had said that day some time back, about a memory being like a "strong rope" attached to the heart. What an amazing picture of freedom, that rope flying up and away from its mooring had been for him! He was learning to pay attention to things and to pray.

The next day Daniel helped Ruth as she created Anna's bouquet and matching headpiece, the attendant's bouquets and the extravagant altar arrangement in its special basket. He trimmed the flowers and prepared them for her. She arranged and attached. He was learning as he watched her execute the designs with an expert eye. Nearly everything was intensely red, with just sparing hints of white and the background shine of green leaves. The exception was Anna's headpiece and her bouquet. They were done completely in the white stephanotis blossoms, tightly nested together. The bride's bouquet was a dome of the pure white stephanotis.

By noon on the wedding day, all the floral work was finished and up in place, in the church and in the tent. Ruth's farm workers came to help them put up the specially created swags in the church and over the door to the tent. The church looked magical even in the daylight. White candles covered the altar where the special vine basket was centered. The arrangement in this basket was spectacular and lavish. Above it on the wall hung the plain wooden cross. The little trees were arranged on the floor where they sparkled with tiny lights on either side of the simple altar. The church was filled with of the fragrance of fir, carnation, orange blossom and exotic greenhouse flowers. Daniel stood, taking in the wonder of it all. Even though he was dirty and sticky with resin from the fir, he didn't want to leave the church, transformed as it was by its wedding beauty. Ruth was grimy too. They didn't mind. It seemed Ruth was not even tired, but energized by the whole process. She sighed and smiled as she looked around at all they had done. Nan was worn out now and sat down in a pew, surveying everything, peacefully smiling.

Daniel sat too. "This is a big deal, even if we are in a little country church. This is a big deal. An event of gravity. I see that now."

"I'm glad you can see that," said Nan turning to look at him intently.

"I was going to wait until after the wedding to talk to you about something, but now seems like the right time."

He told her about his Friday night decision. His turn. His conversion to belief in Christ. His experience of being taken up by Him, adopted really. And he told her about the horrible darkness that had followed and how it had been resisted, how it fled. She listened intently with a grave face. He told her about the revelation on the ferry as he saw the rope break free.

"It was the bitter end," he laughed. "Do you know what that is?" She didn't.

"In sailing, the bitter end of a rope is the cut-off end, like bitten off. It's the final end, fini, no more. No more rope. So it's not a bad thing to be at the bitter end. It's just the absolute end. No mas." He made a sweeping gesture with his hand.

"You are so blessed Daniel," she said with fervor. "So blessed. I knew this was going to happen and now it has. Our God is full of grace, full of mercy and love."

"You are right, Nan. I am so blessed in every way, and you are a big part of the blessing."

She leaned over and put her forehead against his. She took both of his hands in hers. He could tell she was praying.

At noon, Trini and Oscar arrived with the cake. It was a beauty. They had borrowed a friend's van so they could bring the cake tower across on the ferry without mishap. Trini was a nervous wreck until it was installed in the reception tent. She had made three tiers. The top surface of each tier was solidly covered with red icing roses. The side of the layers were smooth, pure white. Instead of two figures, bride and groom, there were two white sugar swans with necks entwined on the very top layer. She put them in place at the last. It was modern, exquisite and completely original. They hid it away in the tent. Trini said she got the idea of the swans from sugar sculpture that nuns created in the convents of Mexico.

Everyone was running around getting last touches done, Daniel took the opportunity to disappear. Without cleaning up, he took the car and dashed down to the marina. He wanted to see Luke and Pete and wish them well before the ceremony. Luke was just sitting on his deck with Pete in the cold afternoon, doing nothing. The groom has little to do the day of the wedding. He just has to get dressed and show up with the ring. They greeted Daniel with shouts as they saw him drive up.

"I'm not bringing beignets!" He yelled back. "Too busy!"

"I could not keep a beignet down today, man. My stomach is in a twist!" said Luke.

"I could," said Pete with a droll look.

They sat on the deck and caught up on life. Daniel had already told them about the condo switch. Now he told them about his plan to get a boat. They were both ecstatic and instantly talking sailing and boats. Imaginations took off conjuring up possible choices for his purchase. They would help him, of course they would.

Luke took him into the houseboat and they showed him all the new changes, the new fixtures and appliances. It was like new, much lighter and streamlined. Anna would add her touches.

Daniel knew he needed to say goodbye, there was still cleanup to do back at the farm. They embraced and he wished Luke the best...the best forever.

The moment had arrived, dusk was falling. It had become bitterly cold. At the farm everyone was cleaning up and dressing for the big event. Sheila had called. She had arrived and was settled in her hotel. She said the town was full of wedding guests and Christmas tourists. She was excited too and said the town was decorated to the hilt with lights. She would be out soon. She asked Daniel to save her a seat with him.

He was cleaned up and trying to get dressed. The fir resin would not come off his hands in the bath. He went down in shirtsleeves to see if Ruth had anything to remove it. He was stunned when he saw her in the kitchen. She was wearing a long, velvet, ultramarine blue gown. It was such a romantic style, with big puffed sleeves tapering down her arms, tight at the wrists and ending in thick, cream-colored lace frills at the cuff. High at the neck, it was a princess cut, just right for her, not bulky. Her hair was arranged in its natural way, like a curly cloud around her head. For the occasion she had put on a little shiny lipstick. She smiled.

"Where did you get that dress!"

"Do you like it? It was Nan's, 'back in the day.' She kept it all these years. I thought I would wear velvet too. Anna inspired me."

"It looks fantastic on you...Shakespearian!"

He showed her his hands. "What can I do with this? It won't come off."

She led him to the sink, pushing up her fancy sleeves she went to work on his hands. She swathed them in Crisco! As she gently rubbed his hands with her little hands, the sticky tar melted off.

"Watch those cuffs! Daniel warned.

She deftly wiped everything clean and buffed his hands in a towel. She grinned.

"An old 'farm' trick. Thank you, Daniel for all your help with the flowers. I needed it."

Trini and Oscar came downstairs; Trini was wearing a silver brocade skirt with an organza blouse, lots of ruffles. Oscar was trim in a black suit and dark tie, his graying hair swept back elegantly. Nan came in exclaiming about how great they all looked!

She was rested and glowing in an emerald green wool pant suit, a flamboyant silk scarf around her neck. She would be pretty and warm. Daniel threw on his elegant cashmere coat and off they went, chattering excitedly.

When they arrived, Ruth went quickly into the tent with the wedding party, to help the girls with their bouquets and to help the men with their boutonnieres. Trini went in too, to arrange the cake in its appointed spot. The rest went on into the church. They were the first to arrive besides Otis, who was stalking around up in the front. This was his son getting married. He was nervous! Nan lit the candles five minutes before she thought people would start arriving. The candle light changed everything. They turned down the overhead lights.

It was a magical environment now! Daniel staked out a pew for himself, Nan, Ruth and Sheila. Trini and Oscar would be right across from them. They were all toward the back but would see everything.

The pianist in the back of the church finally began. The pews were full. Otis, Luke, Pete and Glenn were waiting in the front and the moment arrived. There was a swishing of skirts and the three maids of honor came down first. Their cream colored gowns and tightly-crafted red carnation bouquets were a beautiful surprise, but nothing compared to Anna. That red dress was a complete knockout. She was queenly, with her all-white flower coronet, matching white domed bouquet and stunning red velvet gown. She was wearing her mother's ruby necklace, with new ruby earrings, a gift from her parents. These were her "Something Borrowed, Something New" things that Peg had been talking about. Her father was also tall and regal with an elegant bearing which his daughter had inherited. Daniel looked back at Luke. He was stricken. It was obvious that he was paralyzed.

Otis began, booming and rich. "For this cause a man will leave his father and mother and the two will become one flesh." The ceremony seemed short, but full of meaning. "What God has joined together, let no man put asunder."

They still used those words and Otis delivered the whole thing beautifully. Before you could turn around they were down the aisle and out the door. As they walked out, everyone was gasping and exclaiming. Beautiful big flakes of snow were falling. Soon everyone was safely in the tent, warm with greeting, joy, love...dancing and eating.

There was a disc jockey, apparently still in high school by his looks. No bar was allowed on church grounds, but they did serve champagne. There were toasts and speeches and pictures taken. The food was fine, decent, catering fare. Daniel was glad he had not had to cook for this. He would have been a nervous wreck. He danced with Peg, then with his mother, and with Nan. He danced with Ruth, with Trini and with the Bride! He shook hands repeatedly with Luke and Pete. There was a lot of back-slapping going on. He congratulated Marion. He chatted with Mr. and Mrs. Babineaux and they invited him to come to see them in New Orleans. It was a good time, a wonderfully good time.

Finally, Daniel was standing with Otis. Both of them had plates piled with food. They munched as they watched the festivities.

"We've got to stop meeting like this," Daniel said. "Funerals, graveyards, weddings..."

Otis laughed, "Don't forget the fourth of July and Labor Day!" That's the way life is, m'boy. That's life. Marked by turns, twists, ups and downs. We usually celebrate. Make an event out of 'um, that way we mark 'um, and then we can remember what happened better. Makes life sweeter."

"I guess so. Otis, Listen, there's one other place I would like to meet you. Would you meet me sometime by some water? A place of water somewhere? I would like to be baptized. It's a little cool out right now, but in the spring, would you do it? I'd like to go under the water. I've had what they call a 'conversion experience'. I have gotten connected. I'm a Christian now, Otis. It's happened. I'm trying to read the Bible. I need to be baptized."

"Lord have mercy. LORD...have mercy! Paul, your father, the man who raised you, he desperately wanted this, Daniel. He prayed for this!" Otis was staring at Daniel with wide-open eyes. He was floored. "I have two major events going on tonight. My son married, and you now a citizen of the Kingdom of God! Amen, Amen. My heart is at peace!"

Sheila came by and asked Daniel to dance with her again. He was fine with that.

He could not remember ever having danced with his mother before tonight. They chatted nicely. She looked up at him and he could tell she had something to say. He was steadying himself for it.

"You know Daniel, I have had thoughts since Paul died, thoughts about maybe getting married again."

Now he was floored. He didn't know what to say.

"There are a couple of fellows who have showed an interest in me over time. I couldn't do anything while Paul was alive. I just couldn't. One man is very 'suitable.'

I like him a lot. He is a man of substance, more or less my age. I think this might be coming. I have been thinking that I don't want to grow old alone. What do you think? How would you feel if that happened?"

He was speechless, mouth open. She looked at him nervously.

"You mustn't worry about the money," she hurriedly said. "I would make sure of an iron-clad pre-nuptial before I made any move."

With that Daniel burst out laughing and could not stop. He just swung her around the dance floor even faster, with gusto.

Finally the enormous cake was cut and served. Things were winding down. Daniel was looking for Ruth. He wanted to dance with her one more time. She was nowhere to be found. Maybe she had gone back to make sure candles were all out in the church? He pushed open the tent flap and saw that it was still snowing lightly. So far it was not sticking on the ground. Then he saw her. She was standing off in the dark, just looking off into the distance. He came close and saw that she was weeping. She had her coat wrapped tightly around herself, shoulders hunched, the hood of her coat up over her head.

He came up beside her. She hadn't heard him so she jumped just a bit, then laughed. He put an arm around her. "What is it? Are you thinking about Kevin tonight?"

She threw her head back and laughed up at the sky. "Oh no! Kevin is long gone. That's not it exactly. I don't know. It's just that I've been married and that didn't turn out, in many ways. I'm still young. This has been so much fun, getting all the flowers and things ready for this wedding. Usually things don't get to me like this. I don't know. It's just that I am living and doing and enjoying my life but I don't know where the future is going... what's going to happen, where my life is going." She paused looking up again at the snowy sky. "This earth is hurtling through space and I'm just head down, going forward day by day on it. I'm happy, I love my work, but where am I going?"

"I hear that," Daniel said. He was still trying to hold her, but not so tight. He respected what she had said. He wanted to make space for her, not smother her. So he just took her hand. It was very cold so he took both hands and tucked them inside his jacket, next to his chest for warmth. She had to turn toward him now. She was still crying, just weeping.

"I'm your friend. I am your deep friend now," he said. "This is a beautiful night. Come in and let's dance. Let's enjoy all this."

"O.K.," she smiled, she grinned. "Silly isn't it, to act like this?" She paused. "Let's go look in the church one more time, O.K.? I want to see it one more time before the night ends."

They did look in on the church one more time. It looked different with the lights on, and candles out, but it was still very beautiful and quiet. They had taken the big basket of floral arrangement off the altar and into the reception where people could see it on the main table. The candles were all out and only the cross remained behind the altar now.

"You did a fine job here, Ruth. You're an artist, a designer of natural things. You have great gifts. I am new to this but...God has a plan for your life!"

She looked up at him sharply. "Daniel?" she said.

"Let's talk about it later. Let's go for now. The wedding is over and we're missing the reception."

She dried her eyes and they went back into the tent and danced. They ate cake, they drank champagne. Finally, it was time for the bride and groom to go. Anna tossed her bouquet over her shoulder. Sheila caught it!

The next day was Christmas Eve. Over night the snow had finally begun to stick and now there was a thin white layer on everything. Everyone rested and slept late at the Sloan Farm. Trini and Oscar took off for the mainland after coffee and a few beignets which Daniel had whipped up in Ruth's kitchen. They wanted to get back to be with some family for Christmas.

Ruth and Nan were clearly tired. They planned to rest for the day and return to the church in the evening for Christmas Eve services. Daniel packed up and readied himself and Henry to go in to Friday Harbor to join Sheila at her hotel for the rest of the holiday. It would be the first time in many years that mother and son had spent Christmas together. Daniel promised to return for just a short visit on Christmas Day. They would exchange gifts.

He met Sheila for a late buffet lunch at their inn. It was decorated beautifully for the Christmas guests. Daniel missed the farm, though. And, he was thinking about Glass House and his beach house. He had not been there yet. He and Sheila spent a quiet time together at the inn and watched the spectacular lighted boat parade that night. Daniel did some quick last minute shopping in the town's stores. By ten in the evening, mother and son were ready to turn in. Sheila had been waiting for the right time to give Daniel the gift she had brought. They sat in the sitting area of her room, finishing off hot chocolate drinks. Daniel unwrapped his gift from Sheila. The box was big, and he wondered what she had cooked up. She was shyly smiling. It was an exquisite model sailboat. A single-masted sloop of a racing class. The wood detail work was delicately hand-crafted. He was really touched.

He placed her gift in her lap. She opened it slowly. It was an Italian, filigreed gold bracelet, just the sort of thing Sheila loved. The inside surface had been engraved with the words, "For Mother at Christmas," and the date. She too was pleased.

He gave her a heart-felt embrace. "It is good to be with you, Mother. We should have been doing this all along," he said.

Sheila smiled, "It's never too late to celebrate Christmas."

They had a Christmas breakfast buffet the next morning at the inn. People were singing "Deck the Halls" and cheery things like that. The guests were laughing and friendly, some were wearing Santa Claus hats. Sheila left at noon, wanting to get back home before dark.

As they stood waiting on the dock, Sheila said, "I've been wanting to tell you that I love you, Daniel." She was tearful. "Thanks for spending this time with me. I have loved this holiday." She looked very pretty as she took off on the ferry. She was wearing her new bracelet.

Daniel packed up and got Henry into the car. Henry had received a new Christmas dog sweater in a red and white knit. He was wearing it now. They drove to the Sloan Farm. The fields were beautiful, glittering in the light snow. Ruth and Nan were both dressed in Christmas finery. They were at Nan's little house. She had decorated a tiny Christmas tree there, and she brought out trays of Christmas goodies, including chocolate chip cookies. They sat together in the little parlor, eating, drinking coffee and finally opening presents.

"I hope you like this." Ruth said.

Daniel opened his package to see a black cashmere sweater! It was from both of them. "We wanted to say thank you for all you have done for us this year. I hope it fits." Ruth's eyes were sparkling.

"It's gorgeous!" I'll wear this often!" He was impressed.

He had gotten Nan a gold bracelet too. It had a line of scripture engraved on it.

"*I have loved thee with an everlasting love; therefore with loving-kindness I have drawn thee.*" She was thrilled. "You've made this Christmas a very happy one for us Daniel. Very happy."

Daniel's gift for Ruth was in a small box wrapped with silver paper and silver ribbon. She opened it. It was a gold locket.

Inside he had fitted a tiny picture of the Time Out. He had cut it out himself from a snapshot.

She looked up at him. "That was one of the very best days of my life...our sailing day." She blushed.

He was pleased to the point of blushing himself. It was time to go. They said their good-byes and Christmas wishes. He and Ruth walked out together.

"Let's drive down for just a minute to check on Glass House. Will you? I feel like I need to look it over before I go."

And so, she came along. They left the car and walked, picking their way through remnants of the snow, all around the house, the terrace and then into the orchard. It was so changed in the winter, he could hardly believe it. The orchard was so barren without leaves. The refuse of fallen leaves and debris covered the ground, sodden, with a few patches of snow here and there.

They walked around to the terrace and looked out over a chilly sea. He could see the beach but not the beach house. Henry started to run towards the beach house path, looking back at Daniel. "No!" he called out. "We are not going down today." Henry looked at him strangely, but there was no use in going down there today. It was all locked up and it would make Daniel feel lonely to see it that way.

They were on the terrace, just looking out to the east, towards the mainland. It was cold there and Ruth had her coat wrapped tightly around her. They were shoulder to shoulder, huddled against a chilly wind.

"I want to ask you something, Ruth. I need to try to find Matthew Fleming, my natural father. I'm going to try to search for him." He turned to face her. "If I can find him, would you go with me to meet him? Would you go? It's something I don't want to do alone."

Her face was bright in the afternoon sun, the tip of her nose just a little bit red. She looked up at him steadily.

"Yes, Daniel. I'll go with you."

THE END

*"I was found by those who did not seek me; I revealed myself to those who did not ask for me."*

*The Letter to the Romans, Chapter 10, Verse 20*
*The New International Version of the Bible*

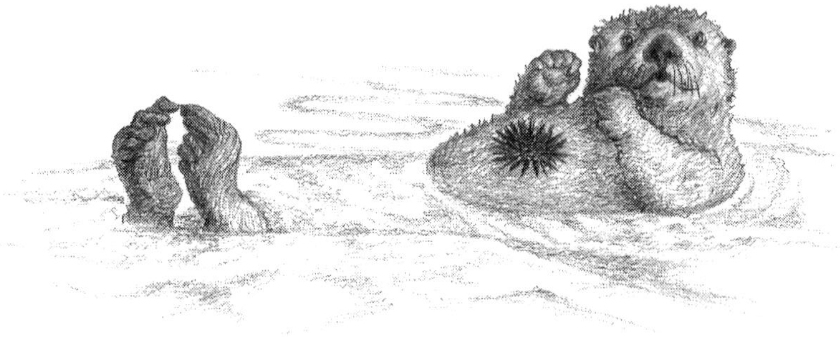

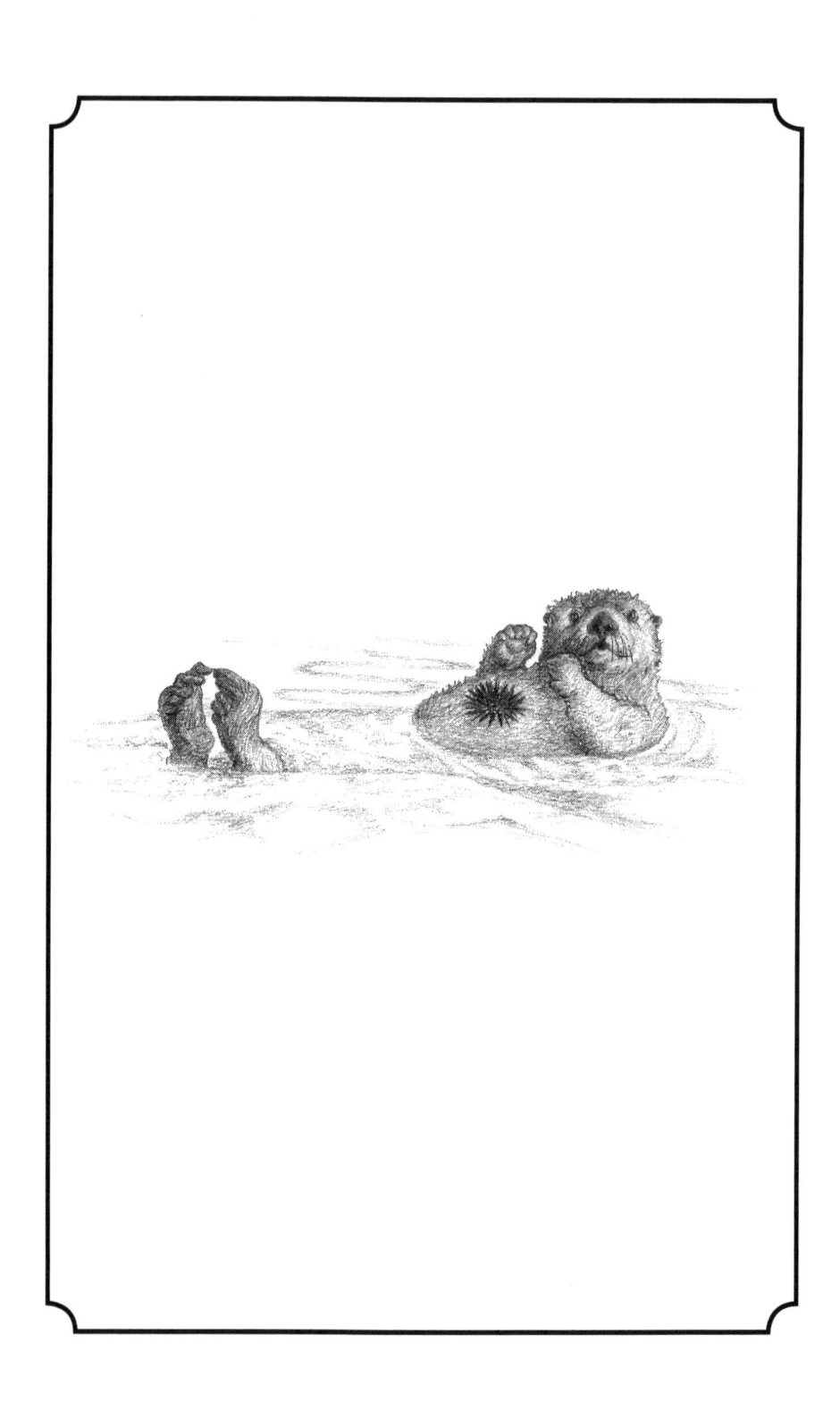

Made in the USA
Lexington, KY
02 February 2017